HETERO Flexible

A NEW **SPRUCE, TEXAS** ROMANCE
BY

DARYL BANNER

AUTHOR OF

FOOTBALL SUNDAE
BORN AGAIN SINNER
HARD FOR MY BOSS
&
BROMOSEXUAL

HETEROFLEXIBLE

Cover Model
Ryan Truong

Cover Photographer
FuriousFotog / Golden Czermak

Cover & Interior Design
Daryl Banner

OTHER WORK by DARYL BANNER

FOREWORD

Hi! I'm Daryl Banner, author of the book you're about to read. If this is our first time together, thank you so much for picking up *Heteroflexible*, and I hope you enjoy your time in Spruce, Texas.

If this isn't your first book of mine, then welcome back!

I'll make this quick. I'm a gay dude. And if you're a gay dude, you *know* what it's like to crush on a straight guy. We've all been there. Hell, if you're a straight woman, I'm sure you've had your fair share of crushes on gay dudes. Or if you're a gay woman, you have probably stared longingly at your straight girl friend now and then. We've all been there, wanting that person we can't have.

It's soul crushing. It hurts. It consumes us. I know.

So with that in mind, I want you to know – *fair warning* – that this story may trigger several of those feelings for you.

But don't worry: It may also heal and warm your heart up.

I like to write my romances in a world generally free from the day-to-day pressures and stresses of homophobia and masculinity crises and gender role expectations. We get enough of that in the real world. I want a break from it, and romance is my escape. In the world I write in, men aren't afraid to show affection – or even love – for one another, regardless of their sexuality.

The world that my romances are set in is a *safe* place.

I want *Heteroflexible*, most of all, to paint that picture loud and clear, because I truly, genuinely, wholeheartedly believe that a homophobia-free world *IS* our future. It may not be tomorrow, or next year, or this lifetime, but it is absolutely inevitable.

And now that I've gotten that out of the way, I'll assure you that, as usual, this foreword is the only 'preaching' or 'soap-boxiness' you'll get from this book.

Because if you know me as an author at all, I'm all about telling stories, not pushing messages. Just set aside your stresses for a while, grab a glass of sweet tea, and come back with me to the small town of Spruce in the dead middle of a hot and sweaty summer, where my other novels *Football Sundae* and *Born Again Sinner* took place. While this book does continue immediately after the events of *Born Again Sinner*, it can be read entirely on its own. Jimmy Strong and Bobby Parker are ready to take the spotlight and tell you their story about a straight dancer and a gay soccer player whose unique friendship defies all definitions.

And if it's your first time here in Spruce, I sure hope you're ready for an abundance of dropped g's and lots of dangs and sassy southern twang.

There's a whole lot of lovin' in this here book.

;-)

Happy reading, always,
Daryl

www.darylbanner.com

HETERO Flexible

PROLOGUE

BOBBY

I ain't gonna lie.

Jimmy Strong is one devastating son of a gun.

Especially with the wind blasting in through the driver's side window, making his short brown hair flip and flop every which way. Well, the bit of his hair that isn't squished down by that dang hideous red-and-white ball cap he stubbornly refuses to retire, despite its threadbare state, weird stains, and a hole in its bill.

But that's the thing about Jimmy Strong: when the boy loves something, he won't ever let it go.

He looks like he's steering a grand chariot one-handed, the way he drives his prized red pickup. It's with authority and pride that he pilots his big metal steed. I don't think he's let another set of feet inside this truck except me and maybe a past girlfriend or three. Ever since he was given this coughing, old piece of rumbly crap on his sixteenth birthday, they've been inseparable.

It's a love story, really. A boy and his truck.

"Think she wanted to suck me off?"

I screw up my forehead. "The hell you talkin' about, Jimmy?"

"You know who. That redhead at the store."

"Who?"

I'm playing dumb. I know damned well who. The last stop we made for gas, the girl at the front counter was a seventeen-or-eighteen-something-year-old with wavy red hair tossed up in a messy ponytail. She had a spatter of freckles over her tiny nose and two sharp eyes. And when I went in to grab me and Jimmy a pair of ice-cold sodas, that redhead was already staring out the storefront window at Jimmy as he filled up his precious truck.

And it wasn't just any stare.

Because when you look at Jimmy, you can't *just stare.* You gotta drink in every damned thing about the boy. You look at his tight gray tank top, stretched over his slender pecs and dancing down his cliff-side abs. You bite your finger as your arrested eyes drag down his long legs and those worn, dusty Wranglers painted down them. You squint your eyes in anguish as you watch the way his ass moves when he struts right up to the pump like it owes him something. His lean, sinewy form holds your gaze so strongly, you forget what you were doing. He's as lithe as a panther, probably as dangerous as one too, and you haven't even seen his face yet.

It's obvious the boy's a dancer.

He's got ass for days and swagger that kills.

And if you've seen him dance like I have—*phew*—all of this is just ten times worse, because you *know* how that boy can move.

I had to go up and damn near slam the two bottles of Pepsi on the counter before that redheaded clerk snapped out of her daze. "H-Hi, did you find everything you needed?" she asked innocently.

"Did you?" I returned sassily.

My mistake was in telling Jimmy all about her ogling after we were back on the highway.

As if Jimmy Strong needed his ego stroked any more than it already is on a daily basis just by existing.

"Whatever," Jimmy finally throws back at me. "You probably made her all up. There wasn't any redhead." He snorts. "Or it was probably a dude."

I shoot him a look. "Would that be a problem if it was?"

Now it's Jimmy's turn to throw me a look of fiery indignance. "Are you serious right now? Tell me your happy ass ain't serious." He twists the radio off so fast, he nearly breaks off the knob. "Who do you think you're riding all the way back home to Spruce with, huh? Am I not the same dude who threw Kenny-fucking-Driver to the dirt the moment he said he was 'sick of playing on the same soccer team as a homo' back in high school?"

I sigh. Jimmy's so easy to set off about this subject. "Okay, I got it, I got it ..."

"Am I not the same dude who took you to prom because my date ditched me and you didn't have one?"

"Ouch."

"Am I not the same dude who's been your roommate at South Wood University for the past two years? I've been naked in the same room with you more times than I can count."

"Are you done?"

"Am I not the same dude—" *Nope, he isn't done.* "—with a gay older brother who's such a football legend at Spruce High that to this day, he's still called the *Spruce Juice*, even while he coaches the team himself now? And I stood next to him, proudly, as his best man, when he got himself married to Billy Tucker. Does that sound like someone who's got a *problem* with gay guys?"

"Good Lord in Heaven, Jimmy, you've made your point."

Satisfied in an instant, he gives me one curt nod, says, "Damn right I did," then cranks the radio right back up, twice as loud as it was before.

I stare at the side of his face for a while, studying the whiskers of hair that now form something of a wispy beard across his cheek and chin and upper lip. That's new as of this past semester, since he'd always been clean-shaven since I've known him. At first, I was certain a sad attempt at growing a beard was going to make him— at long last—look like an unkempt college bum, and the spell he had over me would finally be broken.

I was wrong. So wrong. That boyish beard has done nothing but make him appear stronger, more confident, and sexy in that messy sort of mysterious way.

"Thanks," I tell him.

Jimmy, with one of his toned arms up, fist gripping the wheel, flinches at my one word, heard even through the blast of radio. He squints, eyes still on the road, when he returns, "For what?"

"For bein' that kind of dude who don't care one bit if it's a guy or a gal lookin' your way."

He gives my comment all of two seconds' thought. "Bobby, why you gotta go botherin' me with this feely shit right now? I'm tryin' to enjoy the countryside here."

"Boy, you're gonna get enough countryside when we're back in Spruce. All there is for miles and miles is *corn* and *wheat* and *cow dung*. Can't you just take the compliment and keep driving?"

He shoots me half a look. "There's a helluvalot more than *cow dung* on the Strong ranch."

We ride awhile longer, the rock music blasting from the radio.

"And it isn't a compliment," he adds.

I look at him. "Huh?"

"It's called being a decent, healthy human being. The 'kind of dude I am' shouldn't be anything special. It should just be the way every dude is." Then, for the first time since we left the gas station, he takes his eyes off the road to give me a sincere look of his stunning, warm brown eyes. "I love ya, Bobby. You're my best bud and my man. Ain't nothin' gonna change that."

My heart melts and falls to the floor every time he says that.

I am the luckiest motherfucker in the world, to have a best friend like Jimmy Strong.

He returns his eyes to the road. "Now can we stop with all this feely shit? We got two hundred miles more before we hit Fairview, and then Spruce is just on the other side."

"Feely shit? Pfft. You're the one who just told your gay buddy you're in love with him."

Jimmy rolls his eyes. "I said I *love ya*, I didn't say I'm *in—*"

I crank up the radio, cutting him off with a superior smirk on my lips. Jimmy shoots me a look, then laughs and shakes his head.

The next song comes on, and it's one we both know. In just a few seconds, we're bobbing our heads in sync. Then Jimmy, out of nowhere, starts singing along to it. I join him halfway through the first verse—badly—and by the big chorus, we're singing so dang loud, I'm sure even the coyotes in the prairie are howling back.

1

BOBBY

The door to my screened-in back patio slaps shut harder than I intended, pulled by the wind. Out here in the dusty east suburb of Spruce, the wind's got a bossy little mind of its own.

My mom rushes into the hall from the kitchen, her pink apron covered in flour, her round face red, her mouth agape. "Bobby, my darlin'!" Then she's on me in seconds, her soft and squishy arms around my neck. "I thought you weren't back until tomorrow!"

"Ma, I sent you a text yesterday, and another Wednesday," I say over her shoulder. "What're you makin'? Smells like farts."

"It's fried cauliflower, silly!" Her voice is always so soft and light, like she speaks on half a breath with every word, and her tone is high like a song and fragile as porcelain. "And you know darned well I don't check my phone but once a month."

I manage a laugh and a sigh at the same time. "I got you that iPhone for your birthday so you'd be *out* of the dark ages."

She pulls back and gets a look at my face. Her eyes are shiny with innocence. "Of course, but you haven't shown me how to use it yet, my sweet darlin'."

I'll get her up with the times one of these days. "Where's Pa?"

"He's on a long job in Fairview. He won't be home until nearly midnight, I reckon. We weren't expecting you until tomorrow. Aw, shoot, I bet I got the date wrong and this is all my fault."

"Yep. And the world's gonna end now as a result of it." I give my ma a kiss on the forehead. Seems like just a couple years ago I was looking *up* at her. Now I'm taller by three inches at least. "As you weren't expectin' me until tomorrow anyway, do we have any dinner plans? I was thinkin' I might go over later to—"

"Ooph, already?" my ma squeaks, her face collapsing.

I blink. "What do you mean?"

"Darlin', Bobby, you just got here and you're already makin' plans to spend your whole dang summer at the Strong's?"

Her voice is so dejected, it breaks my heart in an instant. "No, Ma," I throw back softly, my eyebrows pulling together. "I was only askin' about tonight, not the 'whole dang summer'."

"Just like last summer, and one night turns into one week, and one week into a whole month, and suddenly you're goin' back to the university the next morning and I'll feel like I haven't even seen you at all." She sighs and slaps her apron, flour dancing in swirls from her hands like magic smoke, then turns and heads back into the kitchen. "Well, you just do you, Bobby. You just do you, I'm not gonna stand in your way. You're a big boy now."

I frown after her. "Now why you gotta go actin' like I've come home and killed the cat?"

"Didn't you spend enough time with that Strong boy by now? He had you all to himself this whole school year at the university."

"Hey, hey, we came back for Christmas," I remind her.

"And you spent ninety percent of your time over at that ranch just the same," she sings over her shoulder, defeated, as she rolls out a ball of dough on the counter. "They even stole you away for New Year's Eve. Your father and I spent it here, alone."

"But Pa said that's what you wanted to do!" I protest.

"Because he knows how attached you are to that Strong boy. We aren't gonna stand in your way when you get that *look* on your face." She starts cutting the dough into strips.

I'm trying to follow her actions with my eyes, and her words with my ears, but I have no idea what she's doing and less of an idea of what she's saying. "*Look* on my face ...?"

"I didn't get to cleanin' up your room yet, and I'm covered in flour, so it's gonna be a bit of a mess with my craft things. Do you have all your college stuff?" She eyes me over her shoulder. "You don't got a bag or suitcase or nothin' with you."

"It's ..." *Aw, jeez, here we go.* "I left my things in Jimmy's truck."

Her hands stop. Her eyes stay on me. "And where is Jimmy's truck?"

I sigh. "Still in the driveway."

Her eyes flatten. "So you want to go to the Strong ranch *right now* and can't even stay for supper or nothin'?"

"Nadine is ... whippin' up something." I feel so awful. "But I can cancel. I can just go grab my things outta his truck and—"

"That woman can't cook worth a lick of anything." Even in her faint, delicate voice, my ma carries quite a bite. "Y'know she's got that Jacky-Ann doin' her cookin', or some of Billy's creations stashed in her fridge. It isn't *she* who's whippin' up a thing."

If my ma's got a sore spot at all, it's a big-haired, tall, skinny, hot-pink-fingernail-painted, and melon-boobed one called Nadine Strong—Jimmy's ma. It's an odd dynamic, that my pa and Jimmy's pa, Paul Strong, get along so well—having been best buddies themselves back in high school—and the wives hate each other. Something to do with a school bake-off gone wrong. I don't know.

"Well, whoever's cookin' it," I go on, feeling like I'm walking a minefield here, "I can cancel. I can help you cook your, uh ..." I look for a word to describe what she's doing.

She turns away from the counter and crosses her arms. "Your father's favorite. Apple pie."

He and I have had talks about her apple pie. His insistence that it's his favorite is more a thing he says to spare her feelings. *Bless her, I figured the ruse would've been outed by now.* "Well, I can cancel my thing with Jimmy, if you'd rather I—"

"Oh, what's the bother, anyway? I'm gonna be busy with this and the fried foods and the brisket for an hour more or so." She gives me a little brushing-away gesture. "Go and have fun. I'll see you later tonight or ... tomorrow or ..." She sighs and turns back to the counter. "... whenever you decide you can pencil me in."

I frown at her back, wringing my hands with frustration. I glance at the kitchen window, imagining Jimmy getting impatient in his truck, leg kicked up, getting sweatier and sweatier by the minute in his tight gray tank top and Wranglers.

I clench shut my eyes. *Fuck.* "I'll stay, Ma," I decide. "Jimmy's got all summer to hang with me. He and the Strong ranch can miss me a little longer."

At once, my ma's face explodes into something akin to utter elation as she spins around to face me. This woman's just won the son-coming-home-from-college lottery. "Really?"

"I'll go tell Jimmy to skedaddle."

My ma crashes into me with a big hug that slaps all sorts of flour and sticky dough residue all over my clothes. Then she looks up into my eyes with her own beaming ones. "Your daddy's gonna be so pleased to see you when he gets back tonight!"

Two minutes later, I'm walking up to Jimmy's truck. "G'damn, it's about time," groans Jimmy impatiently, his legs propped up on the dashboard just as I predicted they'd be, an elbow hanging out of his window. "I'm melted halfway to nothin' sittin' out here."

Just leaning back like that, he looks like he's posing for the cover of some *"Good Ol' Boys You Can Drool Your Whole Body's Supply Of Water Over"* magazine. He has the drop-dead gorgeous face of a country boy dropped from Heaven itself, and the toned, slender body of a runway model. It isn't so hard to imagine.

I sigh. "Sorry, man. I've gotta cancel. My ma's so excited to see me, I should stay here and keep her company. My pa's not comin' home 'til late tonight from a long job in Fairview, and I—"

Jimmy's face is all wrinkled up with frustration. "Dude, we were gonna throw ball with my bro. And what about my mama's big supper she was plannin' for us? Jacky-Ann's already makin' it."

My ma hit the nail on the head. I smirk. "Sorry, buddy. We gotta wait 'til tomorrow to hang out."

He's about to throw me something else sassy and annoyed when my ma's sweet, singsong voice comes out of the living room window, which she's flung open wide: "Hey there, Jimmy-boy!"

In an instant, Jimmy's legs are swung off the dash and he's straightened his posture. "Hi, Mrs. Parker, ma'am!" he calls out, his tone traded instantly for something chivalrous and polite.

"Sweetheart, you can call me Patricia, you know that!"

"Yes, ma'am, Patricia!"

"Don't go bein' a stranger this summer!" she calls back.

"I won't, ma'am, Patricia!"

She smiles, waves at him, then pulls shut the window and disappears into the house.

Jimmy turns his eyes onto me. "You know my mama's gonna be pissed. She likes showin' off for you every time you come over."

"Just tell her I gotta spend time with my own ma this summer, too. She's ..." I lean in closer, as if she might actually overhear me somehow from inside the house. "... *a bit more clingy than usual.*"

Jimmy cranks on his engine. It coughs and sputters irritably, like it resents having to drive even one more inch today. *That tired old red truck is long overdue to crap out and be put to rest.*

"Better grab your stuff, Bobby my man, before I take off with it all." Jimmy tips his threadbare cap at me.

After I lug my bags and backpack out of the bed of his truck, my heart breaks and falls through the gaps in my ribcage like shards of peanut brittle as Jimmy Strong gently backs out of my driveway. With another cough of the cranky engine, he rumbles off, disappearing slowly around the long, wide bend of my street.

I stand in the driveway staring after him under the hot early-summer sun, beads of sweat slowly crawling down my forehead and back. For a second, I honestly consider pulling out my phone and calling him right up, telling him I'd changed my mind and my ma can just wait another day or two to spend time with me. But sense keeps me rooted—*or just the memory of that look my ma gave me when she thought I'd already had one foot out the door to run off to the Strong ranch with Jimmy*—and I refrain from acting on the impulsive thought. I've resigned to actually spend time with my dear, loving parents tonight like a good boy who's fresh home from college for another long, uneventful summer in Spruce.

And so help me, Jimmy Strong can dang well wait.

2

JIMMY

There was this moment back in January, right after Bobby and I returned to campus from a short winter break in Spruce, when I caught the poor bastard choking his chicken in our dorm.

I get it. We're two horny twenty-year-olds, closed up in a tiny room without a scrap of privacy to even entertain a girlfriend—or boyfriend, in his case. It's inevitable that this would happen.

But I'd just come back from a class on human sexuality—some psych course I had to take to fulfill an honors credit—so my mind was in a particularly strange place already when I pushed open that sad, beige door, and saw what I saw.

Namely: Bobby Parker, on the floor, on his back, with his legs spread as far apart as they go ... and he's naked.

Well, except for a pair of white socks on his feet with red rings around the tops of them, bunched up, one half hanging off.

And he had a happy hand on his dick, jerking it so vigorously, he looked like he was trying to yank the poor fella right off.

The thing is, he didn't hear me come in at all. He didn't see me either, clearly—and for a good reason: his eyes were shut, his head was rocked back, and he looked like he was halfway to Heaven as he shamelessly churned his butter on our dorm room floor.

Now, I'd seen Bobby in his birthday suit before. Several times, in fact. I'd go into his locker room after one of his soccer games, jumping in on him while he's showering or just half-dressed, to congratulate him on another win. He'd come backstage after one of my dance shows, walking in on me while I'm changing into my regular clothes, and shout about how amazing the show was. The girls didn't care a bit; they all knew he was gay and practically welcomed his happy ass in, all of them in their bras or leotards at their make-up stations.

Bobby and I are downright shameless around each other. We are comfortable seeing one another in various states of undress.

But I never quite caught a good look at my buddy's dick.

And phew, *it was quite a dick.*

I could have shed a whole bucket of tears right there, I was so proud. And a bit shocked, if I'm being completely honest. For a split second, I thought he was plunging a toilet. There was dick above *and* below his fist every time he went up and down with another fevered stroke. And that puppy was *fat.*

I had half a conniption wondering how the hell he stuffs it in those tiny soccer shorts so they don't show it off to the world.

Then I spent another hot minute wondering how he hasn't punctured the back of any of his ex-boyfriends' throats and sent them straight to the ER.

Seriously. These were my first thoughts.

And I had them very quickly, in succession.

And like some weirdo creeper, I didn't alert Bobby right away of my weirdo creeper presence. Why ruin the show when I had front row seats to the quidditch match with Harry freakin' Potter riding his big-ass broom on my dorm room floor?

I guess I'd have to accept the fact that my best buddy had a Godzilla dong.

Then came the best part: Bobby let out the most pleasure-filled groan as he, ever so slowly, opened his eyes.

And caught sight of me.

"THE FUCK!" he shrieked as he leapt to his feet with ninja precision and flung himself toward his bed. He fought with his bed sheets until they became a toga, which fell right off his body the moment he stood up straight. Another fumbling of his limbs sent him careening into the bathroom where the door slapped shut with such a boom, the ceiling shook.

And now it was me on that carpet, laughing my ass off so hard and so loud, our hallmates were peeping their heads out of their rooms looking for the fuss.

That day was probably humiliating for poor Bobby Parker. After all, for all the times we've seen each other naked or partially undressed, it's never been in a sexual circumstance.

I called it a moment of male bonding.

Bobby keeps denying it ever happened.

After pulling into the wide gravel driveway of the ranch, I barely have time to slam shut my door and sling a single bag out of the bed of my truck before mama's coming down the steps of our big, recently-renovated wraparound porch. I call it our Porch 2.0.

"Honey, baby, Jimmy, sweetie!" she shouts out as the woman powerwalks over the gravel, stabbing it with her white spike heels every step.

"Goodness, Mama, how many names you gotta give me?"

She's in a tight blue top with white polka-dots, white pants glued to her skinny legs, hoop earrings, and big, big hair that gets right in my face when she throws her arms around my neck. "I'll call you any amount of names I want, baby boy!" She pulls away at once. "Now where's Bobby?"

I knew that'd be the first thing she'd notice, even before my haircut. "He's spending time with his parents tonight."

"But I'm doin' a whole big supper thing!" she protests, her eyes turning harsh at once. Then they narrow with suspicion. "It's that Patricia, isn't it? Patricia had a problem with him comin' on over here, is that it?"

"Can I get a single bag inside at least before ya start *eviscerating'* my best friend's sweet and well-meanin' mama, please?"

She lets out a big dramatic huff before grabbing my first bag right out of my hands and tugging it over her bony shoulder herself, marching up to the porch.

"*Mama,*" I throw tiredly at her, then follow in quickly behind. "Hey, hey, that's heavy! Careful with your back!"

When I come through the door, it's an instant splash of ice cold air over my body—a reprieve from the *Texan Hell* outside.

And that's a lovely reprieve I can't yet enjoy with my mama's fury setting her own hair on fire in front of me. "Hey, if it was the other way around, you'd want *me* to stay here instead of goin' over to Bobby's, no matter how big or fancy his supper is."

She drops my bag on the floor and spins on me. "That Patricia has had it out for me since Junior Prom. I *swear* I didn't know Greg was datin' her, and if I *had* known, I'd have *not* let him kiss me by that punch bowl. I'm a *dignified* lady."

I frown. "I'm ... not even gonna touch that."

"And besides," she goes on, "Patricia knew I'd just gotten out of a long string of *bad* boyfriends, cheaters, and do-no-gooders. I deserved a little lovin'! And *Greg* wasn't anywhere near her all night. And ..." She huffs again. "I need all the joy I can get lately because I'm a dang wreck. What's wrong with wantin' a little more joy? Jacky-Ann made you your lemonade." She marches off to the stairs, leaving me and my bag at the foot of the kitchen.

Why is she a wreck? "Did I miss somethin'? What's goin on? ... Mama!" I call out after her, but she's gone.

I throw a sigh out at the kitchen, then bring myself up to the fridge. The door swings open, and a glorious pitcher of golden-yellow lemonade awaits me—Jacky-Ann's creation I've happily enjoyed since I was a kid. I fetch a glass and serve myself twice in a row, gulping down the first glass faster than I can pour it.

The Texan heat is no joke this time of year. It's a wonder our swimming pool isn't boiling under the summer sunshine.

The sound of nearby laughter outside catches my ear. I turn, cross the kitchen, and peer out the glass doors to the side patio. In a few wicker chairs by the swimming pool, I see my big brother Tanner kicking back with some friends of his: Robby, Kirk, and Joel, from the look of it. Out in the pool, I see Joel's wife Mindy floating on a hot pink inflatable tube. She looks to be sipping a fancy drink through a straw.

My third glass of lemonade in hand, I push open the door and come down the walkway to the pool, the scent of chlorine, beer, and lotion filling my nostrils. Robby spots me first—a wrestler-turned-choirboy with a lady-killer smirk. "Well, here's the man of the hour!" Then everyone else glances my way. "Jim!" shouts Kirk through his lumberjack beard. "Jimmy-boy!" chimes in Joel.

My brother hops out of his seat. "Bro!" he cries out boastfully, spreading his arms while still fisting his beer. "You're back!"

My brother is a total muscular enigma. One summer, he's got the bod of a football god (rhyme intended), then by winter adopts half a dad-bod belly, then tightens right back up the next summer, over and over. No matter where his weight's sitting, however, the bastard is always annoyingly handsome in that women-swooning-everywhere-he-goes-even-though-he's-gay-and-married way.

Right now, his arms are looking big as bowling balls and his shoulders rise like a mountain to the thick cords of his neck when he pulls me in for a big hug.

"What?" I toss over his shoulder as he squeezes my bones to their breaking point. "You didn't hear Old Inferno coughin' up the driveway a minute ago?"

Tanner slaps my back, then wraps his arm around my neck in half a headlock. "Don't call your truck 'Old Inferno'. Sounds like a medical condition you get up your ass after eatin' too much of Billy Senior's level-ten jalapeño dip."

Joel snorts, overhearing that. "Tell that to the wifey! She tried his Tackler the other day and damn near cried herself to death chugging glass after glass of milk! Then needed some 'alone time' in the bathroom a minute later. *She'd kill me if she heard me say—*"

Mindy, still floating on a hot pink tube in the pool, lifts her head up. "You talkin' about me? What was that?"

"Nothin', babe!" Joel calls over his shoulder innocently.

The boys start gabbing about something else, Robby letting out a drunken, watery-eyed laugh every five minutes, while my brother sets down his beer and leads me off to the side near a hedge lining the porch. "Bro, I got some news that you may—"

"Me too," I cut him off. "Bobby isn't comin' for supper."

Tanner's eyes go wide. "You told Mama yet?"

"Is her ice-cold absence right now not makin' it obvious?"

My brother sighs and shakes his head, glancing off at the pool where Mindy just burst into laughter over something Robby said. "Damn, I really needed Mama in a good mood today."

I frown. "Why?"

Tanner faces me. "Billy has this ... *thing* he's gotta tell her, but it kinda involves the McPhersons, and Mama isn't gonna like it."

"Oh, just add it to the list," I let out. "She doesn't like Bobby's mama. She doesn't like Bobby choosing his own family over ours. She doesn't like my bein' at school so far away. She doesn't like—"

"If Mama isn't the center of attention, she don't like much of *anything*."

I nod. "She said she was a wreck earlier. Do you know what's goin' on with her?"

Tanner shrugs. "Could be anything. She's always a wreck." He leans in closer. "To be honest, she's gettin' on Billy's last nerve lately. She's so determined to be Queen Gay of Spruce, I think it's makin' her lose her mind. Especially after Cissy and Marcy teamed up to give one of their gay brothers a giant extravaganza thing, Mama's gotten even worse."

I sigh and whip off my hat to scratch my head. "I thought she was done playin' rivalry games with them years ago."

"Tell me 'bout it. Who knows. Maybe she's just bored." Tanner glances back at the house. "I swear, I think our mama's gayer than me, Billy, Trey, and Cody combined."

Now those are two names I haven't heard in a while. I slap my hat back on my head. "You still hang out with them? Trey and Cody?"

"Sure, when they aren't cooped up in their house or heading some church function. I tried church for a few months," he adds as an aside. "It's great and all, but it just isn't my thing. Mama started goin' every Sunday, but forgive me if I think it's just another of her efforts to *look good* for the community and one-up all the other ladies in town. She's stepped on more toes there than I can count. Even Trey himself came to me privately askin' in his most polite voice how best to handle her 'zealousness', I think he called it."

My phone buzzes in my pocket. I pull it out to find a text from Bobby. Upon opening it, I find a sleepy-faced emoji with a bunch of Z's, and a pair of eggplants. What's that supposed to mean? He's bored and thinking of dicks?

I snort privately to myself and start to type a response.

My brother's next words stop me: "Camille was asking around about you."

I look up at him, my half-written text forgotten. "I thought—"

"That she was still in Europe? Not this summer, apparently. She had a death in the family. Her uncle Juan Carlos, her mama's brother. That was the bit of news I was tryin' to tell you earlier."

"Oh." I glance down at my phone, but am not really seeing it.

Tanner smirks. "Is your heart goin' all pit-pat now? Igniting an old flame in there someplace?"

"Nah, nothin' like that."

"You sure?" He pokes me in the ribs tauntingly. "You *suuure?*"

"Stop it."

"Someone's gonna get it on with his high school sweetheart this summer." Tanner knows when he's found a button, and he's so irritatingly good at pushing it over and over. "Camille and Jim-Jim, sittin' in a tree ..."

He starts laughing when I shove him away. Then he's got me in another headlock, and after three more maneuvers and a few playful shoves, all the guys are cheering us on with shouts, hoots, and whistles—even Mindy from the pool.

Everyone stays for supper, which my mama still serves with a smile on her face, her ire from earlier seemingly forgotten. Jacky-Ann joins us, too, as well as Billy who just finished a ten-hour shift at the T&S Shoppe, which was "downright *hopping* today". He gives me a warm hug and sits across the table from me to chat about all my classes I took this semester. Everyone else is busy yakking about Robby and something big he's planning with his girlfriend Vanessa Evans, whom he *still* hasn't proposed to.

At the head of the table sits Papa, who came back from some errand he was running just in time for supper. Mama and her big hoop earrings sit right next to him, keeping up a conversation with Jacky-Ann. But even sitting halfway down the table from her, I can still tell when my mama's gossiping. I'm sure poor Jacky-Ann is getting an earful about Patricia-this and Patricia-that.

I wonder if my mama has any real friends, or if every woman in town is some kind of sworn enemy of hers, one way or another.

And despite all the joy and chatter and general merriment all around me, I can't help but obsess over the surprise news about Camille. The last time I saw her was two summers ago before I ran off with Bobby for our first year of college together. We weren't really dating, since I was caught up in a tug-of-war between two other chicks who couldn't take no for an answer. I wouldn't even be able to say which one of them won, it's all such a fog. By the time I got to school, I barely remembered either of their names.

But I remembered Camille.

"Yo, Jimmy!" shouts Joel. "Earth to Jimmy Strong!"

I flinch and look up. The table is silent, everyone glancing my way. "Huh?"

"I asked if you're gonna lead the Spruce Ball at the end of the summer. Maybe perform a big number for us."

I blink. "I, uh ..."

"C'mon," coaxes his wife Mindy, her voice lilting. "I'm sure there's a nice girl in town who can match your talent and partner up with you. I hear *Camille's* back from Europe for the summer."

If I have to hear her name said suggestively at me one more time ...

"It's our second annual," Billy points out before I can respond. "You and Bobby had to run off back to school early last summer because of ... well, I forget. The Ball helps raise money to keep the arts alive in the schools. *Everyone* will be there. It's a chance to—"

"—show off, like the cocky bastard you are," finishes Tanner, then gives me a deep elbow-nudge as everyone else shares a laugh at my expense.

Everyone except Mama, who's still the self-crowned Queen of Antarctica down there at the end of the table.

With a cautious look at her, I concede with a, "I'll think about it," to everyone. That's the best I can give them.

I might as well have said yes, because Mindy and Billy high-five, Robby and Kirk and Joel howl their excitement, and Tanner shouts a proud, "Attaboy!" while applauding.

I guess there's worse things I could agree to.

Like giving up my room for another surprise visit from Grandma.

It's late evening by the time our guests clear out of the house. My parents retire to their bedroom, calling it a night. I decide to walk Billy and my brother to their house, which resides down the long dirt road edged by a white picket fence. They live in a shady, picturesque thicket hugging a small boomerang-shaped lake, their house complete with a dock that juts into the water like a finger. The three of us sit on that dock—me between the two of them—and listen to the woods and the water as the stars slowly emerge.

"I wish your school wasn't so freakin' far away," complains my brother. "I'd have come to all your ballet recitals."

I throw him a look. "You know damn well they aren't called *ballet recitals*."

"I know you do the hip-hop and pop-locking and stuff, but you gotta study the basics, too, don't ya? That includes ballet!"

"They're *dance shows*," I go on, "and no, they aren't worth flyin' all the way out there to see. Not yet, at least. I'm no pro."

"Oh, I've seen you dance," he starts, "and you're a total—"

"No," I cut him off. "You've seen me dance in group numbers with girls here in Spruce. You don't know what's out there. There are tons of male dancers in the world, guys who've been training since they were four. I ain't nothin' compared to them."

Billy shakes his head. "Mmm. Sounds like a classic case of big fish gettin' a taste of the bigger pond out there. Jimmy, don't be discouraged. I had the same experience in culinary school. Same as your brother when he went off to do college football. I was suddenly certain that none of my cookin' or bakin' was worth spit compared to the Cordon Bleu caliber stuff I was surrounded by."

I shrug. "Nah, it isn't that. I know I'm good."

Tanner laughs. "*There's* the cocky lil' bro I know so well."

"So what is it?" asks Billy.

I take a deep breath, then let it all out over the water. "In the real world, 'good' doesn't cut it. I guess these past couple of years have given me a reality check. I don't know how I'm gonna make a living doing this. *Dancing.* Whether I'm good or even *great.* There's a gazillion *great* dancers out there who ain't makin' squat, either."

"You never know." Billy nudges me. "Don't go sellin' yourself short, buddy. You've got something to give this boring ol' world."

"Yeah, bro," Tanner chimes in. "You were the first dude to take a dance class in Spruce High history. The following year, four more boys finally grew a set of balls and enrolled, too. You're a real pioneer, my man. A Spruce legend."

I snort and shake my head. "Says the *Spruce Juice* himself."

"Oh, shoot, you didn't tell my mama about your whole thing," my brother says suddenly, peering over at Billy across me.

Billy sighs. "Well, you said she'd be in a mood because ..." He eyes me and winces. "... well, because of, um ..."

I frown. "Sorry. It's my fault, I guess. Or Bobby's."

"Your ma is ... pretty strong-willed," Billy points out. "No one's fault. You pick any day of the week, she'll be set off about somethin' else. Just this morning, I was tryin' to tell her about this sweet sixteen-year-old my pa just hired at Biggie's. He's gettin' picked on at school. I'm pretty sure he's gay. He's ... the kind who's unable to hide it, if you get what I mean."

"Like Lance?" throws in Tanner, smirking. "Remember Lance? He was full of attitude. Never took shit from anyone. Long hair that curled at his shoulders. Hah, I always liked that sassy dude."

Billy shoots him a look. "That makes *one* of us. He gave me the cold shoulder for four years and I still don't know why." Billy faces me again. "Anyway, that poor kid at Biggie's is Toby, and he has this tragic baby face—I swear, he'll look thirty when he's fifty. Anyway, I thought Nadine would have an idea how to help out the kid somehow, but ... well, again, you gotta catch her in the right mood." His feet swing around, dangling over the edge of the dock. "Maybe there won't be a good time to tell her *my* thing at all. My ... other thing, I mean. Not the thing about the Toby kid." Billy starts massaging the bridge of his nose, frustrated.

"What *is* your thing, anyway?" I ask.

"Oh, nothin'. Just that the whole Second Annual Spruce Ball thing-a-ding might have to be held at the McPherson's—Nadine's arch nemesis—instead of here at the ranch."

I roll my eyes. "She's got, like, six arch nemeses."

"'*Thing-a-ding*'," snorts Tanner. "You even *sound* like her."

"I do love your mama," sings Billy in a sweet voice. Then his face collapses. "But she's gonna hate me after this."

I lie back on the dock while Billy and Tanner go on talking about it. Then I pull out my phone and stare at the screen blankly, wondering if Bobby's enjoying his evening with his parents. I can only imagine the stories of this past semester that are being pulled out of him right at this moment over mashed potatoes and spicy brisket. *Except for the one about me walking in on him jerking off.*

I wish I could say I enjoyed my time tonight with my own parents, but my mama's always got her head so deep into her image, her businesses, her gossip, and her own worries that I feel invisible half the time I'm here. Not to mention my papa, who is almost always away in a neighboring town on important business. The only people on this ranch who make me feel worth the shoes on my feet are the two I'm hanging with on the end of this dock.

"It's gettin' kinda late," my brother points out. "Might want to head back to the house, champ, before the evil night opossums come out of the trees to reclaim their territory."

I sit up. "Actually, can I stay here with you guys? Maybe crash on your couch or somethin'?"

Billy and Tanner share a look. It's a look that lasts too long.

"Just for tonight," I quickly throw in. "Mama's in a mood. I don't want to be around that in the mornin', if you get me."

After a complete and entirely wordless conversation goes on between Tanner and Billy's eyes, my brother finally gives me a short nod. "Sure, bud. I'll pull out a blanket and pillow for ya."

I smile, relieved.

An hour later, Tanner and Billy are cooped up in their room with the door closed doing God knows. If it's anything dirty, they are being awful quiet about it, for which I'm thankful.

With their living room all to myself, I pour myself into what I know and do best.

Dancing.

Eyes trained on a mirror hanging in the dining room, I spend an hour or so practicing all my moves while my phone blasts whatever beats I dumped onto it before leaving campus. I definitely have room to improve in my muscle isolations, which my hip-hop dance instructor was all-too-quick to point out to me every damned class in front of everyone. I keep doing the same elbow-popping move over and over, working on getting the timing perfect.

I'm not going to be my brother and give up being the football star. Don't get me wrong; he coaches and he's mighty happy with it, and I'm proud of him. But he got a look at the competition in college and let it psyche him out.

I won't let the other dancers intimidate me.

At least tonight, in my safe space of Spruce, I won't.

After dancing until I'm sweaty, tired, and my legs feel tight enough to snap off of my body like a wishbone, I drop onto the couch on my side with the TV's glow pouring over me. The volume turned down low, which is alright with me since I'm not paying a damned bit of attention to it anyway.

That's on account of me and Bobby throwing funny texts at each other, since apparently his ass can't sleep either. His mama was super giddy and gushy all night and wanted to watch two movies back-to-back. His papa went to bed after just five minutes of hanging out with his son, thoroughly exhausted from some roofing job he had in Fairview. Bobby wants to go for a jog in the morning and invites me to join, but when he mentions how early he's getting up, I decline, insisting that my summers are for sleeping way-the-fuck in every damned day. He sends back a teary-eyed emoji, then says goodnight, since it's getting late.

The sleep timer I set on the TV must have lapsed because it shuts itself off right after that last goodnight text from Bobby, startling me. I sigh and push myself up off the couch, deciding to grab myself a quick glass of water from the kitchen.

Until Billy's raised voice through their closed door catches my attention: "*I'm not upset or anything, babe. It's just that we—*"

"*I know, I know.*"

The two of them have been chatting for a while, but with the TV now off and standing outside the door, I can hear them perfectly. The rest of the house is dead silent, save for crickets chirping outside and little gusts of wind disturbing nearby trees.

"*We went through this last summer. One night turned into a week. I know your little brother misses you, I know he doesn't like sleeping in the main house, but I don't know if I can go another summer like this.*"

"*It wasn't that bad ...*" murmurs Tanner.

"*You don't remember? We went a whole month without having sex. You gave Jimmy about twenty reasons to stay in his own room and he kept insisting to stay here. Not to mention him bringing Bobby by all the time. This place was like a frat house, and it's* your *time off from school, and* our *time to be ... Okay, I mean, I love your brother and all, and sure, maybe I can put up with* some *of his dance music blasting at midnight now and then—like it just was—but goodness, I'm gonna go crazy if he's on that couch for another summer.*"

"*Billy, babe ...*"

"*I know. I'm being so awful. I feel bad even saying it, but ... ugh, I'm an awful husband.*"

"*Yeah, yeah,*" taunts my brother back. "*So awful. The worst.*"

I hear the smacking of lips as they kiss. The springs of their bed creak gently from the movement of their bodies.

"*It's just for a night,*" he says to Billy so softly, I barely hear it. "*Just one quick little night.*"

Then their lips smack again, the bed creaks some more, and I hear nothing else.

I drop back onto the couch and stare up at the ceiling, then throw their cuddly cow-print blanket over my body with my feet sticking out the other end. My heart sinks like a stone dropping slowly through the water to the bed of that dark, lonely lake out there, stared down upon by tall, watchful trees.

I whip my phone back out and send one last text to Bobby:

ME

Yo, can I crash at your place tomorrow?

3

BOBBY

The next day marks my first full day of summer.

And the only person I'm bothering to fill it with is my best buddy Jimmy Strong.

We hit up the only arcade in Spruce, which has been Jimmy's favorite place in the world since he was thirteen. Even now, "*JIMS*" is at the top of every high score of every game—except for *Mortal Kombat II*, where some "*TBOY*" has stolen his top spot. So naturally we spend our time on that game for a solid hour while he reclaims his dignity from this T-Boy kid with a scowl on his face.

That gorgeous, determined scowl is where everything I love about Jimmy Strong starts. I watch him in his sleeveless red shirt and matching backwards cap while he vigorously kicks Sub-Zero's ass, his sinewy arms flexing and tightening as he jams his fingers into the buttons and jerks the joystick every direction. His low-hanging, always-dusty jeans show off a hint of his shiny black underwear, visible because the back of his sleeveless shirt gathers atop his tight dancer glutes, and either Jimmy doesn't notice or doesn't care. *He's always been one to show off what God's given him.*

But it all brings me back to that scowl of his. When he's got his eye on something, a fierce look of unflinching determination takes him over, and he doesn't let go until the job is done. He is the most committed guy I know, which I do understand is ironic to say about your best friend who's had no less than ten girlfriends in his first two years of college. *And those are just the ones I know about.*

I've always admired Jimmy's strength, ever since the day he came out as a dancer, then worked his tight tushie off to prove his worth on the stage in spite of insecure male mockery.

And damn, phew, even off the stage he proves it. He's proving it right now with every twist and thrust of his hip at the arcade game; even the way he games looks choreographed. And once he finally gets his high score back and we leave the arcade, he proves it with just the way he walks, so full of pride and swagger, it makes anyone walking with him feel just as proud. He proves it in the shape of his legs and how they carry his weight with such grace, despite his country-boy, roughed-up, dust-worn appearance.

And when we head down the street, Jimmy can't even leave an innocent lamppost alone. He grabs on and swings around it like a stripper pole, his shirt flipping up for a second by the wind and flashing me the beautiful sight of his toned lower back, his chiseled abs, and his tight buns in those low-hanging jeans, before hopping off and landing on his feet as lightly as a cat, laughing.

Dance is in his blood, and it's evident with every thump of his passionate, boyish heart.

Of course, a highly-inflated sense of over-confidence is in his blood, too. And it's made all the worse when we stop for lunch at Biggie's Bites—Billy's pa's restaurant—and I have to sit there while a bunch of girls two tables over keep looking our way and giggling.

"They still lookin'?" asks Jimmy.

I roll my eyes. "And droolin', and gigglin', and dreamin'."

Jimmy snorts, shakes his head, and takes a one-handed bite of his Touchdown Burger while flipping an arm over the back of his chair—enjoying the attention, from the look of it.

"Don't go encouragin' it," I mumble after taking a sip of water.

Jimmy eyes me. "Why not?" He peers over his shoulder and makes eyes with the girls, giving them a quick chin-lift that makes them all giggle and blush. "It's good to be back home."

I feel my ears flatten like a cat's. "Yeah, sure, right. Back home where everyone and their mother wants your Strong nuts."

He turns back to me. "Depends. Whose mother?"

Despite my annoyance, the look on his face makes us both burst out laughing, and the girls turn our way again, all dreamy-eyed and silly. I'd bet half of them aren't even graduated from Spruce High yet, way too young to bother dreaming of catching a man like Jimmy's attention.

After lunch, we decide to catch a movie, since something's starting in the next five minutes, then sit in the back of the theater with our feet up on the seats in front of us. Only a handful of others are in the theater, scattered among the front and middle rows, including someone I might've had English with junior year.

"Hey, weren't we supposed to throw some ball with your bro today?" I ask him.

Jimmy shifts in his seat with a sigh. His elbow touches mine on the tiny armrest between our seats. "Nah. I was thinkin' I'd give my brother and Billy some space this summer."

I wrinkle up my face. "But you just got here. You haven't seen the pair of 'em since January."

"I don't wanna be all on top of them like I was last summer."

Neither of us are bothering to keep our voices down at all. We have no shame or manners in movie theaters, it turns out. I'm pretty sure we have a reputation for this. I feel like maybe it's our sworn responsibility to hold up that reputation, too.

"Alright, then." I study the side of his face awhile. "Is that why you're wantin' to crash at my place tonight?"

He just shrugs for an answer.

When he shifts in his seat again, his foot on the back of the chair in front of us moves and finds itself resting against mine.

I smile inwardly, noticing that. He doesn't mind when we're touching. He never pulls away. He's so comfortable around me. I wonder why all straight guys can't be like Jimmy Strong, unafraid to show affection for another male, unafraid to just let ourselves fall into each other's spaces.

"I know why you don't wanna play ball. You're afraid I'll kick your ass in soccer again," I taunt him. "Y'know: the *real* football."

Jimmy snorts. "Don't you let my brother hear you sayin' that. He'll kick your soccer-ball butt from here to next Tuesday."

"Hey, all I'm sayin' is dancin' isn't the only sport that requires strong, quick, flexible legs. And my legs are better than yours."

From somewhere in the middle of the theater, an older man turns around and shushes us.

I wince and prepare an apology, but Jimmy leans forward and shouts back, "Shush yourself, *grandpa!*" before kicking back in his seat some more—resulting in his elbow digging worse into my side and his foot leaning fully against mine.

I eye him. "*Didn't your ma teach you to respect your elders?*"

To that, Jimmy only smirks.

After one last swing around town in Jimmy's red truck, we at last stop for the night at my house, coming in just in time for my ma's creamy chicken and dumplings, which we eagerly consume.

It's the crisp, early hour of nine o'clock when my ma retires to her bedroom with an exhausted pa, and Jimmy and I start kicking a ball around my backyard under the young night sky, still bruised by Spruce's nearby streetlights and a hint of distant light from the recently-set sun. The only light we need anyway is the bright-ass one spilling off my porch, lighting us up as I continue to—over and over again—steal the ball right out from between Jimmy's legs.

"Dude, you're cheatin'!" he shouts out for the ninth time.

I laugh and, after a little dance of my own, kick the ball right between his legs and score another "goal" through the middle of the tall, crooked trees behind him.

"Sometimes, you just gotta know when you're beat," I say to him as I gather up the ball and tuck it under an arm.

"I'm not beat. You're just cheatin' with your ... your ..." He can't find the word. "... *lightning legs.*"

"Is that what you call 'em?" I let out a laugh, then toss the ball up and start kicking it hacky sack style, keeping it in the air, going between the sides of my feet to my knees seamlessly. "Lightning legs, you say I've got?"

"Quit doin' that."

"Doin' what?"

He yanks his threadbare hat around in frustration, turning it backwards. "Showin' off."

"This isn't showin' off." I kick the ball a bit higher, then start bouncing it off the top of my head with ease over and over, never letting it touch the ground. "*This* is showin' off."

"You're just *askin'* to be taken down," he warns me.

"Am I?"

"Yeah, Bobby Parker, you are."

"You can't take nothin' down." The ball bounces off my head. "Hell, you can't even—" *Bounce.* "—score a goal when I gave you—" *Bounce.* "—ten and a half opportunities a minute ago."

"You didn't give me squat!"

"Oh, yes, I did, *Jimmy Strong.*" *Bounce.* "Just admit it." *Bounce.* "I'm better with my legs—" *Bounce.* "—than you are." *Bounce.*

"Like hell," he growls back.

The next bounce isn't the ball atop my head.

It's Jimmy Strong against my whole body as he tackles me to the grass.

I laugh out as he wrestles with me, grappling with grunts and jagged breath to pin me to the ground. I keep fighting with him, breaking from his grip easily and nearly managing to topple him off of me. But Jimmy has—and has always had—excellent balance, and the guy is impossible to shake off of my body.

Before I know it, Jimmy Strong is straddling me in his tight Wranglers, his knees pinning my folded arms down to the dirt and the grass, sitting on my chest with his weight. He stares down at me, the chest of his red sleeveless shirt rising and falling with his labored breaths. His backwards cap only holds some of his short hair, the rest sneaking out the front and reaching halfway down his forehead in sweaty tufts. His eyes burn with victory, his nostrils flared and his lips parted as he catches his breath.

Neither of us say anything at first, both of us still recovering from the scuffle. I remain a tightly-kept prisoner between his two strong, firm thighs, my face just inches from his jeaned crotch.

Then he goes and starts taunting me. "Giving up so quickly, Bobby Parker?"

"Shut up."

"What's wrong, Bobby Parker? You were gonna say somethin' about how much better you are, Bobby Parker?"

"Stop sayin' my name like that."

"Why not, Bobby Parker?" He grins cockily and gives my face a light, playful slap. "Feelin' a bit shy suddenly, Bobby Parker?"

"I swear ..."

"Tell you what. Why don't you say I'm better than you, and I'll let you up?"

"Alright." I lift my chin as best as I can while on the ground with my face being hugged tightly by Jimmy Strong's thighs. "I'm better than you. Now let me up."

Jimmy laughs at that. "C'mon, Bobby. You know you wanna admit it." He gives my face another playful swat.

"Stop that!"

"What? Is it botherin' you?" He taps my face two more times in a row on either cheek, harder. "It's like you don't got hands to defend yourself or somethin'."

I struggle feebly under him to free said hands, but Jimmy's strength and weight are too great to match. I'm helpless.

Jimmy's head lowers in one quick movement as he bends forward, his taunting face brought close to mine.

The fight leaves me at once. I stare up into his eyes.

And I'm suddenly aware of how intimate this has gotten in the space of seconds.

That awareness makes my dick flinch.

Oh, God. Not now.

"Well, buddy?" Even his voice lowers as he speaks to me this close. "You got somethin' you want to say to me?"

"Yeah." I eye him. "You need a Mentos."

Jimmy smirks. "Just admit that my legs are better than yours, and I'll let you up."

Suddenly, I find I don't want to be let up.

I don't want to be let up at all.

My dick keeps swelling. It doesn't matter that we're outside. It doesn't matter that Jimmy Strong only has to sit back a little bit to make the discovery on his own of what my dick's doing, since I'm just wearing loose, mesh soccer shorts and not much else in the way of *boner containment*. It doesn't matter that my ma or pa could come out spontaneously and catch us here on the ground—and very visibly see my "enjoyment" of our roughhousing.

I need a figurative splash of cold water—*and quickly.*

"I can keep this goin' *aaaall* night," Jimmy sings, his voice tiny and teasing and full of twang.

My dick flexes urgently at his words.

Stuff is happening in my guts. My heart is thrashing. My face seems to be getting squeezed more and more by his legs, like a vise-grip slowly tightening.

I think he's enjoying this power over me a tad too much.

"Yeah, and I can *last* all night," I throw back at him.

Wait. Why am I taunting him back?

Jimmy smirks with dark amusement. "Good, 'cause I sure ain't lettin' you up 'til I hear the magic words." He flicks my forehead. I flinch and scowl at him from between his thighs. That makes him laugh. "I forgot how much fun it is to play with you like this, Bobs. Why didn't we do this more on campus?"

"Likely 'cause you act like a *dignified human being* on campus, instead of some dominance-seeking *ape* like you are now."

He laughs—finding that hilarious, apparently—then starts to casually play drums on my forehead with his fingertips. "Y'know, Bobby-boy," he goes on, oblivious to my grunting as I struggle to get free again, "it'd really mean a lot to me if you told me—your best friend, your best buddy, your pal—how much better I am at everything than you. It'd mean *so much* to me."

I resort to kicking my legs, trying to throw Jimmy off of me. *I guess that makes me the unruly horse and Jimmy the rider.* It doesn't matter, because it does nothing but make him clamp his thighs tighter around my face and press his ass heavier onto my chest.

He's determined to keep me pinned right where I am.

"Really?" he teases me. "You don't wanna make your best bud feel good? You don't think I deserve that?"

"Jimmy, I swear ..."

"Aww, c'mon. Don't you love me?" He pinches my top and bottom lips, then pretends to speak in my voice. "*'Why yes, Jimmy, I do agree, your legs are so much betterer than my scrawny ones ...'*"

I shake my head, freeing his fingers from my lips. "I swear ..."

"If you keep swearin', Bobby Parker, someone's gonna have to wash your mouth out with soap."

I don't say anything now. I just lie there in the dirt, helplessly caught beneath the weight of Jimmy Strong, and stare up into his rich brown eyes, which are so dark with triumph that he looks like some bully who's just won a schoolyard wrestling match with the shrimp-kid in class.

A decision flickers in his eyes. Then he lifts himself off of my chest, rises to his feet, and extends a hand down to me.

I can thank every gay god from here to Jupiter that my boner is (mostly) gone by the time he gets off of me. Otherwise, we'd be having a totally different conversation right now.

"Given up?" I ask him casually from the ground.

"Nah." He shrugs, all charm and sweetness in his eyes. "Just bein' the better man."

I snort, then reach for his hand.

He retracts it the second I'm about to clasp it, then snatches the soccer ball up off a patch of grass and races away with it.

"Hey!" I shout, then clamber off the ground and chase after him while he laughs. We run around the yard like dogs chasing each other's tails, Jimmy hopping over a tire and twisting his way nimbly around and between trees as I pursue him. I nearly catch him once or twice, but he's always quicker and gets away.

I think this is a perfect representation of my life with Jimmy Strong: always chasing him, just a step or three behind, forever within reach, yet never quite reaching.

A hand always extended, but never taken.

Not that I like to draw symbolism out of every little thing, but you can't help but notice it after a while. *Or maybe it's all of those critical-thinking reading classes I'm taking as part of the honors college.*

Several hours later, it feels like the whole town of Spruce is asleep, and the only motherfuckers awake are me and Jimmy. We are in my bedroom, sprawled out on a sea of mismatched blankets and throw pillows, watching some dumb late-night shit on TV.

He's on his stomach on the floor, elbows propping up his front as he stares up at the TV, and I'm seated next to his feet leaning against the foot of my bed, a big pillow at my back. My legs are crossed with my feet right by his arm. We've since showered and changed out of our clothes and into some comfy gym shorts—his, red and shiny like basketball shorts, and mine, gray and cottony. He's shirtless while I've got on a loose blue tank.

Jimmy laughs every five seconds at the dumb *Adult Swim* show that's on, and every time he laughs, I watch his bare back jerk and jump, little muscles in it flinching and flexing. I also watch his red, shiny bubble butt in those shorts wiggle. I really can't help it; those two shiny red glutes of his in those shorts are practically demanding to be stared at—especially since I'm having doubts he's got on any underwear, as the shiny, slinky, loose material settles between his muscled cheeks, outlining his butt exquisitely.

His short brown hair is freed from his hat for the first time since we set out for our long day this morning, messy and tousled.

Totally uninterested in the show, I decide to make a point and note it out loud: "I like you better with short hair."

Jimmy peers back over his shoulder at me. "You mean instead of that overgrown mess I had over winter break?"

"Your brother called you a hippie."

"What's wrong with hippies? They're all about peace and pot, aren't they?"

"I think you just got lazy and quit carin'." I shrug, then nudge Jimmy's shoulder with the side of my foot. "Not like you needed any help with the ladies, anyway. They'd take you whether you were a *shag master* or not."

"Did you go and tell anyone that I ended things with that girl on campus?"

That girl. His latest "girlfriend" of five weeks at the university doesn't deserve the dignity of a name, apparently.

"I dunno," I mumble. "What's it matter?"

"It matters." Jimmy stares at me severely over his shoulder. "Who'd you go and tell, Bobby?"

I frown. "I have no idea. Who cares?"

"Bobby."

I sigh and give it a moment's thought. "Dude, I don't know. Might've mentioned it to CJ in a message ...?"

"CJ?? Cale Junior, son of barber Cale?? The one with the party tomorrow?" Jimmy gives a huge, demonstrative roll of his eyes, then smacks my leg. "Of all people! That fool has the biggest dang mouth. Fuck. *That's* why the whole town already knows." He sighs. "Including *Camille* ... who's apparently back for the summer."

Oh, shit. "Camille's back? ... Camille Randall?"

"Obviously, bro. What other Camille could I be talkin' about? She had a death in the family. Her uncle on her mama's side. She's here for the summer, and apparently she's been askin' about me."

I glance down at my hands, where I've gone to picking at my nails. *Camille ... I wasn't planning on her to be around this summer. The whole summer before we left for college, people were saying they wouldn't be surprised if she and Jimmy someday had rings on their fingers.*

Of course, the gossipers of Spruce say that about *any* pair who show even a breath of interest toward one another.

Maybe I shouldn't think much of it.

"And now I know *why* she's askin' about me," Jimmy finishes with another harsh look thrown my way.

I screw up my forehead. "What's the problem with that? You love the attention. Now all the ladies of Spruce—Camille or not—will be on you and your dick 'til the end of summer."

"Maybe I wanted a summer to myself. You ever think of that? Maybe I could've gone a few more weeks in peace with everyone thinkin' I was taken." He fidgets and looks back at the TV. "Whole point of the summer is to get *away* from girl drama."

I frown. "Says the guy who was just encouraging and egging on a bunch of *ogling girls* at Biggie's Bites."

"That's different. That's just fun."

Jimmy Strong logic. "Sorry, man. I didn't think it'd matter."

"Sometimes Spruce is the damned worst. Now I'm the freshly single bachelor in town, and everyone's gonna do that annoying matchmaker thing they do. At school, at least people mind their own business. Hell, you could make out with half the class—guys or girls—and ain't no one battin' an eye."

Guys *or* girls, did he just say?

He said all of that to the TV, by the way. Not at me.

I give him another playful shove with my foot. "Oh yeah? That so, Jimmy? Been thinkin' of makin' out with any *guys* lately?"

Jimmy snorts. "You know what I meant."

"Nah, I don't," I taunt him. "I need clarification. Lots of it."

"I'm not makin' out with any guys."

I nudge him with my foot again, this time with enough force to knock him off balance. He scowls. "You sure?" I ask, pushing his buttons. "You just said no one would bat an eye."

He shakes his head, ignoring me.

I stare at Jimmy's bare muscled back. For some reason, my pulse just sped way up—and it's not on account of the sight of his glorious glutes in those red shorts, still as distracting as ever.

A question sits on my tongue. A question that, despite how ridiculously open and comfortable I am around my best friend, I seem to have difficulty asking. Even if it's half a joke. Or all joke.

Or no joke at all.

Another silly thing happens on TV.

Jimmy bursts out laughing, his eyes filling with tears.

I swallow once, tightly. Then I take a breath and, with some invisible fist squeezing my throat, I make myself ask it: "You ever actually think about kissing a dude?"

Jimmy doesn't say anything. He just keeps watching the TV, his eyes hanging on the screen, as if waiting for the next big punchline or stupid thing to happen.

I know damned well he heard me. Is he just ignoring me?

Then—a full fifteen seconds after I ask the question—he says, "Nah, not really."

Nah? Not really? "That doesn't sound like a definitive 'no'."

He peers over his shoulder at me, his dark, blunt eyebrows pulled together. "Why aren't you datin' any dudes lately?"

The abrupt shift of the spotlight throws me. "Huh?"

"It's been a whole year since I've seen you with any guy. And that last boyfriend of yours lasted all of a week before you said— what was it?—'He reminds me too much of your brother. Creepy.' Oh, man, I died laughing."

My eyes turn into two bitter slits. "So glad I could amuse you, Master *Pussy* Hunter. It's a wonder our dorm wasn't equipped with a *revolving door*."

"There are plenty of dudes in Spruce now, ever since Billy and my brother. And Trey and Cody. They're popping up everywhere."

"Oh, now look who's playing matchmaker."

"I heard guys are even coming out like popcorn in Fairview. That isn't that far to travel, y'know."

"I don't got a car."

"I'll drive you. I'll be your summer chauffeur and bodyguard."

"Jimmy, why'd you go changing the subject on me? We were talkin' about *you* and *your girl problems*."

"I don't got any *girl problems*."

"Sure, you do. You've got too many to choose from. That's a problem. You've got so many, you dumped '*that girl*' you were with for over a month back at South Wood."

"I didn't dump her."

He turns and glares at the TV with a grunt.

I blink. "Wait. What?"

"*She* dumped *me*." Jimmy's voice is cold, his whole body gone rigid. "Had stronger feelings for some idiot in her chem class."

Something goofy happens on TV. Jimmy doesn't laugh at it this time, his eyes full of dejection and bitterness.

The Strongs are all hard on each other, I noticed. When one of them is down, they poke each other's buttons until their mood changes—ideally for the better. There aren't apologies exchanged; just sassy eye-rolls, offhanded remarks, and a peace offering of fresh-squeezed lemonade. I've been over there enough.

My family, however, is sensitive, compassionate to a fault, and meek. I get it from my ma. My pa is not too different, being a soft-spoken sort of man despite his rough career in construction and gritty-handed, around-the-town honey-dos he pulls off.

Over the years, Jimmy's really rubbed off on me. I've become rougher, tougher, and harder. My ma notices, and only every now and then says something about it. I never listen.

But I'd like to think I rub off on Jimmy, too. I believe a part of him is tired of all the "hard love" he gets at the Strong ranch.

My voice lowers to something soft and sweet when I pat him on his leg and say, "I'm sorry about that, buddy. I didn't know."

Jimmy just shrugs. "Guess I've dumped enough girls in my life, was only bound to get a taste of my own medicine at some point."

My hand is still on his leg, a perfect handful of his tight and shapely calf I didn't intend to enjoy. "It's still gotta sting, though. I really wish I knew that that had happened."

"Why?"

He keeps staring at the TV while he talks to me, but doesn't seem to be watching it. I shrug. "I might not have been as nice to her when I ran into her at the UC food court our last day."

"Nah. I wouldn't want you to do that."

I lift an eyebrow. "Why not?"

"You don't got a mean bone in you, Bobby Parker."

I smile at the back of his head, touched.

"I'm done with girls for the summer," Jimmy decides. "I'm not playin' this sad-single-dude-datin'-every-chick-in-sight song and dance. Why put myself through that?"

"Yeah!" I cheer him on. "There's the Jimmy I know!"

He sits up at once and puts himself next to me, leaning back against the foot of the bed. Our sides press together as he claims the other half of the pillow I'm leaning against—or rather, *steals* that half from me. "It's just gonna be us this summer, buddy."

Jimmy raises a hand toward me, coming in for one of those half high-five, half handshake bro things he does.

I grin, clasp his hand, and give it a firm shake. "Just us."

The TV takes our attention when another dumb-as-fuck thing happens, and suddenly even I'm laughing at it along with Jimmy. His arm stays pressed firmly against mine, our shoulders dance with each laugh as we share unequal halves of that pillow, and our night stretches into the wee hours of morning before we crash.

4

JIMMY

I pull up against the curb, then turn off the engine.

"You sure you don't wanna—?" I start to ask.

Bobby is already out of the truck with the door slammed shut halfway through my sentence.

—*just head back to your place and play some soccer?* was the rest of my question, but I guess either he didn't hear me, or his mind is made up already.

I hop out of the truck, pocket my keys, then come around the truck to catch up with Bobby, who's already through the double doors of Pepperoni Pirate.

The place is packed and explosively noisy for a late Monday afternoon, and that's for three little reasons: first, it's the summer; second, it's the only place in Spruce that serves both pizza *and* has six pool tables *and* two shuffleboard tables *and* dartboards; third, it's CJ's birthday, and everyone and their damned uncle loves CJ.

Probably because almost everyone in town gets their hair cut by Cale and Edison, and CJ is Cale's only kid—*his pride and joy*. CJ is turning nineteen, and after spending a year being a lazy bum in

Spruce, he's finally heading off to college in the fall—some school for engineers in north Texas, if I heard the rumor right. Cale is super beaten up about it and spends every waking second with his son before shipping him off across the state.

From the looks of it, CJ's birthday bash has taken over the entire restaurant. Tables are shoved together with big platters of differently dressed pizzas laid out. People are gathered in clusters chatting and laughing with giant Pepperoni Pirate mugs of soda and paper plates of pizza in their hands. Paper banners and party streamers and balloons are hung everywhere. The floor is littered with confetti already and the party just started an hour ago.

I find Bobby at one of the pizza-filled tables peering over the choices while Lena, Rhea, and Amber appear to be chewing his ear off about something. Those gossiping girls are a trio of dancers I went to high school with—and who decided they were all Bobby's besties when he came out to everyone three years ago.

"What's goin' on, ladies?" I greet them all, cutting off Rhea in the dead middle of a rant.

Lena shoots me a look. "Oh, I was just asking Bobby here if he's seeing anyone."

Rhea rolls her eyes. "She was askin' if *you're* seein' anyone."

Lena gasps, her face flushing at once. "Rhea! I was not!"

In the middle of Rhea and Lena's back-and-forth, Amber lifts her chin and squints at me. "How's your dancing career over there at South Wood? I hear you're turning into a Californian."

I frown. "My school isn't in California. It's in Arizona."

"Anything west of here is California to us." She pushes in front of her two squabbling friends, bringing herself right up next to me. "Hey, I'm having a little gathering of friends tonight. Just us girls, and a few other dancers from back in the day—those of us still in town. Nothin' big, just wine and finger foods and making fun of our old dance recitals. Are you free? You'll be the only guy there. The girls miss you."

They tried this ruse on me last summer, too. It turned into a night of twenty questions, an unwelcomed kiss in the kitchen, and a ton of gossip firing around town the next morning. I'm not fallin' for that again. "As much as I appreciate the invite ..." I start.

"Camille's gonna be there, too."

Bobby's eyes flick up at the mention of her name, staring hard at the pair of us from across the table.

I wasn't aware that he's paying our chat a lick of mind until now.

I smirk. "That supposed to make a difference? I've got plans."

Amber is persistent. "She hasn't seen you in years, Jimmy. And the girls miss you, like I said. We all do."

I notice that Rhea and Lena stopped arguing, both of their full attentions on me. "Sorry, ladies," I address them all as I slide three narrow slices of thin-crust pepperoni with mushrooms and long green peppers onto my plate. I only wanted two, but the third just hung right on. "Can't tonight. Y'all will have fun without me."

"No, we won't!" blurts Lena, for which Rhea gasps and swats her friend.

Amber crosses her arms. "You think you're better than us."

I eye her. "That ain't it."

"You're all California now," she continues to taunt. "Training at some big, fat, fancy academy. Can't even dare to slum it with a few gals from high school anymore."

"*South Wood isn't in California.*" I pop a garlic breadstick bite into my mouth. "I just have plans tonight with my buddy is all."

"So you're gonna spend all summer with Bobby again?" asks Amber with a suggestive lilt in her voice. "Ignore all of us? Push all the girls aside? Sounds like you don't care a bit about any of us anymore, that's what it sounds like to me."

"Yo, Bobs, my man!" someone shouts out from a table across the room. "Over here!"

Bobby turns around with his plate. It's a table full of his soccer buddies plus a couple others, flagging him over and waving like idiots. Bobby waves back, then heads on over to the table as they shout and hoot like animals, making room for him to join them.

Amber smirks. "Looks like he isn't just *your* man."

I shoot her a look. "The hell you mean by that?"

"Oh, Jimmy, Jimmy ..." She flips her curtain of thin brown hair and lets out a wistful sigh. "If only you knew what the girls say about you. C'mon, Rhea and Lena. This one's a lost cause." And with that, the three of them turn and strut away.

I stare after them, annoyed. "The hell you mean?" I shout at their backs, even long after they've gone. "What do the girls say about me? What do you mean??"

"Jimmy, didn't expect to see ya here," comes another voice at my back.

I whip around to find Joel and Robby at the other end of the table by the breadsticks.

I shift gears at once. "Yeah, wouldn't dare to miss CJ's big ol' birthday bang. His papa would cut all my hair off if I did."

Joel—with his slightly acne-pocked cheeks and a permanently dumbfounded expression—gives my comment a squeaky laugh.

Robby shakes his head, then nods toward the direction where the girls went. "You being *harassed* by your *past*?"

I shrug it off. "I just can't seem to get a summer to myself."

"Dude, you should enjoy the attention!" boasts Robby.

Joel nods. "Yeah, man. Wait a few more years when you've got yourself a wife and kids. I mean, Mindy's not due for, uh, another six months or so, but I look at how much *Kirk's* changed since Kirkland Junior was born, and ... *phew*, I'm petrified, to be honest. Perfectly, rightly petrified. Bonnie's got him whipped. And their little Kirkland Junior? He isn't so little anymore."

"Joel and I got seven or so years on you," Robby points out. "So, y'know, take our damned advice, boy. Let the girls chase after you. Get some tail. You aren't gonna stay pretty all your life."

I chortle and shake my head. "Yes, sir," I mock him right back, saluting him with my free hand.

An explosion of laughter pulls my attention back to Bobby at his table, where his soccer buddies are in the middle of telling him a very animated story involving a lot of hand gestures and facial expressions and obnoxious cackling. I stare at them awhile, lost in a thought or two, my plate of pizza slowly growing limp.

Another hour later, I'm standing by my boy Bobby, and we're watching CJ stare, starry-eyed, at the candle-filled cake his papa ordered special from T&S's Sweet Shoppe. Bobby and I have had about three seconds each to chat with CJ before he was whisked away by someone else, but neither of us seem to mind; Bobby has been more invested in reconnecting with his soccer buds anyway, and I couldn't care less about the bigmouthed barber's kid.

Or the table of dancers in the corner who won't stop sneaking smirking glances my way, then whispering amongst each other.

It's nearly sunset by the time my tires are kicking up dirt off the long country road on our way to the east suburbs. Bobby keeps complaining about how full he feels, mumbling, "Can't remember the last time I ate so much cake in a three-hour period." It felt a lot more like eight hours to me, but I chuckle at him and sing out, "That's Billy's confections for ya!"

It's another night at the Parkers when we come through the back patio door (it's basically the front door at Bobby's house) and drop like a pair of slugs in front of the living room TV, slumped against one another on his old turquoise tweed couch. His gray cat Delilah stares resentfully at us from her perch in the corner of the room while we laugh our asses off at some dumb sitcom Bobby got me hooked on last semester.

Then Mrs. Parker emerges from the hall. "Bobby, hon?"

I grab the remote and turn the volume way down. "Sorry, Patricia, ma'am. Were we too loud?"

"No, no, Jimmy, you're fine. I just need to pull my son aside to speak to him. It'll only take a little nothin' second."

Bobby shrugs at me, then pries himself off the couch where we were pretty much glued to each other's sides, since the middle cushion sinks in a lot. He goes with his mom into the hall.

Despite the volume on the TV being low, I can't eavesdrop, so I just whip out my phone and start playing games, ignoring the show. I glance at the digital clock beneath the TV and realize all the dance girls should be hanging at Amber's by now.

Nah, I'm still not going. Not even thinking about it.

Even if it's just a six-minute drive away.

No desire to spend time with them tonight, anyway.

Except for maybe a mild and stinging curiosity about what Camille is up to. I can't help but think back to that first summer, the one just before I went off to my first year at South Wood with

Bobby, and how she always seemed to be around to laugh at a joke I just made. She had this way of "being one of the guys" whenever she hung out with me and my friends. Even Bobby liked her, especially since she didn't make any deal out of him being gay. Most girls want to turn Bobby into their new shopping buddy, or "talk cute boys" with him, or do a number of other gay-bestie-pigeonholing bull crap that annoys poor Bobby to no end.

But Camille makes him feel normal. Boringly normal, in fact.

And I guess it doesn't hurt that she's cute, too. She's slender, with short and choppy black pixie hair that goes in all directions. She's got a little nose and a permanent smirk on her lips that says "totally over it", yet has a way of also welcoming you into her self-deprecating cynicism, like you're instantly accepted into her inner circle without having to prove yourself in any way. She's also got an older (and slightly less interesting) sister who was once a head cheerleader named Lindsay who happened to be my brother's prom date way back in the day, funny enough.

Camille is, for lack of a more intelligent phrase, "cool as fuck".

I really liked Camille. I hope the past year and a half in Europe hasn't changed her too much.

Somehow, I seriously doubt it.

"Ma, I get it, I understand. I ... I just ..." comes Bobby's voice suddenly from the hallway, his quiet tone from earlier traded for something just loud enough to hear. "I just thought that ... that Pa was getting more work now, since all of that *stuff* in Fairview—"

"I know, sweetie," returns his mama's voice, full of its usual high-pitched soft molasses and love. "I'm afraid it just still isn't enough. South Wood is pretty expensive, hon, and—"

"I know, Ma. I told you I'll transfer somewhere local if—"

"Listen to me, sweetheart. We're gonna keep you going to that school as long as we can. We just need a little help, alright? Start askin' around tomorrow, if you can. Put in some applications. I hear the Loves are in need of a dish washer. Or see if Mr. Tucker's hiring servers at Biggie's Bites. That's within walking distance."

"Walking distance?" Bobby protests. "In this heat??"

A shuffling of clothes indicates a hug.

I bite my lip and glance back down at my phone.

I believe I'm about two more overheard conversations away from earning my official Spruce Eavesdropper Membership Card.

Bobby trudges back into the living room, his mood changed considerably. He plops right back in place next to me on the couch, then just sort of stares at the TV, aloof.

I glance at him. "You alright, bud?" He shrugs. "So what was all that about?" I ask, pretending not to have overheard most of it.

"Nothin' I didn't already see comin'," he answers lamely, then jams a thumb into the remote, turning the volume all the way back up.

I nod with understanding, then throw an arm around my best buddy and pull him against me. "It'll be alright, my man," I assure him, rubbing and patting his arm and shoulder with my hand around him. "I'll take care of ya."

Bobby lets himself sink against me, giving in to my side-hug as his head rests against my chest. The noise of the TV fills our ears, and nothing more is said. Delilah the cat has gone to sleep, the night noises of horny crickets sing through the long wide window at our backs, and the lazy, slumped pair of us sink even deeper into that hungry old couch, though we both seem to be all out of laughs for the night.

5

BOBBY

"Yes, sir, I'm definitely a team player," I answer dutifully.

My ass hasn't been in a job interview since I was sixteen.

"Yes, ma'am, I can work weekends and nights," I answer with a straight back and a charming smile.

But yeah, I still got it.

"Yes, sir, I am a very fast learner!"

My interview at Country Lovin' is at a booth table in the back of the restaurant. My interview at the antique shop on 4ᵗʰ and Apricot is in a musty closet I think is supposed to be the manager's office. My interview at Hadley's Hardware is done while standing with a man in overalls and a stack of two-by-fours piled like an impromptu desk between us, right in the middle of the store.

"Yes, ma'am, I am at least sixteen years of age."

That one was with Patsy herself at Patsy's Pastries & Pies. I should be flattered she asked; I'm always told I have a young face.

With every interview, I'm dismissed with a promise of being called back later. "We just hired a few summer servers," Billy's pa tells me after I finish my interview at Biggie's Bites, which was done in a cramped office off the back of the kitchen, "so I'm not sure if we can squeeze in another just yet, but—"

"I understand," I tell him, same as I told the man at Hadley's Hardware, and Timothy Love from Country Lovin', and Patsy, and the thirty-something with a big brown beard and bigger belly who interviewed me one block down at the antique shop.

I sigh as I come out of the doors of my latest interview—the one with the ten-year-old-trapped-in-a-forty-year-old's-body at the town arcade who thinks I'm "overqualified for sweeping candy and quarters off of floors".

I swing into Jimmy's truck and slam shut the door with a huff, then loosen my stupid tie with an aggravated tug.

Jimmy reads it all off my weary face. "Bummer." He gives his steering wheel a halfhearted smack of his fist. "I was hopin' this one would pan out."

"You just want a hookup to play *Mortal Kombat* free," I throw back, "and ensure 'TBOY' doesn't take your top-spot again."

"Pssh. Mr. T-Boy can *try* to reclaim his throne. He'll lose."

I pull out my phone to check my list. I tap on the last item, marking it as finished. "Well, looks like all the hooks are baited. Now I just play the waiting game, though it's pretty obvious that even *this* early in the summer, everyone's all hired up."

"What about the church? Trey could probably use a—"

"They only do *volunteer* positions. Same as the soccer coaches at the park. Besides, I need *money*, not brownie points with Jesus. Is the AC even on in here?" I check the vents, aiming them at me.

Jimmy pats me on my leg. "We'll find you a job, buddy. And hey, look at it this way: even if it takes a little bit, that gives us more time to hang out!" He smacks my arm so hard, it stings. I retract it with a grimace. "You gotta be *drippin'* in that shirt and tie getup. It's a hundred and fifty degrees! How are you not dead?"

"What did you expect me to do? Wear a tank-top and shorts to my interviews? I'm not tryin' to be a lifeguard at the pool."

"Oh, now *that's* an idea! They hiring?"

"You gotta be CPR-certified. And besides, I'm not gonna sit in a chair and stare at kids picking their noses and peeing in the shallow end all day."

Jimmy snorts and brings his knuckles to his mouth, finding that funny apparently.

I don't.

After grabbing a quick bite for lunch, we decide to spend the afternoon being lazy bums in Jimmy's pool—perhaps inspired by the whole lifeguard thing. It's actually the first time I've been to the Strong ranch since I came back home, but Jimmy's ma isn't even here; she's on some errand to Fairview that has to do with her restaurant, self-titled Nadine's. With my shirt, tie, slacks, and dress shoes sitting on a chair by the pool, I hop into the cool water in my black boxer briefs, then sigh as I lean against the edge of the pool, enjoying myself in the warm afternoon sunlight after a long and tedious day of putting on a smile.

Then Jimmy goes and ruins it by cannonballing into the water right in front of me.

"Dang it, Jimmy!" I shout out, covering my face a second too late to prevent being splashed by water.

Jimmy—stripped down to nothing but his lucky pair of loose plaid boxers with a thick white waistband—only laughs as he hops right back out of the water and sits on the edge of the pool across from me, his legs dangled into the water.

The journey of my eyes up to his face is slow, because they are forced to make a long and lingering pit stop at his endless valley of perfectly chiseled abs, flexed from his torso leaning forward as he grips the edge of the pool with his long, strong arms.

When I finally reach his face, it's like he was patiently waiting for me to get there all this time, enjoying the attention I just gave him with my casual ogling.

Sometimes, I think that might be the only reason he keeps me around. He loves knowing he's irresistible, even to me.

"You went and got chlorine in my eyes," I scold him lamely.

He kicks at the water, sending another spray right at my face.

I flinch away, then glare at him. "Oh, real mature, Jimmy."

"You gonna get yourself a man this summer?"

I wrinkle up my face, as if the question just smacked me in it. "What's with you and your obsession with getting me a boyfriend? I'm not interested in anyone *here*, or in *Fairview*, or *anywhere else*."

"So ... single forever, then? That's your plan?" He kicks lightly at the water again.

I lift a hand to shield my face. "Stop doin' that!"

"There's this gay nightclub halfway to Brookfield. It has a great crowd. Hot fellas. Lotta fun. My brother told me 'bout it."

"A gay nightclub? What are you—Are you seriously suggesting I should whore myself out for a boyfriend at a fuckin' nightclub?"

"I dunno. Is that what you gay guys call it? Look." He leans forward even further, causing his ripped abs to crunch up even more deliciously than they were already. "Even if it's a total, bad nightmare, I kinda thought it'd be fun. You can meet some other gay dudes. I can see what your whole thing is like."

"My whole thing?"

"Yeah, your scene or whatever. Dude, you had to suffer going to so many fuckin' straight bars and clubs and shit out in Arizona. It's only fair that I suffer one of yours."

Jimmy doesn't even hear the words that come out of his own mouth sometimes, I swear. "Jimmy, *every* bar is a straight bar unless it isn't."

"It'll give us a break from Spruce."

"We've only been here barely five days!"

"That's five days too many. C'mon. Let me take you. I wanna."

I push away from the wall and start swimming for the other end, spreading the cool water with my hands. I hear Jimmy jump back into the water behind me, then swim after me.

"C'mon, Parker!" he shouts at my back. "Don't make me beg!"

"Beg?" I throw over my shoulder, still swimming away. "To go to a gay bar with me?"

"There's a million gay fish out there in that sea!"

I stop in the middle of the deep end and spin around, causing Jimmy to stop swimming at once. I'm nearly face-to-face with him now, only inches separating us.

"Is that all I am to you?" I ask him, kicking my feet lightly to stay afloat in the deeper end. "Entertainment?"

"I hooked up with probably five hundred girls since the start of school. You've had ... one boyfriend? Two?"

Talking this close to Jimmy, one miscalculation of my kicking feet or arms could send my lips crashing right into his.

I sigh. "That gay bar has to be at least two hours out of town. Brookfield is fucking far, Jimmy."

"So what? We'll get a hotel room."

Now he's lost me. "Hotel room?"

"Yeah! Then we can hit up this gay bar and have a safe place to crash afterwards. And if you get lucky, well, then I can go get a second room or somethin' and let you have some you-time."

"You've got to be shittin' me, Jimmy Strong."

"Nope. No shittin' is bein' had." Jimmy wiggles his eyebrows. "I told you I was gonna be your chauffeur this summer."

I sigh and shake my head in disbelief. "And when, exactly, was your crazy ass expectin' to take me into the jowls of Hell?"

"Oh, I dunno. This weekend, maybe? Friday?"

"And what if one of these lines I set out today actually bite?" I ask him. "I could be hired in a few days, or a few hours."

"Or a few *weeks*," mumbles Jimmy with a roll of his eyes.

"And if I'm hired, what if they want to go ahead and start me this weekend, right away? I can't be out touring gay bars."

Jimmy gets that obstinate look in his pretty brown eyes when I don't give him what he wants. "Well, maybe you're just makin' up excuses not to go out and live a little. Just say yes, Bobby!"

"Jimmy ..." I start, my voice hardening.

With sudden ninja speed, he jabs his claw-like fingers into my sides under the water, causing me to yelp out with half laughter and half surprise. I fight to get away from him, but the more I kick under the water, the more I seem to get trapped in his relentless finger-clawing, and before I know it, he has me against the edge of the pool, cornered and paralyzed with laughter by his ceaseless underwater tickling and jabbing.

"STOP THAT!" I finally manage to get enough voice to scream out between my forced laughs.

Jimmy stops and slaps his hands onto the edges of the pool on either side of me, his sparkly eyes bearing down on me. "So?"

"For fuck's sake, Jimmy!" I'm still catching my breath from all the unfair tickling and laughter he tortured out of me.

"Knowing all your weaknesses comes in handy," he points out. "Especially when I need to change your mind."

He's so close to me, pinning me against the edge of the pool with the walls of his arms on either side of me and his face inches in front of mine.

It's unfair how much power this boy has over me.

I stare at him hard. "Jimmy ..."

"Truth is," he cuts me off, "you don't really need a job. If it's because of your tuition, I told you, I could easily cover us both. My mama fuckin' adores the shit out of you. You're practically her adopted son by now."

I sigh. *Not this again.* "Your family is *not* payin' a cent for my education, Jimmy Strong."

"Is it the living arrangements? Our dorm?" Jimmy lifts a hand and gives a snap of his fingers. "I can cover that, too. Easy peasy."

"Everything isn't all *'easy peasy'* for everyone else in the world. Not everyone gets their whole damned life and everything they want handed to them on a silver spoon!"

I know I got the saying mixed up.

I don't care. I'm hotheaded and irritated at Jimmy's flippant attitude with regard to my family's finances. It isn't too often that the difference in our upbringing and general privilege is brought into bright, piercing focus. But when it is, I realize how much of life's luxuries he takes for granted.

Jimmy backs away from me in the water, an annoyed look on his face. Maybe I was a bit harsh with my words. Maybe not.

I think I hurt him nonetheless.

Jimmy doesn't really express himself well when he's hurt. Normally, he gets a twisted, indignant look on his face whenever I just say something wrong. But when he's hurt—*truly* hurt—he won't even reply; he'll just give me that look he's got on his face right now as his pretty eyes harden and intensify with frustration.

He looks so beautiful when he hurts.

I sigh, unable (or unwilling) to apologize, and pull myself out of the pool. My feet slap against the hot-as-lava stone as I grab my clothes off the chair and head for the house, not caring if Jimmy's staring at me as I go, or wondering anything, or fuming.

I'm inside his kitchen pouring myself a glass of lemonade when I hear him follow me inside. He stops at the other end of the kitchen island where he leans against it, his lithe, toned, panther-like body on full display, dripping with pool water.

"So I'm nothin' but a spoiled Strong boy, huh?" he asks, his voice soft and thin.

"Oh, here you go," I return as softly, a glass of lemonade in hand. "Bein' all sensitive because I went and hurt your feelings."

"My feelings aren't hurt." He eyes me. "But it isn't my feelings I'm tryin' to do somethin' about here."

My eyebrows pull together. "What do you mean?"

"I mean I'm tired of seein' you alone, Bobs."

The glass I just poured gets set down on the counter, not a sip taken from it. I stare at Jimmy like I didn't just hear his words.

And he's got more of them, apparently: "Don't get me wrong. I want to spend the whole dang summer with you. I don't give a shit about all these Sprucers who want to get all up in our business. But I've seen the way you look at other couples, and I see how you get when we come back here to Spruce and there's, like, no other gay dudes to hang with other than my brother and his husband. You aren't really close with Trey or Cody. C'mon, dude. You need to be around men who'll ... who'll *look back* at you. And since you don't got a car, I wanna be the one to give that to you, and also to bodyguard you or, uh, somethin'."

He really has a way to make my troubles all about him, even when he thinks he's being kind.

I smirk. "Sure, Jimmy. Or maybe you just want a bunch of gay dudes drooling over you, because no matter where the attention is comin' from, you can't get enough."

"So do we got ourselves a plan or not?" he asks, ignoring my taunt. "Friday night? Some seedy downtown hotel? Or do I gotta tickle you some more 'til you give?"

My ribs feel the fresh memories of his fingertips. I'm tempted to dare him to tickle me some more, just to feel his hands on me again, just to be touched, just to see how far he'll go, just because sometimes I love pushing his buttons and having mine pushed in return.

Untimely and fierce blush creeps over my frustrated cheeks at the thought.

Instead, I just shrug at him, lift the lemonade to my lips, and drink.

Jimmy Strong nods victoriously.

He's such a cocky bastard sometimes.

6

JIMMY

I pick through my drawers, thumbing through my underwear choices like pages in a book. I pull out three pairs of black shiny boxer briefs and set them on the bed, followed by four pairs of white ankle socks. Bobby will make fun of me for bringing so much underwear for just an overnight stay, but I'm kind of obsessed with being prepared for anything.

Which is why I also bring three different choices of shirts to wear. With matching skinny-leg jeans, both distressed and not. I throw in a third pair, just in case. I also snag a crisp jacket out of the closet in case I want to dress up any of my shirts a little more.

And let's not forget three choices in shoes.

I'll need plenty of choices in case nothing feels right. I could have asked my brother for advice earlier when he and Billy came to the main house for breakfast, but for some reason, I chickened out when he asked me where I was taking Bobby this weekend. I don't know why I couldn't just tell him it was the gay bar he told me about. What's the big deal, anyway? I'm doing it for my best buddy Bobby. My brother would think it's totally awesome, get that big stupid twinkle in his eye, then trap me in a headlock while he gives me cheeky warnings about not taking any "free drinks" from the men at the bar.

I stand in front of my filled-up suitcase, complete with about a gazillion toiletries, and chew on my lip as I wonder whether I've forgotten anything.

We don't even leave until tomorrow night.

Why am I fretting over this thing so much?

The raised voice of my mother coming from downstairs yanks me clean out of my thoughts. I squint and incline an ear toward my door, just to get a gist of what her latest explosion is about. I pick up a word here or there, a phrase, a glass slamming on the counter too hard, and then I hear Billy's voice.

Oh, shit. He dropped the bomb on her.

I poke my head out of my room, peering over the railing and down into the living room. From this angle, I can't quite see into the kitchen where they're arguing, but I hear them clearly.

And horribly. "But I'm your mother-in-law!! How could you do this to me?? You know what I think of them McPhersons!! You know our horrid history!! Oh my GOD, Billy! Oh my GOD!"

"Mama, you're way overreacting and you know it," comes in my brother's voice tiredly. They've been arguing for a while, it seems, and the argument only moved into the house from outside. "This isn't the snobby Evans. This isn't Marcy Whitman or her equally condescending husband. This is Cissy and Tim McPherson. The ones who actually *did* come to my wedding."

"Yeah, just so they *look* good in front of—"

"Mama, when are you ever gonna give up this silly feud of yours with them?"

"It ain't *my* silly feud! It's them who's the jerks!"

"You were doin' so good for a few years, and then overnight, you decide you've gotta be the queen bee of Spruce all over again. Hell, with the Whitmans' new house—"

"That *gaudy* piece a' property ..."

"—they're closer to Fairview than Spruce anyway. Why can't we just be civilized adults about all this? You'll still highlight the dance the same as you did last year, and you'll be—"

"And all because TJ works at Billy's little dessert store??" she throws back. "That is the dumbest damned excuse for—"

"Mama, now you're talkin' about my husband's pride and joy, and it isn't even just that! Their house is bigger. They also have—"

"Yes, your husband's dessert store, the one that *I* helped put on its feet with *my* funds, and now you're stabbin' me in the back! What's next on our agenda? Are we no longer calling Nadine's the number one romantic spot for prom night dinner? Are we handing over my Spruce chapter of PFLAG because—oh, I don't know— Cissy *Fucking* McPherson decides she wants to run it, too?"

"Mama, for God's sake ..."

"Yes, that's what I need a bit of right now. A bit of God. I need a Hail Mary and a Bloody one, too." The stab of her heels carries her out of the house as my brother follows her out with a, "Mama, c'mon. Mama!" over and over.

Figuring the coast to be clear, I come the rest of the way down the stairs, but stop when I find Billy still in the kitchen, his arms crossed tightly, leaning against the fridge.

Billy looks up. His strained face softens at the sight of me. "Hey there, Jimmy."

I give him a reluctant nod. "Hey, man."

He takes a deep breath. "Well, in other news, I think your mother officially hates me."

"Nah, stop with that nonsense. She can't hate you. She isn't capable of it even if she tried. She's just ... well ..." I come up to the counter. "She's goin' through somethin'."

"Yeah, I found out about the Cold Spoon. That doesn't make this any easier." Billy sighs and pinches the bridge of his nose.

I frown, flicking my eyes to his. "What about the Cold Spoon?"

"About it goin' out of business, I already know."

He says it so flippantly, the spear goes straight through my chest like cold lightning. My eyes avert to the chest of his loose plaid button-up, lost in a whirlwind of thoughts. The Cold Spoon was my mama's baby for years—Spruce's prized ice cream parlor. I remember hanging out there after school when I was just eight or nine, waiting for my mama to finish with the register before she'd leave the store to her workers and take me home.

"Oh, no," murmurs Billy, staring at me as he realizes it. "You didn't know."

I play it off with a little nothing shrug. "Nah, I knew."

Billy's nothing if not smart and sharply observant. He pushes away from the fridge, crosses the kitchen, and stops in front of me with a knowing look. "She kept it to herself until one night when she kinda ... slipped to Tanner. And Tanner, of course, told me. I thought our businesses were complementing each other, but ... it seems like my business sort of stole hers, and now ..." Billy sighs again and slaps hands to his face. "Ugh," he mumbles through them. "I feel responsible for all of this. This is all my fault. Of *course* she's mad at me, and she has every right."

"Nah, man, stop bein' a baby," I say, ignoring my own feelings.

Billy drops his hands and nods with sudden resolve. "You're right. No cryin'," he decides, despite his teary eyes. "I need to do somethin' about all this. I'll find some way to save her business *and* save her, uh, face. With the ..." He gestures at the air. "With the ... the Spruce Ball thing."

I smirk. "Good luck with that."

Billy tries on a smile, then sighs. "Ugh, I knew hirin' TJ way back when was gonna screw me in the end with Nadine. She has never quite forgiven me for that. No offense."

I let out a strained chuckle. "None taken, my man."

"I'm gonna have to make some big changes." Billy wipes off a sheen of sweat from his forehead. "How's Bobby? How are you? I heard you boys are headin' into the city this weekend."

"Yep. Bobby and I are just gettin' away for a bit before he gets hired by ... uh, whoever."

"Y'know, I'd hire him at T&S's in a blink," Billy quickly says, "but we just hired two new girls, and the hours are already spread plenty thin. It'd be an insult to Bobby to offer him five hours a week, if you get what I'm sayin'."

"I do." I give Billy a hearty pat on the shoulder. "I'll put in a word for you with my mama, see if I can smooth things over a bit."

"Lifesaver," he mutters at me, shoots me a smile, then heads on out of the house to join my brother in the front.

I go back up to my room, swipe my phone off the desk, and start texting Bobby a quick message of what happened.

The text is interrupted by a timely one from him:

BOBS

Do you like movies?

I smirk, then type out a reply:

ME
`Of course I do. Why?`

I stare at my phone while he types his response:

BOBS
`How about an endless supply of popcorn?`

I have no idea what he's getting at. He's already typing out another text—a much longer one—which I hope explains the odd questions. Does he want to catch a movie tonight or something? Why doesn't he just come out and say it?

"You're a tough one to catch, Jimmy Strong."

I jump, startled, fumble with my phone, and drop it. At my bedroom door stands a girl in a pair of black army boots, faded black jeans with holes at the knees, a red flannel shirt tied at her waist like a skirt, and a loose white V-neck that plunges down enough to show off her smooth, silky bronze skin she gets from her mother's Mexican side of the family. Her black hair is short and choppy, styled in that I-don't-give-a-fuck way, squished by a gray hat turned backwards. She's got a nose ring now and wears that permanent bad-ass smirk on her face I recognize all too well.

It's the permanent bad-ass smirk of Camille Randall, just the same as I remember it.

"Damn, girl," I exclaim, grabbing my phone off the floor while keeping my widened eyes on her. "You gotta creep up on me like that after two years? Sheesh, you scared the marbles outta me!"

Camille shrugs glibly. "Billy let me in, said you were upstairs. Phew, he's having some words with your mother out there. Didn't want to get in the middle of all that."

"Yeah. They have ..." *She looks really good.* "They have a lot of shit goin' on right now. Business stuff. Drama. Politics." *Like, really good.* "How've you been?"

"Oh, same old me, nothing much to report. Your room smells like an armpit, by the way."

"No, it doesn't."

"It's alright. The French boy I dated last semester smelled worse." She throws a totally "bro" chin-lift at me. "We missed you at Amber's the other night. She said she invited you at CJ's party."

I shove my free hand into my pocket, my other still clutching my phone like a weapon. "Yeah, well, when's the last time I took Amber up on one of her 'intimate gathering' invites?"

Camille chuckles dryly at that and shakes her head. "Amber and the girls have chased your nuts for years. You can't blame the horny bunch of them. They pretty much see your three years of taking high school dance classes with them as foreplay."

That earns a genuine laugh from me. *And she still has that same sassy sense of humor.* "Well, I'm sure y'all gossiped plenty about me that whole night."

"Sure, probably." She glances at her fingernails—painted as red as that flannel shirt around her waist—and smirks as she looks at them thoughtfully. "Not that I was paying any attention to it. The girls could use a little time outside of Spruce. This town has a way of ... *trapping* you ... if you stay in it too long."

I study her, fidgeting with my phone. "Is that how you felt?" I nod at her. "Trapped?"

She lets herself into my room, her eyes peering up at my walls as if to inspect each poster, fissure, and shelf. "Isn't that how *you* felt?" she throws back over her shoulder. "You and Bobby couldn't wait to tear off halfway across the country after we graduated." She gives it a second thought. "Hmm, I guess I *did* feel the same. I couldn't even stay on the same continent."

"I bet Europe's beautiful."

Camille stops at the window and glances back at me. "It is. Well, Germany is. Can't say much about the rest, except for a short weekend in France. Y'know, the countries there are a lot smaller than I expected. I doubt there's a country over there that's bigger than Texas. You could visit five countries in a day if you tried."

I lean my ass against the desk at my back, then cross my feet at the ankles. "You didn't come back last summer."

"Well, I didn't have a dead uncle last summer."

The blunt way in which she says that is *so* Camille. Yet for as much as I'm used to her dry nature, the words still sucker punch me in the gut. I had almost forgotten why she's here. "I'm ... I'm sorry for your loss," I make myself say, albeit awkwardly.

Camille pokes a finger through my curtains. "Your mother is coming back inside," she notes, not acknowledging my sentiment. Then she eyes me coyly. "If I say hi to her, she'll probably invite me to stay for lunch and interrogate me, don't you think?"

She's always shrugged away her feelings like that. It's one of the reasons I probably clicked so well with her back in the day.

I glance down at my phone and the mile-long text Bobby was in the middle of writing me earlier. I read it, then smirk, realizing the point of all of Bobby's seemingly random questions.

At least one of us will get what we want this summer.

"Yeah," I decide, giving her a nod while pocketing my phone. "That sounds about right."

An hour later, Camille *is* proved right: Once Nadine is yanked out of her downward spiral of fury, she finally realizes Camille is under our roof for the first time in two years, and like a rubber band, the woman snaps right back into her happy place. At once, she insists that Camille stay for lunch, orders Jacky-Ann to throw together a nice meal for us, then sits herself right by Camille to pick her brain the whole time about what she's been up to.

I'd figured that Camille might harbor a pinch of regret for inviting this fate onto herself. But from the smart look in her catlike eyes, she doesn't seem to mind my nosy mama's question barrage. In fact, she acts like it was part of her plan all along.

I guess I shouldn't be surprised. That's Camille for you.

It's just a quarter to five when my mama decides she has a headache and heads out to check on some of our recently-hired ranch hands. After helping Jacky-Ann clean up the table and all the dishes—which we insist on doing, despite Jacky-Ann trying to shoo us away and leave the work to her—Camille and I sit up in my room on the edge of my bed with a bunch of dusty yearbooks and old school crap scattered around us, even on the floor at our feet. We sift through the memories and make fun of our worst teachers.

Then she pulls out a photo that was tucked away between two pages of our senior yearbook. She frowns at it, then eyes me. "You ever regret not taking an actual date to your prom?"

I yank the pic from her fingers and give it a look. It's me and Bobby in our fancy totally-not-matching tuxes, our arms around each other's backs, flashing big dorky smiles at the camera.

"Bobby *was* my actual date," I throw back.

"But what if some other girl had asked you? Jazzy was a total twat and shouldn't have dumped you for *Anthony Myers*—of all people—but what if, say, Bekkah Linny asked you? Or Lindsay? Or Laurie? Natty? Tiff? There were, like, a *legion* of options."

I give her a look. "Bobby's my mate. He's my guy. Sure, maybe I had other girls I could have asked, but Bobby didn't have that luxury as a lonely-ass gay dude here in Spruce. And he's my best friend. My pal. I wasn't gonna ditch him on a night like that."

"So, like, what? It was some 'bros before hoes' thing?"

"Nah."

"So it was a 'Bobby before anyone else' thing?"

"Why's it gotta be any kind of thing? I wanted to take Bobby. I took him. I don't regret it a second." I give the photo another look, then catch myself half-smiling at it, some memory resurfacing. "I still remember the look on his face when I got on a knee and asked him in front of the whole soccer team. It was like I was proposing to the motherfucker." I let out a laugh, remembering the gawking faces of all his teammates—and Bobby himself. "Shit, I love that guy like a brother, with all my heart."

I feel Camille studying the side of my face intently. After a minute, it gets to me and I lift my quizzical eyes to her.

Her lips purse. "Like a brother?"

My eyebrows pull together. "Yeah, that's what I said."

She nods slowly, then peers back down at the yearbook on the bed next to her. "There's just no coming between *that*."

I bring the photo down to my lap. "What do you mean?"

"You and Bobby. Your friendship. It's just ..." She softly beats a fist into her palm, like a demonstration. "... impenetrable."

"Yeah, I know that. So?"

Her pretty hazel-eyed gaze lifts up to mine, piercing me. "I'm not saying all this to make you defensive or think I'm trying to get at anything. I mean, look, the guys in Europe ..."

"Guys in Europe?" I cut her off, my heart racing as if my fight or flight response has been triggered somehow, but unsure why.

"They're far more *open* in Europe," she goes on blithely. "Guys are sexually ... *flexible* over there. Guys kiss other guys and it isn't always a gay thing. Guys and girls, girls and girls, guys and guys ..."

"I'm not gay," I blurt out more snappily than I mean to.

"I don't care what you are, Jimmy."

"My brother's the gay one of the family. I'm not gay, Camille. My closeness with Bobby—"

"You don't gotta explain anything."

"—is because *I'm not afraid to show my love for my best friend*. So what if Bobby's gay? My brother set the example for Spruce, and I'm not about to ruin it by perpetuating some homophobic 'dudes can't be close with other dudes' toxic masculinity bull crap. Guys show affection for each other all the time, and they should do it even more. Why else do athletes like slappin' each other's asses after a big game? Or in gym class? We like it when a buddy slaps our ass. It makes us feel good. It makes *me* feel good when a pal smacks my butt cheek with pride. And when I hug my best bud Bobby, I feel fucking great, because I'm showin' him how much I love him. You wanna talk all *European* at me? I'll kiss Bobby if that proves how secure I am, just like your fancy Europeans. I'll call him over right now and kiss that motherfucker on the lips."

After my tirade, Camille just sits there staring at me with this cool-mannered, patient, half-lidded *"Are ya done?"* look on her face that would be comical if her words hadn't just gotten me all hot.

I huff with frustration and stare back down at the photo in my lap, fuming and red-faced.

She says, "You don't have to prove a thing to me, Jimmy."

I don't say anything, my hardened eyes on the photo.

She glances down at her phone, then sets the yearbook aside. "Alright. It's about time I head back home. Mom's waiting."

I look up to watch her rise from the bed, step gracefully over a couple of boxes full of high school trinkets and crap, then stop when she reaches the door.

She turns and eyes me. "I kissed a German girl last summer."

My pulse continues to throb in my ears and I'm still red-faced, but I lift my eyebrows at her words anyway and wait for the rest.

A dreamy look sweeps over her face like a fog. "Her name was Genoveva. Took me saying it about a thousand and a half times to get the pronunciation right. Damned Texas twang never quite gets off your tongue, even across the ocean." Camille shrugs. "She tasted like strawberries and wine. Maybe it was her lip balm."

"Genoveva ..." I murmur, trying it.

"Close." She grips my doorknob, jiggles it for no reason, then eyes me. "Maybe I'm a little gay, a little flexible, or a little nothing at all. Or maybe the better point is, it doesn't matter. You like what you like."

And with another one of her totally-Camille shrugs, she wags a photo in the air that she fished out of the yearbook. It's one of me and her in our first dance routine together sophomore year.

"I'm keeping this one, Jimmy Strong," she says, then swings her way right on out of my room with half a smile on her face.

My heart still beats aggressively inside my chest.

For what, I just don't know.

7

BOBBY

It didn't seem like all that long ago when Jimmy and I were in his beat-up red truck coursing down the open road, music blasting and windows rolled down and Jimmy grandly steering his steed.

Our trip into the city isn't as chill.

Something has clearly been on Jimmy's mind since we left our comfy little hometown. He's snappish and irritable one moment, then chipper and smacking my arm after telling a joke the next. The dude is downright maniacal.

Then Jimmy becomes a furious fireball two hours later when we finally reach the city through a crawling, horn-honking, five-hundred-lane highway. A pinched look of stress paints Jimmy's face redder and redder as we navigate the web of busy downtown streets. He white-knuckles his steering wheel, grits his teeth, and argues with his phone. "I went left already!" he shouts at the poor thing. "We're goin' in a dang circle, ya dumb piece a' metal!"

"Calm down, shoot, Jimmy," I grunt, peering out the window. "Wasn't it the building back there? The hotel parking garage?"

"Which friggin' one?? Boy, you ain't helpin'."

"Why do you sound twice as Texan when you're angry?"

"Not now, Bobby!" A car honks. Jimmy pokes his head out the window. "Go toot at someone else! I ain't from around these here parts! Hey!" He faces front and smacks his steering wheel. "Get out of the dang way! The light's green! *Move yer ass, move, move!*"

I suffer about another forty-four minutes of Jimmy's one-man circus act before we're—*at long last*—dumping ourselves into our hotel room for the night.

A hotel room that smells like soggy wood and condoms.

"I am *not* settin' my bag on that bed," I state.

"Quit your whinin'. It isn't that bad. You want mine instead?" Jimmy pats his, making the old springs squeak and squawk. "The hotel had a four-and-a-half-star rating."

"That's what you call 'a rating bought and paid for'." I set my bag on the desk instead, then wince as I notice a sticky spot under the lamp. I pray that's a coffee ring or dried tea or something.

Jimmy's suitcase is already open—yeah, he couldn't just bring a bag; he needed to bring his whole wardrobe—and he's fished out three shirts, which he slaps to his chest as he faces me. "Alright, bud. You gotta tell me what I should wear tonight. I'm thinkin' the tapered black button-up."

I laugh. "Really, dude?"

"Don't give me that look. I have to look my best. You know I don't half-ass nothin'!"

"Sure. You just want to steal all the attention for yourself."

Jimmy snorts at that. "What're you talkin' about? It isn't my fault if I get stared at everywhere I go. I got Strong genes."

"And *tight jeans*," I add with a roll of my eyes, then peel open my bag and fish around inside.

"Hey, they aren't any tighter than I usually wear!"

"You realize every boy in the nightclub will be starin' hard at that tight Wrangler-clad ass of yours, right?" I throw back at him as I keep looking through my bag. "You're fishing with premium-grade bait in a sea of hungry, hungry fishes."

"So? Isn't that the point? Wait a sec." He turns his ass my way and peers back at me over his shoulder, wiggling his booty in my direction. "Are you sayin' you think my ass is—*what's that phrase you just used?*—'premium-grade' ...?"

"That isn't what I said."

"Are you tellin' me I got a premium butt, Bobby?"

"Ugh, I'm goin' in here to get ready." I grab my bag right back up from the desk—which makes a noise akin to ripping a sticky old Band-Aid off a knee—and push my way into the tiny bathroom.

I start fussing with my hair in the mirror. After trying (and ultimately failing) to get a proper part happening, I resort to just tousling it every which way, going for a "whatever" look.

And that's precisely how I feel right now: *whatever*.

I give up with a demonstrative sigh, slapping my hands to the counter as I lean toward my reflection and glare at my face. "Can you tell me *why* we are even doing this, Jimmy?"

"Aw, don't start with that again," he grunts from the room.

"Seriously," I exclaim to the mirror and the crack in its corner and the shard of rust running down its frame. "I don't need to find myself a boyfriend on some sticky downtown dance floor."

"You're gettin' nervous. That's what this is."

I roll my eyes at the mirror. "No, I'm not."

"Yeah, you're lookin' for excuses to hightail it outta here. I bet you're a minute away from griping about a sudden headache."

I pull away from the mirror to give him a contemptuous look through the opened bathroom door.

Instead, I catch Jimmy facing the bed, his broad back to me, with both his shirt and his pants off.

My eyes drop to his ass in a pair of the tightest, tiniest, black low-rise bikini briefs I have ever seen. They're so low-rise, I can see the tops of his smooth buns and a wink of his crack peeking out of them. His Venus dimples add the perfect punctuation to his exquisitely tapered lower back, tight and cinched and slender.

He's fumbling with a shirt, I imagine unbuttoning it so as to put it on, but his effort takes long enough that he ends up just standing there in those tiny-ass things for *ages* as he figures out the buttons on whatever fancy shirt he finally went with.

I realize after a second that I'm holding my breath.

My eyes are not physically capable of pulling away from that model-boy butt of his. A guy shouldn't have feelings like this for his best friend. A guy shouldn't be *ogling* his best friend like this.

A guy shouldn't be having fantasies of motor-boating his buddy's bountiful butt cheeks.

My heart has lost its way, now somehow lodged in my throat as my increasing pulse threatens to make me explode from within.

Then Jimmy pulls his shirt on one sleeve at a time, and ever so slowly, he turns around to face me as he buttons it up.

His eyes find mine.

I stare back into his, stricken, lost in them.

As if he's blissfully unaware of my staring at his ass a second ago—or perhaps just accepting it with casual flair—Jimmy purses his cute lips with thought, gives me a curt chin-lift, and says, "You gotta tell me which pants go with this shirt, bud. I brought three."

Suddenly, I feel the need to play off my stunned demeanor with a snide-ass comment. "You think you could possibly wear underwear any smaller and tighter than those? Aren't you afraid of suffocating them Strong nuts of yours?"

"What?" He gives his own ass a slap, then lets out a laugh. "I thought these little things would be perfect for tonight. I never wore them before. What do you think? They doin' the trick?"

I blink, my eyes now dropping to the front of them.

And the *generous* bulge of his junk, framed by his tight briefs in such a way that not an inch of it is ignored.

"Trick? What the hell kinda *trick* you hopin' to pull, Jimmy?"

He shrugs. "The kind that makes me fit in with the crowd?"

I eye him with mounting confusion. I wonder sometimes if he enjoys peacocking around me all the time for some deeper reason. I used to think it's because he likes the attention. Then I wondered for a brief spell if Jimmy might be gay and toying with me. Then eight girlfriends later, I dismissed that notion and went back to assuming he's an attention whore. Then I wondered if it was some kind of invisible pissing match with any other man near him, like he has to be sure he's always the hottest dude in the room.

Just how far and big does Jimmy Strong's ego go, I wonder?

Suddenly I find all my fascination gone in an instant. "If you aren't careful, it's gonna be *your* tight little tush gettin' picked up tonight instead of mine." With that, I spin around and face the mirror again, fixing my hair with renewed purpose.

Jimmy isn't done with me. "And what the heck are *you* gonna wear, Bobby? Aren't you supposed to be gettin' ready?"

"I'm already wearing what I'm wearing," I throw back. "What do you mean 'what the heck are you gonna wear'?"

Jimmy's silence makes me pull away from the mirror—yet again—to look at him. He's gazing at my shirt like the mere sight of it deeply offends him. "But ... But you just *rode* here in that. It's all sweaty. Dude, are you *tryin'* to scare away the boys tonight?"

"I look just fine. *You're* the heavy sweater. Not me."

He shakes his head. "Nah, you are *not* going to the nightclub like that."

"I'll go however I damned well like."

Jimmy turns away—again gracing me with the sight of his tight bikini-brief-clad buns—and fishes through the pairs of pants he brought: a pair of skinny blue jeans with stylish horizontal slits running across the thighs, some acid-washed gray jeans, and a darker pair of straight-leg blue jeans. "I'm goin' with these for myself," he announces, tossing aside his signature pair of slashed-up tight jeans that show off his dancer legs, of course. "And you are gonna wear one of the other two, plus one of my tops. We're the same size," he adds over his shoulder—again catching me staring at his ass and not mentioning it, "so you'll look great."

I walk right up to that bed and pick up one of his shirts—a sleek blue button-up with stripes running up just the middle of it, the sleeves left solid. "The Strongs are never wanting for clothes."

"Blame me for havin' a gay brother who never let me walk out of the house lookin' half-assed." He picks up the pair of gray jeans and slaps them against my chest. "And neither are you."

I give him half a scowl of defiance, then relent at once with a huffed, "*Fine,*" as I toss the jeans back onto the bed, then proceed to undo my own pants and tug them right down. Jimmy just grins a knowing, cocky grin as he continues to dress himself.

Jimmy Strong always gets his way in the end.

After we grab a bite at a diner on the corner, the (now totally Jimmy-approved and swanky) pair of us walk down five crowded streets through smoke, body odor, cars honking, and loud city chatter. When we reach the nightclub, I'm almost disappointed at its unassuming entrance, wondering what all the fuss is about. But when the man at the door checks our IDs and lets us through, I find the nightclub's interior throbbing with colorful lights and deafening music. Through the flashing lights, I see a dance floor flooded with bodies, and the longest bar I've ever seen lining the perimeter of the space, interrupted here and there by sections with tall tables, moody lighting, and more bodies.

"Hooooo-wee!" cries Jimmy in my ear, laughing. "Now if *this* isn't a total change of pace ...!"

Bodies, that's all I see. Not faces. Not people. Just bodies with glittered shirts, tank tops, and nothing at all. Legs with underwear and heads with leather-daddy caps. Loose gold chains. Sweat and shiny muscles that look made of wax, or actual bronze, or pure oil.

"C'mon! Let's go out onto that dance floor and live it up!"

I shoot him a look. "Let's not."

Jimmy grabs my hand, and like some sad, forlorn dog being dragged on a leash, he yanks me through the room until the pair of us are surrounded on all sides by dancing bodies.

I haven't been in this kind of environment, ever.

I don't know what I'm supposed to be doing with my hands or my legs or my hips.

I'm a soccer player, not a dancer.

Yet there Jimmy goes, having the time of his life, feeling right in his element in the middle of a sea of sweaty gay men, dancing his tight tushie off in those stylishly ripped-up skinny-leg jeans.

Whenever Jimmy dances, he puts every part of his body into it: his arms as they pop with the beat, his legs as they bend in and out, his feet as they twist and do all this crazy cool shit—hell, even his face gives this total stank-eye to nothing in particular as he gets his moves on and grinds the space like he's fucking it in his mind.

It's totally intoxicating. Well, whatever is the equivalent of intoxication by drinking through one's eyes.

"You aren't movin'!" he shouts at me. "C'mon, Bobby!"

I start nodding my head to the beat, glancing to my left, then to my right. Guys are looking at us. Sweat is already creeping up my neck. *Or is that some heavy-breathing dude behind me?*

"Don't worry 'bout no one else. Just move. Dance."

"I ..." My throat's closing in. I've never been around so many gay guys before. I can't even focus my attention on a single one of them, let alone move my damned hips. "It's ..."

"What?" shouts Jimmy through the noise. "I can't hear you!"

"I can't ... I just—"

The next instant, Jimmy grips me by my hips.

I snap my eyes to his at once, startled.

Then he starts to guide me, rocking me with every four-count to the throbbing trance music that aggressively fills our ears and threatens to make them bleed. He tugs me one way, then tugs me the other.

He never looks away from my eyes.

"You got it!" he shouts at me encouragingly. "C'mon, get your hips moving! Yeah, like that! Like that!"

And indeed, just like that, Jimmy's got me dancing with him. With each step, I gain confidence, With each bob of my head and thrust of an elbow or arm, my heart warms to the music.

Suddenly, I'm another dancing fool in the sweaty crowd.

And it's all thanks to Jimmy who, once again, finds a way to pull me out of my own head.

Didn't I already say Jimmy always gets his way in the end?

About four songs later (It's difficult to say when one song ends and the next begins; they're all sort of expertly blended together by the DJ.) Jimmy and I take a seat at the bar where we order a pair of sodas, since we're both a year shy of the drinking age.

The energy between me and Jimmy tonight is something I am not used to. My being gay isn't ever something that's so—how do I put this?—*spotlighted* as it is right now. I feel strangely attended to, and I'm not sure yet whether it's a pleasant thing.

As we sit there sipping our lame sodas, Jimmy surveys the bar with his keen eyes, then nudges me when he thinks he's found me a guy to approach. Three times, I give said prospect a look across the smoky haze, then shrug, or shake my head, or sigh and look away. "You're so picky," Jimmy keeps muttering at me, then looks around for some other handsome dude with potential.

This hunting routine goes on for the better part of an hour.

During which, the pair of us get hit on. Several times, in fact.

But they all go something like: "Hey there, boys." That came from a thirty-something with a flat, greasy part, a silver button-up shirt opened halfway down his chest, and a unibrow.

Jimmy was quick to say: "He's taken, and I'm straight."

Five minutes later came an older man who put a hand on both our shoulders. "How about I treat the sexy pair of you to a drink?"

Jimmy shot him a deadly look over his shoulder. "How about you buy yourself a pair of glasses and see that we ain't your age?"

"Age is just a number," the man returned with a soft smile.

"And so's 'one'," Jimmy retorted, "which is the exact number of times I'll punch you in the nuts before you fold in half."

Then there came the tweaked-out party boy who—shirtless and sweaty and sunken-eyed and bone-thin—slammed right up against the counter next to me. The white cockeyed visor-cap he wore nearly fell right off. "Hey, baby. You and your hot friend look bored. Looking for a way to spice up your night?"

Jimmy didn't even let him get out another word before he stood between us, coming to my rescue. "He's got enough *spice*."

The boy's hands were in the air in surrender at once, backing away and disappearing into the noisy throng.

After a while, I sigh and give Jimmy a look. "Are you plannin' to scare away *everyone* who approaches us? Wasn't that the whole point of this? To get me a *guy* or something?"

Jimmy snorts. "The way you say *guy*, you make it sound like *gonorrhea*."

"Well, in a place like this ..." I start.

He swats my arm. "Look, you just need to be patient. Besides, if this doesn't work out, we can just go back to the hotel and make fun of skeazy *Skinemax* movies until three in the morning. This is our big night out! We can do whatever we want with it!"

"Alright," I concede with a shrug.

It only takes three more minutes before another body slides onto the tall empty stool at my side. "Hey."

I turn and look his way. I'm surprised to find a young guy my age with sandy blond hair and a zillion freckles peppering his cheeks before me. I wouldn't say he's my type—if I *have* one—but he isn't a bad-looking fellow by any means. Especially compared to all of the recent hits I (or Jimmy) have had to bat away.

I give him a tentative chin-lift of a greeting. "Hey."

The guy takes a breath. He's nervous. "So, um ... like, can I buy you a drink, maybe?"

I give him a tightened smile in return. "I'm only twenty, and I already have a drink," I point out, giving my glass a tap.

The guy flashes me a smile I think is supposed to be charming. "You mean that murky watered-down Pepsi you're holding?"

I laugh, then turn my body his way. "Well, honestly, even if I *was* old enough, I don't think I'd be drinking anything stronger."

"Yeah?" He props his elbow up on the bar, also inclining his body toward mine. "And why not?"

I'm about to respond with something witty when Jimmy at once appears, having slid off his own seat to come right between us. "Sorry, dudes, emergency," he blurts, then slaps a hand onto my shoulder and pries me away from the bar.

I frown at him as he pulls me away. "What the heck was that for? I was actually talking to a nice guy who—"

"You aren't lookin' for a *'nice guy'*, Bobby. You need a *man*."

I try to peer back at Mr. Freckles, but Jimmy's got such a grip around my shoulders that I can barely manage a peek. "I left my drink! You did, too!"

"They were gross."

"Well, they cost us an overpriced six dollars apiece."

Jimmy stops us by a wall with a giant neon dick-shaped light glowing over his head. I don't think he notices. "Look, we're gonna need to find you *quality*, Bobby. I'm not lettin' you settle for no loser whose opening line is about how *watered down your Pepsi is*."

I frown. "But it *was* watered down."

He grabs my shoulders and brings his face close to mine. "I'm tellin' you, Bobby, I don't want you settling for just anyone. I have had my fair share of mediocre girls, and it just isn't worth all the effort. I'm givin' you priceless advice that I wish *I* was given when I first put myself out there to date."

"Yeah, how old were you? Twelve?" I sass back at him.

He ignores my quip. "You've got to hold out for the right one. You need someone who's going to worship you, but not like some kind of precious thing to put on a shelf. He's gotta worship you in the way that makes you *know your worth*. He's gotta set your soul on fire. He has to *know* what he's got in you. Get what I'm sayin'?"

I stare into Jimmy's eyes, a bit taken by the oddly poetic way in which he's talking to me right now.

But something about Jimmy's constant control of my life— even the way he's gripping my shoulders right now, after having physically pulled me away from a potential date—suddenly has me feeling hot with resentment.

Why does he get to call all the shots?

Who named him King of every choice I make with my life?

"You've got a lot of nerve, Jimmy Strong," I throw at his face.

His whole forehead wrinkles up in a frustratingly adorable way as he blinks. "Say what?"

"This whole stupid thing was *your* idea. And now that we're here, you won't let a single guy come near me!"

"They aren't good enough for you! Were you even listening to anything I just said? You need to hold out for—"

"I'm not gonna find the perfect boyfriend here in a downtown nightclub, Jimmy. I'm gonna find exactly what we *have* found: old horny men, young tweaked-out party monsters, and the whole spectrum of '*weirdo*' in between."

Jimmy huffs frustratedly at me. "You've gotta keep lookin'!"

I swat his hands right off my shoulders, fed up. "And who are you expecting me to find in here?" I shout at him. "You?"

Jimmy had his mouth open already to say something else, but those next words are now frozen to his tongue.

After an eternity, his face moves again. "The hell you mean?"

I cross my arms. "No one's gonna meet your standards," I tell him, "because you won't settle for me being with anyone who isn't like you. And guess what, Jimmy? *No one's* like you."

"And how—" Jimmy swallows, interrupting himself, and shifts his weight from one leg to the other. "And how am I, exactly?"

"Fiercely devoted," I answer dryly.

Jimmy lets on a tiny smile of pride.

"*To a fault*," I add, my eyes narrowing.

His face falters.

"Totally irritating, in fact," I go on. "Won't just let things be, *ever*. Needs everything in its right place or else. Needs reassurance all the time. Insecure as all get-out."

He lifts a hand. "Now wait a minute ..."

"Needs to be in the spotlight all day long. Full of himself. Can't stand the idea of his best friend having a life of his own. Needs—"

"Hold on, wait a sec, whoa ..."

"—everyone to drop everything at his beck and call. And why do I put up with it? Why am I letting this happen? I don't need a boyfriend. Hell, I don't even know if I *want* one."

"Bobby, stop."

"I'm goin' back to the hotel room."

With that, I ditch Jimmy, push through the doors, and march my way down the crowded street, the city smog baking my face.

8

JIMMY

Now wait a dang minute.

Slow down. What the fuck?

I chase him right out of the club, but *Lightning Legs* hurried out so fast, I don't even see him on the street. I dodge weird looks while searching for any sign of Bobby—and narrowly avoid a car that flies right on by suspiciously close to the curb.

Bobby got out of there fast.

Well, at least I know where he's headed.

After a brisk fifteen-minute jog, I'm racing up the stairwell—listening to my feet stick on every gummy, stained step all the way up to the third floor—and finally reach our room.

I turn the key and push inside. I find Bobby chilling on the bed in just a pair of white boxer briefs and a tank top, the TV on, and the remote in his hand. His arms are crossed as well as his legs at the ankle, making his thighs look huge.

Goodness, he sure whipped out of his clothes fast enough.

I don't come too far into the room, standing at the door and staring in at him. "Look, dude ..." I start.

"Can we skip the whole conversation and just kick back and watch the dumb TV?" Bobby cuts me off. "Y'know, like we said we would do if your whole nightclub scheme didn't work out?"

I wrinkle my face. "It wasn't no *scheme*."

"I'm tired, Jimmy. I'm just tired and not in the mood."

"What was that crap you went on about at the club?" I press on, coming into the room and letting the door close behind me.

He purses his lips in frustration and doesn't answer.

"Bobby." I sit on the edge of my bed, facing his. The springs creak and groan under my ass. "Full of myself? Can't stand the idea of you havin' a life of your own? *Insecure?* What was all that?"

"I shouldn't have said it, sorry," he mumbles, looking away.

"Nah, don't close up. Tell me what you really think."

"Didn't I, already?"

"Bobby ..."

Then, at once, he swings his legs around and now sits on the edge of his own bed, facing me directly, his face tensed up. "You ever felt like the minor character in your own damned life?"

I stare at him. "Say what?"

"That's what being your friend feels like sometimes," he goes on. "It feels like the Jimmy Strong show all day, every day. Even at South Wood. I'm always hangin' with *your* friends, following what *you're* doing, going to *your* friends' parties ... The second I try to do somethin' on my own, you've got a problem with it."

"That isn't true," I blurt at once.

"Yeah, it is." Bobby tosses the remote behind him, freeing his hands so as to clutch the edge of the bed. "You don't know what it's like to not have the spotlight on you. Hell, even on a night that is *supposed* to be all about me, you make it all about you."

I gape at him, struck by his words. "What the—?"

"How many guys were you gonna shoo off? Five more? Ten? Would we have to go through the whole population of that nightclub before you were satisfied with whatever guy showed interest in me? And besides, what gives you the right to choose for me?" Bobby's eyes are on fire as he rises from the bed suddenly and stands over me. "I deserve the right to make my own stupid decisions. To make my own mistakes. To go home with whoever the hell I want. You aren't the boss of me, Jimmy Strong."

Standing over me like this in just his underwear and a tight-fitting tank, his crotch is just a foot or two from my face. I only notice it because suddenly I have this overwhelming desire to apologize to him, and it's making my arms want to reach out and hug him aggressively, or tackle him to the bed to make him laugh, or do anything to change that unhappy look in his eyes.

I hate it when Bobby Parker's unhappy.

And I hate it even worse when I'm the cause of it.

This sure as shit isn't our first fight. It isn't the first time I've pissed him off, or vice versa. But for some reason or another, it's the first time it hurts me so deeply that all I want to do is squeeze my pal until it's all better and he's smiling again.

"I *do* know what it's like," I tell him, looking up his long, lean torso to his eyes. "Being the minor character or whatever."

His eyes soften. He doesn't say anything, but he's listening.

I look down at my hands. "Growing up as Tanner Strong's lil' bro ..." I let out half a sigh and half a laugh. "Wasn't always easy. Being compared to the Spruce Juice my whole life. The big college football star. Tan the Man. So many stupid nicknames. I mean, I love my big brother," I add quickly, peering back up at Bobby, "but it gets to you after a while. How was I ever gonna climb out from under his huge shadow? Dude, you remember that one year when Mama forgot it was my birthday because she was all caught up in planning Billy and Tanner's wedding? It was my sixteenth."

"I remember."

Good, I've got him talking again. "Everyone's always fussin' about my brother, my whole life. I wasn't Jimmy back then. I was just the Spruce Juice's lil' bro. I was Tanner's little brother. So yeah, I think I have an idea of what that's like." I eye him importantly. "And I don't want you feelin' like second to *anything*, Bobby Parker."

His mouth crinkles up with frustration. "Yeah, well, maybe it was like that for you while growin' up, but it sure as hell isn't like that anymore."

"No, it isn't. And do you know when it changed?" I stand up, bringing my eyes level with his. "The day I asked you to prom."

Bobby's eyes cast downward, a look of self-consciousness reddening his face suddenly.

I put a finger under his chin and lift it, bringing his eyes back to mine. "What I'm sayin' is," I tell him, looking him right in those warm, muddy brown eyes of his, "*you're* the reason I'm someone now, Bobby Parker."

Bobby's lips twitch.

Maybe I could even call it an attempt at a smile.

It's all I need to feel reassured—that dumb little nothing smile on Bobby Parker's face. "I became someone that day, a person totally apart from my big bro. It was somethin' that gave me an identity, somethin' even my being the first dude to enroll in *dance* at Spruce High couldn't do. And you?" I shake my head. "Bobby. You aren't a minor character in anyone's story."

Bobby tilts his head and crosses his arms again. "So you're saying that your huge, overinflated ego now is basically my fault?"

The pair of us stare at each other.

Then we both burst out laughing together.

Suddenly, I chase a thought I had a second ago and tackle him to the bed, causing him to shriek out in surprise. Then I straddle him on top of that bed and attack his bare, exposed sides and ribs with my evil fingers, tickling poor Bobby into a state of screaming, choked cackling, and tears.

When my fingers mercifully stop, we're both out of breath, and he's staring up at me with a frozen smile on his face.

I shrug. "Yeah. I guess it *is* all your fault, huh?"

Bobby is still catching his breath when he shakes his head and laughingly hisses out, "You're a fuckin' monster."

There's a twinkle in his eye. It's probably a stray tear from his having laughed so much. A little parting gift of my relentless tickle attack. A tiny, liquid gem of hysteria.

But there's also all the words we just shared.

And his pain that he won't show, that lonesomeness inside of him, that part that I was supposed to help alleviate by taking him all the way to this downtown club, far away from home.

That lonesomeness I've been trying to kill inside of him since the day I asked him to our high school prom.

I want to kill it for good.

I *need* to kill it for good.

Isn't Bobby depending on me to do just that?

Before I know it, my face is descending.

Bobby's tiny little laughs cease at once, and his eyes snap to mine, startled, confused.

And we kiss.

My eyes close as I taste Bobby on my lips. I feel a surge of emotion rushing up through me. His lips are so soft to the touch, yet firm and resistant, like muscle. Even the energy coming off his skin is prickly and exciting, something new that I've never known.

I feel so good to do this for Bobby.

And it feels so good to kiss my best friend and know that this kiss is more meaningful than any I've ever shared before.

I want to kill that lonesomeness inside him.

I never want him to feel lonely again.

"Jimmy, wait," he says against my mouth. "What're you—?"

Still straddling him at the waist, one hand propping me up, I bring my other to his face, caressing it as I keep kissing him. "*It's alright,*" I whisper between kisses, my words nothing more than breath in his mouth. "*Just let it happen, buddy. We're okay.*"

"J-Jimmy ..." he tries again.

"*We're okay.*"

I deepen the kiss, pressing my lips harder against his. There is only a second's worth of fight before he gives in completely, his body slackening beneath my weight, and his soft mouth opening up to mine.

Kill it. Kill the loneliness.

My heart slams against my chest over and over as I kiss him.

My pulse beats in my ears like war drums.

This feels so fucking good, to do this for my best buddy Bobby.

My lips must be charged with electricity, because they crackle and tingle as I continue to kiss Bobby, turning my head one way and the other, tenderly caressing his mouth.

Kill it.

I keep thinking those words to myself, but with each kiss, I grow more confused about whose loneliness I'm trying to kill.

"Jimmy ..." he whispers.

I lift my face from his at last and stare down into his warm, bewildered eyes as they slowly open, as if emerging from a deep, deep pool.

Nothing passes between us for a while.

Not even breath, or air, or sound.

I don't hear the TV. I don't hear the weird chatter through the wall from the room next to us. I don't hear the city noise through the window, or the distant police siren, or the hum of the air conditioning unit churning across the room.

Bobby's face is my whole world right now—and what's going on in his head, my one and only concern.

And finally: "What was that?"

I lift an eyebrow. "What was what?"

"That." Bobby's gaze flits down to my lips, then back up to my eyes. "What was that?"

I'm not sure what it was. "A kiss," I answer lamely. "What do you think it was?"

He huffs, frustrated. "Obviously. I meant ... what was—?" His demeanor changes suddenly. "Stop being so ..." He says the words almost sweetly. "... w-weird and coy and ... and casual about this."

I drop onto the bed next to him, propping my head up with a hand, my elbow digging into the mattress. "What's the big deal? Can't we just be a little spontaneous? Dude, I felt like you were sufferin', I saw all that emptiness in your eyes, you were talkin' about feeling like a minor character in your own life, and I just ..." I shrug. "... wanted to take it all away."

Bobby, still on his back, snaps just his head my way and eyes me harshly. "Oh, don't go actin' like that's all that was just now. 'Taking away my suffering.' There was something else goin' on there. Straight guys don't just go kissin' their best friends."

"Says who? Can't a guy just do something to make his friend feel better? What's the big deal?"

He lets out a choked laugh of disbelief. He's completely beside himself. "Jimmy, you were on top of me tickling the shit outta me a second ago, and now you just went and ... and ... and ..."

"Kissed you. Yeah, I know, I was there. Tonight was supposed to be about gettin' you a guy," I point out to him, my voice turning light. "And I feel like I've let you down on that. So ... I guess *I'm* your guy tonight. You've got a boner, by the way."

Bobby doesn't seem to know which of my words to give his attention to, confusion twisting his face, and then suddenly both his hands shoot down to cover the pointy bulge he's making in those tight white boxer briefs of his.

He glares at me. "Of *course* I'm hard. *You just made out with me.*"

"See? It's already working. You look like you feel superb right now. And besides," I quickly add as I watch his face grow redder, "that was *way* too short to be called makin' out. That was just a kiss or two. A couple pecks, at the most."

Bobby sits up suddenly, his back to me. He sits there, silent.

I quirk an eyebrow, studying his tense back. "What's wrong, dude? Don't make a big deal out of it. I just wanted to ... make you feel good, that's all."

"This isn't ..." Bobby's back muscles contract, his head bowed. "This isn't some fuckin' *game* to me, Jimmy. This isn't some ..." He struggles to find the words. "I've been single a long time, man."

"I know."

"Like, a fucking *long* time."

"I know, dude, chill."

"So it *means* something to me when ..." He sighs. "... when you go and ... and kiss me like that."

"I just wanted to make you feel good." I put my hands behind my head and lean back on the bed, staring up at his back, which swells and slowly deflates with his every breath. "That's it."

He doesn't say anything.

My legs are half hanging off the bed, my thigh near his hip. So I give his side a nudge with it. "So?" I prod him.

"So ... what?"

"So did it make you feel good?"

Bobby takes a minute. Then he peers only halfway over his shoulder, but his eyes still don't meet mine. He doesn't respond.

"Well? Did it?" I ask again.

He licks his lips absently, his mind seeming somewhere else. And then, almost distractedly: "Yeah."

"Good." I sit up right then and slap a hand to Bobby's bare back, startling him and making him snap his eyes to mine, wide open. "That's all that matters, isn't it? It felt good. That's the only thing that matters."

Bobby stares back at me, clearly unsure of what to say.

There's a part of me that *loves* how freaked out he is.

I mean, who knew that with just a few kisses, I could have my buddy's mind twisted up with so much excitement and pleasure that he doesn't even know what to say?

There is another part of me that's worried I'm crossing a line I'll never be able to uncross.

A part of me that feels like everything changed between us in one reckless instant.

And that's a part of me I'll blissfully ignore for now.

I slap a hand onto his firm, muscled thigh. "Tell you what. You went and got all comfortable, so I'm gonna go do the same. Then you and I can watch TV all night long and chat about what a bad idea tonight was and laugh it all off, alright?"

He takes a minute to sort a thought or two. He doesn't look finished when he absentmindedly mutters, "Yeah, alright."

With that, I leave him there on the bed and head for the bathroom. I peel off all my clothes, splash water on my face and in my hair, dry off with a towel, then tug on a loose pair of gym shorts I tucked away in my suitcase.

Coming out of the bathroom, I find Bobby exactly where I left him: sitting there on the edge of the bed, lost in his head. He looks up when I come out of the bathroom, and his eyes drop to my bare chest. He has this totally blank, adorably faraway look on his face.

"C'mon, let's cuddle up," I say as I hop right back onto his bed and lean against the headboard. "It's *our* night, now!"

Bobby glances at me over his shoulder. "Uh ... what?"

I reach out and grab him without warning, then pull his body up against my side. After throwing an arm around him, I've got him held against me in half a hug, cuddling him. He seems to have a second of confusion before he finally gives in, resting his head back on the headboard next to mine. Nestled on the bed now, we stare at the TV as it plays some nearly-muted game show at us.

During the commercial break, Bobby breaks the silence. "You got your prized, banged-up truck."

I turn to him, confused. Our faces are very close. "What?"

"On your sixteenth birthday. The one your family forgot." He looks my way, too. A corner of his lips curl up. "That was the year you got your prized, banged-up truck, remember?"

The memory clicks. "Oh, yeah. You're right."

"Guess it pays to be Jimmy Strong," he teases flatly. "When a birthday is forgotten, the bastard gets gifted a truck."

I smirk. "Having car-envy now, are we?"

"Nah." Bobby picks at his fingers, then shifts his weight next to me. "I don't mind walkin' everywhere, or being driven around by you. You make a decent chauffeur."

"Do I? Just decent?"

"Yeah. You just need to do one more thing and you'll be the *perfect* chauffeur."

"Oh yeah? What's that?"

He eyes me. "Lose that damned ratty-ass hat of yours."

I laugh and shake my head. "Never."

Bobby stares ahead at the TV, giving up his sudden fight with a soft chuckle. I peer at the side of his face, moved suddenly by all the emotion that's passed between us tonight. It's something new, yet feels like it's somehow been there since forever.

I give him another kiss on the side of his head, then hug him against me tighter. "I'm your man, now and always." I feel totally proud of us and right with the world. "Fuck the losers at the club. None of 'em are good enough for you anyway."

Bobby doesn't say anything, but I swear I feel him cling to my side tighter after those words. Or maybe it's just my imagination.

Three minutes later, he goes: "Shoot, you're gettin' hot. Why the hell you sweat so dang much?"

I shrug. "It's a Strong thing."

9

BOBBY

I smooth out my black pleated slacks, then do up the last few buttons on my mustard yellow uniform shirt. My fingers fumble at first with the shiny black bowtie around my neck, but I finally get it even on both sides, despite feeling like its suffocating me. I can never get anything to fit right around my neck.

Or maybe I'm just in a zone right now and *nothing* feels right.

A zone called: *my straight best friend just kissed me two nights ago in a dirty hotel room, then cuddled me to sleep.*

All yesterday after we got back to Spruce and he dropped me off here at my house, I've been in this totally alien state of mind. I keep stopping in place for no reason, my mind going back to that hotel room. It's like I've been stirred awake from a deeply moving dream and am now being haunted by it all day long.

I literally question at times whether it actually happened.

If Jimmy Strong ... actually kissed me.

"Hon, you ready yet?" comes my ma's voice through the door.

I yank at the straps of my dumb shiny red suspenders, making them snap. The things keep tugging on my shoulders all weird.

Maybe everything's going to feel weird for a while.

Or maybe the sadistic manager of the movie theater is just trying to humiliate all the swagger out of his employees.

Seriously, I look ridiculous.

"Oh, you look so *cuuute* in your uniform!" cries my mother when I finally emerge from my bedroom. "Oh my goodness, I gotta take a picture on my new smartphone!" She races to the kitchen to fetch it, nearly tripping over a meowing Delilah on her way.

I roll my eyes, standing awkwardly in the living room, ready to go and get my first day started. "I think you lost the right to call it your '*new* smartphone' six months ago when I first got it for ya."

She rushes back into the living room. "Oh, you're so funny! Now how do I take pictures on this thing? Do I gotta talk to it?"

I snort. "Here, bring it here. Let me show you."

Showing her takes ten minutes. Then suddenly I peek at the clock and realize I'm going to be late if I don't head out right now.

"Your pa will give you a ride on his way back out to Fairview. Traffic should be light since everyone's at church." My ma gives me a big kiss on the cheek, then does a giddy little dance with her feet. "I just can't wait to hear about your first day! Do you get off at five or six? Tell Mr. Lemon I said hi and asked about his kiddos!"

A minute later, I'm in the car with my pa, who's as silent and stoic as a stone. He just gives me a few eye-scrunching smiles that come out of nowhere as the radio gently plays music. We drive the seven blocks and the one main street to the theater. Really, I could have easily walked, but I think my pa feels guilty for working all the time and wants to spend any spare minute he can with me.

"Thanks, Pa," I say when we pull up to the curb. "I can walk home after my shift. It's just a little bit of a walk, and—"

"Nonsense, son. Not in this heat." My pa gives me yet another squishy smile. "I should be back this evening sometime around six. If you get off early, just wait for me at Biggie's down the road."

There's no sense in arguing—or turning down an opportunity to dodge some harsh summer sun. "Yes, sir."

"Now you have yourself a good first day, alright? Remember to respect your superiors, like I've always taught you."

"Yes, sir." I pop open the car door and step out.

"And son?"

I shut the door behind me, then peer in through the rolled-down window. "Yes, Pa?"

"Don't you worry 'bout money. Just have fun at work. Enjoy it, make some new friends. You used to love goin' to the movies. Now you get to see all the behind-the-scenes. And Mr. Lemon is a nice man! When you love your job, you don't work a day, right?"

His warm, dopey brown eyes have a glaze of guilt across them, which his words only make worse. I wonder if he and Ma actually had an argument or two about whether or not I should go and get a job this summer. Maybe he wanted me to stay home and enjoy my time with Ma and Jimmy and my friends. Maybe he resents that we're in such a position where I have to pitch in, too.

I don't resent him for anything. It's time I contribute to the household. Not everyone can have it as easily as Jimmy, who—*ugh, do all thoughts have to lead back to him lately??* I shake my brain like an *Etch A Sketch* and put on a big smile—my most convincing yet. "Oh, I'm gonna have a blast, Pa. I just hope you're ready for all the movie posters I'm gonna sneak home after my shifts."

To that, he laughs warmly and shakes his head. "Don't you go gettin' yourself into trouble now!"

"No way," I return through a chuckle.

My pa drives off, and then all the humor drops off my face like rain off a windshield. I turn to face the building with a sigh. It's Spruce's only movie theater, boasting five proud screens and a lot of outdated technology. The big glass windows of the box office face me with one sad-looking, tired young teenager sitting there in a suspender-and-bowtie outfit that matches mine. She's half-asleep, her big curly bush of red hair nearly drowning her round face, and she's got her head propped up at the chin with one crooked, lazy hand. She might be drooling, but the glare of the sunlight off the glass prevents me from seeing clearly.

I wonder suddenly if Jimmy is still asleep at his house, or if he has woken up by now. Maybe he's in the shower, washing away his thoughts. Or he could be hanging with his brother, who's a totally annoying early-riser. Or he might be lazing around on his bed, just staring up at the ceiling, bored, sucking on his tongue. Maybe he went to church with his ma, sitting on a bench listening to Trey or Reverend Arnold talk about God and preaching their Sunday love.

Why do I care so much what Jimmy Strong is doing right now?

I blink away the thoughts, then proceed through the glass doors into the movie theater, ready to begin my first day at the Spruce Cinema 5.

After ten minutes with the manager Mr. Lemon, I find him to be starkly different than he was when he interviewed me. He is a stress-ball of uptightness this morning whose perfect part of hair is the only part of him under control; his off-centered tie, the sweat stains under his pits, and the scuffs on his dress shoes reveal a man who's barely got it together. His tour of the building with me is ripe with about a hundred-thousand fatal warnings.

Such as: "You do *not* want to dump the popcorn kettle early, because the oil will burn your hands right off, and the hot seeds will jump down your shirt like molten pellets of lava. And *don't* bump the popcorn tray. It's *loose* and all your *popcorn* will fall *out*."

Then in a supply closet: "You do *not* want to mix the wrong chemicals or forgo gloves, because these acids *will* make you go blind, sear your skin, or cause diarrhea if just a drop is ingested."

And finally upstairs in the projectionist room: "You do *not* want to be caught with your hand here, here, here, or here." He points at each area of the huge, clacking projector for emphasis, his eyes manic and his jaw clenched. "Or else you'll lose a limb. And your job. And mine."

The man has a phone call with the corporate office suddenly, so he leaves me with one of the ushers, who takes me from theater to theater to demonstrate how to sweep up popcorn off the floor, how to check cupholders for hidden napkins and candy wrappers, how to sweep *under* the seats as well as around them, how to hold open a door (seriously), and finally how to tell guests to have a lovely day after their feature film has ended without looking like a soulless goon in a bowtie.

There's a perfected science to all of that, apparently.

Since there's still twenty minutes before the next movie ends, the usher takes me to the scullery behind the concession stand where we sit atop a stack of popcorn seed bags like a pair of bums and lounge with our broom and dustpans rested by our sides.

And I'm totally not thinking about Jimmy.

Nor the sweet taste of his soft lips on mine, for that brief and fleeting moment in which our mouths were one.

Nor the feel of his breath against my face.

Nor the embrace of his strong, tight arms around me.

I'm such a fucking mess and it's all his fault.

"This is really the majority of what your day will be like," the usher tells me. His name is Vince, by the way, and his voice is the rope I climb to get the hell out of this thought hole I've fallen into. "Sitting around and waiting on the next movie to drop."

I glance around the scullery itself, troubled. "Isn't there, like, somethin' to clean, or organize, or—?"

"You'll get used to it." Vince lets out a soft chuckle. "This is the best damned blow-off job in town. You're fuckin' lucky."

"What're you bitches doin'??" comes the voice of the blond-haired concessionist out of nowhere, bursting in through the tall swinging door that leads out to the concession stand. His uniform is the same, except he's got a bright red apron on over his clothes. "Bein' a lazy pair of bitches? Or you bitches got work to do?"

"That's ... three times too many that you used that word," says Vince with his half-lidded, bored-as-hell eyes. "Seriously, open a dictionary. Don't you have a customer to scoop popcorn for?"

"It's Sunday morning, man. No one comes to the theater except all the sinners. Hey," he greets me with sudden courtesy. "I'm Anthony. You're the new guy, huh?"

I frown. "Really, Anthony? We graduated together."

He wrinkles up his face, as if I just gave him the world's most complicated math problem to work out. Then he goes, "Wait. Wait a damn sec." It clicks. "Bobby? ... Bobby Parker?"

I give him a straight-lipped smile. "Don't go pretending like you didn't recognize me, Anthony Myers," I sass him.

"Oh, shit." His whole demeanor changes. He's working out ten or eleven things in his head all at once. It's an effort for him. "It's been ... Y-You're Jimmy's friend ... Jimmy fuckin' Strong."

I give yet another nod of confirmation. "You and I had English together, too. And Spanish sophomore year."

"Shit, you remember that?" Anthony snorts, gives a peek out the small circular window in the door to check for customers, then gazes back at me with wonder. "The hell you doin' here?"

"He works here, numbnuts," Vince tiredly retorts at him.

Anthony still seems perplexed. *You really need to give this one extra time to make thoughts.* "Huh. Which department?"

"Mr. Lemon hasn't decided yet," says Vince. "But probably the usher department. Mr. Lemon left him with me to train."

"Huh." Anthony crosses his arms and leans against the door frame, studying me with mounting frustration. "Huh."

Vince lifts an eyebrow. "You gonna just stand there grunting for an hour? 'Huh'? 'Huh'? Didn't Mr. Lemon tell you to restock the sodas when you didn't have any customers?"

"I've got all day," Anthony fires back. "Besides, I just spent all morning detail-cleaning the butter pumps. How 'bout you go—"

Vince and Anthony go at each other a few times more before a "Hello? Anyone?" from a customer outside catches Anthony by surprise, and he quickly shoves back through the swinging door to greet them with a hearty, "Welcome to Spruce Cinema 5! Can I get you a large drink and popcorn today?"

After a moment, Vince nudges me. "What was that about?"

Vince is a few years younger than me, seventeen or eighteen if I had to guess, so he probably doesn't know the whole drama. I fill him in. "Jimmy Strong was supposed to go to prom with this girl named Jazzy. She dumped him last minute for your friend out there, Anthony Myers. Whole town was talkin' about it."

Vince's eyes go wide. "Oh, shit. That *does* sound familiar …"

"Yeah, it ought to. The next thing Jimmy did was ask *me* to prom instead."

A chuckle jumps out of his chest. "Wow. Yeah, I remember all that. I was in gym class when I heard. We talked about it through a whole match of dodgeball. Couldn't believe it." He eyes me. "So you're that same gay Bobby dude, huh?"

Gay Bobby dude. Somehow, coming from this totally laidback Vince guy, I don't mind the phrasing. "Yep."

"Phew. No wonder Anthony hates Jimmy so much."

I frown and shoot Vince a look. "Huh? He hates him? Why?"

"Anthony's loud n' rude n' hates being shown up by anyone. I bet he felt like a king for a day, the day a girl dumped *the Jimmy Strong* for him. Then Jimmy stole all his thunder by prom-posing to you." He shakes his head and kicks at a stray popcorn seed on the floor, sending it scuttling across the tile. "Jimmy not only stole all of the glory back for himself. He also made Anthony and Jazzy look like loser villains, all in one big prom-posing fell swoop."

I bite my lip in thought and stare down at my hands. "Hmm. Never thought of it that way."

"Don't let it get to you, man. Anthony only works part-time, anyway. You'll barely see him, I'm sure."

I bite the inside of my cheek and glance up at that swinging concession door, doubting it very much. *My whole summer's gonna be plagued with dirty looks from Anthony Myers. I can see it now.*

Five long hours later, my training day comes to an end, and the manager Mr. Lemon is too busy to even come downstairs from the office to give me a last word, so Vince is the one who pats me on the shoulder, says, "Great first day. See you tomorrow," and leads me to the employee lounge to show me how to clock out.

When I'm on the curb at fifteen past five, I realize it'll be a while before my pa arrives to scoop me up. I take his instruction and start heading down the street toward Biggie's, letting the evening sunlight wash over my head. Halfway down the first block, I pop off my suspenders, letting them hang down my sides, and roll up my sleeves past my elbows. The bowtie is pretty much permanently fixed to my neck until I can find a mirror, which I plan to do once I get to Biggie's.

Then I realize I never turned my phone back on. I stop on the corner of Main Street and 2nd to pull it out of my pocket, then click it on. At once, I'm flooded with twenty texts from Jimmy, who is wondering what I'm up to, wondering why I'm not answering him, remembering my job and asking how my first day is going, asking when my lunch break is, asking why I'm not answering again, then finally sending a bunch of pics of himself around the Strong ranch: three selfies with some cows, another of him lazing by the pool pretending to be dead, and finally one with his brother where they appear to be chilling on his back patio with a plate of nachos.

I stare at one of his selfies, watching him look back into my eyes through the screen of my phone. I stare into those eyes for far too long, the evening sun beating down on my neck.

And I wonder what the hell is going on in that boy's mind.

Did he seriously kiss me? Did that actually happen?

Did he enjoy it? Did his dick jump at all, or was it all just some selfless, friendly act like he claims?

Why do I find that so difficult to believe?

And seriously, how the fuck can Jimmy act like nothing at all is different between us?

The whole world is different now. Maybe it means less to him, to put his lips on me and kiss me.

He doesn't realize at all the storm gates of repressed emotion, longing, and painful desperation he's opened with that seemingly innocent kiss—and the night that followed of long, warm cuddling in his arms. He fell asleep with his face against mine, snoring into my ear, his arm resting over my stomach and his other tucked beneath my pillow, hugging me against his body, trapping me.

I couldn't go to sleep for the longest time. I just stayed there with this semi-boner in my underwear—a boner that both wanted to be pleasured as much as it wanted to pee, because for the love of God I had to pee so damned bad, but I wasn't about to destroy the Heaven we made on that bed just to relieve myself.

I could have just closed my eyes and pretended that Jimmy Strong was my boyfriend. I would have believed it. Not a muscle in my body would have told me otherwise—not with that boy's arms around me.

He more or less said he'd be mine.

For the night, at least.

Then came the morning. I don't even know how or when I fell asleep, but I must have, because I woke to the sight of Jimmy in his underwear doing some sexy elbow-popping dance moves in the body-length mirror that hung on the back of the closet door. He was turned away, so he didn't see me, but I sure saw him.

And I watched him.

When Jimmy Strong dances, phew, you can't do a damned thing but watch his beautiful body move.

The evening sun still burns my back as I shut my eyes, overwhelmed with so many confusing emotions I have yet to take a proper moment to sort. Who could I even talk to about this? Who could I trust? Who, except for Jimmy himself, and will I even be able to get the truth out of him?

Is there some part of my best friend that truly has feelings for me? *And not just in the frustratingly straight-boy platonic sort of way?*

I decide to march the rest of the way to Biggie's before taking the effort to respond to any of his texts. I need to get out of this heat, first and foremost. Being Sunday evening, Biggie's Bites is slammed with customers when I arrive, so I just take a seat in the small waiting area by the door out of the way of the madness, pull out my phone, and think up something to text Jimmy.

I draw a total blank.

Do I go on as blithely as he is, pretending we're all cool and nothing's changed?

Suddenly my phone buzzes in my hand.

Of course, it's a text from Jimmy.

> **JIMMY**
> Are U off work yet? I'm at your house.

I sigh. *That boy, I swear.* After glancing behind me when a table of teenagers bursts into laughter, I type out a response:

> **ME**
> At Biggie's waiting on my pa to get me.

> **JIMMY**
> Why? It's just a ten minute walk to your house. Fifteen tops.

ME

My pa said he'd pick me up at 6.

JIMMY

Screw that. I'm coming to get U.

I frown at my phone. Once again, that insufferable Jimmy-always-gets-his-way thing.

But on the other hand, it saves my pa the extra five minutes to swing by Biggie's and grab me. Plus, I think I need a little time with my friend to figure things out. My mind's been pretty shot all day, dreading what I'll say to Jimmy when I finally see him.

Maybe he has a thing or two to get off his chest as well.

That's probably why he's been hounding me all day.

After shooting my pa a quick text telling him that Jimmy's giving me a ride, I rise from my seat to pocket my phone. My eyes catch sight of Mrs. Tucker through the kitchen window, where she spots me through a haze of grill steam and smoke, then gives me a quick wave and a smile. "Hey there, Bobby!" she shouts out, her cheeks rosy and her forehead covered in sweaty bangs.

I give her a warm smile and a wave back before she rings the bell with someone's order, then disappears. I'm sure she would've offered me a bite, but the place is busting at the seams already with hungry mouths and a zillion orders, and she's so busy she can't even pull out of the kitchen for a proper hello.

Sunday evenings are no joke in Spruce; every food place is exploding with people, and Biggie's is at the top of the list.

A new teenage server I've never seen before—probably one of Mr. Tucker's new hires—rushes up to the counter, out of breath, to collect the order and hurry off to a table with it. He's got a total baby face, cute smallish ears, and a sweet demeanor that makes his cheeks look permanently flushed.

I watch him, curious. After just a few seconds of observing the stressed-out kid, I'm already fairly sure he's gay, but hate jumping to such a hasty conclusion. Just because he walks a certain way and carries dishes a certain way doesn't mean—

The teen flicks his eyes in my direction.

He throws me a tight-lipped, nervous smile, fusses with his hair for a second, then wrings his hands as he approaches another table, greeting them cheerily.

Okay, definitely gay.

The growl of Jimmy's engine is my cue. I bid a silent goodbye to the mystery overworked server, wishing him well as a young maybe-gay teen at Spruce High, then push my way out of the door.

I find Jimmy's truck parked right there on the curb, as well as Mr. Jimmy Strong himself leaning against the side of his vehicle with his arms crossed and a foot propped up on the wheel like he thinks he's some country boy model posing for a photo shoot. He's wearing a tight pair of his jeans, brown boots, and a tattered tank top with some greasy dark stain right near the hip. His signature threadbare red-and-white cap sits atop his proud head, squashing down his short, sweaty hair.

He gives me a charming smirk and a chin-lift. "Hey, Bobs." His eyes drop to my shirt, and suddenly his look changes. "Good Lord in Heaven, what do they got you wearin' at that place?"

"If I got hired a year earlier, it would've just been a nice polo shirt," I point out. "Now the uniform is all fancy and annoying and totally—Ugh, it's hot out here. Can we just go?"

Jimmy gives me a cute little obedient salute, then pops open the passenger side door for me. I hop inside. He slams it shut, then comes around and slides into the driver's seat.

He cranks his truck into gear. "So your mama says dinner's about to be ready any minute. Gave her one *flashy* flash of my eyes and I'm invited."

I smirk. "You're flirtin' up my ma now for dinner?"

"Nah, just bein' myself. Y'know how it is. The Strong charm."

I roll my eyes as he drives off down the road. "You and I gotta have a talk about that totally out-of-check ego of yours."

Stupid country boys and their big pretty brown eyes.

I give the side of Jimmy's face a look. Is it a bad time to bring up the whole hotel-room thing? How do I even bring it up? *Hey, uh, so you remember that night you kissed me?* No, that's stupid. *Hey, Jimmy, so listen, I want to talk about that semi you gave me when you put your lips on mine, and*—No, definitely not. *Hey, Jimmy, remember when you cuddled me to sleep, and I felt like your boyfriend?*

"You look constipated."

I blink. "Say what?"

"You." He throws me a look as he turns the corner, his truck rumbling as it coughs and spits from the strain of accelerating. "I said you look constipated."

I turn away with a sigh. "Just a long day, I guess."

"Long day, is it?" He chuckles to himself. "I'm sure you could have at least sent one dang text back instead of leaving me in the dust all day. You know how restless I get."

Seriously, with this boy. "Uh, sorry, maybe you've never actually had a job," I retort, "but you're not supposed to have your phone out while you're on the clock, and—"

"I'm just messin' with you. Still, you look constipated. Should probably check that out. Maybe eat some Raisin Bran, I dunno."

I close my eyes, my face flushing.

Now's definitely not the time.

The house is filled with the aroma of braised beef, potatoes, and buttered corn. My pa shows up only minutes after we do, and the four of us are deep into our dishes of food in no time. My ma asks a hundred and a half questions about my day at the theater while Jimmy smacks obnoxiously on his food and grunts, "Mmm-*mmm*, so good," every ten seconds.

When my parents are in the living room, I retire to my room with Jimmy. He's squished into a turquoise beanbag chair by the window while I'm on my bed, my back against the headboard and my arms folded tightly over my chest. I changed into a pair of red shorts and a loose t-shirt. Jimmy's playing some game on his phone, its noises rattling my ears and drowning out whatever's on the TV (that I'm totally not paying attention to anyway).

Still, I let out a sigh and blurt, "Can you be any louder?"

Jimmy grunts, his eyes not peeling away from his phone for even a second. "Just one more level."

I force myself to swallow. *Hey, Jimmy, about the other night ...* My heart picks up pace. My mouth runs dry. *Hey, Jimmy, I want to talk about the night in the hotel when we ... when you ... when the two of us ...* My lungs force a deep breath into them and out of them.

Jimmy throws his phone suddenly with an angry huff. "Damn game cheats." He scowls and crosses his arms like a petulant kid. "Fuckin' unfair."

"Jimmy."

He lifts his eyes to me, still scowling.

I stare at him across the room, then take a quick breath. *Just say it. Just say it, you idiot.*

"What?" he says impatiently.

"Jimmy. Can we ..." *Why is this so hard?* "Can we talk?"

His eyes harden at once. There wasn't a tense bone or muscle in his whole body, and in an instant—and without him seeming to move a muscle—I see him tense right up.

He swallows. It seems to be an effort. "Talk 'bout what?"

"You know what."

His eyes scrunch up, as if waiting for me to just let it out.

Is that sweat under my arms already? Am I sweating? "About the other night," I elaborate. At the sight of his still-scrunched-up face, I just say it: "The kiss."

Jimmy swallows again, then shrugs. "What about it?"

He's not going to make this easy. "Why did you do it? Didn't it make you ... uncomfortable?"

"No."

"Like, at all?"

"I said no."

"You're saying it didn't freak you out, to kiss another guy?"

Jimmy leans forward in the beanbag chair. "That's what I'm sayin', isn't it? How many more ways do I have to say it?"

"Why did you do it?"

"I already told you why. I told you the moment I did it, and probably ten-hundred times afterwards. I wanted to be your man that night because we found fuck-all at that dumb club."

I could strangle him. "Jimmy, you ... *kissed* me."

"I know that." His voice grows harder. He spreads his hands. "What's your point?"

"My point?" I'm off the bed suddenly. "My point is, did you ever consider how that'd make me feel?"

"Yeah. It should've made you feel good."

I slap my own forehead and shut my eyes. "*Jimmy* ..." I growl.

"That was the fucking point, dude. To make you feel good."

"Do you not see how that might ... totally fuck with my head?" I say, trying (and failing) to keep my voice even. "To have my best friend kiss me like that? And then hold me all night long?"

"Well ... I ..." He draws quiet.

I open my eyes and look down at him. He's staring somewhere at my knees, perplexed, his hands still spread as if in a showing of innocence and disbelief. I can feel my pulse in my fingertips and my toes, and my stomach feels like it wants to squeeze out every bit of my ma's dinner.

With Jimmy continuing to not say anything, I just sit myself down on the edge of my bed and stare at the TV, frustrated and at a loss for any more words myself.

"I'm gay," I finally let out.

Jimmy's face scrunches up when he looks up at me.

"I know you know that," I go on. "I mean, everyone knows. But I'm not sure you really ... get what it means." I eye him. "To be attracted to other guys. And to have someone like you as my best friend—as a *gay guy's* best friend."

He pokes a finger at his chest. "Someone like me?"

"Yeah. Someone like you. Someone who's ..." I suddenly find I can't look him in the eye when I say these next words, so I glance over at a bright yellow sneaker on the floor that I'd kicked off. "Someone who's ... so annoyingly good-lookin'."

"Annoyingly good-lookin'?"

"Yeah. With your stupid, pretty brown eyes. Your body. Your cute hair and your sexy dance moves."

"Sexy dance moves?"

I snap my eyes at him. "Can you quit repeatin' everything I'm sayin'? What are you, a parrot?"

"What are you saying, then?" Jimmy brings both his hands to his chest now. "You're holdin' my God-given beauty against me?"

"It's just a fact, Jimmy, and it's a fact that happens to ... make a difference in this ... situation. You're good-looking. You're a guy that girls *and* guys ... happen to enjoy looking at. I mean, did you not notice how you got hit on as much as I did at the club?"

"So are you sayin' I can't help my buddy out? I can't just hold you when I know you're feeling lonely? I can't just kiss you so you feel good for a single night?"

"Jimmy, it ain't right."

"It ain't right??" He's on his feet now. "The hell? It ain't right? What are we, fuckin' pastors in Fairview with their 'hate the sin' bullshit? Since when did kissing a guy become 'not right'?"

I'm on my feet, too, and with just a few steps, I'm nearly nose to nose with him. "You want to tell me with a straight face that the guys on your brother's high school football team are gonna *kiss* each other when they don't have girlfriends?—y'know, just to relieve some of that *loneliness* inside them? Think that's normal? Tell that to me with a straight face."

His fingers are balled up into fists. His eyes are burning and his face is so intense, especially this close to mine. "Well, maybe it *ought* to be normal. Who the hell decided straight guys can't hold hands when girls do it all the time? Who decided we can't fuckin' show affection for one another? I sure didn't."

"But you're straight, Jimmy. I'm not. It makes a difference."

"So the fuck what?" He grabs me by the waist and tugs me against him, our bodies crashing together at the hip. "Who says it's wrong?"

"Jimmy ..."

He brings his mouth to mine.

I try to push away from him, but Jimmy pulls my body against his with even more force, pressing a forceful kiss to my lips.

It takes a lot of effort to push away a kiss from Jimmy Strong.

Because for one, Jimmy Strong *is strong.*

And two: *Jimmy's the best goddamned kisser I have ever known.*

"Well?" he says when he pulls his mouth away for one brief instant. I'm out of breath. My head spins. "Who says it's wrong?" He kisses me again, destroying me. "What's wrong with it? You're my friend. I fucking love you. So what's wrong with wanting to show it?" He forces another kiss on me.

"J-Jimmy, stop," I protest against his soft, perfect lips.

He lets go of my waist, but stays right there in my face. "I'm not the one with the problem. You are."

I'm stunned. My lips still crackle with the energy of his forced kisses. "S-So that's it?" I fire back into his intense eyes. "You're gonna show your love by kissin' your *gay* best friend? Really? You don't think anyone might think—"

"Fuck what anyone thinks."

"Then why not go all the way with it?" I challenge him, taking a step forward, forcing Jimmy to take a step back. It's like our own little dance; I'll call it *Cat & Mouse.* "Why not just be my boyfriend for real, then? Kiss me all the time? Sleep with me? Tell me, what's stopping you from doing that?"

My words strangle Jimmy, closing up his throat and causing his eyes to harden.

"You're so comfortable kissing me, after all," I go on. "Your *gay* best friend."

"Stop callin' yourself that."

"Well, I am. I'm your *gay* best friend, Jimmy."

"I know that. It's *how* you're sayin' it, like it's wrong, or bad, or something scandalous."

I let out one dry laugh. "We live in Spruce, Texas. *Everything* is scandalous here."

He half turns away, throwing his eyes to the window where he glares beautifully through the glass.

I have to stare at him awhile, wondering how someone can look so beautiful when they're angry.

Was he really just doing something he thought would make me feel nice? Is that really all this is? Am I just angry because of how *not* homophobic my best friend is?

Fuck. Am *I* the homophobic one?

All the fight leaves me at once. "I'm sorry, Jimmy."

"Nah."

"Seriously. I'm sorry. I blew this way out of proportion."

"Nah, don't be sorry."

"I've just been mulling over it all damned day ..."

"Bobby, it's fine ..."

"I mean, we didn't even talk about it *once* on Saturday. We just let it happen, then moved on like it was nothin'."

"I should've been more ... careful with your feelings." He lets out a sigh at the window, then peers over his shoulder at me. "I'm sorry I kissed you, Bobby."

His intense eyes are on me, burning me, petrifying me.

Hearing him say those precise words, I suddenly find myself lost in a tumbling stack of backpedaling thoughts. *I'm not sorry you kissed me*, I suddenly want to say.

I'm not sorry at all.

Jimmy turns to face me completely, then sticks out a hand toward mine. "I promise not to go forcin' any kisses on you again."

My eyes drop to his outstretched hand.

I swallow once.

"I'll be your best buddy again," he goes on. "I've learned my lesson. I overstepped. I crossed a line. Won't happen again."

My heart pounds like a drum.

I'm fishing for words to say, searching for a length of rope to climb myself out of this hole, but I've gone and dug myself in it too deep with all those protests I made just minutes ago.

Suddenly all of my resolve breaks. A bitter pinch of regret sits in my stomach where my dinner's supposed to be. It weighs three hundred pounds, and it's as prickly as a cactus.

Is this really what I wanted?

"Do we have a deal?" Jimmy asks me.

I gently accept his hand and give it a loose shake. I don't look into his eyes when I quietly reply: "Deal."

10

JIMMY

I stir my bowl of cereal, staring at the little Cheerios dancing lazily around each other in a shallow pool of milk.

Mama's been at the kitchen counter jotting notes into her big yellow spiral notebook, making tiny sighs now and then. She leans one way on the counter, then another way, then props an elbow on it and rests her chin on her hand sulkily.

She's in a mood.

After her nineteenth sigh, I've had enough. "Mama."

"Sweetheart, I'm tryin' to concentrate." She squints down at her notebook, bouncing the pen on her lips like a bongo.

I lay my spoon in the bowl, letting the Cheerios claim their victory over me, and get up from the table to cross the kitchen. I hop onto the counter by her.

She looks up at me, mildly annoyed, her face pinched. "Get off the counter, boy, didn't I raise you right?"

"Mama, what's going on with you lately? I hate seein' you like this, all bothered and bad-mooded all the time."

"Why aren't you bringin' Bobby by the house anymore?"

She can never just answer a question. "He's got a job now."

"So? Have him stop by after work. I'll have Jacky-Ann cook us up a lovely dinner." Her eyes narrow. "Or is *Patricia* going to have some problem with that?"

"Mama, you can't fault her for wanting her son around. Bobby was here all last summer, and that was just as much my fault as it was yours."

To my surprise, her eyes soften at my words, and then just as quickly, she shrugs. "Sure, maybe you're right. I ought to make amends with Patricia."

I quirk an eyebrow. "Make amends ...? For what? Y'all aren't enemies. The battle's all in your head, Mama."

"She raised a sweet boy in that Bobby," she says, ignoring my question. "I'll have Jacky-Ann make her a pie and send it to her house. Maybe I can have his parents over for dinner sometime. You and Bobby are such good friends, we all oughta be friends."

This is certainly a sharp change in pace. "Well, Papa and *his* papa are friends since school. Guess it makes sense, don't it?"

"It sure does," she agrees, her voice flat and tired. "He seein' anyone, that Bobby boy? Any pretty young man caught his eye?"

Suddenly I'm back in the hotel room staring Bobby in his eyes. And he's staring back, uncertain, the tension ripe between us.

"No," I answer. "He isn't seein' anyone. Single as a Pringle."

"Hmm." She jots another quick thing down in her spiral, like something interesting just occurred to her.

I glance down at her notebook, my eyebrows pulling together. "What're you busyin' yourself with, anyway?"

"Plans."

My mama's so helpfully vague sometimes. "With what?"

"Oh, you know." Her jaw tightens and her tone turns smart. "Just 'cause Billy decides he wants to hold the Spruce Ball at the McPherson's doesn't mean I can't still have my part in it, doing all the heavy-lifting. They need my connections, anyway."

Despite the slightly embittered edge in her voice, I give her an approving nod. "That's mighty big of you, Mama."

"Oh, I know." She jots down something else, then sucks on the end of her pen thoughtfully.

I pull my phone out, check it one more time, then pocket it with an inner sigh and stare off at the glass doors leading out to the patio, the stone walkway, and the blinding, sun-sparkling pool beyond. It's Wednesday, and I haven't gotten to hang with Bobby at all since that tension-filled Sunday night when I shook his hand and agreed never to kiss him again.

Boy, if I had a nickel.

Then I'd have exactly one nickel.

I mean, what a hilarious thing for a straight dude to promise his gay friend. I wonder if there's another pair of guys anywhere on this whole damned planet who shook hands in a bedroom and made that same promise.

"You're smiling."

I ditch my thoughts and the sight of the sunlit patio to turn to my mama, who's staring at me searchingly.

After a second, I shrug. "Didn't notice."

"What're you smiling about, hon? Did you get a chance finally to spend some time with Camille?"

My eyes detach at the mention of her name. I haven't given her a speck of thought in days, strange enough.

"No."

"Then what is it?" she prods, setting down her pen to give me her full attention. "Is it something funny Bobby did? You boys went off somewhere last weekend."

"It's nothin', Mama."

"Hmm." After studying me for a bit longer, she finally gives up her prying—a lot sooner than she normally would. "Alright. I'll set up a nice dinner next time you get Bobby over here, whenever that is. Just let me know." She reaches out and gives my cheek a quick peck, then returns her attention to her notebook.

I watch her fret for a while over a note she's jotting down and wonder if she knows that I heard about the Cold Spoon. I suddenly want to bring it up and ask her about it, but just as quickly the impulse is gone; the last thing I need is to ruin her mood when it looks like she's inspired for the first time in over a week.

I wander around outside for a while, my phone glued to my pocket as I sweat through my tank top. I take a seat at the edge of the woods leading to my brother's house under the shade of a tree and just let the warm summer air waft over my face, lazily tossing around a few bangs of hair my hat isn't claiming.

I check my phone again.

Nothing.

That's all it's been for days now: nearly nothing. I try to catch him after work, and he has plans to stay and learn some other thing. Or he's gotta race home for dinner. Or his papa needs him for something.

If I was smart, I'd notice he was avoiding me.

But I'm not smart. I'm insisting to myself that he really is so busy with his new job, and maybe he's taken me down a notch or two on his priority list.

I turn my head at the sound of a flock of birds bursting from a nearby thicket, then watch them ascend into the sky as I consider why it bothers me so much when Bobby doesn't put me first.

Is what he said true? Am I obsessed with being the first and last thing in Bobby's life?

What am I without him?

Maybe this is his way of forcing me to find out.

I scratch at something imaginary on my arm, then flick away a bug that's not even there with a grimace.

I'm so fucking restless, I'm imagining insects.

The next minute, I'm back at the main house making use of the gym equipment that's set up in the garage. After just two sets of squats, I realize how dehydrated I am and end up going back to the kitchen to chug down three glasses of cold water. My mama has relocated to the back patio now, sipping a glass of sweet tea while wagging her pen between her fingers. I stare at her through the back window while chugging my last glass of water.

Maybe I should go out and get a job, too.

Bobby did it. Why can't I?

I'm back in the garage, but this time, I'm practicing my moves on a stretch of hardwood flooring in front of the body-length mirrors. In just seventeen and a half minutes, I'm sweating through my tank top and gym shorts and smelling ripe.

I check my phone one more time.

Stop always checking your phone one more time. He's at work.

I make my phone play some tunes and set it on the weight bench nearest to me before I go and get even more sweaty with my dancing. The music pops and snaps, and I pop and snap my arms along with it, my feet twisting on each hard downbeat.

With every pop, kick, and thrust, my face tightens more.

I'm determined to do something.

I just don't know what that something is.

I mean, seriously, what the fuck? How does showing your best fucking friend affection make him not want to hang out with you anymore? Why is he so scared and bothered and emotional over a little cuddling and a kiss? Shouldn't he be over the gay moon? Isn't a deep and meaningful kiss from a decent-looking fellow something he dreams about?

I dance harder, feeling more pissed off the longer I think.

Then the door from the garage to the house bursts open, and in struts my brother. He stops after taking just two steps in, gives the room one hearty sniff, then gags as he eyes me. "Good Lord in Heaven, bro. What kind of funk you buildin' up in here?"

I sigh, tap a finger on my phone to stop the music, and face my brother with a hard smirk, out of breath. "What d'you want?"

He's lifted an arm to his nose. "Literally, my eyes are waterin'. My *eyes* ... are fuckin' *waterin'* ..."

"You're interrupting my moves."

"You're interrupting all of the oxygen supply in this garage. Dude, how are you even breathing?"

"I had to put up with *your* musky man-funk for years every time you'd work out in here. Isn't my fault you've let yourself go and forgot what a real man in a gym smells like."

Tanner drops his arm from his face, gives me a stare, then yanks up his shirt to reveal a set of abs. "Really? This is what you call 'letting myself go'?" He drops his shirt with a tickled laugh. "Hey, listen, I'm running a little errand. Wanna come with?"

"Why don't you take Billy? Where is he?"

"At the Shoppe. C'mon, you know you're bored as shit up in this place, nothing to do all summer. Bobby's got his job, and—"

"So?" I spit back, turning defensive in an instant. "I got moves to perfect. I can't just *laze* around all summer and ..." I wave a hand everywhere. "... be a bum on the ranch. I've got work to do, too."

"Sure you do."

"I do!" I insist, my tone harsher.

"I don't doubt it," he says tiredly, yet still sounds mighty unconvinced. "Still, it's Wednesday, it's the dead of summer, and you're here at home dancing with yourself in mirrors. It's sad."

I blow him off with an eye-roll and a mumbled, "Shut up."

"Seriously. You're breakin' my heart here."

"Tanner, I'm warnin' you ..."

"So I'll ask again. Wanna come with me, ballerina bro?"

It never used to bother me when he'd call me that. We even had an inside bro-bro thing with it, him calling me that all the time, me laughing, us thinking it's our little thing we do. Hell, I even liked it. It reminded me of the important precedent I set in this town, being the first boy ever to enroll in dance and have that count as my physical education credit while all the other loser boys took PE and played idiotic games of dodgeball, climbed cargo nets, and threw three-pointers with half-deflated basketballs.

But right now, suddenly the nickname *does* bother me.

It bothers me a hell of a lot.

"I ain't no fuckin' ballerina," I spit back at him.

My brother studies me awhile, his steady eyes searching my face for something. Then he folds his arms. "Alright, tell you what. Come with me on my little errand, and I'll let you fill my ears with whatever's going on with you lately."

My eyebrows pull together. "Who says anything's going on with me?"

"Your whole face." He turns back toward the door, then beckons me with a nod. "C'mon, Jimmy. We'll be back before you can do a single pirouette." His heavy footsteps carry him off. He leaves the door open—for me, presumably.

I stare down at my phone—and its totally blank screen, save for the name of the song I was just playing and the play/pause icon next to it—then let out the world's longest sigh. "What errand?" I call out as I grab up my phone and head on after him.

We take his new white Subaru, both the windows rolled down so the air drowns out all noise and sense from me on the road. It's nothing but a hurricane of oblivion in my ears as I lean my head back in the passenger seat and let my brother steer us into town. I don't feel a drop of sweat on me in just a matter of seconds, the tunnel of wind that this vehicle has become drying me completely.

Despite his promise, Tanner doesn't ask me anything, perhaps changing his mind and choosing not to pry.

That's just as well, because I'm not in the mood for a feely talk with my brother. How can I even begin to put into words the thing that's going on in my head?

I can't tell my gay brother that I kissed my gay best friend.

That's literally a Spruce-caliber recipe for scandal.

Because then he'll have to tell Billy, who will gasp and tell his friend Mindy, who will spill it to her husband Joel, who won't be able to keep his mouth shut the next time he's at the church, and then by morning, the whole town will think the Strong ranch is breeding gay dudes left and right.

But if I can't tell my own brother, then who the hell *can* I tell?

When Tanner pulls into the parking lot of Spruce High, I have to admit this wasn't the "errand" I was expecting—as obvious as it seems now, in retrospect. "Some kinda mid-summer coach errand thing?" I throw at him with half a pout.

"Just 'cause it's summer doesn't mean the school's all closed down. They hold classes still for summer school in the freshman wing, plus the theatre department is puttin' on some production of Shakespeare, and—" He turns and looks at me. "The hell do you care anyway? I got you out of the house, didn't I? Thank me later when you realize you *didn't* waste your day doing the *orange justice* in the mirror." He turns off the engine, then swings out of the car.

"That wasn't no damned *Fortnite* dance I was practicing!" I shout back at him, but it's no use; he's already halfway down the path to the school.

I follow him begrudgingly, kicking the dirt with my sneakers as I go. I'm surprised to find the school looking exactly the way it did when I left the proud, squatty building just a couple years ago. Its front wears the school colors in stripes of complementary paint that outline the foundation, windows, and awnings.

But it isn't the front through which we enter. *Coach* Tanner has keys that get us in through the back where the locker rooms and gym storage areas reside. "Not sure if Coach Larry is here or not," my brother grunts as he takes me down a few dark hallways, only a strip of the piercing sunlight outside coming in through some office windows. "He's such a lazy bum sometimes. Don't tell Bobby I said that. I know Coach Larry *loves* Bobby, being his star soccer player and all, but phew, Coach Larry gets on my nerves."

He can't go five seconds without mentioning Bobby around me. Hell, even when I'm *not* obsessing over why Bobby's icing me out, the world finds a way to shove him back in my face.

I check my phone again.

Nothing.

The scent of sweat, bleach, and generic laundry detergent assaults my nose long before we even make it to the gymnasium, flooding me with an overwhelming sense of nostalgia. That sense is made all the worse when we enter the actual gymnasium itself, and I find that just like the outside of the school, the inside is exactly the same, too, right down to the chips of paint and small cracks that trace the gym walls near the floor from all the wear and tear of basketballs and bodies slamming against them.

"Hard to believe it's only been a couple years," I murmur.

"Yeah? Feelin' your memory strings gettin' tugged?" Tanner smiles knowingly. "Bro, and this isn't even the dance gym."

Our footsteps echo and fill the space. Ghostly sunlight pours in from the windows up above the bleachers, obscured slightly by the unclean glass. "What are we doing, exactly?"

"Errands. Coach stuff. Boring summer stuff."

We exit the gymnasium through its front, emptying into the long main hall that runs down the heart of the school. "So what do you need me to do?" I ask him distractedly, still looking all around me at the lockers lining the halls, the posters hanging from the ceiling, and the small display cases with trophies that punctuate the hall every one or two classrooms. Everything looks different with the lights off—almost creepy, even during the day.

"Oh, I didn't bring you to put you to work, dude. I brought you just to get your sad ass out of the house, like I said."

"My ass isn't sad," I retort—still distracted, staring all around me. "Shoot, that's where I had English. Is that one still Ms. Bean's room? Oh, fuck, no way, Mr. Robin used to be in this one!" I peer through the tall skinny window in one of the classroom doors, my eyes searching through the glass. "What happened to Mr. Robin?"

Tanner squints at the room, then nods. "Yeah, he moved out to Brookfield, last I heard. Still teaches French, now at some fancy uppity private school where the bathrooms have gold toilets."

I peel my face from the window. "Gold toilets?"

Tanner shakes his head and snorts. "You're so damn gullible sometimes, Jimmy. Really, where'd your sense of humor go? Did California steal it from you?"

I frown at him. "My school isn't in *Cali-fuckin'-fornia*, I've said a hundred times."

"You're usually quicker than this, man. Phew, I'm gonna have fun with you this summer." He laughs again, beside himself, then continues on down the hall.

I roll my eyes and follow him.

I don't follow him for long. We stop in front of a set of office doors, the windows of which reveal that it's the only room with its lights actually on. "Alright, this is where I do a bunch of boring shit in an office and make a few calls. So you're officially free to roam the halls, break shit, draw graffiti on your old locker, whatever your heart desires. I shouldn't be more than an hour, tops."

"Oh, alright," I say with a nod. "Good thing I still have my old cans of spray paint stored in the janitor closet down the hall."

My brother blinks. "Really?"

I smirk at him. "And *now* who's the gullible one?"

He lets out one hearty laugh, then reaches out to grab me in a headlock, but I'm quicker and parry, leaving him bent over and off-balance. I playfully give his butt a kick, nudging him toward the door to the office. Tanner reacts with a choked laugh and gasp. Then he points at me with a, "You're gettin' quick on them feet of yours, boy!" before he laughs again and disappears into the office, grinning and chuckling openmouthed.

With a renewed smile on my face, I take off strolling down the hall, drinking in all the sights my eyes can find. The freshman wing—otherwise known as the "fish bowl"—is far away, so all the halls and rooms are dark as I pass them. It gives me a strangely mischievous feeling, like I'm not supposed to be here.

Wish Bobby was with me so we could have fun, race each other down the halls, and reminisce like a pair of memory-drunk fools. I bet he'd fucking have a blast here with me.

I check my phone.

For fuck's sake, keep the damned thing away.

I stop at the doors to the main cafeteria. The only thing I hear is the soft hum of machinery somewhere—an air conditioning unit if I had to guess—but I swear if I close my eyes, I can almost hear the loud chatter of the cafeteria during lunchtime. I can hear a girl scream from across the room, shouting at her friends. I can hear guys beating their fists on the tables, causing everyone's trays to rattle. I can hear laughter and gasping and more laughter. I can hear the scrapes and taps of spoons and forks.

And then I'm back where I am, and I hear nothing but that distant hum of machinery, all the memories turning into ghosts.

Ghosts of jokes that make a whole table burst into laughter.

Ghosts of stories told over bread rolls, dry cheese pizza, and stale chicken nuggets.

Ghosts of anxiety that swims in the bellies of the outcasts and awkward sophomores who aren't sure where to sit.

Ghosts of the way things used to be.

It's all just ghosts and weirdness in this place. I bet I wouldn't recognize a single kid if I were here during the actual school year, listening to the actual noise. I would feel as lost and clueless as any freshman, looking around for something familiar, desperate for emotional comfort, in need of constant reassurance.

It's strange, how it takes coming back to this place to realize how much I don't miss it.

Without Bobby, reminiscing sure ain't fun at all.

I put a hand to my pocket where my phone is, tempted, then sigh and leave that damned thing right where it is.

Then I go farther down the hall and arrive at the double doors to the dance gym, which the wrestlers happened to also utilize in the early mornings and the afterschool hours. The locker room is exclusively for girls, so I was given the back of the teacher's closet to change every day for dance. The memory of that first day when I exclaimed, "I'm changin' in a freakin' closet??" at my teacher— and the incredulous look on her face—earns the first smile on my face since Tanner left me to wander these halls.

By total impulse, I whip my phone out, snap a selfie in front of the double doors, then shoot it straight to Bobby with a message:

ME
Give U one guess where I'm at, bro!!!

I grin, satisfied with myself, then wait for a response.

I bite my lip, standing there in front of the doors to the dance gym, and wait a bit longer.

My foot taps impatiently.

Three minutes later, he hasn't even seen the message.

Fuck it. I push into the gym.

Wow. It's instant, the effect. So many fucking memories. The awkward stares I got that first day I showed up for dance class junior year. The first time I tried my hand at a pirouette and fell on my dumbfounded face. Only some of the girls laughed.

Camille was there that day. I can picture her gentle face right now, staring at me from across the room, curious.

She didn't laugh.

I got right the fuck back up and tried again. I remember it, the feeling in my chest, the knot of determination in me.

I tried everything I failed at again and again.

I refused to accept that I couldn't do it.

Just a month after that, I was the one being called up in front of the class to show off my skills as the shining example.

Ballerina bro.

I chuckle at that, biting my lip and shaking my head.

The mirrors still line the front of the gym from one end to the other, punctuated only by an exit and the door to the girls' locker room. I saunter along in front of that endless mirror, watching my reflection as it hops between the divisions from one wide mirror to the next.

I stop at the middle one. Imaginary spotlight clicks on.

I really wish Bobby was here.

Feeling inspired, I pull out my phone—*Bobby still hasn't seen or responded to my pic, too busy at the movie theater, I guess*—and tap on my music app. Soon, my favorite beats fill the giant gymnasium from my tiny phone. I face that mirror proudly.

Then, on the eighth count: *Snap!*—my body moves.

And I'm dancing.

Pop! I hit the beat right on-time, twist my body to perfection, then kick the floor, sending me right into the next move.

I'm improvising every twist, pop, and snap of my feet. I let the music take me away, bobbing my head, curling up my lips with attitude, and stank-facing the mirror.

Music is attitude.

Dance is my armor.

My body is the weapon.

With every hit, I attack the space. I attack that stupid feeling of loneliness in me. I attack all my awkward moments and also my proud ones. I attack every label that tries to stick to me like a bug. I attack all the sidelong looks, all the glances and whispers, and all the giggling from girls at nearby tables in restaurants.

As long as I'm dancing, nothing can touch me.

When I'm one with the beat, I become completely unaware of myself. I'm not some guy who went to this high school. I'm not the younger brother of some local football legend. I'm not best friends with Bobby Parker—or anyone, for that matter.

I'm something completely different.

I'm something that can't be contained with—*Why isn't Bobby looking at any of my texts?*—achievements and desires and—*Did I do something wrong?*—lifelong plans.

I'm something beyond the definition of a person.

I'm—*Bobby, would it fucking hurt you to simply acknowledge me, see my text, give me a laugh or a hello or a selfie back?*—the weapon and the armor and the attitude, rolled into one.

I'm invincible when I move my—*Seriously Bobby, what the fuck?*

We could be enjoying this moment together right now. We could—body to the music. *Damn it, Bobby.*

... until something goes wrong with my foot.

"FUCK!" I cry out as I twist like a snake, drop onto my ass, and grab my ankle with a hiss squeezing out of my clenched teeth.

In an instant, fuck all that shit I just said: I'm Jimmy Strong.

The idiot who just danced too hard.

Fuck, fuck, fuck, what did I just do?

My ankle throbs and screams at me.

Nerve endings send a flood of telegrams up to my brain, each of them louder than the last.

Has anyone ever mentioned that the ankle is the hardest part of your body to hug when it hurts?

Throbbing, throbbing, throbbing.

"SHIT, PISS, FUCK, GOD-DOG!"

The tunes play on obliviously—suddenly sounding obnoxious and mocking somehow—as I struggle to hold and nurture my poor ankle like a precious, crying baby. I inspect it, checking it on one side, then the other. *Is it sprained? Did I just fucking sprain my ankle? Did I break it? Did it come off? What the fuck was I even doing that was so strenuous that I injured it?*

Was I even paying attention to my dancing?

Is it bad that I don't even know which move I did that made my leg go all wrong? Did I kick into the floor at a bad angle?

I look off to my left, then to my right. Suddenly, the gym feels vast and empty and dangerous. Every shadow looks suspicious. All the walls look far, far, far away.

I stare ahead at the mirror—at the reflection of myself curled up on the floor and clutching my ankle, my phone sitting off to my side, still blaring the music, careless of my plight.

"God-*dog*-it," I let out, angry. *Your ankle is fine,* I tell myself right away—my defense mechanisms kicking in. *You're fine. Just get up. Walk it off. You just landed on it wrong. No big deal.*

Despite the throbbing, I brace myself, then rise with all my weight on my good leg. I let my throbbing ankle hang for a second, staring down at it with mounting skepticism.

After a breath, I gently set it down on the ground and apply a tiny bit of weight.

Pain.

Ache.

Throb.

PAIN.

I wince, sucking in air through my teeth. "For fuck's sake," I let out. "Fuck, fuck, *fuck me,* fuck." I try a little more weight on it, determined. It throbs just the same. I take one tentative little step.

I nearly fold myself in half.

"FUCK!" I shout out, lifting my bad foot from the ground.

I shouldn't have left the house. I should've stayed home.

I crouch down carefully, all my weight on my good leg, and swipe my phone off the ground. With a resentful jab of my thumb into its screen, the music is silenced at last.

This is Tanner's fault. I shouldn't be here. I shouldn't have come.

I let out a steeling huff, then proceed to hop across the gym.

This isn't *Tanner's fault. This is* your *fault, Jimmy. You're a reckless dancing maniac fool.*

Crossing the gym one-legged takes an eternity, by the way. And after that eternity, I finally push through its doors—which feel twenty times heavier—and hop my way down the long hall.

I stop in front of a water fountain, holding it for support.

I try my weight down on that whiny ankle again.

Pain. Throb.

"Fuck you," I yell down at it. "Just fuck you, you whiny thing."
I push away from the fountain and start to hop again, making my
way down the hall—which seems to stretch on forever now.

When I reach the one lit-up office down the dark hall, I find
my brother at a computer, pinching the bridge of his nose as he
stares at a screen full of spreadsheets and numbers. He glances
over at me, seems for a second to want to make a joke, then sobers
up at once. "What's wrong? What happened?"

"Danced too hard," I growl.

"Jimmy, for Pete's sake, really?" He gets up from his desk and
rushes to me. "Sit down, sit down," he tells me, throwing an arm
over my back and guiding me to a chair. My weight drops into it,
and he gently picks up my bad foot by the heel, then tries to
remove my shoe for a closer inspection.

I shout out when the pain hits me. "Tanner, what the fuck?!"

He stops at once, flicks his wide-open eyes up to mine. "Dude,
we've gotta get you to the clinic if it hurts that bad."

"I'm fine. It's ... fine. I just need to—" I wince when he adjusts
his hold on my ankle. "Need to ice it and keep off of it for the rest
of the day. This happens all the time. It's a dancer thing."

Tanner twists up his face. "Dancer thing? Really?"

"Yeah, sure. Toe injuries. Ankle rolling. Whatever. I'm fine. I'll
just ..." I gesture tiredly at his computer. "I'll just sit here while
you finish up your stuff. I'll be fine."

"You realize I'm a coach and former football player and deal
with injuries all the time, right?"

"Nah, totally forgot." I wince again, all the nerves in my ankle shouting at me in a pulsing, thumping chorus.

Tanner sighs. "Jimmy, you want me to get you some ice? The teacher lounge is just down the hall," he points out, poking a big thumb over his shoulder. "Just five seconds away."

"Nah, I'm fine."

"You sure?"

"Yeah, Tan, I'm fine."

"I'll get you some ice," he decides anyway, hopping to his feet and charging through the door before I can protest.

Typical Tanner.

I bite the inside of my cheek and scowl at my stupid feet. *What did I do wrong?* I keep asking myself over and over. I try to replay my dance moves in my head, but I was improvising so fast, and going at it in such an out-of-body way, I can't even determine if it was a leg twist or a foot jab that did the trick. Or neither.

I feel my phone buzz. I yank it out of my pocket at once.

BOBS
What are you doing at Spruce High?

What lovely timing, right? I type out a response.

ME
Came here with my brother. So many memories
here. Also I think I just broke my ankle.

BOBS
What??? Are you OK??

I smirk, then decide to play with him a bit.

ME

```
No, man. U should prolly come over when U
get off work. I need a thorough foot rub.
```

There's a long pause after he sees the message. Then I watch him type, stop, type, stop, then type again. And finally:

BOBS

```
Nice try. Not funny, btw.
```

I try on a smile, but feel a pinch of awkwardness in my chest. Again, I can't help but feel like Bobby is completely shrugging me away like some pariah who's gone and done something utterly unforgivable by all the laws of man.

"I just kissed you," I say at my phone, annoyed. "That's all. What's the big fuckin' deal?"

Then I wince when I forget about my ankle for a second and let it touch the ground.

If he had answered sooner, you never would have gone into that gym.

I clench my eyes shut, frustrated.

My brother is back the next second with a pack of ice. After a second of me holding it against my ankle, a permanent grimace painted over my face, Tanner lets out the world's longest big-brother sigh, throws me a harsh look, then says, "Yeah, this isn't gonna do. We're going to the clinic. Now."

Two and a half minutes of arguing and nine minutes of very awkward hopping through the school later, we're back in Tanner's Subaru and driving down the four quick blocks to the clinic.

Tanner sweet-talks the woman at the front desk, Marybeth, who's going on about something to do with the doctor being out for lunch. "But Trey's in the back. Maybe he can give him a quick looking at before the doctor does? Run an X-Ray?"

"Yeah, that's perfect," decides my brother on my behalf.

A minute later, Trey himself emerges from the back. I haven't seen the guy since last summer. As Reverend Arnold's son, and a nurse, he's Godly, kind, and known for having the biggest heart in all of Spruce. I've never really had a chance to get to know him all that personally or one-on-one, but if there's one thing I'm aware of, it's how big of a scandal it was when his and Cody Davis's relationship was outed.

And when Trey's eyes meet mine, and I feel all that kindness and compassion in them, it suddenly occurs to me.

He's the guy I need to see right now about my problems.

And I'm not talking about my ankle.

"Jimmy," he greets me courteously with a nod, then turns to my brother. "Tanner, hey there."

"It's his ankle," Tanner says for me. "He turned it wrong or landed on it wrong while he was dancin', something like that. Can we get him looked at? I understand the doctor's out."

"Sure, of course." Trey smiles at me, then comes to my side to help support me as I rise up onto my good foot.

When Tanner also comes to my side, I quickly blurt, "Thanks, but I'll go with Trey alone. I appreciate it."

Tanner's face turns into a crinkled grocery bag. "Dude, let me help you. You need—"

"I got it, thanks."

"You sure?"

"Yep." I turn and give Marybeth a quick nod at the counter. "Thanks a bunch, Marybeth."

"Tell Bobby I said hi!" she says right back, giving me a wiggly-fingered wave. "Phew, I haven't seen that sweet boy in too long." She smiles broadly and rests her chin on a propped-up hand, her eyes batting wistfully at me as I go. My brother just stares at me, baffled, as I leave him with Marybeth and head back with Trey.

Trey leads me into one of the rooms with an arm over my back, guiding me. I sit on the examination bench thing, the rolled-out paper crinkling under my ass, and rest my left leg on the table with my bad foot. In a few words, I tell him what happened, and Trey inspects my ankle to the best of his ability, now and then stopping to apologize and say something like, "When the doctor's back from his lunch, he'll be able to give you a more thorough check and say all the things I'm not authorized to conclude or say." Then he eyes me and adds, "*Yet,*" with a coy smile. Trey turns my whole leg delicately one way, then the other, constantly asking if it hurts, if he's hurting me, or if he needs to be gentler.

He's the nicest person I've ever known. It's no wonder that his life's calling is to be a nurse and, well, literally save lives.

Not that my ankle is any life-or-death situation, mind you.

"I can't say anything definitively until Dr. Emory's back from his lunch—*protocol and all,*" says Trey dutifully, "but from what I can tell here, I'd say you're just looking at a minor sprain."

"Minor sprain?"

"Yep. We should go ahead and do an X-Ray to be sure, but ..." Trey smiles. "I'd say the doctor's gonna suggest a painkiller and just tell you to keep off it for a few days, maybe a week to be safe."

"What a relief," I sigh out.

Trey smiles and rises. "Well, if you want to come with, we can run a quick X-Ray before Dr. Emory's back. We sent him a text, and he responded saying he's headin' back this way for you."

Well, nice to see some *people in Spruce actually respond to their texts on time.* "Thanks, Trey. I really appreciate it."

"No problem. Now let's go ahead and get you into the other room for an X-Ray. Ready?" He prepares to help me off the table.

"Trey?"

He stops and peers at me. "Yes, Jimmy?"

"I ..." *Shit, am I really gonna do this?* "I, uh ... I need some ..."

"Yes?"

"Advice," I finally get out. "I need some serious advice. It's on a thing I can't really talk to my brother about. Or, well, anyone."

Trey steps back, his lips pursed together in thought.

"Like, I know I don't go to church or nothin'," I add, "but uh ... I mean, people confess stuff to you, right? And you ... keep it to yourself? You don't go and tell anybody? Like, confidential and ... and confessional stuff ... uh, right?"

Trey gives a nervous glance out the door, then gently shuts it. "I think that's more a Catholic thing, really, but—"

"Can I confess somethin' to you anyway? I need to get it off my chest. I need advice, and I ..." *Shit, my ankle's throbbing.* "I can't tell my brother. He isn't any help sometimes."

Trey gives me a tiny, tight smile of compassion, then takes a seat on the little rolling doctor stool. After a second's breath, he lifts his face to mine. "I'm all yours. Shoot."

I carefully think over my words. Then I start to speak while staring at my bad foot. "I ... have a situation. With my best friend. It's my fault. But I don't know what to do."

"You mean with Bobby?"

"Yeah, that's the guy. Uh, and also, I wanna preface this by saying that I'm not gay."

Trey blinks. That threw him off. "A-Alright. Noted."

"I love gay dudes. Obviously. I'm talkin' to you. There's my big brother. My best friend's Bobby. It ain't nothin' like that. It's just ... It's just that I need to preface what I'm about to say."

"That's fine."

Trey's the most patient person in the damned world. This is exactly what I needed. "Alright." I slap my thighs, steeling myself, then bring my eyes up from my feet to meet Trey's. "So I kissed Bobby last weekend."

Trey lifts his eyebrows in reaction. When I don't say anything more, he inclines his head toward me. "Okay. And ...?"

"I took him to a big gay nightclub. It was a bad idea. But I just wanted to, like, get Bobby out there in the world, find him a guy, make him happy, y'know? And I failed. So later that night in the hotel room, I ... kissed him."

Trey's facial expression hasn't changed. At all. "Okay."

"The thing is, I think it made him go all weird. Now I made a deal with him not to kiss him anymore. And he looked relieved, I think. Fuck knows why. I mean, *I'd* like kissing me, but whatever, if he isn't into it, fine. The thing is, he's kinda cold shouldering me. Or ... well, it's more like a warm shoulder. I mean, he's just ... he's not prioritizing our time together anymore. He's always busy."

Trey bites his lip in thought for a second, then asks, "He got a job down at the Cinema, didn't he? Isn't he just busy with that?"

"Well, yeah, but ..." I stare at my foot again. "I mean, I know the difference between him being busy at work and ..." I let out a sigh and stare hard at Trey. "Look, I just gotta know if I went and did something super wrong by kissing him."

Trey shrugs. "Well, I guess that depends on a lot of factors."

"Such as?"

"Such as, how did the kiss make *you* feel?"

"Good. It made me feel really good. I felt like I was his hero for a second, saving him from ... his own loneliness, or something."

"Alright. And how do you think the kiss made *him* feel?"

I take a second to consider it. "Uh ... good at first, I think."

"At first?"

"Well, then he got all weird." I glance off at the closed door, my mind wandering to that night in the hotel room, then when I forced a few more kisses on him in his bedroom Sunday night. "I mean ... I don't know. Maybe it wasn't a good thing for him."

"Why do you think it wasn't a good thing for him?"

"I ..." A stroke of worry dances through my body. "I dunno."

"Well, let's put you in his shoes for a second," suggests Trey, his voice light and patient. "If you were gay, and your straight best friend kissed you ..."

I snort. "Shoot, if I was best friends with a good-lookin' guy, and I was gay and single for as long as Bobby's been single, I'd ..." My voice breaks. "I'd probably ... have feelings for him."

"You think Bobby has feelings for you?"

Now I'm staring at nothing, those words of Trey's striking me the hardest of all, that seemingly innocent question.

"I mean ..." I start to say. *There's no way Bobby has feelings for me. Not in that way. We're like brothers.* "I mean, no. No, because ..." *Because why? Why wouldn't he have feelings for me? It's obvious.* "No. I don't think he ..." *It makes perfect sense, doesn't it?*

Doesn't it?

"I'm not trying to say anything," insists Trey. "I'm just—"

"You're asking me questions. And I'm ... I'm answering them. And ..." *Is that why he's gotten all weird? He has feelings for me, I went and kissed him, and now he's hurt?* "And I think what you're asking me is ..." *Shit.* "... makin' a whole lotta sense all of a sudden."

Trey winces. "I'm just trying to help, like you wanted me to."

"I know." I stare down at my lap, at a complete loss.

I hear Trey make a short sigh. He shifts in the doctor's stool, then gently rolls up next to me. "I can't say I got the answers, but I might suggest—as a gay man himself who has had his fair share of crushes on straight guys his whole life—that perhaps giving Bobby his space to figure things out is just what you both need."

"He's *gotten* his space," I throw back. "Almost three days of it. What the heck else does he need to get back to normal?"

Trey smiles patiently at me. "Maybe just try to let *him* be the one to come to *you*."

"Wait for him to come to me? Shoot, I'll be waitin' forever for that. He's as stubborn as a ..." I sigh frustratedly. "... as stubborn as somethin' that's really stubborn."

"I know it's hard," Trey assures me, "but sometimes, you just can't force a thing. Even with a close friend."

"We're closer than close. We're like brothers."

"Well, even more so. You ... just need to let it happen in its own time. Absence makes the heart grow fonder, right?"

"Nah." I look down at my bad foot, angry at it all over again. "I don't want to just sit around waitin'. I don't *wait*. I *do* things."

"And sometimes you do too much, as is evidenced by the fact that you're here in this office at all," Trey points out smartly. "And if anyone's an expert at guys just doin' what they want without a care about their own bodily injuries, it's me, seein' as I'm married to the *stubbornest* of all."

I smirk. Cody's a bullheaded guy, I know that much. But I just don't care right now; I need a solution to Bobby, and "waiting" is simply not gonna do.

"So just give him some time," Trey finishes. "The ball is, more or less, in Bobby's court."

"Bobby *hates* basketball." I huff and cross my arms, unsatisfied with his advice.

"It's a tennis reference, actually."

"He hates tennis, too."

Trey rises from his stool, then gives me a reassuring nod. "Well, I gave you my advice, but ... I'm just one guy in a crowded little town, growing more crowded by the day. Take my words with a grain of salt, alright?" He shrugs. "Or pepper, if you hate salt. Or sugar. Whatever grain you want." He smiles, then reaches to help me off the table. "You ready for your X-Ray?"

I stare at my foot. Somehow, I hear the distant laughter of my brother and Marybeth cutting it up at the counter through the closed door. Their merriment makes the frustration in me mount further for some reason. The frustration is like some itchy thing that's crawling over me bit by bit, something I can't properly scratch at no matter where I dig my nails, something without even a shape.

But it sure has a name.

Bobby fuckin' Parker.

11

BOBBY

I hold open one door, Vince holds open the other.

"I hope you enjoyed your show. Thanks for coming."

That's what I say to each customer, exactly the same as I said to each departing customer in the previous four showings in which I've dutifully held the door open before cleaning.

Which is similar and yet slightly different from the thing I say when I stand at the front podium to tear the customers' tickets:

"Thanks for coming. I hope you enjoy your show."

I don't suspect my brain is going to be getting much exercise as an usher at this movie theater.

My vocab sure isn't expanding exponentially.

"How're you holding up on your first Friday night shift?" asks Vince when we take a short on-the-clock break at 8:15, the pair of us sitting in the back row of a theater we just cleaned. "See what I mean about how hectic it can get?"

I don't want to disappoint him, but the workload feels like a lot of the same as the weekdays, only with more popcorn to sweep. Still, I give him an assuring nod. "Definitely."

"Don't get overwhelmed, though. Tonight's the worst of it. Saturday nights die down fast because everyone goes to church early the next morning." He starts scrolling through his phone, bored, then yawns tiredly. "Shift can't end fast enough. Hey, you aren't squeamish, right? Dumpster duty is the worst on Fridays."

I make a fake gagging sound. "Lookin' forward to it," I reply dryly, earning a chuckle from Vince.

With him busy on his phone, I pull out my own.

Unless one of my friends from college actually bothers to hit me up, say hi, or shoot me some random message, there's really only one person I'd be sure to have a message from, and we all know who that super, special, cocky individual is.

But my phone shows no notifications.

Just like it did this afternoon. And this morning at breakfast. And right when I woke up early for a little jog.

And last night before I went to bed.

And yesterday after dinner.

And during my shift.

In fact, I haven't gotten a dang thing from him since he sent me that weird text joking about breaking his ankle Wednesday.

What a weird thing to joke about, by the way.

"Waiting on your boyfriend to text you?"

I flinch, then give Vince side-eye. "He's not my boyfriend."

"Who?"

"Jimmy."

"No, I meant your actual boyfriend. Aren't you seeing a guy?"

I stare at him fully. "Uh, no. I'm not. Who told you that?"

"My sister. She said you've got plans to go on a date with him tomorrow on your day off, in fact. Out in Fairview."

Now I'm completely lost. "Say what?"

Vince gives me a long, skeptical look. "You mean ... that's not true? Are you saying my sister's lying to me?"

"I have no idea what I'm saying," I reply, "but I am sure not seeing any guy in *Fairview*. Hell, I haven't been out that way since the high school days when we had a soccer match out there."

Vince chews on that for a second, then shrugs it off. "Alright. I'll tell my sis she's got her head messed up, or you mixed up with some other Bobby Parker."

"Yeah. Mixed up with someone else, definitely." I give it three dry chuckles, then turn away, baffled.

Minutes later, we're out of auditoriums to clean until all the last showings end in another couple of hours. Vince and I (along with some sixteen-year-old usher named George who the others call G-man for some reason) stroll around the lobby sweeping up stray kernels of popcorn. It isn't long before there's nothing left to sweep, and eleven o'clock rolls around when the last tickets are sold and the box office is closed down. G-man is sent home, and I'm left with Vince to perform closing duties.

But the noise of someone banging on the locked front glass doors of the lobby stop me near the concession stand. I turn at the sound, squinting across the lobby.

My eyes flash when I see Jimmy—in a pair of skinny jeans, a form-hugging red shirt, and that ratty-ass hat on top of his head—waving at me through the glass.

"Your not-boyfriend's here," teases Vince dryly.

I shoot him a look. "Think you can give me five?"

"Closing duties aren't going anywhere, don't worry. We got all night to do them. Just don't let Mr. Lemon catch you letting him in after closing hours. He gets weird about that, ever since that one security issue two years back when a dumb pair of teens—"

"Don't worry, I'm not inviting him in," I assure Vince before heading across the narrow lobby to the doors.

That's when I notice the crutches.

I pop the door open and stare at his crutches, confused. "What the hell happened, Jimmy?"

"Told ya already," he fires back. "Destroyed my pretty ankle."

"I thought—" *I thought he was kidding, considering the way he just dropped that bit of information on me.* "Jimmy, if I'd known you had *really* hurt your ankle ..."

"Isn't a big deal," he says dismissively, leaning against the edge of the door and glancing off. "Went to the clinic and the doc gave me painkillers, crutches, and said to keep off of it for a week."

I narrow my eyes. "And *this* is you 'keepin' off of it'?"

"Yeah, well, when have I been known to follow the rules?" He hops his way into the theater, pushing past me. "How do you like your job, my man? You own the place yet? Spliced frames of porn into the Disney movies? C'mon, show me something cool."

"Jimmy, I'm in the middle of ..."

I try to protest, but my eyes drop down to his ass in those tight jeans. With his arms over those crutches, his already-too-small shirt is pulled up, revealing a wink of his back muscles, those Venus dimples of his, and those pert, tight, jeaned, perfect buns.

My throat closes up at once, like I'm allergic to the sight.

I come around to the front of him, determined not to be (as usual) hypnotized by his butt. "Jimmy, what're you doing here? I got work to do."

"No, he don't," calls Vince from behind the concession stand.

I throw Vince a look. "And what was this business about not lettin' Mr. Lemon catch me letting in a friend afterhours?"

"It was me joshin' you," he calls back. "He don't give a lick."

Jimmy starts swinging across the lobby on his crutches, half-hopping, half walking. "C'mon, Bobby! Show me cool stuff!"

Ignoring the amused look Vince is giving us, I hurry after Jimmy, coming up to his side and lowering my voice. "Dude, what about the doctor's orders? You shouldn't be runnin' around like this. You gotta take care of—Wait, how'd you even get here?"

"Borrowed my mama's car. It's a bitch, not drivin' my truck, but since it's standard and requires two feet, well ..." He gives a nod at one of the auditorium doors. "Show me the big projector room. I wanna see the projectors."

I sigh. "First off, I can't take you up there. Second off, you don't get there through the *auditoriums.* You get there by going up the stairs toward the *office* where my *boss* is, and I can't risk—"

"Well, then, let's go!" Jimmy hobbles his way to the other side of the concession stand. "Where is it? Where's the stairs? I'll hop."

"Jimmy, I got work to do. Can't you just wait down here until I'm finished or something?"

He stops and looks at me. "Why can't I come with?"

Oh my God, he's so infuriating sometimes. "I'm at my job, Jimmy."

For the first time since he pushed into the theater, his eyes cast down in thought and he starts doing that thing with his mouth—I can't tell if it's biting the inside of his cheek, sucking his own tongue, or working something out from between his teeth.

I come up closer to him. "Seriously, man, what are you doing here? Y'know I can't just mess around on the clock. I need this job.

This isn't some ... blow-off thing to me."

"Yeah, it is," interjects Vince from halfway across the lobby where he's playing basketball with balled-up trash and a trashcan.

With a sigh, I lower my voice and come really close to Jimmy, close enough to smell his deodorant. *"Jimmy, can we put a rain check on hanging out for now, please?"*

From the tightened look on his face, he's mighty unsatisfied with that request.

Still, I press on. *"I know I've not really been around much ..."*

"We've put a rain check on our friendship for a whole week."

"I know." I peer over my shoulder at Vince, who's still pulling napkins out of a nearby dispenser, crumpling them up, then tossing them at the trashcan. He pumps the air with his fist every time he makes one in. I turn back to Jimmy. *"This is the first week at my job, so it's all kinds of ... hectic. I can't focus on much else."*

"Too busy to focus on your best friend's broken ankle?"

My eyes flash. "Really? It's broken?"

Jimmy smirks, lightness returning to his eyes. "It could be."

I'm convinced he enjoys toying with my emotions sometimes. This is the same guy who woke me from a dead sleep at two in the morning freshman year because he nicked himself while trying to snip off a loose thread from his sleeve. *"I can see bone! I cut myself to the bone! Do I need to call 9-1-1?!"* I'd had worse paper cuts than that.

Still, I might complain a lot lately about Jimmy's big spotlight obsession, but there's also something weirdly endearing about it. Because even when he woke me up, I bandaged his finger for him, talked him down, and assured him it was just a minor cut. *"Ugh, I hate blood, I fuckin' hate blood,"* he kept saying, and I just chuckled to myself, rubbed him on the back, and stayed up with him until he was alright, despite my being tired as hell.

Yes, I think he occasionally overdramatizes his issues for the attention. Yes, sometimes it's more obvious than other times.

But in the end, I find I don't care as much as I maybe ought to.

Maybe I even kinda like how much he needs me at times.

Suddenly, Jimmy relents with a sigh. "It's sprained, that's all. My foot will be better before the Spruce Ball, don't you worry one bit about *that*. I already had my mama and Billy *both* flip out when they heard about my dumb ankle." He gives a cheesy wink, then nods toward the door. "Now you gonna show me a projector or what? Surely you got at least a few minutes to blow off, right?"

I glance over my shoulder at Vince. Ever the eavesdropper, he has all but completely stopped his trash-themed basketball game to pay attention to us. When our eyes meet, he gives me a shrug and a nod, more or less permitting me to fuck off for a bit.

My heart's light the next instant. I give Jimmy a smack on the arm. "You'd better still be able to keep up on those crutches of yours!" as I head toward the door that leads upstairs.

Jimmy blows air out of his lips, then hurries on behind me, hopping half of the way.

We blow off more than just a few minutes. I don't even pay attention to the time as I show off all my recently-acquired film and projector knowhow, pointing out and identifying (with chin-lifted confidence and prestige) each part's name that I recall. "This part right in the middle of the film platter is called the *brain*," I expertly tell Jimmy, "which feeds all the film into ... *here, come 'round to this side* ... which feeds into this thingy here, around these gears—you gotta make sure the tension is *just right*—and then ..."

Over and over, I keep telling Jimmy not to touch this, or not to touch that, or to keep away from this or that because he'll lose a finger. "It's way, way hot to the touch," I warn him when he gets too close to one of the projector lamps, "so you better stay back."

I love being the expert for once.

I've got Jimmy's attention right in the palm of my hands.

Jimmy and I end up at one of the projector windows, through which we can peer down into one of the auditoriums, or watch the movie up on the silver screen. It's like the two of us are in a secret back row *behind* the back row.

The projector windows are considerably small, so we have to stand super close to both look through it. At one point, Jimmy goes off-balance a bit, and by reflex, I throw an arm around his waist to catch him, and then my arm just sort of stays there, holding him in place, while we both stare through the window, watching the movie.

My hand stays there at his lower waist, just inches away from his butt, holding him.

Just a couple weeks ago, this act wouldn't be such a big deal.

Just two buddies in front of a window.

Me, holding on to him to keep his balance.

It's an act of friendship. An act of courtesy, of compassion.

But now—after that kiss in the hotel room, after that kiss in my bedroom, and after that cruel pact he made me make after all of it—everything feels so different. Just the act of having my hand around his waist, my arm against his back, holding him up ... it all seems so intimate now.

Like I'm holding a boyfriend—a real boyfriend.

My lover. *Jimmy.*

"How much you think them Hollywood actors get paid?" he

ask suddenly.

"*Shh*," I hush him. "*This is just glass. They can still hear you down there in the auditorium.*"

Jimmy peers into the window, his nose pressed against it. "I think I see two teens makin' out in the third row."

"*Jimmy ...*" I whisper warningly.

"Hey! I see you two horny hooligans!" he shouts. "Quit makin' your mamas blush! God's watchin' you! God's watchin'!!"

I yank Jimmy away from the window just in time to avoid the heads that turn. "*Jimmy!*" I hiss at him, furious.

We lock eyes.

He cracks a smile.

I do, too.

Then the pair of us break into laughter so loud, we have to slap hands to each other's mouths to keep from making more of a scene than we just did. I laugh so hard that I fall to the floor, and without a way to balance himself, Jimmy falls right down with me, laughing so hard he doesn't seem to care. His crutches are lost. We're on the tiled floor that hasn't been properly mopped in months. We just don't give a flying filmy fuck.

"Bobby Parker."

I lift my tear-ridden face up.

Mr. Lemon stands at the door to the office, staring down at the pile of clothing and limbs that is me and Jimmy.

Oh, fuck.

My laughter ceases at once. I clamber to my feet, smooth out my clothes, and give a stuttering, "S-Sir, Mr. Lemon," in return, followed by a hard, throat-tightened swallow.

Jimmy is still recovering from his laughter when he sits up, also teary-eyed, and takes a look at my manager. He wipes his eyes and hugs his knees, his bad leg hovering off the ground. "Hey," he mutters, then smiles dumbly.

Mr. Lemon recognizes him. "Jimmy Strong?"

"That's me. And ... wait." He looks around. "The fuck is my ...? Oh, there it is." He grabs the ends of his crutches, which somehow got flung five feet away from us, and uses them to rise back up to his feet. "Damned stupid sticks."

My face grows redder and redder by the second.

My only saving grace is that the projectionist hall is dark—as it ought to be, since the light would pour into each auditorium.

But Mr. Lemon has the light of the office pouring over him, and it creates a menacing shadow that stretches across the room to the tips of my toes, making him look a hundred feet tall.

"S-Sir, sorry," I manage, taking a second to wipe the tears of laughter from my eyes. "I got carried away. I shouldn't have—"

"It's fine," says Mr. Lemon at once. "Just ... um ..." He licks his lips, wipes his brow agitatedly, sighs, then finishes: "Just ... don't make a habit of this, please. Okay?"

I swallow hard. "Y-Yes, sir."

"Thank you. Did you ..." He looks tired and overworked, his eyes going crossed as he tries to finish his sentence. "... uh, finish your ... your usher duties downstairs?"

Oh my God, what time is it? How long have we been fucking off up here? "I'll ... I'll go check with Vince right now to make sure it's all done, sir."

"Good, good. That sounds all good." Mr. Lemon gives Jimmy a hardened smile. "Nice to see you, Mr. Strong. Give your best to my mother. *Err ...*" He slaps his forehead. "*My* best ... to *your* mother."

Jimmy smiles. "Sure thing."

"Yes, good." Then, with another stiff-necked look at the pair of us, he turns and disappears back into the office, the door slowly closing and taking all the light with it.

I let out a deep sigh at his departure, then turn to Jimmy with a look of *oops* in my eyes.

Jimmy looks at me the same. "Looks like we *funned* too hard."

"We *funned* way too hard," I agree. "I should head back down. To, um ... check on Vince and stuff."

"Yeah, dude." Jimmy slaps me on the back, then starts on his way, his crutches stabbing the ground every step he takes.

After hopping down a flight of stairs—me figuratively, Jimmy literally—I find Vince sitting on the concession counter, his legs dangling off.

When I come up closer, I discover someone else with him.

"Hey, Vince," I say quickly, hoping to diffuse any tension at once. "I'm really sorry, I got busy upstairs with showing off the projectors, and I lost track of time, and—"

Anthony Myers—the someone else with Vince, sitting next to him on that concession counter—is the one who cuts me off. "You know, it's enough work to close down the concession stand on your own, but to make me have to step out of my position to help out the lone usher with his duties, too?" Anthony shakes his head, tsk-tsking me. "That's messed up."

I stop in front of them, my face hardened. "I said I'm sorry."

Vince shrugs, not adding anything to the conversation. I can't tell if he's actually bothered by my absence, or is truly indifferent to it and it's just Anthony making the big deal out of it.

Jimmy catches up and plants himself right next to me. When

his eyes meet Anthony's, I watch Jimmy's face turn into hardened granite, his eyes narrow darkly, and his lips tighten—everything short of a cat's ears folding back.

Anthony, likely shocked at the sight of Jimmy Strong in the flesh before him, has much the same reaction—except I might say it's more in fear than it is indignance.

Vince seems to notice the sudden monumental increase in tension, because rather suddenly he *does* care about everything and quickly blurts out, "Nah, it's no big deal, Bobby. Don't worry about it. I'll show you the dumpster routine later after we clean the last movie. It drops in, like, fourteen more minutes."

"Okay, Vince. Again, I'm sorry, truly."

"No sweat off my back, man. I mean ... other than the literal sweat dripping off my back from hauling four bags by myself."

I wince. "Sorry."

Vince quickly amends himself with, "Like I said, no problem. We're all good." He glances at Anthony. He glances at Jimmy. "We are all ... totally ... totally good."

Exactly seven and a half seconds of pure, wire-tight silence passes. Then Anthony gives a curt nod with a clipped, "Jimmy."

Jimmy returns the nod with a tilt of his head and an almost smarmy, "Myers," in reply.

Those are all the words that are exchanged between them.

And the fourteen minutes that pass are the longest in history. They crawl by slower than years on Neptune and Pluto. Jimmy and I find a hundred and one different positions to lean on the counter in, now and then exchanging a few words about something utterly useless and unimportant. Vince and Anthony chat back and forth about the bushy-haired girl who works in box office, and Anthony sneaks a dark-eyed glance or two at Jimmy.

What a strange night this has turned out to be.

It's while I'm cleaning the last theater that I get the text.

I pull my phone out, wondering if Jimmy is texting me some snide comment about Anthony from the lobby where he's waiting patiently—and find myself surprised at what I see.

> **NADINE STRONG**
> Hi there Bobby sweetie. Clear your Saturday night plans, because I made you some.

The text begins and ends with three kissy-faces.

I read it a hundred zillion times in a row.

What the heck is she talking about?

Vince, having come up to read the message over my shoulder, chuckles and shakes his head. "Well, well. Looks like your buddy's mama is looking out for you after all."

I snap my face to Vince's. I'm still in a distracted daze, totally not following anything at all. "W-What?"

"You haven't connected the dots?" He nods at my phone. "It's your best friend's mama who set you up on a date with that dude out in Fairview—my sister's friend. I knew my sister wasn't lying. She never lies. You got yourself a date tomorrow night, homie."

I open my mouth to protest.

Nothing comes out.

What the fuck ...?

12

JIMMY

"Don't worry, Bobs, I'll sort this shit out."

I drove Bobby home in my mama's borrowed car. *I already miss my truck—badly.* Now we're sitting in his bedroom with the TV on in the background, though neither of us are paying attention to it. It's ten or twenty past two in the morning—and I think Bobby *still* might not have closed his mouth since he got the text.

"Seriously, I'll sort it out," I repeat, trying to assure him. "My mama's known for this. It's like, her fucking second job. *Meddling.* That woman's ... *ugh, fuck man* ... That woman's been meddling in everyone's business ever since Spruce had a name."

"She set me up on a date. Tomorrow night." Bobby looks up from his phone and stares at me from the bed. I'm across the room, squished into his beanbag chair like I always am. "How did she know I'm off tomorrow night, anyway?"

I snort. "You kiddin'? My mama knows everything. Besides, Mr. Lemon knows her. She and my papa used a fund or somethin' to help repair the seats in the auditoriums when they got water damage from that bad storm ten-fifteen-something years ago."

"Oh, Hurricane Hailey, right." Bobby nods distractedly, then peers back down at his phone.

I shake my head. "Staring at that text a hundred times isn't gonna change the words in it, y'know." I frown and glance at the window to my side, listening to the night breeze disturb the trees in Bobby's front lawn. "What's my restless mama doin' awake so late, anyway?" I wonder out loud. *Probably planning stuff for the Ball while inventing a hundred more reasons to hate the McPhersons.*

"I mean, I should go on it, right?"

I face Bobby at once. "Huh?"

"The date." He sets his phone down next to him and crosses his arms tightly over his chest, his oversized white t-shirt that he changed into after his shower crinkling up. "I should go ahead and go on it, right?"

For a second, the words *"Hell no!"* are on the tip of my tongue. I picture the most pretentious, annoying gay guy my mama might have found through a friend-of-a-friend, and don't want Bobby to be put through that headache of a bad date.

Then there's the opposite extreme: some gorgeous, handsome motherfucker in fancy clothes making Bobby swoon and gush afterwards over how amazing his date was.

Both possibilities bother me immensely.

"Well?" Bobby prods me, impatient. "Should I? Shouldn't I?"

"I ..." My words come out weirdly deflated and sad. "I think ... it's, uh ... up to you, I guess."

Bobby looks troubled by my answer or tone of voice, his lips curling into his mouth as he mulls it over, frustrated.

My heart turns into a full-on drum solo in a marching band. What the hell am I panicking about? "Listen ..." I start, sitting up from the beanbag chair and leaning forward. "It's really up to you, alright? But ... also consider that my mama has a certain kind of taste. An *uppity* kind of taste. A refined and ... and ..."

"Jimmy, are you tryin' to call your own mother stuck-up?"

"No." I shake my head too quickly. "Nah, wouldn't dare." My shoulders rise and drop with a sigh. "But you know my mama. I think you need to consider that if you go on this date—which is a *blind date*, by the way—it might be with someone you won't like, and then there you go, wastin' a perfectly good Saturday night."

Bobby quirks an eyebrow, confused. "So ... I *shouldn't go* ...?"

"I'm not tellin' you what to do. And I'm not tellin' you what *not* to do. I'm just ..." My tongue trips me, and I'm left staring at the floor, searching for words and coming up empty.

"Well, gee, you sure aren't any help," mumbles Bobby with a sigh, glancing away.

I stare at Bobby looking confused and lost. A fire sets within me, which pushes my body out of the hungry beanbag chair. I hop across the room and plop down on the bed next to him. Bobby looks at me as I lean back against the headboard, then throw a lazy arm around him, pulling him against me.

"Um ..."

"What?" I throw at him. "I just wanna comfort you for a sec. You're freaking out about this whole date thing, and—"

"But we made that deal, didn't we? Last weekend?"

I turn my head toward him. "Do you see me tryin' to kiss you? I'm keeping my end of the deal. I learned my lesson."

Bobby gives me a long, quizzical look. Then, after a moment of indecision, he finally gives in, allowing me to hold him, his head resting against my chest.

We spend some time just like that, Bobby cuddled against me, my arm around him, and the murmur of the too-soft TV in front of us. The only other light in the room is a tiny lamp near the bed with a soccer-ball-print lampshade I'm pretty sure he's had since before he sprouted hair in his armpits.

Instinctually, my hand starts to rub up and down his back comfortingly. It's barely a thought; I just start doing it.

"I'm sorry if I've been ignoring you."

I peer down at the top of his head. "Yeah?"

"Yeah. I didn't mean to."

Those words mean so much to me right now. "Thanks, Bobs. I know you've been pretty busy with your new job and all. They had you working the whole dang week, you realize that?"

"Well, I have tomorrow and Sunday off," he points out.

"Sure, but ... that's still six days in a row they worked you."

"Sunday was just a training and orientation thing." After a bit, he reconsiders. "Well, an eight-hour-long training and orientation thing ... I guess. Yikes, you're right. Six days straight."

I chuckle softly. My hand still rubs up and down his back. I fucking love this guy. I want everything in the world for him. "You seem to fit right in there. That projector hall was really cool. I just hope I didn't make your boss have a bad impression of you."

"No, I'm sure it's fine."

"Really, though. I feel bad about that." My hand runs up to his shoulder, giving it a massaging squeeze. "I should've been more responsible or somethin'."

"Mr. Lemon is super forgiving. Heck, he probably won't even remember it when I come in for work Monday morning."

"And you don't have to apologize to me for nothin', Bobby."

He shifts slightly. "Huh?"

"The whole 'ignoring me' thing." My fingers dig and play into the muscles in his back, turning the soft rub into a one-handed massage. "I'm a big boy. I oughta be able to take—"

"That feels good."

"Does it?" I dig my fingers into his back with more intent, focusing all the strength of my hand into his muscles. "Anyway, I was saying, I oughta be able to take care of myself."

"Yeah, but now you've got a gimpy foot."

"It's fine. Just needs a little lovin'." I give it a wiggle. "Speakin' of, is that offer for a foot rub still on the table?"

"That was *you* asking for one, wise guy. Not *me* offering one."

I chuckle softly. My hand works its way down to his lower back muscles, which is just a bit of a reach. He lets out a soft sigh when I dig into them, which I take to be an admission of, *"Damn, that feels good,"* so I knead my fingers even deeper.

He shifts slightly, and his arm slinks across my waist.

By instinct, I reach for it with my other hand. Now clutching his arm, I start gently rubbing it, too.

"You're like a mini massage parlor," Bobby mumbles against my chest.

"I'm a lot of things, I guess," I murmur back as I press a thumb deep into a muscle in his lower back. Bobby hums softly in reply, melting into it. "I'm also a space heater, according to you."

"A *wet n' sweaty* one. Mmm."

His words are starting to turn into milk and nothing.

He's really enjoying my massage, by the sound of it.

My fingers go even deeper, working down to the very bottom of his back where the muscles end and meet the top of his ass. He groans the deepest when I press my thumb right into that knot of muscles where all his tension gathers.

Ah, there's the sweet spot.

When my eyes meet the top of his shorts, and I see a tiny peek of his ass crack—just inches from where my fingers are digging—I find my mind straying.

My heart's light right now. So light, I could float away.

And my chest is finally relieved of every bit of the stress of this past week—now that I've got Bobby here in my arms.

And my mind keeps wandering off, curious about things.

Things like, this feels so fucking good, spending time with my man and making him comfortable.

Things like, I wonder what's so damned different about Bobby and me. Sure, he's gay and I'm straight. But I love Bobby just as much as I've loved any one of my past girlfriends. I care for him deeply. I like holding him.

Things like, why do we have to put this big wall of labels between us? Straight, gay ... Hell, back when I played football my freshman and sophomore years of high school, I know how it felt when a teammate slapped my ass. It made me proud. It made me feel loved—in that brotherly, teammate-like way. And I would return the love, too, showing my encouragement and team pride with a hearty smack right on the ass of another teammate.

That's how you do it as a dude. It feels great.

All guys like it. All guys think it feels great, too.

Maybe men feel this need to toughen up their showings of affection to prove their masculinity—or some other dumb shit. But the bottom line is the same: we care about each other. And if we were brave enough to admit it, we can love each other, too.

Same as I love Bobby Parker.

He's always gonna be in my life, and I'm always gonna be in his, no matter what that means for the both of us.

Even if that means ... having to let him go a bit.

"You're holding me a lot lately," Bobby murmurs softly.

I shrug. "I like holding you."

"Do you?"

"Yep."

"Why?"

"It feels good." I give his lower back another deep, massaging squeeze. "Don't you think it feels good?"

Bobby gives it a thought, then nods. "Yeah, it does."

"Good. You should go on the date."

He flinches at my abrupt shift in topics, for a second looking like he's been shaken out of a trance. "Uh ... wait, what?"

"What else do you think I'm talkin' about? The date tomorrow night. You should go."

He shifts himself around, rolling onto my lap and turning to face me. His face reflects confusion. "Why are you saying I should go, right after warning me about your ma's 'uppity taste'?"

I shrug. "Maybe this is the nice deed I was tryin' to do for you down at the nightclub. Maybe this guy's a super nice guy who'll do you good, I don't know. But you'll never know unless you try."

Bobby's eyes cast down to my chest, as if reading his thoughts off my red shirt.

My hand's somewhere on his leg now after he shifted, so I give him an encouraging pat on his thigh. "C'mon. It'll be fun. You can tell me how it went when it's over. We can make fun of him together if it all goes south."

That makes Bobby break a little smile. After a second more of thought, he looks up at me. "Jimmy?"

I lift an eyebrow. "Yeah?"

"Will you take me? Like, be my chauffeur again?"

My heart swells up. "Sure thing, man. I'll drive you and wait in the parking lot of whatever restaurant it is, or something. I'm assuming—if my mama really had a hand in this—she'll probably have set you guys up on a date at her own restaurant: Nadine's."

Bobby rolls his eyes endearingly. "That sounds like Nadine."

"Nadine 101, right there," I agree with a chuckle.

Bobby nods. "Alright, then. I'll go. And you'll take me. And ..." He bites his lip in thought, then meets my eyes again. "We should have a code or something. Like, for when it goes bad."

"*If* it goes bad," I amend for him.

"And if I give you that code—like a text or something—then you'll know to make up some emergency and come in and get me. You can pretend you drove in from Spruce, and there's, like, some emergency I gotta go home for."

"Already planning your escape route, huh?"

"It pays to be prepared!" Bobby smiles at me. "I think I feel pretty good about this, now. Maybe it'll turn out alright after all."

"Maybe," I agree lightly, my hand rubbing his thigh firmer.

Bobby swallows, then glances over at my hand. "Uh, Jimmy?"

"Yeah?"

"Your hand is on my butt."

My eyebrows pull together in confusion. I follow his eyes to my hand.

And I realize that I've been rubbing his ass, not his thigh.

Oops.

I slide my hand back to his thigh, then laugh it off and shoot him a look. "What's wrong with rubbin' your ass? You got a good one. All those years of squats and soccer playin' did it well."

Bobby bursts into laughter, his whole face going red, and he rolls right off of my lap, shaking his head. "Dude," he tries to say between his bouts of laughter, "the things you say sometimes ..."

I grin and fold my arms, watching him as he laughs, amused.

He stops suddenly, somewhere near the end of the bed, then looks up at me. "You crashin' here tonight?"

I shrug. "Figured it's a bit late to be driving home down those unlit country roads. Is it alright with you if I stay over?"

"Sure. That's ... uh, fine. Just ..."

Bobby hops off the bed suddenly, rushes to his closet, and starts searching around inside it for something. I watch a blanket get tossed to the floor, followed by a jacket, followed by a striped scarf I've never seen him wear, followed by another puffier jacket. I watch him for all of ten seconds more before I go, "Did you lose an eyeball or somethin'? What the hell you lookin' for?"

"I had an *air mattress*," he grunts, still pulling things out of his closet, "*somewhere* in this *mess* ..."

"Why do we need an air mattress?"

He stops and glances back at me over his shoulder, silent.

I gesture at his bed. "Your double-size spread here is enough for both of us. I slept on it with your snoring ass last couple times I crashed here, too."

"Yes, but—" He cuts himself off and eyes me. "I do *not* snore."

"Yeah, you do."

He ignores me and goes back to rummaging through his closet like a maniac. "I'm gonna find that air mattress. You'll love it. It's really super ..." Out flies a jacket. "... *duper* ..." Out flies the empty box to a PlayStation. "... comfortable."

"Get your butt back over here, Bobby. I told you we don't need it. We've got your bed. Why are you bein' all weird, suddenly?"

He stops, lets out a sigh, then shuts his closet door in defeat. "Alright," he mutters, then spins around with another sigh and returns to the bed, where he leaves a notable amount of space between us when he sits down and leans against the headboard. "But you and I are not cuddlin' like we did in the hotel room."

I lift my hands in surrender. "Hey, I can't help it if I'm so dang irresistible that a dude's gotta look for an *air mattress* for me so he can behave."

Bobby shoots me a sharp, knowing look, though I see a glint of playfulness in his eyes. "You better watch it before I challenge you to another soccer match in my backyard and dance circles around you with my *lightnin' legs*."

I smirk. "Yeah, yeah. Just wait 'til my foot's all better."

He lets out a chuckle, then crosses his legs at the ankles, his thigh muscles popping out when he does. Despite our best efforts to leave room between us, our arms touch when we both lean back against the headboard together, our arms crossed over our chests. I lean forward briefly to tuck a pillow underneath my left leg so that my bad ankle is supported. It's throbbing a bit, but I think I can manage without one of those dumb painkillers tonight. They make me all heady, anyway.

Bobby nudges me with his arm. "Hey, Jimmy."

I glance at him. "Yeah?"

"What if I hit it off with this guy tomorrow? Maybe, like, we could go on a double date sometime."

I don't follow. "Double date with ... who?"

"Me and this guy. You and Camille."

My stomach drops a bit at the mention of her name.

Or maybe it's those cryptic words she left me with when she last spoke to me in my bedroom. Those words about not caring what I am. That story she told me so casually and coyly about her and a German girl getting it on. The way she just stared at me so knowingly, her eyes piercing and prying into all my secrets.

It left me feeling so damned uneasy.

"Or not," Bobby adds, taking a look at my very sudden change in facial expression.

I laugh it off. "I dunno. Camille's a bit ... strange."

"Really? Strange?"

"Yeah. I mean, I don't know. I feel like Europe kind of changed her a bit."

"Changed her? How?"

"I don't know. It just did."

"Well, that doesn't say anything."

I sigh. "You gonna make me spell it out? Camille's not really the same gal she was when we all grew up in Spruce together. She practically lost all her Texan drawl."

"But maybe you two could—"

"Hey, I told you, I'm staying single this summer, remember? No girls means no drama." I sink into his bed with a shift of my body, inadvertently shoving my side against his some more.

Bobby doesn't seem to mind, because he doesn't flinch away.

Maybe he even sinks a bit against my side, too, like a pillow.

"No girls, no drama," recites Bobby, then nods knowingly, leaning his weight more into me. "Yeah, I remember that talk."

"The only important thing you and I need to worry about," I tell him, leaning my head towards his, "is what you're gonna wear tomorrow for your date. And *how*."

Even without looking at his face, I can feel his attitude.

"Don't get smart with me," I throw at him. "I know how you get when you're about to go on a date. All crazy and nervous and fretting. We'll have none of that."

Bobby scoffs. "I didn't say nothin'!"

"I *felt* your thoughts. We've got that *psychic* connection, you and I. Or telepathic or whatever. You're judging me hard for being fashion conscious, same as you did downtown at the hotel. You'll thank me one day for having a sense of these things."

Bobby snorts, but he doesn't respond.

A moment goes by with the TV murmuring incoherently at us. In the noise of whatever show we're *not* watching, I feel another bolt of pride inside me at being here on this bed with my best bud. I don't know what it is, but I feel absolutely complete when I'm with Bobby Parker. I'm sure some psychologist somewhere would say it isn't healthy for me to feel totally lost and incomplete without my best friend at my side, but I'd tell that man or woman I don't care one bit; I feel perfectly at home right now on this bed, and that's all that matters to me.

Finally, Bobby shrugs and says, "Alright, maybe I judged you a *little* bit."

"Judgment or not, you're gonna have *style* tomorrow, bro," I insist proudly. "And whether your date's a dud or a total catch, you'll make him *cry* and *bite his fist* at how much of a *stud* you are."

I feel his head turn my way. "You're a good friend, Jimmy."

"And don't you forget it," I spit back at him.

13

BOBBY

Jimmy's ma's car rumbles awkwardly, casting all these weird vibrations through its small body all the way out to Fairview.

Even the car is nervous about this date.

"Don't be nervous," Jimmy tells me for the fourteenth damn time since we left the Spruce city limits. "You're way studlier than whatever guy awaits you at the restaurant, I can already tell."

I snort. "How can you possibly know? Neither of us have seen a pic of him, and we're still ten minutes away from Nadine's."

We were right, by the way.

Mrs. Strong herself set up the date at her own restaurant.

The bill is going to be covered too, I've been told.

How romantic. Insert eye roll. And a sigh.

And an extra plate of buttered lobster tails, please and thank you.

"I just know these things, man," Jimmy insists. "I mean, I'm not tryin' to sabotage your date before it's even started ..."

"Sure you're not."

"... but my mama doesn't have some stash of single gay men hidden in her address book. So what you're gettin' with this date you're about to meet is ... probably some lady's older brother's gay nephew who's single and desperate."

"Some lady's brother's nephew ...?" I work it out. "So it's the lady's own son? Why didn't you just say the lady's son?"

"It was a hypothetical, I got confused. Jeez, stop bein' so smart with me! You get what I'm trying to say here."

I shrug, then prop an elbow up on the window. "Anyway, I'm not nervous. I'm ... curious."

Jimmy grips the steering wheel in that one-handed, muscular way of his, proudly commanding the vehicle even if it isn't his own. He gives his hat one anxious tug and, with his eyes still focused on the road, half-turns his face to me. "You're curious ...?"

"Yeah. Curious." I fiddle with the sleeves to my fitted blue button-up I'm wearing. It's one of Jimmy's. He took me back to his ranch to dress me from his own collection of stylish threads. "It's been a while, y'know?"

"A while since what?"

"Since I've met a new guy. And I don't mean at a nightclub setting where everyone's lookin' at everyone. I mean ... a tabletop, in a restaurant, where you and your date and a nice meal over conversation are your only focuses. No one and nothing else."

Jimmy drives in silence for a while after that, chewing on his inner cheek in thought. "Hmm," he grunts eventually, then shrugs and nods. "Sure. Yeah."

We don't say much else.

Until ten minutes later when the warm and romantic lighting that pours out of the windows of Nadine's washes over the car. Jimmy pulls into a spot right by the front and kills the engine.

"You ready, my man?"

Despite my nervousness—*yes, of course I'm nervous*—I shrug and play it off like it's just another Saturday night. Bored, even. "You remember the signal, right?"

Jimmy smirks at me. "You realize you can literally just text me 'Hey, come save me' and that would suffice? We don't need a special *signal* or something. I'll be right out here in the car."

"Yeah, I know. But just in case."

"Just in case of what? An alien invasion or electromagnetic explosion that disrupts all our cell signals and renders all forms of communication futile?"

I stare at Jimmy.

He shrugs. "Star Trek was on last night after you fell asleep. I stayed up and watched an episode. Or two."

"Wow. That's even nerdy for your standards."

Jimmy's face screws up. "For *my* standards?"

"Wait, that means you were up *really* late. Did you have some trouble sleeping last night?"

He peers off through the windshield at the restaurant. "I slept just fine," he mutters vaguely.

I study the side of his face awhile, just a tinge of frustration building up in me. I knew this was going to be hard on Jimmy, not being the center of my universe for four and a half seconds. But I think a little resistance from his side is to be expected.

And I should allow him his space to be moody.

And sleepless. And restless. And watching late-night Star Trek for God-knows-why.

And all those other endearingly Jimmy Strong qualities.

"I should probably go on inside. You sure you're just gonna sit out here the whole time? You can go run an errand if you want."

"Nah, I'm just fine here." He cranks his chair back and kicks his feet up onto the dash suddenly, legs crossed in his torn skinny jeans, and webs his fingers together over his lap. "Got music, got games on my phone, I'll just chill 'til you're done with Ding-Dong."

"His name isn't *Ding-Dong*."

"You don't know *what* his name is. My mama didn't even give you *that* courtesy, huh? It's a double-blind, no-name date. What if his name's Elvis?"

"His name isn't gonna be *Elvis*."

"Or Leroy. Can you date a Leroy? What about a Jim? What if his name's Jim, and you gotta deal with everyone confusing the two of us when you start datin' for serious?"

"Dang it, shush your mouth."

"Oh, God. Even worse, what if his name's *Bobby*?" Jimmy gasps. "Can you date yourself, Bobby? Can you do it?"

After a deep breath, I give Jimmy a stern pat on his shoulder. "Alright, Professor Panic. I think it's about time I head in before you run through the names of everyone we know in Spruce. Have fun with your games and your tunes. Oh, and ..." I give him a tiny smile. "Thanks for the snazzy threads."

He whips out his phone and starts playing a game already. "Go and be your bad-ass self, Bobby Parker," he throws my way without even looking at me.

That's Jimmy Strong for you.

All attitude, sass, and skintight Wranglers.

Professor Panic. I gotta remember that one.

I slip out of the car, shut the door, take a deeper breath than my lungs have the capacity for, and let it all out as I stroll up to the ornate front glass doors of Nadine's.

Fairview is basically a twin cousin of Spruce, except with a big dark underbelly no one really talks about, and unless you're from the town, the only reason you drive here is to drive through it.

Unless you're going to the oasis that is Nadine's—a little pinch of Spruce-lovin' in the middle of an otherwise strange, sometimes unfriendly, occasionally elitist little town.

And it is an oasis both in culture and in grace. The second you step through its doors, you feel underdressed or fancy, depending on your attire. Thanks to Jimmy, I feel just one single notch below adequate, which is pretty much my sweet spot; not too cocky, not too awkward. So I feel a stroke of confidence when I walk up to the hostess and tell her that I'm here to see someone, a young man who's waiting for a Bobby Parker. She smiles knowingly, murmurs, "Right this way," and kindly leads me through the restaurant.

My pulse is pounding something awful in my neck. I know it's my imagination, but it feels like everyone in the restaurant—all these married couples and business suits and gowns—are looking my way. I don't pay any attention to them, because if I do, I might trip over my shoes (Jimmy's shoes, rather; we *are* the same size in practically every dimension) and humiliate myself royally.

I don't know who to expect, but my mind flaps through a twenty-photos-a-second slideshow of possibilities. A cute blond? A square-jawed brunet? A curly-haired dude with freckles like the one at the nightclub? A fashionably tragic boy-next-door like me? A hulking brute with muscles for days? A pencil-thin fashionista who wears scarves in July? A dad-bod bear with sweet eyes?

After winding through one section to another, at last we come to a sea of tiny round two-person tables, all white tablecloths and candlelight. She leads me to a table in the dead center.

It's empty.

"Um ..." I start.

"He must've stepped away to the restroom." She smiles, her eyes squeezing halfway shut when she does, then gestures at my seat. "Your server will be with you two shortly."

I take my seat, then accept a menu from her. "Thank you," I say belatedly to her back after she promptly walks away.

I don't even look at the menu. I just glance around myself, not comfortable in the least. I have no idea who's about to come back to the table and join me for my date. Added to that the fact that we're seated at a tiny table right in the middle of the room, with straight couples on all sides of us. Older ones with wrinkles around their eyes and mouths. Middle-aged ones who look bored of each other. Ritzy wives who put on every piece of jewelry they own. Stiff, suited men who dab at the corners of their lips after each bite with their beige cloth napkins.

Suddenly, a guy approaches my table, handsome, sweet-eyed, and full-lipped.

My heart jumps. My mouth spreads into a smile. *Oh, wow.*

And then he passes right by to meet with his girlfriend—an equally pretty vision in green and silver, and the pair of them take a seat at a table together.

Sigh.

Still have no idea who I'm looking for.

Someone else passes by my table, but he's old enough to be my grandpa. Another guy my age strolls by—dark hair, dark eyes, shiny gold watch and swagger—but he's heading for the exit.

I bite my lip and stare at the menu, not really reading it.

My leg bounces in place.

I think about Jimmy lounging out there in his ma's car, his feet kicked up—good foot *and* bad one—relaxed as a cat with its face stuffed in a warm shoe. I envy him right about now.

Maybe it isn't too late to stand up my date.

That doesn't make me a bad person, does it? To even consider doing something like that?

Stop it. Don't even think of doing that. How rude. I lift my menu to my face and turn all my focus onto it. Even if our meal is covered, it doesn't save me from the awkwardness of the server showing up too soon and staring at me for an hour while I still haven't made up my mind between the salmon or the steak.

I really could just go.

Couldn't I ...?

I could just get right up, scurry outside, hop right in the car, and tell Jimmy to hightail it back to Spruce. He'd probably be all over that idea in a hot second. Then we'd plan out our night like a pair of free birds. I'm off tomorrow, so we could hit up the arcade, or go out to the Strong ranch—which I've spent approximately half an hour at this whole summer so far, and that half hour was today when Jimmy dressed me with his vast wardrobe.

The thought comforts me instantly. All my anxiety is gone at the thought of running off with Jimmy and foregoing this foolish blind date. I mean, really, I love her and all, but what was Nadine thinking? How presumptuous of her, to think I need a guy, right?

Right ...?

If only I could stop my foot from bouncing maniacally in place.

"Hi."

The single, blunt, deep-voiced syllable comes from the chair across the table from me.

I drop my menu and stare ahead, wide-eyed.

Sitting there at my table is a young man of twenty-something with a wide face and tiny features. My instinct is to say he's cute, but his lips and nose are a pinch too small, and his eyes are farther apart by a hair than you want them to be. His eyebrows are thick, long, and wide, yet strangely proportionate to the spread of his facial features, and while technically he looks clean-cut and put-together, there's something immediately *off* about his face, like it's too stiff, or too groomed, or too *something*.

And then there's the gelled-to-the-side dark hair, which has been touched by a professional stylist, no doubt. I can literally *see* the hours that went into fixing himself up for our date, though something tells me he'd put just as much effort into his looks to go to Wal-Mart at two in the morning. And that's a far stretch, to assume he'd even *deign* to go to a place like Wal-Mart.

Yes, I get all of this in a split second just from a peek at his face from across the candlelit tabletop.

I can't see what he's wearing from the waist down, since he's seated, but he's got on a fitted black designer polo that's so small, it reveals his bodyweight to be exactly ninety-three and a half pounds. I'd literally put money on that.

I feel like if I hugged him, he'd break.

He doesn't look like a hugger, anyway.

"Hi," I return tentatively.

He doesn't smile. He simply tilts his head exactly one inch to the right, then extends a hand across the table. "Malcolm."

Well, at least I'm saved from dating a Jim or an Elvis. *Or myself.* I reach for the handshake, which is a short and light-handed one on his account, and then we retract hands swiftly. "I'm Bobby."

"Pleasure. Have you eaten here before?"

Seriously, his voice is so staggeringly, unexpectedly deep for that tiny frame of a body he's got. It's a complete disconnect. I'm having a lot of trouble believing that it's his real voice at all and that there isn't some high-tech Mission Impossible voice-changing device strapped underneath the table, or that his *cojones* aren't the size of yoga balls. Seriously, should I check?

"Yes, long while ago," I answer. "My best friend's parents own the place. It's named after his mother."

"I know."

He picks up his glass of water, takes a brief, calculated sip from it, then sets it back down perfectly in place. I have a sudden suspicion that Malcolm irons his underwear and matches them to his shoes. Just a suspicion. Totally unimportant.

"Well, it's a pretty decent establishment," says Malcolm as he flicks a finger near his cheek, as if to swat away a rogue eyelash. "I am never disappointed with the service, though I did get a steak medium-rare once when I ordered medium-well."

Hmm, he's one of those types. *Hey, don't judge him so quickly.* "Well, I know Mrs. Strong personally, and that woman's nothing if not committed to making people happy," I assure him, then smile and add, "and that includes every person who walks in through those pretty doors."

I notice my Texan twang is heavily buried far beneath this … weirdly stiff conversationalist I'm trying to be right now. I haven't dropped a single "g" nor uttered a single "dang" since we started talking, for Pete's sake.

I do this at South Wood sometimes, too. I notice it.

And Jimmy is physically incapable of losing the Texan twang.

"Well, aren't you a walking *Nadine's* commercial," he teases.

His teasing intent, by the way, is revealed only by the slightest twitch of an eyebrow and nothing else. He neither smiles nor lilts his voice. His default state is a total deep-voiced deadpan.

I laugh, receiving his joke the way a polite person does. "Yeah, I guess I'm a big fan of the Strongs. I mean, you kinda have to be if you're gonna be best friends with one of them."

"Charming." Malcolm helps himself to another rigid sip of his glass of water.

I stare at mine, not having realized it's been sitting there the whole time. I go for it, taking a sip myself to wet my fast-drying tongue. It's an awful side effect of my nerves; my mouth goes as dry as the Sahara.

My phone buzzes in my pocket.

I let it peek out just enough to read the message.

JIMMY

Make sure U don't do that thing U do with UR hands. Also make sure U ask him some questions about himself cuz U don't want to be just all about urself. Also

Thing with my hands? What thing with my hands?

I stare at my phone and his incomplete text, waiting for him to send another with the rest. He doesn't. *Also ... what?*

"Something wrong?"

I glance up at Malcolm. "Hmm?"

The tiniest trace of annoyance flickers over his face. "You're checking your phone."

"Oh. It's ..." I shove my phone back into my pocket. "Just my ma checkin' ..." *There it is.* "My ... mother checking ... up on me."

"Right. I heard how you guys are in Spruce. I've never been."

I quirk an eyebrow. "How we are ...?"

"You're so ... family-oriented," clarifies Malcolm. "Everyone in Spruce keeps connected with their families. Mothers and fathers and uncles and aunts and siblings, they all know your business."

I make myself chuckle. "I guess there's no denying that. It's a restless town. Everyone's up in everything."

"So how many people know we're on this date right now?"

With his flat, dry affect, it's difficult to say whether I'm being mocked right now, or if he's genuinely curious.

I clear my throat before answering. "I'd say just a small little tiny handful." *Small little tiny handful?* "My ma. My pa. My best friend Jimmy and his mother, obviously."

"And my father, who obviously knows Nadine," Malcolm adds, "since he's the executive chef here."

My heart stops.

I stare at him.

"W-Wait a second." I lean forward and bring down my voice. "You're Malcolm ... *Tucci* ...? Chef Mario Tucci's son?"

"Yes."

"Oh, wow," I nearly sing, unable to close my mouth. "Wow. I didn't ..." *Shut your jaw before you swallow the candle on your table.* I do. Shut my jaw, that is, not swallow the candle. "I did *not* know Chef Mario had a son."

"And a daughter, too," Malcolm points out. "My sister Aurora. But she lives in Maine going to school for zoology, so ..."

"Oh, I like animals!" I smile cheerily.

"I don't. They make me sneeze." He goes for his water again.

I bite my lip, then nod. "Sure, they have lots of ..." *Um.* "... fur. Hair. Whiskers. Sneezy things."

I guess I shouldn't be surprised that Nadine set me up on a date with someone so uppity and important as her executive chef's son, who I didn't know was gay—or existed at all.

It shouldn't change anything, but suddenly I feel like I'm on a date with some kind of prince. A culinary master's offspring. A boy who was born with privilege.

He flicks at his cheek again, then goes for yet another sip.

The prince is thirsty.

I peer down at my pocket while I bring my hands to the table and start tapping my fingers on its edge. Jimmy hasn't texted again. I know because otherwise I would've felt it.

I stop tapping my fingers at once.

Oh. *Is that the thing I do with my hands? Is that what he meant?*

The server comes by, and our orders are taken. And just as I predicted, I suddenly have to fumble with the menu and endure the stress of making a hasty choice of what I'll be eating. With a muted thank-you, the server departs, and Malcolm and I return to glancing awkwardly at each other over the table.

"So have you—" I start.

"Why haven't you—" he starts at the same time.

I chuckle. "Sorry. You first."

"I was going to ask why you haven't found a boyfriend at college yet. Or in Spruce. Do you not go on dates?"

"I ... well, it's ..." *Way to put me on the spot.* "There aren't very many *options* in Spruce," I finally settle with. "And I haven't really found anyone I want to pursue a relationship with on campus."

"So why are we here tonight?"

I don't know if he realizes how bluntly he comes off, or if that is just one of his "endearing traits" that people around him have to put up with. If what I've heard about Mario Tucci is true, then the rest of the family may likely be as brusque and curt as he is.

"Because Nadine set us up?" I reluctantly offer for an answer.

Strangely, he accepts my honesty at once. "Fair enough," he states, then goes for another precise sip of water.

I catch sight of someone coming in from the other side of the room, far behind Malcolm. Someone who has a limp and is way too underdressed to be in a place like this. He's wearing a skintight pair of Wranglers, a t-shirt, a threadbare red cap, a—

Oh.

My eyes flash wide.

What the hell is he doing here? Why did he come inside?

"So do you have a job?" asks Malcolm.

Jimmy spots me. Like a stealthy cat, he slips onto the chair of an empty table by the wall in the corner, far behind Malcolm so that I'm the only one in his view. He picks up a menu to shield half his face, then proceeds to peer over its top, watching us.

I force my eyes back onto my date. "Yes. A summer job at the, uh ..." Jimmy's sneak entrance rattled me. "I have a summer job at the movie theater. At Juice Cinema 6. I mean 5. I mean Spruce."

"I'm a coffee barista, also a summer job. It's humiliating."

"Humiliating? To work? Why?" My eyes steal a quick glance at Jimmy, who's still hiding ridiculously behind that menu.

"Me? A barista?" Malcolm scoffs. "I should *own* my own coffee shop. My father insists that I follow in his footsteps, but that bores me, even if I *could* tell you forty-two different names for pasta."

"Bores you?" I murmur distractedly, sneaking another peek.

"Bores me. To the *death*."

I keep the convo going. My leg is bouncing in place again. "I like the smell of brewing coffee, but I never drink it." When I take another peek at Jimmy, he's nodding toward my date, then doing some kind of hand signal I don't understand. I frown his way, then turn my eyes back to Malcolm. "But I *do* like Frappuccinos."

"Hmm," is all Malcolm replies.

I hear a bucketful of judgment in that one miniscule "*Hmm*".

Jimmy waves his arms in the air, which succeeds in attracting about half the room his way before I ever look. When I do, he nods over his shoulder, then points down at his dick, then points away.

What in the ever living fuck is he trying to communicate?

Malcolm clears his throat. "Something wrong?"

That would be the second time Malcolm has uttered those exact words to me.

This doesn't bode well for a first date. "N-No," I insist. "I'm waving. I mean *fine*—I'm *fine*. Not waving."

No, it's *Jimmy* who's waving his arms again. *What in the hell?*

"You sure?" asks Malcolm dryly.

"Yep, totally sure. So ..." My eyes flick over to Jimmy again.

Malcolm notices this time, then peeks over his own shoulder, following my line of sight. Jimmy stops waving his arms just in time to pick up his menu and shield his face so fast, he smacks himself in the head with the heavy thing.

None the wiser, Malcolm glances around, uncertain where I'm looking, then returns his attention to me. "Is there someone here you recognize? Isn't that one of those weird things in Spruce, that everyone recognizes everyone?"

His questions *are* starting to sound mocking. "No, no one."

"You keep peeking over my shoulder."

"I'm fine, I was just ..." Jimmy's back to waving his arms. *For the love of baby Jesus ...* "Actually, can you excuse me? I need to use the boy's room."

"Mmm-hmm," mumbles Malcolm, then folds his hands in his lap and detaches his eyes.

I give him an apologetic smile he doesn't see, then slip off my chair and make a casual, unhurried walk down the aisle to the men's restroom. I slip quickly through its doors.

Someone slips in just as fast behind me.

I spin on him in front of the sinks. "What the fuck, Jimmy?"

Jimmy sighs. "Sorry, man, it's just that my phone died. I was playing too many games, I drained it down to nothin'. It died."

Really? This is what he so urgently needed to tell me? "Why didn't you just plug it in? Your ma's car has two USB ports."

"Left my charger in my truck. Do you need rescuing yet?" he asks abruptly, his eyebrows lifting halfway up his forehead. "Is it going really bad? The date?"

"It's ..." *It could be a lot worse, right? Like, this date could be a hot mess of a disaster compared to what it is, right?* "It's fine, Jimmy."

"Fine? Just fine?"

"Yeah, it's fine. Can I go back now?"

"No way. You got up to pee. You've gotta stay in here at least three more minutes now."

"Why?"

"Because if you return too quickly, he'll think you didn't wash your hands after you tinkled, and that's just plain gross." Jimmy crosses his arms, satisfied with himself.

I narrow my eyes. "'*Tinkled*'...?"

"Look, we're gonna have to use your signal thing now if you want an out," he goes on. "Since my phone's dead, we can't text. I will keep an eye out while I'm eatin' my steak. Now, if you—"

"Wait a sec. What?"

Jimmy blinks. "I'm gonna stay at that empty table during your whole date."

"How? You're—" I gesture at him. "You're *way* underdressed for this place. How'd they even let you in, dressed like that??"

Jimmy rolls his eyes. "My mama owns the place. Duh."

Okay, yeah, that was a stupid question. "You can't eat a meal back there and stare at me the whole time, Jimmy. I don't need a damned babysitter for my date."

"Yeah, you do. So just like we said, if you need rescuing ..."

"No."

"... then just make some special signal with your hands ..."

"I said no."

"... and I'll come over with some fake emergency. Oh, you can drop your napkin on the ground! That's a *perfect* sign, and I can—"

"*JIMMY.*" I put my hands on his shoulders and get up close to his face. "I don't need any rescuing. I'm fine. Just go back to your car, and I'll finish up with this date, see how it goes, and then you and I can drive on back to Spruce afterwards."

He huffs in frustration, causing the bangs of my hair to dance. "But what if you like him too much? What if you wanna go back to his place or somethin'? How will I know?"

"Well, first off, that's not likely. Second off, you'd literally see me leave the restaurant—as you are parked right in front of the entrance doors."

"I ... but I ..." Jimmy presses his lips together, frowning.

He looks so stinking cute when he pouts.

"Besides," I go on, "it's Saturday and the restaurant is busy. You don't want to occupy a table that a *paying* customer could sit at, and interfere with your ma's business, now do you?"

Jimmy sounds hurt I'd even put it that way. "I'm not hurtin' no one's nothin'. I'm always welcome here. It's my mama's place and I know everyone. Besides, you and your lil' date aren't *paying customers* either, dummy."

Oh, yeah. Forgot that bit. "Jimmy, it doesn't matter. I'm—"

"And what if I worked up a little appetite out there?" he goes on, straightening up his back indignantly. "I deserve to get a nice and tasty meal on the house, too, now don't I? Haven't I earned it, being the owner's son and all?—*and your chauffeur tonight?*"

I roll my eyes. "You shouldn't even be walking around. What are you doing racing around a restaurant on your bad foot?"

"It's fine. I don't feel a thing. I can walk normal already."

"Jimmy, you should be in the car with your foot up, resting it. Don't you give a damn about not damaging your dancing feet any more than you already have? Those are your moneymakers!"

"I said it's fine. I could do a tap dance right now if I wanted."

I roll my eyes. Again. Second time in the space of ten seconds. "Jimmy, you and I *both* know you aren't hungry. You're just—"

"Maybe I don't have some *fancy date* to share a meal with," he says, "but it doesn't mean I can't enjoy a high-class and super juicy medium-rare steak. They are *killer* here, by the way. *Killer.* Mario Tucci, I swear by everythin' good and tasty, is a damned *genius* in the kitchen. *Ooph,* the things he can do to a cut of sirloin ..."

If he only knew who my date is.

I let go of Jimmy, AKA the lost cause, and step up to a sink to wash my hands for whatever reason. "I think the issue here is just obvious as all get-out," I tell Jimmy's reflection in front of me.

Jimmy stares back at me through the mirror. "Issue? What issue is so obvious?"

"You're jealous."

"J—" He can't even say the word. "J—" He sputters five more times like a buffoon. "What does that even mean?? Why? What?"

"You don't like it when I'm seein' guys. I noticed it all the time back at South Wood. You *hated* when guys showed me attention or when I went on dates, as sadly seldom as it was that I did." I finish and snatch a paper towel off a stack of them in a fancy red wicker basket on the counter. "You're as predictable as the rain, Jimmy."

"The rain isn't predictable," he spits back. "Weathermen get it wrong all the damned time."

I turn around to face him, then drop all the attitude and speak to him sincerely. "Jimmy, can you just let me have this date? Just one little dumb date with this Malcolm guy, just to see where it might possibly go?"

Jimmy studies my face long and hard.

"I'm genuinely curious, believe it or not," I add. "I mean, it has been half a century since I've been on a date, anyway."

"Humph," he grunts. "Malcolm, you said?"

I nod. "Yes. Malcolm."

"Stupid name," he mumbles, takes a step back from me, then says, "I'm eatin' a meal. And that napkin drop is still your signal, Bobby."

Seriously, with his stubbornness. "Jimmy ..."

"So you go on then and enjoy your date."

The glare I give him seems to melt something inside him.

Jimmy's demeanor changes. "I mean, I *want* you to enjoy it. I told you, I'm here for you. Ain't nothin' about that's changed. It's just ... I want you to be smart about it, alright? Don't go givin' your heart away for free or nothin'."

"Oh, I sure as heck won't be doin' that," I assure him. "Not with Malcolm Tucci as my date."

Jimmy huffs, then limps over to the door to see himself out.

Then he stops. "Wait." He turns back to me. "Tucci? Malcolm Tucci? As in ... Mario Tucci's *son* Malcolm?"

Ah, finally it's clicked. I gain a spring in my step when I saunter up to the door myself, then throw Jimmy a self-assured smirk right in his face. "You bet your ass that's who my date is." I push through the heavy bathroom door ahead of him, then throw over my shoulder, "Enjoy your steak."

The gawping look he gives me as he watches me walk away is as hilarious as it is heartbreaking.

Eat your heart out, Jimmy Strong.

14

JIMMY

I've never chewed on a piece of succulent, perfectly-cooked, exquisitely-seasoned steak so angrily in my life.

While watching my best friend on a date.

With the most insufferably self-absorbed little twat in all of Fairview and Spruce combined.

My mama didn't let me down, that's for sure. She really does know how to pick them. Why on *Earth* she'd pick Malcolm as an ideal date for Bobby, I have no idea. Is she trying to punish him? Is she trying to punish Patricia and the rest of the Parker family?

Is she trying to punish me?

I watch Bobby laugh at some joke or something. Even the rigid shoulders of Malcolm move with a cool-mannered chuckle.

Not that I can see much, over here in the corner of the room, three rows away and by the wall, like I'm in fucking time-out.

A server passes by one aisle over—it's some new girl I don't recognize. I flag her down with a wave of my hand. She spots me at once, then makes her way to my table.

"Hello, sir," she greets me. "Is there something I can get you?"

She's a gorgeous blonde with wavy hair that cascades down her breasts, framing a modest slice of cleavage that shows right in between her partly-unbuttoned blouse. She is the stuff of every boy's dreams, from her pouty lips to her sparkling blue eyes to her curvy, synched hips and the southern twang in her voice.

Ain't none of that sexiness touching me right now. I jab a fork in the general direction of Bobby and his date. "Hey, you see that couple over there? At that table in the middle of the room?"

She lifts her face and follows where I'm pointing. "Um ..."

"Yeah, them right there. The two boys on a date."

"Oh!" She brings a hand to her mouth and flashes her eyes at me. "They're a gay couple? Them two boys?"

"Yeah, *them two boys.*"

"Are you sure?" She takes another peek.

"Yes. Are you listening? Hey." I swallow my bite finally and nod their way. "You wanna do me a favor?"

"You can't tell they're gay." She studies them from afar while hugging one of those leather-bound check presenters against her chest with someone's credit card sticking out of the top. "Like, at all. I mean, I'd never have guessed."

"Okay, well, that's beside the point. Can you do me a—"

"I mean, they're both super handsome. Especially the one in the blue button shirt."

"That's my best friend Bobby."

"Ooh!" She gives me a face of two starry, excited eyes. "He is just the *cutest!* He definitely works out. I mean, look at that cute body of his!"

Jesus, lady, reel it in. "Ma'am, can you do me a favor or not?"

She turns back to me. "What kind of favor?"

"The kind that involves you goin' over to that table, checking on them, and then dumping water over the other guy's head and calling it an accident?"

Her lips form a perfect O. Then she lets out a giggly laugh and shakes her head. "A-And why would I do that?"

"Never mind. Listen, can you tell the guy—*not* Bobby in the blue shirt, but the other one—that his *daddy* has some emergency and needs him in the kitchen?"

"His daddy?" She blinks and peers back over her shoulder at them, confused.

I study her patiently. "You're new here, right?"

She stares back at me, eyes wide and defensive. "No."

"How long've you worked here at Nadine's?"

"One and a half weeks."

Good Lord in Heaven, give me strength. "Listen. That little shrimp right there in the tiny black shirt is the son of the executive chef."

After another quick glance at them, a light flickers in her big bright eyes. "Ooh. So, like ... are you wantin' to speak to your best friend, but don't want the other guy to know ...?"

"That'd be the plan."

"Ooh! Excitin'!" She grimaces. "I don't know if I can do that, though. I could get in trouble, you know? I'm new here."

Oh my good God make up your mind. "Sure you can do it. It'll take you all of two seconds, and it's easy as pumpkin pie. Or apple pie. Banana cream. Whatever's an easy pie. Do you know who I am?" I put a hand to my chest. "My mother is who this place is named after. Nadine Strong. It's how I was able to get a table—" I snap my fingers. "—just like that, without a reservation. I can put in a word for you to the *owner* of the whole dang shebang, alright? Wouldn't that be amazing? I just need you to get that *fellow* away from my best friend for, like, three minutes tops. Pretty please."

The boys laugh again, drawing our attention. Bobby shakes his head, then says something back to Malcolm, who then lets out one curt little laugh before neatly cutting another bite of his steak.

My stomach twists at the sight of them *enjoying themselves.*

Bobby, don't be a fool. Open them eyes your mama gave you.

"Hmm. Hmm." She considers it again, glancing back and forth between me and the boys. "Hmm." She bites her lip, looking awful troubled for five more long and excruciating seconds. "Fine. I'll do it. Yes!" she decides at once. "Yes! I'll just go and do it! Yes!"

"Yes!" I agree, not meaning to mimic her, my eyes lighting up.

"Yes!" She gives me a wrinkly-faced look. "Now wish me luck. I haven't done anything like this before. *Ooh, so exciting!*" She goes off at once, cutting between the tables, heading straight for theirs.

I crouch down, as if trying to hide again—this time behind my steak and a modest mound of garlic mashed potatoes with skins— and watch my plan take root. The server reaches their table. The boys look up at her. They proceed to exchange some words. Then she lets out a musical little laugh, nods at them, and walks away.

The boys stay at the table, resuming their chat.

What the fuck.

I stare at the server incredulously as she walks away, then look back at the table, wide-eyed and frustrated. What the hell did she tell them? What did they tell her? Why isn't that damned Malcolm fucking off yet?

Bobby looks my way.

I meet his eyes, hopeful. I lift my eyebrows encouragingly at him and give him my knowing, Strong-caliber smirk.

Without acknowledging me, he turns his face back to Malcolm just in time to hear something. It makes him smile, whatever the moron said, then nod in agreement before cutting another bite.

I frown across the room at them, certain that just my glare alone could set a fire between this table and that one.

The next instant, the server returns carrying a pitcher of ice water. *Oh. She asked them if they needed anything, and they said refills. She's literally doing her job. Okay, good.* When she refills their glasses on the table, she seems to take an unnecessary amount of time to steel herself and gather some breath before, with a stiff and tragically awkward face, she says a few words to Malcolm. He frowns up at her—for the first time revealing half his face to my field of vision—and asks something back. She shrugs and gestures off toward nowhere in particular. Malcolm excuses himself curtly from the table—at which point I quickly turn away and shield myself by scratching at a spot on my face with my whole hand.

When I drop my hand and glance back at the table, Bobby is there, all alone, both Malcolm and the server gone.

And Bobby is staring right at me from across the sea of tables, suspicion burning in his eyes.

Let him be suspicious.

I rise from my table at once, cut hurriedly across the aisles, and beg someone's apology when I half-hump their chair with my dick in trying to squeeze between two tables. (It's an older woman of maybe eighty-five or ninety years of age; really it's probably the most action she's gotten in a while and she ought to thank me.)

I plop into Malcolm's seat. "Bobby."

He's already at level-five mad. "Really? An emergency in the kitchen? Can't you just leave me alone for one measly little date?"

"That's exactly what I'm comin' over here to tell you. He is a *measly* little date."

"Jimmy ..."

"I didn't know your date was *Malcolm-fuckin'-Tucci* or else I'd have warned you not to come. I've known the twerp for years."

Bobby sighs. "Yes, he's a little twerpy. Yes, he's full of himself. Yes, he's annoying."

I blink, startled. "Then why are you lookin' like the two of you are laughin' and havin' a great time over here, cuttin' it up? I keep watching the two of you."

"Because I'm *polite*, Jimmy. Because I'm *trying* to have a good time, despite the fact that this date is just—"

"Awful? Terrible? Uncomfortable? Irritating? Dude, just ask me to come rescue you. You remember the signal, right?"

"Yeah. It's like a white flag of surrender, practically."

"Drop your napkin. Right. So, like, when you're finally *up to here* with his pretentiousness, drop that damned napkin and let's get our asses out of this town."

"But maybe—"

"Maybe? There's no maybe."

"MAYBE—!" Bobby closes his eyes after that one outburst of a word—which silences me utterly, by the way—and after he takes a short breath, he brings his voice way down and finishes: "Maybe I want to live out the fantasy for a bit, alright?"

I stare at him, ignoring the one or two heads that just turned our way at his outburst. "Fantasy? ... What fantasy?"

"That I actually *do* have options for love, even if they're shitty. That guys actually *do* want to be with me, even bad ones. That ..." Bobby blinks a few times, then wipes a finger at the corner of his eye. *Was that a tear? Was that a fucking tear?* "That maybe I *could* someday have a real and actual boyfriend. A special guy who loves me as much as I love him. Unconditionally. The forever thing."

The forever thing ... "Bobby. The world's full of special guys."

"Yeah, yeah. And here I am at a table with Malcolm Tucci."

"Nah, you're at a table with Jimmy Strong right now," I tell him, leaning forward, "and I'm tellin' you, you're not gonna go the rest of your life being alone. That isn't your fate. *You're* a special guy, too. Remember that." I reach across the table and take his hand in mine, squeezing it. "You deserve the forever thing."

Bobby looks down at our clasped hands.

My thumb rubs over the top of his soothingly. "C'mon, Bobs. I want you to have it. Just ... *not* with this idiot."

"Just ..." Bobby shuts his eyes again, then opens them onto me with a hardness. "Just go back to your table and let me pretend for a little bit longer, alright?"

My stomach twists again. "Bobby ..."

He jerks his hand away from mine and crosses his arms tightly across his chest, staring at his half-eaten dinner with frustration.

I can't stand to see that hurt in his eyes. "C'mon, man. Don't be like this. All you gotta do—"

"Just go."

"—is drop that dumb napkin."

"I don't want to surrender. Go." He nods toward my table. "Go before Malcolm comes back and this already awkward nightmare becomes a goddamned *ménage à trois of horrors*."

I lean back. I guess there's no more words to say when Bobby has made up his mind—*especially when he's on the verge of tears, and it has anything at all to do with me.*

With a heavy heart, I rise from the table.

Then I stop.

Just before turning to go, I tell him, "I don't ever want to hurt you, Bobby. I've always had you in my heart, right here, right in here, *unconditionally*, and ..."

My own words are starting to lose themselves. My heart races. I want to hold Bobby. I want to touch him and break our dumb deal and kiss him just to make that light burst in his eyes again.

That isn't a weird desire, is it?

To want to make my best friend feel better?

"You deserve ..." I sigh. "You deserve to have the perfect guy, the forever thing, the everything. Bobby Parker, you deserve it more than anyone I know or will ever know."

He peers searchingly into my eyes. Something touches them— an emotion, or a bit of pain, or a bit of wonder.

I give him a touch of a smile, which is probably more of a wince of apology, before I leave him at that table, just like he requested of me. I cut back across the aisles to my own seat—and I mercifully don't hump any old ladies this time.

I hope Bobby really can handle it from here on out, because that's the last time I'll interfere tonight.

When I plop back down at my table, I notice that my ankle is throbbing. It gets worse whenever my heart beats faster.

And it's sure beating fast right now.

I must've left just in time, because when I dare to sneak a tiny glance Bobby's way, I find that jerk-wad Malcolm already returned from the kitchen, seated, and the pair of them chatting on.

There's no way I'll finish my delicious steak now.

Nor my savory, perfectly-seasoned potatoes.

What a waste of a meal I'm not even allowed to pay for.

Ten long minutes crawl by as I poke at my steak, mourning an appetite that's utterly fucking lost. Then twenty minutes, as I keep sneaking glances at Bobby's table and watching him interact with that smarmy McSmarm.

I rest my chin on the table like a pouty child, glaring at my tall glass of water. I watch as a single bead of condensation crawls, crawls, crawls down the side like a tiny glass beetle.

Comically, the tables of couples that were between me and Bobby have all left, and there's this annoyingly perfect line of sight now between us. I let my eyes wander back to his table, and for a second I think I see them holding hands, but it turns out to be Bobby holding his fork in a weird way, with his balled up cloth napkin right next to his hand on the table.

I snort. *Better not be holding my Bobby's hand,* I think bitterly, *or I'll make sure it's the last hand you ever hold, Tucci-boy.*

Then Bobby shifts his arm, bumping the napkin.

It drops to the floor.

I lift my head like an alerted dog, wide-eyed, staring.

Bobby scratches at his nose, then smiles politely at something Malcolm says.

My eyes dart down to the napkin, then back up to Bobby. Back and forth, back and forth.

Was that the signal? Or a total *actual* accident?

Do I go? Do I stay? Do I act? Do I wait?

I'll wait, I decide. *If it was the signal, Bobby will look my way. I know it. He'll look my way and wonder why I haven't come yet.*

I stare at him with intense, piercing focus, waiting for a sign.

Y'know. For a sign that his sign was a sign.

The minutes crawl by. Bobby never once looks my way to give any indication, nor even acknowledges the fallen napkin. Then a totally different server walks by and picks it right up off the floor, sets a new one on the table for him with a smile, and is on his way. Malcolm and Bobby are talking on like they don't even notice.

I sigh and lean back in my seat.

"You want a to-go box for that, Jimmy Strong?"

I glance up. It's the pretty server with the boobs and the wavy blonde hair. Apparently she learned my name since performing my requested task, likely after having gathered intel from the rest of the staff who know me quite well.

I barely give the poor girl an acknowledgement other than a tiny sigh and a lazy gesture at my plate.

She folds her hands over her front. "So, did you get done what you needed to get done? With your best friend over there?"

I give him a tortured look from across the room. He's fully involved with the stuffy moron now, chatting away. "Don't matter much, apparently."

"Why's that?"

I shrug. "He doesn't need the help I thought he needed."

"Hmm. Shame." She peers at them herself for a second, then faces me again. "Well, I think you're a sweet guy, Jimmy, to go all out for your best friend. It's just the sweetest, nicest thing."

"Is it?" I ask lamely, not really caring for an answer, still raw and staring at their table.

"Oh, yes! The sweetest!" she answers chirpily. "I mean, that kind of friendship y'all got, that's a real special thing, I can feel it. A real lifelong thing ... a forever thing."

My eyes meet hers at those words, struck.

She leans down, her boobs nearly spilling from that tight top of hers, and lowers her voice to a whisper. *"My name's Cindy. Cindy Anne Thorpe."*

I peer into her pretty, glistening eyes. Maybe there's a silver lining in all this after all, even if I'm feeling nothing but pain about my best friend across the room. "Cindy," I murmur thoughtfully.

"Yeah. Y'know." She shrugs, then nods at me. "For when you talk to your mama and put in a good word about me."

My heart sinks.

"Oh," I grunt. "Uh ... right." I nod slowly, then glance down at my plate. "That thing."

She makes a tiny scoff of disbelief. "You done already forgot your deal with me?"

"No, no. I got it. I'll ..." *I'm the master of keeping deals, apparently.* "I'll put in a good word for you. Trust me, it'll make a difference."

The smile returns instantly to her face. She takes my plate. "I'll put this in a to-go box for you, Mr. Strong. Thanks." She leans in again. "I could *really* use that good word. My last job sucked, and I do *not* want to go back there. The staff here is *so* much kinder."

And off she goes with my unfinished meal.

And there I sit, alone again, and feeling the sting of regret for suggesting this whole thing was a good idea.

What a cruddy night this has turned out to be.

Another couple of minutes, and I've got a fancy container in my hand I've seen only a hundred thousand times, as it's been the same exact branding ever since the place opened however many odd years ago. Armed with it, I leave a tip for Cindy—or whoever claims it—and make my limping, roundabout, behind-Malcolm's-unsuspecting-back escape from the restaurant.

I don't bother to look at Bobby, figuring he'd rather keep up the illusion that he's all on his own, that this is a real date, that he might actually be able to feel like he's got a boyfriend in Malcolm.

Or whatever other crazy delusions he's telling himself.

Just let me pretend, he said.

If only he could hear himself sometimes.

I pop open my ma's car, toss my leftovers into the backseat, then pull shut the door and prop my feet up on the dash, just like they were before I felt so inspired to enter the place. I pull out my phone to play a game, remind myself it's one-hundred-percent dead, and toss it onto the passenger seat with a huff. I yank down my hat over my face, cross my arms, and drift off.

Except there isn't any way I'm possibly drifting off to sleep when my heart's pounding this madly.

And when I can feel my pulse in my ears like anxious fingers drumming on a tabletop—*Bobby's annoying habit.*

And when all my thoughts are on wanting to protect my best friend, and my best friend denying me even that right.

And when I want to punch a certain kid in the nostrils.

The passenger seat door flies open.

I jerk my feet right off the dash—causing my bad one to bump against my good one—and yank my hat off my face, alarmed.

Bobby's face hovers at the opened door, furious, glaring, his breaths pulling in and shoving out of his nostrils like dragon fire.

"What is it??" I ask, wide-eyed. "Did he do somethin' to you?? Don't tell me he put a hand on you, or said somethin' awful, or—" I pop my door open at once and hop right out of the car, fuming, then slam it shut behind me as I limp around it. "I'll beat his face in, dude. I warned you, Bobby. I said he was a little shit, and I—"

"Jimmy."

I stop in front of my car, two steps from the door to Nadine's, and face him. "What?"

"I gave the signal." Bobby spreads his hands. "Why didn't you come and do your thing?"

I blink. "It *was* your signal? It looked like an actual accident! I thought—"

"Seriously, Jimmy?" He sighs, shuts the passenger side door, then comes around the car and puts himself in front of me. "I give up. That's what that white-fuckin'-flag-napkin-drop means. I give the hell up. I give up on tryin' to find the perfect guy. I give up on boyfriends completely. I give up on love."

I want to reach out and hug him, but our big dumb deal sits dauntingly between us like a brick wall. And even if I can't see that wall, I feel the cold, hard strength of it. "Bobby, don't give up. C'mon. I'm sorry I interfered in there, like I always do. Ugh." I hit my own face with my hands, then drop them to my sides. "I'm the worst fuckin' friend, Bobby. I keep getting in your way."

"You were *supposed* to get in my way when I dropped the dang napkin on the floor, you dummy!"

"I'm sorry! I thought—" I let out an honest to goodness growl, like I'm turning into a canine. My frustration level is about to set my hat on fire. I give it an angry tug on its bill for emphasis. "Just tell me what you want me to do, Bobby. You want me to go punch the son of the executive chef of my mama's restaurant in the face? I will. I'll do that for you and spend a night in jail."

Bobby sighs and shakes his head. "Don't do that."

"It's me who's the problem," I go on, talking to him even as he drops his head with another sigh and stares forlornly down at the pavement. "It's me who's always the problem, Bobs. Not you. Not Malcolm. Not any of those guys who hit on you at the club."

He closes his eyes.

"Bobby, I care about you. I love you like a brother."

"I *know* that." He says those words with an unexpected anger, like his jaw is clenched tight. He brings his hurt eyes up to mine. "I just ... need to accept the fact that it's pointless, doing this."

"Doing what?"

"Looking." He gestures angrily at the front door to Nadine's. "Going on stupid dates ..."

"These aren't stupid. Your *date* is stupid."

"And trying to find a dumb boyfriend ..."

"Bobby ..."

"It's just pointless."

"It ain't pointless!"

"Yeah, it is!" he snaps.

"No, it's not!" I snap right back.

"It *is* pointless, for a guy like me!"

"The fuck does that mean! 'A guy like you'??"

"A GUY WHO'S IN LOVE WITH HIS BEST FRIEND!"

My mouth is open with whatever I was about to shout back at him, the words now trapped in my throat. I stare at Bobby's stern, pained face while he stands there, his shoulders rising and falling with his heavy breaths and ire. His eyes are two balls of liquid fire, wet with his emotion, even though no tears fall from them.

"Bobby ..." I choke, the word barely there.

He looks ashamed suddenly. His gaze detaches and drops to my chest. "I'm ... I just ... I ..." He closes his eyes at once. "I can't believe I just said that."

I don't give it another thought. I wrap up Bobby in my arms, standing in front of Nadine's big glass doors, and hold him against my body in the tightest, protective embrace.

And right there, listening to his breaths as they crash over my shoulder near my ear ...

Right there, feeling his body against mine, feeling the urgent, panicked thumping of his own heart, feeling his warmth ...

Right there, filling with that unequivocal sense of home, of belonging, of completion ...

That's when something clicks.

It's very quick, like an instant the answer occurs to you to a lifelong puzzle of half-explained truths and a lot of quick denials. It's this mental key that slides right where it needs to go in my brain, unlocking a great big door that's never been opened, light pouring in like a golden flood.

All of these feelings I gave one name all my life that deserved another.

Some words Camille said in my room that day, words that resonate as deeply and as truthfully as the touch of my hands on Bobby, the feel of him in my arms, the way he makes me so happy.

Words that Trey said in that little room in the clinic, about putting myself in Bobby's shoes, about feelings and truths and how a lonely gay boy might feel about his straight best friend.

And how I feel about my best friend, about my man, my guy.

Words I've said and meant—*more so than maybe I realized.*

The desperate thumping of my heart.

As desperate as Bobby's right now.

It makes sense. Everything makes sense, all at once. In a quick and surprising instant, I feel absolutely sure.

"Bobby ..." I try again, my lips near his ear.

"Don't," he begs.

"You've felt like this for a while, huh."

"Please. Please just ... don't."

"I should've seen it."

"Just let me be. Just let me—"

"You're the most important person in my life. You've always been number one, Bobby." I kiss the top of his head. "I should've known that you ..." I kiss his forehead, squeezing him tighter. "I should've known that you had feelings—"

"S-Stop talking." He's sputtering. His throat is closing up. Is he trying not to cry? *Is he even listening to what I'm saying?* "I don't want to talk about it, Jimmy. It was stupid to look for a boyfriend. I don't have it in me, this dating thing. I can't do it. I just can't."

"Maybe you don't have to."

My arms loosen, allowing Bobby to pull his face away to get a look at mine. He stares into my eyes, confused, wondering. "What do you mean ...?"

That wild heart of mine is trapped in my throat, thumping frantically. I have never been more terrified to say a few simple words in my life. "I'm sayin' ... maybe you don't have to go lookin' for a boyfriend, Bobby ... because there might be one standing right in front of you."

Bobby's stare hardens. He is utterly lost.

So I find him by bringing my lips to his, kissing my best friend yet again—but this time with more *need* than I've ever given a kiss before—and breaking that stupid fucking deal of ours for good.

15

BOBBY

Lightning courses down my body, from my lips to my toes to my fingertips and back to my lips again.

Jimmy Strong is kissing me.

What did he just say?

What were all those words he just said?

I bring my hands up to his face, holding his body against mine as the kiss deepens, our breath crashing against each other's faces.

I forget who he is. The kiss has me trapped so suddenly, I can easily believe we've been in a relationship for over ten years, and this is the special, perfect guy I was always meant to be with, my boyfriend, my lover, my man.

Except we *have* been in a relationship for over ten years.

We just never dared to call it that, because we never dared to cross that definitive line.

Not until now.

His hand slides down my back, reaches the top of my ass, then pulls me tighter against him, pinning our crotches together.

Is he hard, or is that his belt buckle? Shouldn't I be able to tell?

He pulls away from my face with one loud and hungry smack against my lips.

My eyes open slowly, emerging from it. I look upon his out-of-breath face, his now-rosy cheeks, his full, parted lips.

Neither of us say anything, just staring at each other's eyes in a total state of *what-the-fuck-just-happened.* His tattered red-and-white hat is nearly knocked off his head, tufts of his bangs messily flipped out from under it. His nostrils are flared from the effort of catching his breath. His muddy brown eyes look freaked.

The doors to Nadine's calmly open, and a middle-aged couple depart—providing a sharp, comical contrast to our moment of fevered kissing. They give us a diminutive, nonexistent look as they pass, blissfully unaware of the profound, momentous thing that just transpired between a pair of best friends before they stepped out of that restaurant.

We're still holding each other.

Maybe we just finished a hug. Maybe he's teaching me square dancing in front of the restaurant. Maybe I almost fell down, and he caught me.

Maybe that last sentence is truer than I intended it to be.

"That ..." I start to say.

"Was amazing?" breathes Jimmy quickly.

I stare at him, then finish my sentence: "... isn't how brothers love each other."

He squints at me, not following.

"You said you love me like a brother," I explain.

"Oh. Right." His eyes drop to my chin.

I can literally see the terror painting his face. Reality returns to him. "That was the third time you've kissed me," I point out.

"I know." He reluctantly meets my eyes again.

"Jimmy, what are we doing?" I ask unblinkingly.

"I don't know."

The doors open again. This time, it's not a couple departing the restaurant to make way for their car after a nice fine-dining experience at Nadine's.

It's Malcolm, who stands at the opened door and stares at me with his eyebrows pulled together. Then, as if the first thing he noticed wasn't actually the sexy dude attached to me, Malcolm slowly turns his eyes onto Jimmy. Recognition is slow to dawn, but it dawns, and the boy's already stiff posture grows stiffer still. He says nothing at all.

Jimmy and I both stare back at him, wordless ourselves.

Then, as if coming out of a weird dream, Malcolm squints at Jimmy suddenly. "You're Nadine Strong's other son, aren't you?"

Jimmy's eyes narrow darkly.

Nadine's *"other"* son. Yeah, I heard it, too. *And Malcolm knows damned well who Jimmy is.*

I let go of Jimmy—or perhaps it's more accurate to say that we let go of each other—and I face Malcolm. "I'm sorry for leaving so abruptly."

Malcolm studies him for exactly two and a half seconds before he turns back to me. "So are we ready to continue, then? There is still dessert to be had, and my father—"

"It's his mama," Jimmy blurts out suddenly. His voice carries a far less polite edge than mine did. "She needs him back in Spruce. Family emergency."

Malcolm appears annoyed. "What kind of emergency?"

"The family kind." Jimmy faces me. "Ready to go?"

I nod at Jimmy, then give Malcolm an apologetic wince. "I'm sorry, Malcolm. I've gotta go. Maybe we can take a rain check on that dessert? I'm so sorry to run off like this. My ..." I give Jimmy a quick look. "My ma needs me."

"Okay, then." Malcolm's words are cold and dry as a picked-over T-bone. "Give your mother my regards."

Jimmy barely lets me get a, "Thank you for understanding," out before he's ushering me to the car—hobbling still on his bad foot, damn his stubbornness—then shutting both our doors and cranking on the engine.

We're out of the parking lot and on the road in seconds.

Neither of us speak, the hum of the car and the night wind squealing its way in through one of the windows which must not be shut all the way. Cars whiz by as Jimmy gets on the highway, and then we're hightailing it to Spruce.

"Watch your speed," I choke out.

Jimmy gives his odometer half a glance, then lets off the gas a little bit.

Silence persists.

"Don't wanna, um ... get a ticket," I explain.

More silence, whirring wind, and engine purring.

Then: "Jimmy ..."

"I don't know," he says at once.

I peer cautiously at him. "What's going on with us, Jimmy?"

"I said I don't know."

"Was that another kiss just to ... make me feel good?" I don't realize I'm drumming the fingers of my left hand anxiously on the center console. "Or was it something else?"

Jimmy's gripping the steering wheel two-handed.

That means business.

"Jimmy ...?" I try again.

"I don't know. I don't know." He swallows hard, then squeezes the wheel with such force, his knuckles bleed white.

"You can't *I-don't-know* your way out of this one."

"Just let me think. Let me think."

He hasn't looked at me once.

The road rushing under our feet has his full attention.

I keep drumming away one-handed. My heart hasn't slowed down a single beat since we left the restaurant.

Good Lord, this is torture.

"Jimmy ..."

"Still thinkin'," he grunts.

"You're speeding again."

He slows down with one jerk of the brake, causing us both to lurch forward, then bites his lip as he stares ahead, driving five *under* the speed limit now. His eyebrow keeps twitching under that hat of his.

The tall metal lampposts that light the highway periodically throw waves of sickly yellow across our faces.

I'm dyin' here.

"You realize Malcolm will probably report to his own pa that I had to cut our date short," I point out with mounting frustration, "due to an emergency with my ma, right? That hot piece of news is gonna reach *your* ma's ears in no time, no doubt, and then she'll know that I basically ditched my date halfway through, because if anyone's a bullshit-sniffer, it's your ma." I glance at the side of Jimmy's tightened face. "You listening over there?"

"Loud n' clear."

"Loud n' clear, alright. Well. You and I need to figure this out, what to say to them, because—"

"That's what we gotta figure out first?" he blurts, turning his face halfway toward me with his eyes still on the road. "What my ridiculous mama thinks? I'll handle her, don't you worry one lick about that. What you and I need to figure out is ... is what I ... what I'm ..." His face seems to lose its color again. "Well, I guess *I'm* the one who needs to figure out what's goin' on with me, actually."

"We can figure it out together," I tell him. "You and I ..."

"You're doing that thing again."

I stop drumming my fingers, retracting my hand into my lap. "You and I just need to spend some time together and ... and have a bit of a talk, y'know? Figure things out. You don't have to sit in that driver's seat and freak out all by yourself."

"Oh, thanks for the permission," he says, his voice cracking, as out of breath as if he just ran the whole way down this highway.

I ignore his attitude; that's to be expected. "Let's go back to your place, Jimmy, and just ... relax for a bit. My ma expects me to be out all night anyway, so she won't miss me. And I haven't spent much time at all at your house this summer, and—"

"I gotta get my mama her car back, anyway," Jimmy reasons, nodding his head a bit too fast. His nerves are consuming him. "I'll do that, then. Good idea. Alright."

"To the Strong ranch," I confirm, studying him with concern.

"To the Strong—" His own swallow cuts him off. "—the Strong ranch, yeah."

I nod, then cross my arms and peer out the window, watching the cars and trucks out late on a Saturday night whiz by on the old two-lane highway.

Nothing more is said at all.

But a lot more is thought.

And felt. And worried over.

I can't say what's likely going on in Jimmy's mind other than the obvious, but I know what's going on in mine.

I can still taste him on my lips.

That wasn't just another kiss in a bedroom.

Jimmy Strong put fucking everything into that kiss. He took complete command of me with his arms around my body, with his hands at the small of my back, and with the way he possessively held me against him, our hips crashed together and our crotches grinding one another's in those few, fleeting seconds.

He owned me.

And he totally fucking has me.

I close my eyes and feel his lips on mine again.

I feel the shock that raced through me when he took hold of me and kissed me.

My dick jumps, straining against my underwear, and against these tight, fitted slacks of Jimmy's that I'm wearing.

This fitted blue button-up of his, too.

These shoes on my feet. Even the chic dress socks.

It's like Jimmy's already all around me, holding me in place.

My eyes pop open, and the highway still surrounds us, roaring under our feet with the engine, and I'm still at a loss.

I mean, this is the same Jimmy Strong who brought girls to our dorm and made out with them in front of me. The same one who regularly shared his sexcapades with me. The one who had a panty collection of his exes. The one who went all the way with a girlfriend freshman year in the parking lot of a Wendy's.

How does that boy reconcile with the one who just kissed me passionately in front of an upscale restaurant in Fairview?

The two versions of Jimmy are completely incongruous.

I close my eyes, rest my head against the window, and let the steady white-noise moan of the car carry me off.

The jarring difference between smoothly paved streets and the bumpy, gravelly country roads leading out to the ranch stirs me out of my half-nap. Soon, his headlights pour over the front of the Strong ranch and its pretty, newly-renovated front porch that I spent so much of last summer on, lounging around with a laptop, a book, or Jimmy himself, staring off into the countryside.

He pulls off somewhere on the gravel, then kills the engine. We get out of the car, are swallowed at once by cricket songs and the noise of restless trees in the warm summer night, then head up the steps of the porch—which no longer creak.

After Jimmy unlocks and opens the door to let us in, we find a single lamp on in the living room as well as a small nightlight in the kitchen. His parents don't seem to be home. "Probably are out with some friends themselves," he mumbles to himself, tossing his ma's keys on the counter and turning to me. "You thirsty, my man? We might have some of my mama's lemonade."

"You mean Jacky-Ann's lemonade," I can't help but correct him, "and no, I'm fine."

"Alright." He stares at the counter, blank-faced as a stone, not seeming to have even heard my subtle correction.

I shuffle my feet awkwardly, then scratch at something on my arm as I search around with my eyes, looking for anything that's different or changed, since I didn't get much of a chance to do it earlier when Jimmy rushed me here to dress me.

It's difficult to do in the dim lighting.

"How about we go to your room and ... chat?"

"Yeah, good. That sounds good." Jimmy starts limping up the stairs, leading the way. He goes slowly, taking each step one at a time, for once giving his bad foot the attention it needs.

Which forces me to head up right behind him just as slowly, granting me a view of his snugly-fit buns in those skinny jeans the whole way as he hops from step to step with care.

Bad timing for a generous view like that. *Aren't my emotions already all scrambled up enough like a Sunday omelet as it is ...?*

At the end of the landing, we enter his room. I shut the door behind us as he flicks on a lamp, drops into a stylish wicker chair by the window, then props up his bad foot on his bed.

For as much time as I spent in this room last summer, it's strange how it always takes me by surprise how big the bedrooms in this house are. Jimmy's room—which used to be Tanner's years ago before he moved into his own house—is at least twice the size of my own. This boy's got enough room for two beds, a pool table if he wanted, and maybe even an area to set up a gym with mats. His room's so big, he's had friends over to practice dance routines in here his senior year of high school. I guess he and his friends got tired of using the oversized gym in the garage (complete with wall mirrors and a length of smooth, hardwood flooring) his junior year. I remember so many times when I came over to watch them, how I felt so in awe of Jimmy's talent.

"You gonna sit down?"

I'm jerked right out of memory lane with his question. "Yeah. I was just ..." I give a chuckle at the giant mirror by his walk-in closet. "I keep forgetting how big your room is."

"Yeah, I guess," mumbles Jimmy, distracted, staring off.

With that, I take a seat in the matching wicker chair near him right by the window and prop my feet up on the bed next to his.

Then we proceed to sit there in the warm, strange, thought-filled silence, and say not a damned word.

Minutes flow by.

All we do is sit here and breathe, and think, and breathe some more, and think a lot more.

Then he touches my hand.

I flinch and turn my head his way, looking at him.

The touch turns into something else as Jimmy slips his fingers into my palm, then takes hold of my hand completely.

It feels so good when he holds my hand.

I lift an eyebrow. "Jimmy ..."

"I don't know where to begin," he blurts. "I just know I gotta hold your hand or something while I'm doin' it, 'cause otherwise I'll totally freak the fuck out over here."

"It's fine." I give his hand a little reassuring shake and a firm squeeze, then let him hold that hand hostage as long as he needs. "Just ... tell me what it is you need to say."

"I think I might be bi."

16

BOBBY

My entire soul drops through the floor and crashes through the earth at that one word Jimmy just uttered: bi.

As calm as I was a second ago, at once my heart jumps into my throat and my stomach flips over.

Bi.

Just giving it a name, this thing that's been going on ...

In my heart, a door flies open, a door I didn't even know was there, a door I kept shut because I thought it wasn't possible.

"Bi?" I murmur back, stunned.

Even saying the word out loud, my feelings can hardly contain themselves. All those wishes, all those cravings, all those long nights of wondering what *could be* ... *if only* ...

He isn't saying anything. Keep him talking. "You think you're bi?"

"I dunno how else to explain what's goin' on with me."

We're still holding hands. That act suddenly becomes so much more meaningful, just from that one blunt word. *Bi.* "Well, why don't you make it super simple and just ... *say* what's going on with you, Jimmy? Tell me what you're thinking about."

"I'm thinking about that kiss."

Me too. "I wonder if Malcolm knows what he almost saw."

"Not *that* kiss. The one back at the hotel." His hand flinches. Our palms are so sweaty suddenly. "The first one."

I shift my weight slightly, causing the wicker chair to groan under me, and watch him, listening.

A flicker of pain enters his eyes as he searches for the words. "Do you remember in eighth grade when we went to that big end-of-the-school-year party at Carter's?"

I remember it instantly. "The one where Michael stood watch at the stairs for the parents while we all played spin-the-bottle in the living room, unsupervised for all of ten minutes."

"And I spun the bottle in those ten minutes, and it landed on Darcy Pryor, the girl I'd had a crush on all year ...?"

I nod. "And you kissed her. And when we went home later in the back of your ma's car, you wouldn't shut up about how it felt."

"It was amazing. It changed my life. Girls were everything to me from then on. Freshman year football, all of my buddies had girlfriends, and I wanted one, too. Darcy had moved away, but the spark she ignited in me was something I chased for years. I was so girl-crazy. I couldn't get enough."

"I remember."

"And ..." Jimmy gazes at his foot, but his eyes are far away in the memory of it all. His face hardens. "And I think ... I think I had feelings for guys, too. My teammates ... Guys in general ... I'd just always excused it, thinking, 'Oh, all guys feel this way. All guys like gettin' their asses slapped. All guys feel a rush of excitement when they hug their friends.' I've ... I've been tellin' myself those lies for fuckin' years. I never let myself even consider another possibility for these feelings, that ... that I might actually ..." Jimmy lets out a long, jagged breath. "Wow, Bobby."

I swallow hard, then grip his hand even firmer, despite all the sweat between our palms growing more slippery. "What?"

"I'm just shocked that it's taken me all this time to say this." He turns to look at me. "The reason I brought up my first kiss with Darcy ..." His watery brown eyes search mine for a while before he finishes: "... is because I felt that same serge of excitement inside me when I kissed you in that hotel."

Those words do something to my heart.

And my stomach.

And the half-eaten dinner I'm still trying to digest.

"I want to do it again," he says.

I stare back at him. "D-Do what?"

"Kiss you." His fingers in my hand twitch, then squeeze. "I ... I want to kiss you again, Bobby. Just to see."

"J-Just to see ...?"

My words aren't conscious choices. I'm just repeating what I hear from those beautiful lips of his I've been staring at for years, lips that never belonged to me, lips that only touched girls who were lucky enough to be Jimmy's type.

Until recently.

"Can we just try this?" he softly asks, nearly pleading. "Can I kiss you and we just ... see where this goes? Can we, Bobby?"

I swallow once, lick my lips, then lamely say, "O-Okay."

Jimmy rises from his chair.

I rise from mine at the same time, a perfect mirror of him.

Our sweaty hands still grip one another's as our bodies slowly draw close.

There is an uncertainty and an excitement swirling in his eyes. The Jimmy Strong cockiness is nowhere to be found.

This boy in front of me is walking into all-new territory.

Before he appears to be ready, he drops his lips to mine and takes my mouth with his own.

I shut my eyes and give in to the warmth of his kiss.

It is the fullest kiss my lips have ever felt.

I tilt my head, letting him press deeper into my face. Waves of warm breath crash over my cheek as our lips dance. It's no telling which of us is leading. I feel commanded one minute by his mouth, and then I'm in charge the next.

The kiss ends at once, and he pulls away.

I open my eyes on his face, flushed and rosy, the same way he gets when he works out, or dances too hard, or jogs with me.

I feel a private satisfaction in how much I've worked him up.

"Bobby ..."

That one uttering of my name splits me open, the sensitive, almost broken tone in his voice. "Yeah?"

"Can we ...?" He seems to nod toward his bed.

That nod could mean a million things. But I take it at its most innocent interpretation. "Yeah, let's get you off your feet."

Jimmy sits down on the edge.

I sit down right next to him.

Then our mouths are on one another's the very next second.

Jimmy falls back on the bed, taking me with him and pulling me atop him, straddling him. He works his lips against mine in a fevered kiss twice the strength of the last one.

I've probably dreamed of his moment ten thousand times.

This is better than any of those ten thousand times.

Except I never quite pictured myself on top of him like this. Somehow, even while straddling him, Jimmy seems to be taking charge, his hands running up and down my back as my palms press into the mattress on either side of his head, holding up my body in half a push-up as I keep my lips on his. Our heads tilt one way and the other, each of our kisses growing more frustrated and desperate as the last one, like we can never quite manage the right position to completely satisfy ourselves.

We just can't seem to get enough. Each kiss is a restless and hungry attempt at perfection.

Has he wanted this as badly as I have?

Where were the signs?

Did I miss each and every one of them?

At once, he lets go of my back and grips my face, cradling it in his big hands as our lips separate. He stares into my eyes, as if he's searching for me.

I'm right here.

His fingers adjust to a more caring hold of my face, like a bit of a loving caress, and then he runs a hand through my hair at the side of my head, right by my ear.

I'm always surprised anew at how big Jimmy's hands are. It's a wonder he didn't continue pursuing football like his brother did.

Just a side thought, a totally unimportant thought.

And then his hand clasps the back of my head and draws me in for another kiss.

And once again, I'm his prisoner.

"Jimmy ..." I breathe against his lips as we kiss.

"*I don't know what I'm doin'*," he breathes against mine, the tiny wisps of words coming out between the smacking of our lips.

"*You're kissin' me,*" I breathe back.

"*Mmm, I know that, smartass.*"

I love how croaky and gruff his words come out when he calls me a smartass, almost like a moan. "*You kiss so good.*"

"*You do, too,*" he moans back against my lips.

We make out so much, I lose track of time. I'm not even aware that time exists. I don't count seconds or minutes. I barely even acknowledge when we shift slightly and I end up on the bed next to him, our bodies turned on their sides as we continue to kiss uninhibitedly. Maybe we've been making out for ten solid minutes. I wouldn't know. Our hands caress one another's backs, and we both keep grinding our hips at one another's, like we can't manage to get them close enough.

He's hard—as hard as I am.

I feel it through his skinny jeans.

Is this the first time he's ever gotten hard with another guy? Or has he simply ignored all his male-inspired boners, writing it off as something that "happens to all guys", like everything else he's so flippantly written off?

I'm so hard that my entire crotch is starting to ache.

I feel like my balls are so swollen, they could burst.

I've never come from dry-humping, but with as charged up as I am right now, I feel like I just might experience it if we don't stop what we're doing soon.

He pulls away and gets a look at me. "Bobby, I don't know if—"

"It's okay," I tell him without even hearing what he was going to say. "We can just do whatever you want. We don't have to rush anything, or feel pressure to do anything else, or even—"

"I'm havin' such a great time just kissing the fuck out of you."

"Me too," I agree. Our hands are all over our lower backs still, pulling our crotches firmly against one another on the bed.

"I've never thought of guys sexually before," Jimmy admits as his eyebrows pinch together. "I mean, I don't *think* I have. I don't really fantasize or anything. I don't know what I'm doin'."

"Other than kissing the fuck out of me."

"Are you sure this is okay?" I've never heard Jimmy sound so worried or panicky before. "I mean, what if this is all we do? What if all we do is kiss for hours? Is this totally fucking lame?"

"Jimmy, only do what you want. Don't worry about anything else at all. Just do what feels good."

"This feels really fuckin' good."

"Then let's keep—"

Jimmy doesn't let me get the words out before he's on my lips once more, right where he belongs. And I melt all over again, my heart surging and my stomach dancing with excitement—and my swelling, hard cock throbbing.

I've never wanted to burst in my pants as badly as I do now.

I do realize how much of an unnecessary mess that'd make, and I really don't fucking care. I have this painful, crushing feeling inside that what I'm experiencing is a once-in-a-lifetime, fleeting moment of opportunity that, if missed, I'll never have again.

I need to seize this moment.

My hand slowly slides down his muscled, sinewy back until a finger touches the top of his jeans. Then I push my bravery to the max, invite my fingers onto the round, supple, tight denim landscape of Jimmy's ass.

And I give him one firm, experimental squeeze.

"*Mmm ...*" he moans against my lips.

Wow.

I think he likes it.

I give his ass another finger-curled, palm-of-my-hand, *oh-my-God-I-can't-believe-I'm-doing-this* squeeze—and yet again, he moans.

Is he encouraging me? Should I keep going?

Then Jimmy catches me off-guard as he shifts his body, rolls on top of me, and caresses my face as he deepens the kiss.

With his weight over me, our crotches are inevitably united, and his muscular, lean body is pressed against mine. Jimmy owns every bit of me now, trapping me against his bed with his long and powerful body, his strong arms, his caressing fingers, his lips.

And I've still got his ass in the palm of my hand.

Maybe he's giving me access to all of it.

While he continues to pin my face against his with his breath-stealing, all-devouring lips, both my hands start to massage and rub his meaty ass, every inch of it, every curve of Jimmy Strong's perfect buns that I've lusted over for years and years and years.

I'm not me. I can't possibly be me.

I've never been allowed into the land of Jimmy Strong's body.

Not like this, with free reign and total abandon.

Following an instinct, my hands slide up his hips, then slowly start to drag his shirt up with them. My fingers touch his smooth, silky skin now, drawing his shirt up even more, exposing his lithe, long, smooth back.

When his shirt is tugged up halfway up his torso to his chest, Jimmy follows the lead by lifting off of me to allow the shirt over his head and off his arms, where it's then flung away, never to be heard of again, and he's on my lips once more.

But shirtless now.

Good Lord, Jimmy, and it ain't even my birthday.

My hands patiently glide up and down his back, exploring it from underneath his body. I feel his stomach billow out against mine with his every hot, labored breath as he kisses me—and feels the soft touch of my fingertips along his back. I imagine the chills of excitement I must be giving him as I drag my fingers along his skin, exploring him in a way I've never been allowed to before.

My hands catch on the rim of his pants. I tease my fingertips underneath, caressing the waistband of his tight, soft briefs. With gentle, rubbing strokes, my fingers slowly find their way in, sliding as best as they can inside his tight jeans.

They don't get far.

More clothes are going to need to come off if I'm to explore him all the way.

And I think he wants it, too. He just doesn't know how to ask, except to assist in my accessing his ass, and taking off his shirt.

His body's asking.

"Jimmy ..."

"*It feels so good,*" he whispers against my lips. "*What you're doin' to me. It feels so good, Bobby.*"

"*Let me make you feel better,*" I beg him.

"Jimmy ..."

"*Let me make you feel really, really good.*"

He takes the hint of my hands as I push at his hips, rolling us over again to bring myself on top of him. With Jimmy on his back, I gaze on his exposed chest, his cute nipples, and his tight abs that ripple down like arrows to the swelling crotch of his dark skinny jeans and the white waistband of his underwear that peeks out like a wink from under them.

I straddle his legs as I gently pop open his jeans a button at a time. Jimmy lifts his ass as I tug them down, exposing his briefs to my hungering eyes.

Jimmy watches me.

It makes me feel like I have an audience, unlike every other time I've done what I'm about to do. Jimmy watches me with an excited, intense curiosity like he can't believe his eyes. He watches me like he isn't even sure I'm about to do what I'm about to do.

I need to get him to relax.

I can't have him freak out.

I pull my eyes away from his and bring them to his tight briefs and the swelling crotch of them. Then, as if approaching a lover's face, I bring my warm mouth to his bulge and plant a firm, open-mouthed kiss.

His cock flexes against my lips.

Jimmy's head rocks back with a sigh.

Success.

I mouth his crotch over and over, never quite closing my lips, breathing and kissing and loving on his bulge over and over, and every time, his dick flexes against my face and Jimmy lets out a deep-throated moan.

I can't tell whether the wetness of his crotch is my saliva or his dick pre-leaking with anticipation.

Not to mention how urgent the throbbing in my own pants has gotten. I feel like just sucking on the outside of Jimmy's briefs is enough to make me spill prematurely.

I've never been this excited to do something in my life.

And if Jimmy's constant grunting and hisses of breath are any indication, neither has he.

I reach down with a free hand and pop the button of my own pants, then unzip them and work my cock out from my confining underwear. With my hand around my swollen, steel-hard, freed cock that's as warm as a fire with pumping blood, I already feel miles of relief and haven't even stroked it yet.

I curl my fingers into the waistband of his underwear.

Still no objections from Jimmy—just half-moans and grunts and an occasional sputtering of breath.

I'm not me, and he's not him.

I pull down his underwear just enough to expose the head of his cock. *Wow, what a beautiful head.* Then I slide his underwear down some more, like a horizontal curtain of cotton, and observe all of Jimmy Strong's infamous cock inch by inch, as hard as it can get, throbbing with his pulse, desperate and flexed to its max.

I could spend an hour describing what the sight of it does to me. Instead, I'll put it into one word: perfect.

Jimmy Strong's dick is *perfect.*

I bring my lips to his cockhead, giving it a gentle kiss.

All of Jimmy's sighing and grunting ceases at once.

The very touch of my lips on his dick has paralyzed him.

It's like he's entered a true state of disbelief.

A state of oh-my-God-is-this-really-about-to-happen.

Yeah, buddy. This is about to happen.

My fingers gently wrap around it—Jimmy is still perfectly silent and still—and I kiss it again, like another little test. I turn my head and kiss it at another angle, feeling my lips touch the warm, soft flesh of his cockhead.

It's so intimate, Jimmy letting me do this to him—*or for him.* I bend my head the other way and kiss under the head where it's most sensitive, and his dick flexes with anticipation within my hand. We're the only two people in the entire world right now.

I bring my lips to the tip, then open my mouth.

Jimmy is completely paralyzed as I let in the first few inches of his cock into my mouth. The sensation is so much that he can't even move, his mouth locked open in a permanent, soundless gasp and his eyes clamped shut.

You'd think the boy never got a blowjob before.

With every descent of my lips around his cock, I take in a little bit more until I'm sucking as much of it as I can without gagging.

Let's be honest here. There's more of it than I can handle.

My hand slides down to the base to cup his balls, making room for my mouth to go as far as it can.

I think Jimmy's still holding his breath. *He needs to relax.*

I let go of his balls and slide my hand up and down the side of his body, rubbing him with a soothing motion.

As if my arm is a lifeline thrown out and Jimmy is lost at sea, he reaches down at once and firmly clasps my arm with his hand, squeezing it appreciatively.

I don't even realize I've started jerking myself with my other hand, unable to contain my horniness any longer.

He's worked me up faster than anyone I have ever known, and my poor dick can only contain so much fucking pressure.

Apparently so can Jimmy's.

I feel the throb and flex of a dick that's already so close, I may twist my mouth a certain way at its head and send it shooting. So I slow down my pace and let my free hand graze across his chest. My fingers catch at one of his nipples, causing Jimmy to breathe out with a pleasured gasp.

I bring that finger right back to his sensitive nipple. Like some kind of automatic response, Jimmy moans when my fingers touch it. *I'm learning so much about you, Jimmy Strong.* The evil guys they are, my fingertips gently pinch and play with his nipple, making him thrust his crotch up at my face all the more, gagging me with his cock when he goes too far.

Jerking mindlessly as I am, I get too close twice in a row, and have to slow down to bring myself back. I have never ridden the edge and been so turned on for this long, nor in this manner. It's always another person pleasuring me that gets me this close.

Maybe I've always been with the wrong kind of men.

Maybe no one's touched me the way Jimmy touches me.

Maybe no one's let me in the way Jimmy has let me in.

"I'm gonna come," Jimmy announces. "Oh, God ..."

Jimmy clenches his legs closed around my body, scissoring me in a vise-tight grip with his crazy-powerful dancer thighs as I continue to swallow down his dick, sucking it to the end.

The trap I suddenly find myself in makes my own edging all the more erotic somehow, being held prisoner in Jimmy's long, lithe dancer legs while sucking his slippery manhood and jerking my own toward the precipice.

"B-Bobby ..." he moans—my last warning.

And then he shoots into my mouth.

I take it all in, every shot that fires from his pulsating dick.

And as a direct reaction to his busting, I follow immediately afterward, shooting my load all over the side of his bed. I moan with my mouth still wrapped around his cock, grunting with deep relief as I empty myself just as plentifully as Jimmy just emptied in my mouth.

I swallow as I gently bring my mouth off his dick, then slowly lick the end, as if to clean off every last drop.

His legs relax, total bliss washing over his body.

I collapse right there, my hand still gripping my dick, now wet and sticky, my come turning cool on the tops of my fingers. I lay my head on his upper thigh as I slowly collect my breath. Jimmy, somewhere far above me, breathes deeply as he catches his own.

"*Wow ...*" he says finally, part breath, part word.

I smile against his thigh. I reach up and give his wet dick two gentle little strokes, which makes poor Jimmy buck his hips due to the sensitivity.

His reaction makes me smile more.

I give him three more slow strokes, making his legs squirm beneath me, but he's too spent to fight me off, so he just has to take it.

I lift my head and look up the rippling, leanly-muscled valley of his body at his face. He's staring up at the ceiling, looking as if he sees faraway galaxies.

Maybe he does.

"You alright up there?"

"Bobby, wow ..."

"Yeah?"

"I didn't ..." He shakes his head. "... expect you to ..."

"To what?"

I watch his lips curl. "*Swallow.*"

I smile, then glance down my own body. "Well, I, um ..."

"Yeah?"

"I ... might've ... made a big ol' mess on your bed. Sorry, but I think I just made us some laundry."

Jimmy lets out a deep-throated chuckle that shakes the whole mattress. "Well, we'd better change the sheets, then, huh?"

The next moment, we're off the bed like we do this every day. Still floating in the euphoria of it all, we wash up in the bathroom next-door to his room—Jimmy taking a washcloth to his thighs, stomach, and now-deflated dick, while I carefully wash my hands in the sink—then proceed to change his bed together.

He gives me these funny, adoring looks over the bed as we change his sheets.

I shoot them right back, feeling content.

We lie down side-by-side on top of the sheets, then stare up at the ceiling, our shoulders pressed together. After the mess we made, we're down to our underwear, our clothes in a balled-up tangle on the floor.

In the cool, still silence of his room, the reality seems to wash over us both at once. We've said maybe ten words since we got up off the bed, cleaned up in the bathroom, and changed the sheets.

The room fills with our individual breaths.

I'm counting each and every one of them as they draw into our heavy lungs, then spill out gently from our nostrils. Thirty-six for Jimmy. Forty-one for me.

Forty-two. Thirty-seven.

Forty-three. Thirty-eight.

Forty-four ...

"What does this mean now?" I ask quietly.

Jimmy tilts his head slightly, leaning it against mine. "I think we're gonna have to figure it out as we go along, huh?"

"Yeah."

The silence swells between us again.

Forty-eight. Thirty-nine.

Forty-nine. Forty.

Fifty.

"I really like you, Jimmy," I tell him.

"I like you, too, Bobby. That ain't nothin new."

"I know, but—"

"I know," he says, his tone more sincere.

A moment of significance passes.

"I don't want this to ... to change things between us," I tell him in that moment. "I don't want—"

"Neither do I," Jimmy blurts at once, as if he was thinking the same things and is desperate to agree with me. "What we've got between us? That's too fuckin' precious. It's the most important thing to me, you and I."

"Me too."

"I love you, Bobby." He reaches over to give me a light slap and a bro-ish squeeze on my arm. His hand stays there, hooked on my arm, not wanting to let go of me. "You and I, we're gonna be alright, no matter what. I've got you."

I've got you.

I can't help but smile, exploding inside at the sound of those words, said in his voice. "I've got you, too, Jimmy Strong."

17

JIMMY

We were too spent to even take showers.

We fell asleep just like that: in our underwear, lazy and tired, full of dreams in our eyes. Thank God we shut and locked my door before drifting off, because my parents came home from their thing at around one in the morning. I woke to the sound of the front door slamming shut (Bobby stayed completely asleep, softly snoring in my ear) and then the loud and clacking footsteps of my mama's heels as she checked things downstairs, then eventually the heavy-footed sound of my papa as he came up the stairs. He likely observed that my door was shut before slowly padding back downstairs to join my mama in their bedroom, the door shutting with a distant *thump*. All fell silent again, and I closed my eyes.

When the morning light is pouring obnoxiously over my face (I sometimes hate having a bedroom that faces east), I open my eyes to find Bobby turned away with his smooth back cuddled against me. We must've gotten warm during the night and separated, because I'm hugging myself.

I rectify that by facing him and bringing an arm around him.

Bobby shifts slightly, but stays asleep while I spoon him. I tuck him into me, nestle my face in his neck, and close my eyes, wondering if I can catch another hour or so of sleep. There's no telling how little of it we got last night.

But I'm just too damned restless to sleep anymore.

In my restlessness, thoughts of last night flood right back into me. I feel his soft and careful lips on mine, our fingertips all over each other's bodies, that thing he was doing with my nipple ...

And his mouth on my dick.

Who am I ...?

My eyes wander across the room and land on my half-open closet door, thinking suddenly of Camille when she was here and we were dumping out all that memorabilia from back in the day. The way she looked at me that night, it was like she figured out a secret about me—something I didn't even know. A few years spent in Europe, and suddenly she's got an up on me.

How could she possibly tell?

Is it how I treat Bobby? Is it what I say when I talk about him, the words I use, the expression on my face? What is it about me that gives it away?

Has anyone else suspected? My parents? My brother? Trey, or Billy, or any other gay dude in town who's given me and my friendship with Bobby a second or third thought?

Not that it particularly matters, I guess.

Especially when I'm not even sure what it all means.

Am I really bi? I haven't wanted to stick it in any dudes' butts I've ever known, Bobby included. Though I *do* like how it feels to grab a nice handful of Bobby's ass, but is that the same?

I don't suddenly want to suck any dicks, as far as I can tell.

But the idea of sucking Bobby's isn't repulsive at all. I feel like I'd get a crazy hot thrill from watching his eyes roll into the back of his head, assuming I'm any good.

Why is it all about Bobby?

Why have I never felt like this for any other guy before?

He sucked my dick, and I was so excited, I came in his mouth.

Despite all of my self-denials and stubborn insistence, even I know that isn't normal for a straight dude.

At least, I don't think it is.

Or is that just some other stupid thing I was taught?

Great. Now I'm thinking about Bobby sucking me off again.

My dick flexes.

Great. Now I'm hard again. And in this little-spoon, big-spoon position, my boner is pressed right up against Bobby's ass.

It flexes again without my permission, throbbing desperately.

I close my eyes and suppress a moan.

Maybe I can picture sticking it up Bobby's ass easier than I realized.

My dick flexes yet again.

It's completely out of control. The thing has a mind of its own, and unless I pee, get off, or stick it inside something, I'm going to bite Bobby's ear to wake him up and demand he sucks it again.

No, you're not.

Jesus, what kind of horny animal am I turning into?

And then I can't contain myself: "*Bobby ...*" I hiss urgently.

His slow, quiet, blissful breathing is my reply.

"*Bobby ... Bobby ... Wake up ... Bobby ...*"

Ever so slowly, he starts to squirm in my arms. His eyes open in a flutter of blinking, and then he turns his face to look at me. He is just his sleepy, red-eyed self when he wakes up at first.

Then last night's events play past his eyes in a split second, and a look of curiosity mixed with worry takes over his face. He gives his throat a meager and inadequate clearing before gruffly whispering, "*Hmm? What? Are you okay?*"

"*No, I'm not okay,*" I whisper back.

I allow my dick three solid flexes against Bobby's ass.

Y'know, like *knock-knock-knock.*

Bobby's sleepy eyes go wide, he takes a peek down our bodies, likely sees nothing, then blushes as he eyes me. "*Dude, really?*"

"*I can't help it.*"

"*It's morning wood. It's 'cause you gotta pee.*"

"*It's more than that,*" I hiss back, my lips right by his ear. "*I have got a boner this morning that is an untamable goddamned monster.*"

"*Jimmy ...*"

"*Help me out, dude! What do you think?*"

Bobby turns a bit more onto his back to better face me. "*I ain't even woken up yet, Jimmy. And I think ... I think we're—*"

I interrupt him with a kiss.

A firm, hard, full-mouthed kiss on the lips.

That melts poor Bobby right down to nothing, all his protests turned into small whimpers and breath on my face.

When I pull away, I smile down at him. "*I like kissing you. A lot.*"

He returns an awkward smile of his own. "*And maybe I'll like it better when we both aren't plagued with morning breath.*"

I gently hump his side. "*C'mon, buddy. I'm achin' down there.*"

Finally, I see that all-too-familiar hint of mischief enter his cute brown eyes. He bites his lip and glances down, then back up at me. "*You're really aching bad, huh?*"

"*Can you get me off, dude? Please?*"

While staring me right in the eyes, Bobby reaches down and, without warning, grabs a big old mighty handful of my junk, then gives it a massaging squeeze.

I groan, folding in half against his side, clinging to him, my fingers and toes curling.

"*You really want it?*" he asks me.

"*Yes. God yes. Please yes.*"

Suddenly—morning breath or not—I press my lips against his with a hungry, furious urgency.

The kiss is greedily received and quick to deepen, as if Bobby's been just as desperately hungry for it ever since we fell asleep late last night.

Both my hands draw to his face, cradling him, and then his hands find my chest. My kisses stray from his mouth and start to work down his neck, hungry for every inch of Bobby's skin.

I'm a fucking maniac for this guy.

Somehow, when we finish making out, half of the new sheets we'd put on the bed end up on the floor, and his underwear is tugged halfway down his ass, like my hands made plans to rip them off his body without my even knowing.

I stare into his eyes, catching my breath. "*I've never been blue-balled this badly before,*" I confess to him, a wet spot forming on the bulge of my underwear, my hard cock throbbing relentlessly. "*I have to come, man.*"

"*We ...*" Bobby sighs, closes his eyes, then flips onto his back with a huff. "*We need to slow down.*"

I stare at him incredulously. "*Slow down?*" I prop myself up to get a better look at his face. "*Dude, my dick doesn't do slow. It's crying right now. I'm literally leaking. Slow down??*"

"*We're losing our heads, Jimmy. We ...*" He lets out another sigh, then gazes at me with worry. "*We can't just mess around all the time. We're actin' like rabbits.*"

"*Rabbits are the healthiest and happiest gosh-darned creatures on God's green Earth,*" I spit back. "*You want me to give you a handy or somethin'? Are you feelin' left out?*"

Without waiting for his reply, I thrust a hand into his crotch.

He squeezes his thighs shut with a gasp, trapping my hand.

"*Jimmy!*" he scolds me—while also suppressing a deep and obvious grunt of pleasure.

I smirk. "*What? You can touch and feel me all over, and I can't reciprocate? You scared I don't know what to do with a dick, Bobby? I've had one my whole life too, you know.*"

"*I just ...*" He shuts his eyes, pained.

And then his dick flexes against my hand.

I lift an eyebrow. "*You're sayin' one thing, and it's sayin' another.*"

He opens his legs, grabs my wrist, and tries to pull my hand out of his crotch. I keep it right where it is, clinging to my handful of his swelling Parker jewels through his tight underwear.

He turns two cold eyes onto me. "*I said we need to slow down.*"

"Why?"

"*Because I said so.*"

"*That isn't a good enough answer for me.*"

"*Because what if this is all just sex and fun for you, we burn out, and suddenly you're in Camille's bed by the end of the summer?*"

My eyes soften.

That wasn't exactly the direction I thought he was going.

"Bobby, I'm not gonna—"

"You don't know."

"Why would I even—?"

"What if this is just what happens 'cause you've been single so long?" he throws at me. We're not whispering anymore. We're full-on talking. "What if you're just horny and any hole on Earth would do? I've seen how you are these past two years at South Wood. From one girl to the next."

"I'm not *that* much of a man-whore, dude. C'mon."

"All semester long. I couldn't keep up with you, Jimmy!"

"You aren't just another—!" I give a glance at my closed door, growl with frustration, then lower my voice to a hush. "*You are* not *just another girl to me.*"

"You remember that *phase* you went through at the beginning of last year?" He crosses his arms. "When suddenly you wanted a set of handcuffs, all 'cause you met that one kinky girl with a lip ring from your poli-sci class who was 'into stuff'?"

"*Keep your voice down! You wouldn't think it, but sound travels in this big-ass, echoey house.*"

"And what about that other phase, the one when you only had sex with girls in your truck, playin' it all risky in parking lots?"

Now *I* can't even keep my voice to a whisper. "You are *not* callin' yourself or us or whatever I'm going through no damned *phase*, Bobby Parker."

"But what if it is? How would I know? You're the horniest guy I've ever met."

I let go of his crotch, grab the side of his face, and steer his eyes right into mine. "Look at me, Bobby. Look right at me and tell me what you see."

His eyes search mine, clueless. Slowly, I watch his stubborn resolve begin to melt. "I see you, Jimmy."

"Nah, not yet, you don't." My fingers slide into his soft hair. "I know this is all new for me, and I know you know me better than anyone on Earth, even better than my parents or my own brother knows me. Girls come and girls go, I know that. I've never had one that stuck. But you ...? You've always been there, Bobby, and you always will be. We're a ... a forever thing, y'know what I mean?"

A flicker of uncertainty touches his eyes.

I lift my eyebrows and touch our foreheads together, then whisper the rest: "*The only thing that can pull me away from you is if you tell me you don't want this as badly as I do.*"

"*Jimmy ...*"

"*And even then, I don't know if I can turn away from you, Bobby. I just don't have it in me. When I want somethin' ...*"

"*It's just ...*"

"*What?*"

He closes his eyes. "*It's too much. Too quick. I'm freakin' out.*"

I let out a sigh, then remind myself that Bobby always sees things more clearly than I do. He always has. He's like a fucking psychic sometimes, the way he foresees trouble.

Maybe he has a point.

I slump onto my pillow and roll onto my back with a sigh. "*I won't lie and say there isn't a part of me that's ... probably a bit in shock. Over all of this. And whatever's goin' on with ... with me.*"

Bobby sighs up at the ceiling. "*Yeah, I know.*"

"*I mean, this is totally new territory for me, man.*"

"*I know that, too.*"

"*So I get why you're freakin' out. Maybe it's kinda weird that I'm not freakin' out. Maybe that's why you're questioning this so much.*"

"*Can we just take this slower?*"

I turn my head to face him.

He turns his, almost putting his lips to mine when he does. We search into each other's eyes for a while, as if looking for the answer somewhere in them.

"*That's all I'm askin',*" he whispers so softly, I barely catch the words.

I press my lips into a flat line. "*Yeah ... yeah, alright.*"

"*Yeah? You mean you will? You'll slow down for me?*"

My dick throbs. My balls ache. My insides are yearning for him in ways I've never felt before. "*Yeah, I will,*" I insist anyway, swallowing down all that bottomless desire.

Bobby bites his lip, then gives a gentle nod. "*Alright.*"

Then we both lie back, detaching from each other, and stare upwards some more, letting all our thoughts and troubles float off to that endless, colorless oblivion that is my ceiling.

His stomach growls.

Mine does immediately after.

"Breakfast time?" I mutter.

"Sure," he agrees with a tentative smile.

The pair of us climb out of bed, then proceed to fetch some clothes from my drawer. I toss him a pair of gym shorts and a light tank, then pull out the same for myself. While we get dressed, we keep sneaking glances at once another.

Bobby cracks a smile.

I do, too.

Once we're dressed, I grab one of my crutches off the wall and decide to be a good boy. *No use having my mama and Bobby scold me for not using it to get around today.* Bobby heads out of the room first and right on down the stairs. I lag behind a bit, using the dumb stick to help myself out of my bedroom, across the long L-shaped landing, and carefully down the stairs.

The whole way down, I can hear my mama already hounding poor Bobby in the kitchen about his date last night, Lord help him.

"You didn't even kiss?" she's in the middle of asking him.

"Nah, we didn't get that far. I'm sorry it didn't work out with the Tucci boy, I just—"

"But he's prime datin' material, ain't he? He's intelligent, he's got a good family, he's as handsome as a pineapple ..."

"Mama, give it a *rest*," I call out as I hobble my way into the kitchen, "and there ain't *nothin'* handsome about a pineapple."

She quirks a sharp eyebrow at me. "You look like you wrestled with an alligator and lost, and good mornin' to you, too."

"Sorry for our condition," says Bobby on my behalf. "After we got back from Fairview last night, the pair of us just crashed."

"Crashed," I agree lamely, then eye Bobby.

He gives me a muted, cautious smile in return.

My mama lifts an eyebrow at me. "You went to Fairview with Bobby on his date? Why?"

I shrug. "I was his chauffeur. You knew that. He doesn't have a car. Oh, and uh, by the way," I quickly add, "Cindy is a *great* server. Treated me super well. Just puttin' in a good word for her. Jimmy-Strong approved." I put on a tight, *not-anxious-at-all* smile.

My mama gives it one more second of thought, then shrugs it off. "Well, anyway, it's been—*Jacky-Ann, the boys are up!*" she calls out suddenly, interrupting herself, "It's been far too long a time since I've seen you, Bobby. What'd you think of Malcolm?"

"Oh, Mama," I grunt as I hop past her to the counter and slap down two glasses from the cupboard, then pull open the fridge.

"What?" she sings innocently, then ushers Bobby over to the table where they take a seat. "Malcolm's a handsome young man."

"*If you can get past how much of a dick-sneeze he is,*" I mutter over my shoulder as I pour us a couple glasses of orange juice.

She ignores me. "I'd think that you'd have a hundred boys lining up to be your boyfriend at South Wood. What gives?"

Bobby notices what I'm doing and quickly rises from the table to get his own glass so I don't have to carry them both. "I've got this," I insist to him. "I'm just gonna—"

"Yeah," he mutters back, "until you go hoppin' over to the table and spill half our juice down your front." He grabs both of them out of my hands. "I'll take these."

I smile at his back for a bit, watching him head back over to the table with the glasses, strutting all cutely in those shorts of mine that fit him so damned well, you'd think they were stitched right on his body. With a chuckle, I follow on my crutch and sit at the table across from them.

My mama, who I didn't realize was avidly watching us during that exchange, starts glancing back and forth between us, chewing on her lip with growing agitation. "Somethin' is goin' on."

Bobby and I share a look. "Hmm?" I mumble right after taking a sip of orange juice. "What do you mean ...?" asks Bobby lightly on top of my grunt, lifting an eyebrow.

She shakes her head while wagging a long finger, making her hoops jangle against her neck, and eyes the pair of us. "You two. I can smell it. Somethin' is up, and I want to know."

"Nothing's up, Mama," I'm first to say, an annoyed edge to my voice. "We just didn't get all that much sleep last night."

She eyes Bobby. "You're seein' someone already, aren't you."

I choke on the sip of orange juice I just took. Bobby freezes in place, his eyes as wide as my mama's hoop earrings.

"I ..." Bobby swallows. "I'm, uh ..."

"I *knew* it!" She slaps the table once for punctuation and gives a nod of victory. "I got a fifth sense with these things."

"*Sixth*," I mutter, narrowing my eyes.

Then, to my surprise, Bobby goes right along with it. "Yeah, I'm really sorry, Mrs. Strong. I just didn't want to tell anybody. I need to keep the news to myself for now. It's for the best."

"But why?? Goodness, it's such great news!" She applauds for no reason other than to fill the kitchen with her obnoxious, ear-splitting claps. "I want to meet him! Who is he? Is he a boy back at school, is that why you—Well, that don't make sense, why would you keep *that* a secret if he isn't even here? Oh my God, that means he *is* here!" She gasps. "He's here in Spruce and *that's* why you want to keep it a secret! Oh, you *have* to tell me, Bobby. Who is he? Is he the new boy they hired down at the Marvin brothers' market? I always thought that boy had a look about him."

Bobby knew better than to give my mama a juicy, steaming cup of tea like that. That woman is an atom bomb of world-ruining proportions when she gets excited.

"I really don't want to say anything," he calmly replies. "It's still very ..." He bites his lip, then drags his sad brown eyes across the table until they're on me. "... new."

I stare back, frozen in place, drops of orange juice still drip-drip-dripping off my chin.

I think I might be holding my breath.

My mama sputters about twenty more times and does half a backflip in her seat before she finally reels it in with a, "Alright, I'll behave, okay, alright. I am very mad at you, Bobby, but okay, if you insist on keeping it a secret—*Urgh!*—I'll just have to deal." She runs a hand through her hair, anxiously adjusts three of the rings on her fingers, then huffs. "I'll respect your privacy."

Bobby takes one of her hands. "Thank you, Mrs. Strong."

"Oh, shush with that *Mrs. Strong* formality mango-jumbo. You call me Nadine, you know better." She rises from the table.

"Mama."

She looks my way. "What?"

"The sayin' is *mumbo*-jumbo." I give her a shriveled smile. "Not mango-jumbo. That's a fruit."

"I know dang well what I said." She eyes Bobby. "You sure you can't just give me a hint? Ugh, never mind, you boys are cruel." She saunters out of the kitchen while calling out at us over her shoulder. "You two'd better get cleaned up in a hurry then if we're gonna make it to church on-time for the noon service. *Jacky-Ann! Good Lord, are you dead? The boys! The boys!*"

Bobby and I share a look. "Uh, Mama," I call back, "we weren't plannin' on going to church with—"

"*Well, ya are now!*" she calls out at her bedroom door before it slaps shut.

The two of us are left at the table, staring at each other over glasses of barely-sipped orange juice. My crutch loses its balance leaning against the kitchen table and falls to the hard tile below with a loud, echoing clack.

I narrow my eyes. "You're ... 'seein' someone' ...?"

Bobby shrugs.

I sigh, shake my head, then lean over the table and lower my voice. "*You realize she ain't gonna sleep a wink 'til she finds out who the* hell you're seeing? That involves a thorough and invasive investigation, and what's your plan when she gets too close to the truth for comfort?"

"*Calm your tits,*" he retorts. "*Last person she'd suspect is* you."

"*And are we seein' each other suddenly? Are we a thing? When did we ...*" I swallow, struck by the concept of it. "*... decide that?*"

Bobby's eyes cloud over. "Oh." He forgets to whisper. "I ... I just thought ... uh, that we ..."

"*I mean, I want to be a thing, don't get me wrong,*" I quickly add, my tone softening. "*I just meant—I mean, we never said we, uh ...*"

"*So we are?*" Bobby starts drumming his fingers on the table, his foot bouncing in place below. "*We're ... like, whatever we are? A thing? Friends with benefits? Close buddies? Boy ... friends ...?*"

"*We are whatever we are,*" I agree.

And I place a hand on his drumming fingers, stopping them.

The pair of us smile at each other, relieved somehow.

Fifteen minutes later—after a hasty breakfast of burnt toast and eggs we fry up ourselves in a big pan—Bobby and I take turns showering and throwing on some Sunday clothes fresh from my closet. When I go to help Bobby do his tie right, he blushes and gets awkward. Then he sighs at the way I always sag my dress slacks and yanks them right where they belong, which leaves us in a position of him having his arms around my waist, and me staring down into his eyes, like a high school slow dance frozen in place.

So much is said without a single word coming out of our lips.

Then my mama calls for us from the foot of the stairs.

And the moment's over.

Twenty minutes later—and a very uncomfortable ride in the car with my mama chewing Bobby's ear off about a hundred and one different things—we're heading into Spruce Fellowship in a crowd of giggling ladies, all of them fluttering excitedly around my mama like starved pigeons and she's got a bag of bird seed.

"Where's your pa?" asks Bobby as we enter the church, all the noise of chatter following us into the echoey, small space. "Doesn't he go to church with your ma?"

"He kinda leaves my mama to her church thing every Sunday, as far as I understand it. Something to do with *him-and-her* time. I never really took much effort in understanding my own parents' idiosyncrasies over the years."

"I don't understand my parents either," confesses Bobby.

Suddenly my mama comes to a stop, staring across the lobby. "Now what's your mother doin' all by herself, Bobby?"

Bobby lifts his face. "What? Where?" He looks off.

I follow their line of sight. Mrs. Patricia Parker stands at the other end of the lobby, fidgeting with her purse and glancing around herself, looking like a sweet, lost lady in a sea of strangers, despite her likely knowing each and every face here.

"That ain't right," my mama decides. "That woman looks like she could use a bit of company, poor thing." She turns back to give a wink at Bobby. "You boys find yourselves a seat. I'll go have a little girl-talk with Patricia and keep her company, then sit with her inside. Go on, now."

With that, my mama beelines through the lobby like she owns the church, and soon, the ladies are having a pleasant exchange at the other side of the lobby. In no time, Patricia is laughing merrily and wearing a smile that looks too big for her sweet face.

Even all the way across the lobby, it makes me smile.

My mama does do a nice thing or two, now and then.

The ladies, both husband-free, take a seat inside together—at my mama's insistence—while Bobby and I find a small available spot near the front, all the way to the side by the windows.

We're squeezed so tightly on this long crowded bench, our shoulders and arms find themselves pressed together, and our faces are super close whenever we turn to each other to speak.

Or whisper. *"You look really handsome today, Bobby Parker."*

He turns and peers into my eyes adoringly. *"You look mighty handsome yourself, Jimmy Strong,"* he whispers back.

The service is long, but Reverend Arnold keeps it entertaining when he invites his son Trey up to say a few words of his own on the subject of family, which is this week's theme. With a witty joke and intelligent aside here and there, Trey talks about appreciating the family we have, and how sometimes "family" can include the special people we invite into our lives—loved ones, close friends, and lost souls who "find themselves in you".

I don't know if it's just me, but every word that comes out of Trey's mouth seems to carry a deep and weighted significance that resonates, as if the sermon is specifically meant for me.

Have I been lost for years, and searching for myself in Bobby somehow?

Am I still searching?

"Now how about some brunch?" chirps my mama when we're gathered outside the church. "I propose Biggie's, since I can get us a good deal with Mr. Tucker." She leans into Patricia. *"That's my son-in-law's father. He's such a sweet man, that William Tucker."*

Mrs. Parker seems privately amused that my mama wouldn't think she—along with the rest of the town—already knows who the infamous William Tucker is, but she indulges her with a sweetly-voiced, "Ooh, that sounds lovely," anyway, then peers at her son. "Bobby, how's that sound to you?"

Bobby and I share a look.

We had a private discussion of our own before meeting up here, anticipating this very thing.

"I think Bobby and I were gonna—"

"—catch a movie," Bobby picks up right on cue. "Jimmy hasn't seen the one about the—"

"—that heist one starring what's-his-name," I say, half on top of his words, half cutting him off.

"Yeah, what's-his-name," Bobby agrees, then turns smilingly to his mama and gives her a kiss on the cheek. "The theater is just down the road, not too far. We can walk there. But you two can go and have some brunch, if you like. I'm not really that hungry."

"Me neither," I throw in unnecessarily.

"And we can come meet you at Biggie's after the movie to head back home. I have employee privileges now," he points out, satisfied with himself, "and I can get us in for free."

To my surprise, my mama doesn't seem to mind in the least. She gives a light little laugh—the same kind when she's had a glass or two of wine—then faces Bobby's mama cheerily. "Well, I don't have a problem with that if you don't, Patricia?"

"Not at all! Nadine and I have so much to chat about," Patricia sings in her high, feathery voice. "I'm sure we'll be brunchin' away for at least a good hour or two. That's long enough for them to see their movie with what's-his-name!"

"What's-his-name!" agrees Nadine, and the two ladies laugh.

Bobby and I stare at each other, unsure whether to be pleased or alarmed at how well our mamas are suddenly getting along.

We decide to be pleased.

The ladies leave arm-in-arm while Bobby and I make a short two-minute trip down the road to the movie theater, me stabbing the pavement with my crutch the whole way there. At the box office, Bobby greets the bushy-haired girl who always seems to be working there, gets his two allotted employee passes for the day, and leads the way inside by holding open the door for me to carefully crutch my way through. *What a gentleman.*

Unlike the crowded church, Bobby and I enjoy a whole back row to ourselves in our auditorium. I even kick my bad foot up on the seat ahead of me, since the only other people in the theater are an older couple near the front who pay us no mind at all every time we laugh at the movie—*it's way super awfully bad*—and heckle the actors on the screen.

It's just about twenty minutes into the movie when I shift in my seat and throw an arm around the back of Bobby's chair—a totally casual, reflexive move I make without thinking.

Bobby freezes at first. But after a glance to the left and right, he gives in, sinking his body into mine.

And I, barely aware that I had thrown my arm around him in the first place, decide to follow through with my own spontaneity, turning the maneuver into a cuddling half-hug, holding my Bobby against my side like a proper movie date.

I plant a kiss right on the top of his head, then face the silver screen with renewed confidence.

Maybe this can work after all.

18

BOBBY

Sunday afternoon spent in the movie theater snuggled up to Jimmy Strong is an absolute dream.

And I've had many dreams.

When we meet up with our parents at Biggie's afterwards, the pair of us are in such blissful moods, we don't even care about our mothers talking our ears off about nothing important. I just keep shooting Jimmy these knowing looks, and he shoots them right back at me, his eyes full of mischief.

We need to take it slow, I had insisted.

Yet from the looks in our eyes, it seems like we already can't wait until our next sleepover.

The whole rest of the evening and night, I text a storm back and forth with Jimmy. He was invited over to his brother's for dinner, then discovered it was an ambush attempt by Billy to find out if his ankle was going to be healed for the big Spruce Ball—and also whether his dance would be a sexy solo or romantic duet.

"I guess I need to keep off my foot," Jimmy tells me a bit later when texting is too slow and I suggest we talk on the phone. "The fate of the whole town of Spruce depends on it, according to Mr. Billy Tucker-Strong, unofficial dance coordinator."

I laugh and shake my head, clutching my pillow tightly on my bed while peering out the window, wondering if he can see the same half-moon I'm looking at. "So which is it, then?"

Jimmy grunts. "Hmm?"

"Solo? ... Or duet?"

He hears the innuendo in my voice. "Well, I guess it depends how daring-as-fuck a certain someone wants to be."

"You mean me? Seriously?" I snort. "These legs aren't meant for dancing. At least not like yours are."

"All legs are meant for dancing. You don't even have to learn how. Just put on the right music and start movin' your tush."

That makes me smile.

I guess he's got a point there.

"The second you pull me up there to dance with you, Jimmy, there won't be a question anymore whether there's something going on between us."

"So?" Jimmy snorts. "Haven't they been thinkin' that ever since I took you to prom? Let them think what they want."

I can imagine Jimmy getting quite a thrill out of making all the folk of Spruce whisper and gasp, then talk about it for days on end after the big dance is long over. What a totally Jimmy Strong way to end the summer: leaving your hometown talking about you for weeks after you've run off back to college.

"Hey, Bobby?"

We've been talking awhile. It's almost one in the morning. My TV is shut off, the house is silent, and I'm having trouble keeping my eyes open.

"Yeah, Jimmy?"

"Do you ever wonder ..." His voice is croaky and low, sleep's heavy fingers having a hold on him, too. "... what your life would be like if you, like ... made different choices?"

"Hmm? How do you mean?"

"Like ..." He moans. I hear him shifting on his bed, then settle in place. "Like if you just had this totally different life. And people saw you a different way. And you lived somewhere else. And you did things that scare you, things you would never, ever do. And you had ... different friends ..." His voice drifts off.

At once, I'm no longer sleepy, my eyes open. "W-What ...?"

Jimmy takes a long, lazy breath, groans, then says, "It's weird, 'cause ... no matter how differently I picture my life, you're ..." A sleepy sort of chuckle escapes his lips, then silence.

I blink. "I'm ...?"

So sleepily, somewhere between being awake and dreaming, Jimmy finishes: "You're always in it."

Oh.

Wow.

A smile slowly spreads over my face. I close my eyes and hug my phone to my ear. "Jimmy, that ... that really means a lot to me. I know things have been kind of complicated between the two of us lately, and ..." I bite my lip, thinking. "... and I know we've got a lot to figure out together. Maybe whatever's going on between us has a shelf life. Maybe it doesn't. I don't know. But I think I've ..." I feel so safe with him. I can tell Jimmy anything. "I think I've felt strongly about you for a long time. Maybe ever since we first met as clueless kids. And I think ... maybe I've *always* loved you."

I listen for his reply.

There is nothing.

"Jimmy?" Still nothing. "Jimmy ...? Are you still—?"

Then the calm sound of deep breathing passes through the phone like soft, white noise.

The boy's fallen asleep.

As if the phone is his face, I softly whisper, "Goodnight," to it before closing my eyes and turning over in the bed. Then I listen to the gentle sound of Jimmy breathing as I drift off.

If only every night could be as peaceful as Sunday's.

Monday morning is a harsh and unkind wake-up call of spilled soda on four seats in auditorium two, puking kids in auditorium three, and a leaky, spraying soda fountain that I'm somehow given the task of figuring out how to fix. Vince is off, and it's the power-tripping Anthony who shrugs, makes some excuse about having to man the concession stand during the busy afternoon rush (it isn't busy at all), then tosses me a set of tools. Anthony might be an enemy of Jimmy's, but he sure is doing his best to antagonize me, too. *So much for keeping the peace at work.* After getting home, I can't get into the shower fast enough.

Then wash, rinse, repeat for Tuesday morning: another day without Vince, and *up to here* with Anthony Myer's smug bossing me around and shoving off the worst, most disgusting, and tedious of tasks onto my shoulders. I'm not one to complain or cause a scene, so I take each and every one of them and perform to my best, even if I don't know what the hell I'm doing.

And Wednesday isn't any damn better.

Can someone remind me why I took this job again ...?

The saving grace each day is texting back and forth with Jimmy on my breaks. He's decided to take my advice and keep off of his foot for the week, to everyone's surprise. He sends me funny selfies from the ranch where he's been kept busy on a laptop or at a table full of crafty things by his ma, who needs this and that to be done for the Spruce Ball. Jimmy's convinced his ma has totally lost her mind or else is in complete denial that it isn't she who's running the event this summer.

And each time my break ends and my fun text-tennis with Jimmy's over, I'm already excited for the next time I'll get to chat with him about my day, which is going to be whenever I finally clock out and head home. I've talked my pa out of coming by and picking me up every day, preferring to do the seventeen-minute-walk home—which turns into a half-hour walk, since I like to take my time. It gives me a chance to text back and forth with Jimmy some more before I get home and am bombarded by my ma's love and dinner plans and spilling all about her own (comparatively uneventful) day.

Then comes Thursday: my last day of work this week before I get both Friday *and* Saturday off.

It would be the perfect day if it weren't for Anthony Myers—once more—being a total and unnecessary dick.

Like when he hounds me about emptying the trash in the concession scullery. "Isn't that your job?" he asks pseudo-politely while leaning halfway over the counter, flippantly tossing kernels of popcorn in the air and catching them with his mouth. "Your job is trash, right? It's been full-up for almost an hour with empty syrup boxes and popcorn seed bags. The trash doesn't take out itself. I mean ..." He shrugs at me. "... unless you're too busy with another *tour* of the projectionist booth that you're wanting to give some other *friend* of yours."

Or every time I walk by in front of the concession stand, and Anthony—totally busy with nothing at all whatsoever—points at a stray popcorn kernel on the ground (that he likely tossed there) and says, "Hey, sweeper boy, don't miss that spot right there."

Or whenever I'm already lugging two full, heavy, smelly bags of trash over my back like Movie Theater Santa Claus across the lobby, and Anthony flags me down from the concession stand to say, "I'd offer to help, but Mr. Lemon gave me strict orders to stay back here and inventory my popcorn bags and candy. I've already counted them twice, but y'know: manager's orders! I'm so bored and tired back here! Nothing to do! Should I take a nap?"

Constant antagonizing.

Constant taunting and sneering.

Constant Anthony Myers, every day this week.

Doesn't anyone else work that damned concession stand??

The end of my long shift Thursday afternoon couldn't come fast enough. I clock out quicker than I've ever clocked out before, wash my hands after dealing with an unusually sticky job of taking trash out to the dumpster, then hurry out the doors to the tune of Anthony calling at my back: "See you Sunday, trash boy!"

I hope the only capacity in which he sees me is my knuckles when they kiss his annoyingly high cheekbones.

I don't vent a word of my frustrations to Jimmy, because that would basically be an open invitation for him to come down to the theater, kick Anthony's ass, and cause another big Spruce-caliber scandal with me and Jimmy at its center.

Besides, don't I have enough to worry about?

Like the fact that Jimmy and I haven't seen each other since we said goodbye at the movie theater Sunday?

Getting home, however, I find myself caught in a different predicament entirely. "But sweetie," my ma sings in her light and plumy tone, "I was really hoping you'd stay in tonight and relax with your father and I. We haven't seen you all week."

"Ma, you've *only* seen me all week," I argue back, unable to keep the whininess out of my voice. "Every day after work, in fact. I've stayed in every night, too. I've got two full days off, and I want to spend them with Jimmy."

"Always that Strong boy. Jimmy, Jimmy, Jimmy." She's sitting in a chair by the living room window, some multicolored mess of a crochet dropped into her lap. "Honey, I don't want to be the one to say it, really, but—"

"What is it, Ma?" My frustration from the day I've had at work has built up to the exploding point already. I'm so tired, I can feel an ache in my *toes*. All my patience is sapped.

My sweet, well-meaning ma doesn't seem to notice any of it, obliviously prattling on. "I'd just hoped by now that you'd—"

"That I'd what, Ma?"

She doesn't notice how terse I'm getting, how I'm cutting off everything she's saying. "I wish you would have realized that the Strong boy isn't ... *like* you, in *that* way."

I shut my eyes and let out the most aggravated sigh. "What do you even mean, Ma? I've had a long day."

"Sweetheart, he can't love you in the way you want him to."

I pop my eyes open and look at her. She isn't looking back at me, however; her gaze is lost somewhere around my knees, her lips pursed with a wistful little frown to them.

"Ma," I start, "I don't know what you're thinkin', but I—"

"You like him, sweetheart. I know you do."

"Ma ..."

"He's a handsome young man, it makes sense. You've been inseparable ever since you were kids. He took you to prom. But sweetie, I think that prom night meant more to you than to him."

The explosion is inevitable. Between the day I've had and the things she's saying, and the uncertainty that still pulsates in the air between me and Jimmy ... "Ma, I'm tellin' you ..."

"Nadine and I were talkin', and really, she's on the same page as I am. It's not that I don't value your friendship. I do. I just think you should be careful with your heart, and your—"

"MA." *She won't stop talking until I explode. She won't stop with her soft, insistent, endless and sweet barrage of reason.* "PLEASE. MA."

"—feelings with that boy. I don't want him breakin' your little heart because he can't love you the way you want him to. He just can't, sweetheart. He can't love you in the way—"

"HE ALREADY DOES!"

For the first time since she started talking, her eyes snap up to mine with surprise, her jaw dropped.

I grit my teeth.

I shouldn't have said that.

After a moment of silence fills the room from one blank-faced wall to the other, she brings a hand to her mouth, then murmurs through her fingers: "How do you mean, sweetheart?"

"Never mind," I quickly say. "I don't know. I'm stressed, and— Never mind. I've had a long day at the theater."

"Bobby, how do you mean he already does?"

"I just ..." I drop on the couch behind me. My ass nearly misses the cushion, catching clumsily on the arm. I shut my eyes. "I'm ..."

"You can tell me, sweetheart."

My eyes are still closed. My heart drums frantically in my chest. *She isn't like the gossips of Spruce,* I reassure myself. *If you tell her what's going on, she won't spill it to anyone else.*

She's your Ma. You can trust her.

Just say it.

"Jimmy ... has feelings for me," I murmur, almost a whisper, to the back of my eyelids.

I don't hear any noise, like every muscle in her body is as still as an iron piece of furniture across the room.

And then: "Well, of course he does, honey."

"No." I keep talking with my eyes closed. "Actual feelings. The ones you have for a ... for a boyfriend. He has feelings for me. Real ones. Real and actual ones."

Really, how many more ways can I say it?

I hear her hands drop to her lap. "Are you sure?"

"He's kissed me. More than once." I take a deep breath. "He and I are ... figuring things out right now. It's complicated."

"Okay." I hear shuffling, her rising from her chair, and then there's a set of arms wrapping around me, hugging me close.

I lean into her hug.

Why was that so difficult, yet so easy to say out loud?

Strangely, I feel little relief. I don't think I'll feel relief until I know for sure that this isn't just some exciting new sexual game Jimmy is playing with me.

I want to know it's for real.

I want to know that Jimmy isn't going to break my heart, in the same way he's broken countless girls' hearts at school. I had the pleasure of watching each and every one of them break. Some girls didn't get the hint, and they'd puppy-dog me all the time, saying things like, "You're close to him. Can you find out what I did wrong? Why he isn't returning my calls? Please, Bobby, you're my only hope. I'm crazy for him." Over and over, girls would come to me, their new gay best friend, begging to know what they did wrong with the infamous Jimmy Strong.

What if it was none of their faults?

What if Jimmy is just a professional heartbreaker?

Then my ma goes: "So is he a good kisser?"

My eyes pop open. I pull away and give her a look.

She shrugs innocently, then sits on the couch next to me. "I'm just tryin' to have a little conversation. This is ... This is not what I was expectin' to hear. About you and Jimmy. I need to *process*."

There's a buzz in my pocket. A text from Jimmy, I'm certain of it. "Ma, I know you've probably got a lot of questions, but—"

"Ya darn tootin' I do," she sings in her cute, feathery voice.

"—I really just want to clean up, shower, and go spend some time with Jimmy tonight at his place. We've got a lot to figure out. And I think the only way to really do it is to ... well ..." My heart still races. "... to spend time together. Just me ... and Jimmy."

"Mmm." My ma fidgets with her fingers for a while. Then she nods, rises off the couch, and stops by the kitchen. "Well, go take your shower, and at least I can warm you up some casserole before you go. You've got to be hungry after your long day."

I smile wanly. "Starved."

"And I guess Jimmy will be comin' by to scoop you up? Or do you need me to take you?"

"I'm sure he'll come get me. He's ... probably sufferin' from a bit of cabin fever. His ma's workin' him to the bone on dance stuff and farmhand management, far as I know."

"Mmm, to own a farm." My ma shrugs, then disappears.

And I pull out my phone to check the buzz from earlier. Just as I predicted, it's Jimmy telling me he's already halfway to my house. *By the time I'm showered and dinner's ready, Jimmy will be here before I even take my first bite.*

I text him back, then call out, "You got space for one more at the table, Ma?"

Of course she does.

After taking a speedy shower to wash off the filth of being a movie theater usher with questionable stains all over my body and grease marks all over my uniform, I feverishly dry off. Then I go and throw on a pair of tight red boxer-briefs, denim shorts, and a fitted red-and-blue soccer jersey top with yellow trim at the neck and the ends of the sleeves, which cling to my arms.

Then I stare at myself in the bathroom mirror, unsure.

What's missing?

I pull my shorts open and take a peek down at my dick.

Should I manscape a little? Squirt a spritz of cologne down in the jungle? Massage in a little oil or cream?

I haven't had to worry about these things in a long, long time.

And certainly never before with Jimmy.

I lift an arm and take a sniff of my pit. *Soapy and fresh from the shower, good.* I check my breath. *Not so fresh.* I decide to brush my teeth, even though I haven't eaten dinner yet. I take a comb to my hair too and give it a better shape, fussing with it.

I take more care with my hair tonight than I did for my date with Malcolm Tucci.

When I'm done, I'm back to staring at myself. Another breath draws in through my nostrils, then slowly out my parted lips.

My heart's racing so fast, I feel like I could pass out.

What's the big deal? Just be yourself, and relax.

I let myself out of the bathroom, and already I hear Jimmy chatting away with my ma. They appear to be talking about the pros and cons of running a ranch the size of the Strong's. When I come into view at the small archway to the dining room, Jimmy stops talking at once and gazes at me with this beautiful, faraway expression, like the sight of me has taken him somewhere.

Lord knows why. I'm just my same old self. "Hey, Jimmy."

My greeting breaks him from his trance. His words come out in half a croak: "Hey there, Bobs."

My ma brings dinner to the table, but stops for a second at the exit to the kitchen, her eyes observing the pair of us. Then, with a coy little smile on her face, she slaps down a potholder, then sets a casserole on top of it. Jimmy turns back to her with wide eyes, then gets straight to serving himself, mumbling, "Good Lord, ma'am, Patricia, this smells heavenly!" And my ma is too quick to mutter, "*Just Patricia.* You know better than to *ma'am* me!"

I find I barely have an appetite, what with all the excitement and anticipation of my first night off squirreling through my guts, but I make myself eat at least one serving before calling it quits. The whole dinner's conversation is occupied with Jimmy and my ma exchanging pleasantries about farm life, interrupted just for a moment by my pa's late return from a job. He joins us at the table, gives Jimmy a hearty greeting, and the four of us finish eating like one big, happy family, just like we used to do back in the day.

And after my pa mentions "odd shenanigans out in Fairview", Jimmy nudges me and says, "Tell that to this one. He was almost married to the chef's son at *Nadine's*, thanks to my mama."

I snort halfway through a sip of my water. "I wasn't *married* to *anyone*, thank you very much. It was just a date with a guy I likely won't be seein' again."

Unbeknownst to myself or Jimmy, my ma is staring at us from across the table, this teary-eyed, happy expression pasted over her face. Then, like a balloon pricked by a needle, she explodes with, "Oh, I just love the pair of you together!"

My eyes flash. I stare at her. "Ma ..." I start.

Jimmy, oblivious to what my ma is now privy to, smirks and punches me in the arm. "We make a great team, don't we? Too bad I wasn't in soccer, or this one wasn't in dance. Then we could be an actual team."

For a second, I breathe a sigh of relief that the comment goes right on by without any deeper implication revealed.

Until my ma goes and says: "Oh, you're just so cute together, I can't wait to see the sweet pair a' *you* married!"

Jimmy's eyebrows pull together, the first trace of suspicion crossing his face. He eyes me, concerned.

And I'm staring hard at my ma, clenching my fork so tightly, it might bend in half. "*Ma*," I press even harder.

Then my pa chuckles deeply, amused. "Well, you can wish it all you want, Patricia, but Jimmy here's going to be married to a lovely girl someday, not our son." He gives me a wink. "And you'll have yourself a handsome lad who prefers boys over girls."

In the past three years since I've come out, I *still* haven't corrected my pa's use of words like "prefer" and "preference". I guess there's more dire things to focus on than a choice of words.

Like my ma slipping up at the dinner table—without even realizing she has. "Ma, I think it's time for me and Jimmy to—"

"Yes, yes," she agrees, her eyes still twinkling. "You two need your alone time. Just you boys." She giggles. "Don't touch a thing, Jimmy, I'll get all the plates. Oh, you two!" She titters again, then starts cleaning up the table.

And Jimmy still hasn't stopped giving me that hardened look in his eyes.

Shit.

After the table's cleaned up and I've gathered my stuff, I give my ma a kiss on the cheek and my pa a tight hug before Jimmy and I head out the door.

He doesn't say a thing to me as we walk down the driveway to his truck.

Double shit.

I swing into the passenger seat, and before I can take a breath, the pair of us are speeding off to his ranch in the waning sunlight. The uneven hum of the engine fills our ears along with the wind that blasts in through the rolled-down windows, tossing my hair in every damned direction it pleases.

So much for taking all of that time in the bathroom mirror to fix it up nicely.

"I see you're back in your truck," I note, attempting a casual dialogue, dipping a toe in the figurative waters.

He takes a minute to respond. "Yep."

"So ... you're recovering then?"

"Yep." He's gripping the steering wheel especially tight. "Foot's pretty much back to normal now."

"Yeah, 'cause you kept off of it this past week like you were supposed to in the first place."

"Did you tell your mama?"

The sudden question hits me right in the belly button. I close my eyes. I can't lie to him. "Yeah."

"Why?"

I sigh. "It's just my ma. She doesn't talk to anyone. It isn't a big deal, Jimmy, and I only told her that we—"

"That we what?"

"That we ..." I open my eyes and face him. "We had a few real feelings to work out between us. That maybe there's something going on. And to keep it quiet."

Jimmy brings both his hands to the steering wheel, wringing it as he mulls over that information with a sternness in his pretty brown eyes.

He doesn't say anything.

"I swear, Jimmy, it isn't a big deal."

The noise of blasting wind still fills the car without a word from Jimmy Strong to join it.

I sigh. "Are you mad at me?"

He gives it a second of thought. "Nah," Jimmy decides. "Not mad. I just didn't realize we were tellin' anyone anything yet."

I watch the side of his face. "This isn't one of those situations where you tell me you aren't mad, then sulk all evening and act like I've gone and killed your cat, is it?"

Jimmy smirks. "No. I'm not mad. And you know I've never had a cat." Then he eyes me. "You look cute tonight."

I fight a smile, then nod at him. "Keep your eyes on the road."

"I am." After a second, he lets one of his hands drop back to the gear shift, returning to his usual method of driving in that one-handed, proud, chariot-commanding way of his.

"And ... thanks," I add belatedly.

That makes Jimmy chuckle. Then he bites his lip, gives his hat a tug, and continues on driving, half a smile on his face.

I feel a wash of relief that he isn't mad about the telling-my-ma thing. The relief carries me all the way out to the Strong ranch where we find a spot in the gravel, kill the engine, then hop out of his truck and head up to the house.

Jimmy stops me before we reach the porch with a tug on my arm. "C'mon. This way." Then he heads around the porch to the other side of the house.

I follow him to the pool, where he stops, then proceeds to kick off his shoes, yank off his socks, drop his pants, and peel off his shirt right there.

My pulse accelerates at once. My eyes are glued to his figure as he stands there in just a pair of skimpy, tight black briefs—the same ones he wore to the gay nightclub. They could be Speedos, for as low-cut and ass-squeezing as they are.

Then, with a coy look over his shoulder, he asks, "You ready for a dip?" before diving right into the pool.

I glance toward the house. There's a light on in the kitchen, but I don't see any activity. I look the other way toward the long path that leads to the woods in the distance where Tanner and Billy's house is. Nothing but gently swaying trees meet my eyes.

No one's around us. Nothing. Not even birds. It's rare that you find yourself all alone with the one person you want to be with in a place like Spruce—where there are always eyes.

Today, there's only us.

With a smirk, I bravely kick off my shoes, peel off my shorts, then take off my soccer jersey shirt.

So much for painstakingly choosing what to wear tonight.

I throw the ball of them at a nearby pool chair, then slide right into the cool, glistening water wearing just my tight red boxer-briefs. The water swallows me up in its cool embrace, casting little ripples across the surface.

Jimmy swims a lap around the pool, then slows down to a stop in front of me, beads of water dripping from his hair. His brown eyes sparkle as he stares into mine.

"Hey there, boy," he says to me.

I shoot out one tiny, nervous breath out my nostrils. "Hey."

A faint smile curls his lips.

The cool water laps at my bare skin as I float there in front of him, mesmerized by his dreamy gaze. He's always had this way of putting me completely at ease, no matter what. Jimmy Strong makes you know you're in his circle without doing a thing at all. Just floating right here in front of him in the middle of summer's sweetest oblivion, Jimmy makes me know I belong in this moment, in this place, with this special guy.

He's made sure no one comes near me who will hurt me.

He's made sure I'm always safe and taken care of.

He's always been my—

"Protector," I murmur.

Jimmy lifts an eyebrow and makes a deep grunt: "Hmm?"

"First word that comes to mind when I think of you."

He gives it a moment's thought. His eyes never leave mine. "Is that so? Protector? You think I protect you?"

"I sure do."

After another moment passes, his arms come out of the water and rest over my shoulders. "I think it's gonna come soon that *you* are gonna need to protect *me*."

I love the feeling of his arms on my shoulders, bringing his face so close to mine. I'm his one and only man. "Protect you?"

"Yep."

"How?"

"There's things I don't know. Lots of things. About how all of this works. Between two guys."

Under the water, my hands find his hips. Our lower bodies have gravitated together, the wet, swelling underwater bulges of our underwear pressed against each other's.

"Like, what I'm supposed to do," he goes on. "And what I need to be careful of. Or whatever."

"As usual, you're worryin' too much, Jimmy. There isn't some *special list of things* you gotta do."

"Yeah, but—"

"You just do what you want. You just do what feels right."

Jimmy shrugs. "Alright."

Then his arms close around me, and with me locked firmly against his body, Jimmy brings his soft, warm lips right to mine.

Our bare chests press against one another's.

He tilts his head to get a better angle, working the kiss with strength and muscularity. I feel his jaw tighten on every kiss he presses to my lips.

Blood rushes through my body. My heart beats with hunger. Every tip of my toes and fingers are charged at once as I cling to his body. I can't get close enough to it as we kiss.

Jimmy takes what he wants when he wants it.

Is now an inappropriate time to mention how, ever since the beginning, I've always wondered what it would be like to be one of Jimmy Strong's ever-so-lucky girlfriends?

To be on the receiving end of one of Jimmy Strong's passion-filled, hyper-aggressive, power-packed kisses?

To be the object of Jimmy's boundless adoration?

And here I am, once again living my own dream.

His hands slide off my shoulders, then hungrily drag down my sides under the water, coming to rest at the small of my back.

I have never really taken time to appreciate how big Jimmy's hands are. They are so big and strong and commanding.

And they are all over me.

And his strength is proven the next moment when he takes hold of my hips and pulls our crotches even tighter against each other, humping me with mounting aggression.

He is rock hard.

So am I.

As if it's physically possible to not be hard in a situation like this.

When our lips separate, our heads are still together, touching at the forehead. His eyes are in another world every time he opens them onto my face, out of breath, water still dripping down his cheeks and off the wispy, curled ends of his wet hair.

"You're, like, the perfect teammate," he murmurs.

I have no hope to follow Jimmy's sex-drunk logic. "What?"

"You and I. We're ... We're like the perfect teammates." He kisses me again. "On a team." Another kiss. "Just you and me."

"Yeah? What sport?"

"Not important." Another deep and breathless kiss. "It doesn't matter what game we play. We always—"

"Yeah?"

"We always win."

He kisses me again.

Before I know it, my back is pressed against the edge of the pool. Jimmy's big hands have worked their fingers under the wide waistband of my boxer-briefs. He grips the top of my ass cheeks powerfully, holding me in place as he makes love to my lips.

Suddenly I'm doing the same. My fingers have been teasing at the rim of his tight, skimpy underwear. I let them slip underneath it, gently teasing the tiny things down his hips.

I know his dick is freed when he humps me under the water, then parts his lips against my face with a sigh of relief.

I grip him under the water.

Jimmy pulls away and stares at my face, his eyes drunk with the lust exploding between us.

"See?" I smile. "You just do whatever feels good."

I give his hard cock a stroke under the water.

Jimmy moans.

"Whatever you want," I go on softly, my voice barely there.

Then I give him another stroke.

Again, Jimmy melts against me. So much power I have, just holding his throbbing dick under the water and giving it an innocent stroke or two.

"Bobby ..." he murmurs.

"Yeah?"

"I wanna do somethin' that feels good."

"And what's that?"

His eyes meet mine importantly. "We need to go inside for it."

19

JIMMY

My heart is pounding in my chest as we enter the house.

Our damp feet slap the wood flooring as we head up the steps to my room.

The door shuts behind us and our lips reconnect in a sweep of breath and passion. I move backwards as we kiss, dragging Bobby along with me to the bed.

We're just in our wet underwear.

Only thin, nothing bits of fabric separate our dicks.

I pull him on top of me as I fall backwards on the bed, then let my hands roam freely over his body as I kiss him aggressively.

I can't get enough of Bobby.

"If only things had been different ..." I mumble against his lips as we kiss.

"Different?" he moans back on my lips, also not bothering to interrupt our kisses to speak.

"So much of our friendship spent without doin' what we're doin' right now." My hands are slowly creeping down to his ass, where I take a big handful of each cheek. "So much *time* ..."

"Better late than—*mmm*—never," he murmurs back.

I squeeze those ass cheeks of his.

I pull away from his lips to get a look into his eyes. "I want this ass."

"It's yours," says Bobby. "All yours."

"I want it right now."

"Mmm—yeah?"

"Like, I *want-it* want it."

"I—" His eyes flash. "Wait, what?"

"I want to have sex with you, Bobby Parker."

He doesn't seem capable of closing his mouth suddenly.

I roll him over to bring myself on top of him, causing him to suck in a lungful of air in surprise. My fingers hook into his tight red boxer-briefs, then gently slide them down his legs. They stick to his thighs, being wet, but as soon as they clear his feet, I throw those suckers aside like nothing.

Bobby lies there on his back, completely naked, beautiful, and staring at me in wonder. His huge cock is fully erect, his legs slightly spread and bent over the edge of the bed, thigh muscles popped, and feet dangling.

The longer I look down at his body—and that sweet, curious face of his that burns with desire for me—the more I want him.

"Jimmy, I've ... I-I've wanted this for a really long time," he murmurs. "I just want to make sure—"

"—that it's what I want?" I point at my dick, which is poking fiercely outward from within the restrictive confines of my bikini briefs. "It's clearly the *only* fucking thing I want."

"Jimmy ..."

"My body doesn't lie."

"I just want to make sure ..."

I climb over him and put a kiss on his lips, shutting him up.

All the other arguments and worries and concerns he was probably planning to voice seem to have lost all importance to him, because at once, he gives in to my kiss, and his hands are all over me again.

His bravery finds him the same way it did in the pool. He puts a hand at my crotch, then works my cock right out of my briefs. When his fingers wrap around it, an overwhelming sigh of relief escapes my lungs, and I swear my dick gets twice as hard.

"I can't stand waiting anymore," I groan.

"Where are your parents? Are they *always* out at night?"

"Pretty much. Why the hell you worryin' about all that right now? My mama and my papa aren't on my mind. Your ass is."

Bobby quickly picks his head up off the bed and gives a look at my nightstand. "You're, uh ... gonna need lube."

"I know that."

"And a condom."

"Bobby."

"Well, I don't know," he exclaims. "All of this is happenin' so damned fast, I feel like I need to, like, teach you or show you some things first, or at the very least give you some pointers on how—"

I silence him with another kiss.

He melts in an instant.

Then I lean into his ear, my lips right against the lobe when I whisper, *"I'm gonna take care of you tonight."*

A faint smile spreads Bobby's lips apart.

I kiss them right then. *He looks so damned cute when he smiles in that sleepy, awkward sort of way.*

"Now you just lie here like a good boy," I tell him, "while I—"

"Jimmy?"

"Yeah, Bobs? What is it?"

His dreamy eyes find mine. He bites his lip, then lets out the words, "Go slow. It's ... been a while."

I return his smile with one of my own. "*I'm not gonna let a dang thing hurt you, Bobby—not even me. Protector, remember?*"

I pull open a drawer by the nightstand and take out my bottle of late-night-bored-as-fuck jerking lube. *I figure this works for butt stuff, too.* Then I pull out a condom, tear it open, and slowly roll the thing over my dick.

"Jimmy?"

I let out a snort as I start lubing up my cock. "Boy, you've got about a hundred and twelve worries a second."

"You've also gotta put some lube on my, uh ..." He gestures awkwardly between his legs. "On my hole. In it. Sorta. Let me do it," he says suddenly, extending his hand for the bottle.

I smirk. *This guy.* Ignoring his offer, I squirt a dollop on my own palm, then put myself between his legs and slide my lubed fingers right into his smooth, exposed crack.

Bobby gasps, his eyes widening.

"Like this?" I ask saucily.

Then slowly I begin to move my fingers, massaging the lube in his sensitive, tight hole. From the look on Bobby's face, this is half the fun for him. His eyes and half-open mouth are exploding with all kinds of pleasure and my dick hasn't even touched him yet.

I lean over him and put my lips to his left nipple, catching him by surprise. I watch his face dance with the sensations I'm giving him. Air hisses out of his mouth as I turn the kiss into a lick.

He tastes perfect no matter which inch of him I'm licking.

I move to the other nipple. Anticipating it, Bobby squirms under my weight and gasps with delight. My fingers slowly start to move at his hole, teasing it in their slippery, frictionless way.

It's making him squirm and moan and gasp so much, I wonder if it's all I gotta do to get him there.

The moans I make this boy sing is my favorite fucking soundtrack.

"This doin' it for ya?" I tease him, coming up from licking his other nipple. "I'm not a virgin, y'know."

"You kinda are," he argues back, though his voice has no fight in it, his body in a total state of bliss after my tongue-torturing his sensitive nipples.

"If you say so."

"I say so. I gay-say so."

Each time I rub my fingers back and forth over his hole, I feel his muscles loosening for me. Each pass earns me a half-sigh, half-moan that delights my ears, too.

It's practically an invitation.

"Work me with your finger a bit," he tells me. "You gotta—"

I let one of my fingers slip halfway in.

Bobby moans with a sudden explosion of pleasure.

"Wow," I exclaim, surprised. "That went in so easy. You sound ready for the real deal already. Hmm, how 'bout another?" I gently begin to work in a second finger, teasing it inside. I almost have Bobby singing bass tones with what I'm doing. "Goodness, are you gonna last when I finally get myself in you?"

"Just do it," he lets out suddenly. "I'm ready, I'm ready."

"You sure?"

"God, yes."

I can't keep teasing him. I'm growing too impatient myself to keep this up much longer and can't let my fingers have all the fun.

I've never been jealous of my own fingers before.

"Bobby."

He's still lost in his own head, blissful and dreamy. "Yeah?"

"Look at me."

He opens his eyes. They snap right onto mine. "Something wrong?" he asks at once, serious. "You okay?"

"Perfect." I give him a lopsided, cocky smile as I hook my hands under his spread legs and pull his hole right up to my dick. "I just want you looking into my eyes when I enter you."

Bobby is stunned silent at those words.

My fingers slide out as easily as they slid in, and then the tip of my throbbing hard cock replaces them. With just a little hump of my hips, I feel the cockhead trying to push its way in, but the tightness of Bobby's hole keeps it right there.

He's so tight.

Just one more little hump is all it'll take.

I can tell. I'm right there on the precipice of sliding into him. Just one miniscule thrust of my hips will give the pair of us what we've been wanting. I feel the pressure building up in my dick from pressing the head against his tight hole, like any sudden movement will cause it to slip right in.

The anticipation is agony.

Bobby bites his lip as he stares into my eyes. Stars of desire sparkle in his cute brown eyes.

It's almost automatic when my hips give a gentle thrust, like my body betrays me, unable to wait, and pushes my cock past the point of breaking ...

And my cock pops partway in.

"Oh my God, Jimmy ..." groans Bobby, his eyes screwing up.

The sensation of his hole around my cockhead throws me into a state of unmatched pleasure. Prickles of ecstasy chase their way up and down my legs and arms.

"Am I hurtin' you?" I ask him, out of breath, trying not to rock my eyes back from the pleasure. "Are you okay?"

"*PERFECT*," he exclaims.

I grin and lean forward some more, pressing my weight into him as I bring my face closer to his for a kiss.

My dick unintentionally slides in another few inches from the innocent effort.

Bobby moans out and gasps.

"Does this feel good?" I ask him. "Are you—?"

"I'm okay. Yes, *God*, it feels good, it feels—*mmph*—good."

I let go one of his legs to cradle his head with a hand, then kiss his parted lips, desperate to know Bobby in every way possible. I want his lips on mine while my cock is inside him. I want to feel as close to Bobby as I've ever felt, in body and mind.

I don't know what I was expecting this to feel like.

But no expectation could possibly match the real thing.

"This feels so good for me, too," I breathe against his lips.

"Keep going," Bobby begs me, his soft eyes reeling back as he struggles to keep them on me like I wanted. "Please. *Mmm, please.*"

My dick slides out a bit, then right back in deeper than before.

Bobby's legs squeeze around my waist, muscular and tight, as he moans. He is slowly being driven as mad as I am with every gentle thrust of my dick inside him.

"H-Harder," he cries.

I lift an eyebrow. "Harder?"

"God, yes."

I kiss him deeply, then eye him. "First, you wanted me to take it easy with you and go slow, and now—"

Bobby's hands reach around me, grab hold of my hips the best he can from this angle, then hungrily pull my hips against him as powerfully as he can.

My dick slides as far in as I think it can go.

"*GOD!*" he cries out.

His passion ignites my own, and suddenly I've got him cradled in my arms, half-lifted off the bed and held against my body like a toy as I pump him greedily.

Bobby clings to me however he can as I gently ride him, every inch of my dick filling every inch of him.

I hold on to him like my most precious possession.

I have never felt closer to another human being like I do now.

It's minutes later when he breathes out, "You're doing good." He's half out of his mind with euphoria. "You're doing *so* good."

"It's not too rough?"

"It's perfect, perfect, *perfect* ..."

We fuck for so damned long, it's a wonder I haven't nut inside him yet. I feel like I'm already riding the edge, worked right up to it before I even slid inside him.

Then his soft, parted lips find mine, kissing me with a breath-stealing desperation as he whispers, "*I need you to come inside me, Jimmy.*" He moans as I ram him deeply. "*Please.*"

I lay him down on the bed, then stare into his eyes as I reach between our bodies for his dick.

His mouth pops open as my fingers wrap around it.

"I want you to remember this, Bobby."

I start stroking his dick.

"Jimmy ..." His eyes are rocking back again.

"Bobby, look at me."

His eyes snap to mine again. He's completely beside himself. He can't believe this is happening.

That makes two of us.

I've seen him work his huge dick before. I walked right in on him that one day this past semester, right after we returned to campus from winter break. I watched him get halfway to Heaven, working his big meat with such eye-rocking ecstasy.

Now I'm the one who's about to take him there.

Bobby's every ounce of pleasure is mine to give.

"You're gonna look in my eyes when you come," I tell him.

"Are you close?" he asks suddenly, wide-eyed.

"Yeah." I keep pumping him while I stroke his big, hard dick. "I am, buddy. Any second now. I'm right there with you."

"Stay with me," he begs.

"I'm right there, right there with you."

"S-Stay with—" He chokes himself with a gasp, eyes rocking back, then snapping onto mine. "J-Jimmy ... Stay with me. *Oh, God.*"

"I'm with you."

"I'm so close, Jimmy. I'm right there."

"Me, too."

"I know I'm ... I-I'm difficult sometimes ..."

I catch myself smiling as I pump him harder. "You always get this talkative when you're riding the edge?"

"Jimmy, I never thought ..." His voice breaks off in a series of incoherent moans and shivers. "I-I never thought ..."

His dick pulses in my fast-stroking hand.

He's about to rocket all over his chest.

And he's still trying to speak. "I ... I never ..."

"Bobby, buddy ..."

"I never thought ... that I'd finally know ... what it's like."

It's becoming a struggle to hold off with every movement of my throbbing, aching dick.

The inevitable is coming for me, too, and it's only a matter of seconds now.

"I love you, Jimmy Strong," he breathes, eyes rocking back.

"I love you, too, buddy. Eyes on me."

"E-Eyes on you!" he cries out as his gaze snaps back to mine.

"Come for me."

"C-Coming!" His mouth opens. "J-Jimmy." His eyebrows crawl up his forehead. "Oh, God."

The moment I feel him explode between our bodies, I let loose inside of him in a series of desperate, excited breaths. I can barely pump anymore, instead just thrusting my dick as deep into him as I possibly can, prodding him right in the prostate as he hollers out with his release.

And despite all my demands and best intentions, both our love-drunk eyes rock back as we empty ourselves.

I collapse on my man when I'm through, utterly spent.

The pair of us breathe heavily, our sweaty heads side-by-side. My chin rests over his shoulder, and his face is tucked into the nape of my neck like it was made to fit there. Our tired bodies are embraced in each other's arms, the mess of sticky desire between us forgotten, quickly cooling, while sweat drips from our brows.

We don't move for the longest while.

We just listen to each other breathe in the wholesome, safe, beautiful silence of my bedroom.

"I'm all yours," I tell him, my voice muffled by the sheets.

"Jimmy ..."

"Every part of me." *Has this always been true, and I'm only now putting it to words?* "Every single part of me. It belongs to you."

His hand finds my back where he starts to gently rub. "Jimmy. We're more—"

"What?"

"We're more, now." His head shifts slightly, his lips touching my ear now. "More than buddies. We crossed a line."

Lying on him, I feel like we're one being, one body, one breath and mouth and set of ears. "Yeah?"

"I want you to ..." He takes a breath. "... to be my boyfriend."

The word isn't strange when used to describe me. I've been many people's boyfriends.

But I've never had one myself.

"I want you to be—" I start.

"Yeah?"

I lift myself off of him to get a look at his face.

Bobby's starry, sparkly brown eyes meet mine, curious and excited for the rest of my sentence.

I run a few fingers over his forehead, drawing some of his unruly strands of hair aside. Then, to that precious face, I say: "I want you to be my dance partner for the Spruce Ball."

To that, Bobby Parker's face freezes.

He sure as hell wasn't expecting that.

20

JIMMY

I'm not sure how it happened.

Or when.

Or why.

Or for what greater, unknowable purpose.

But Bobby Parker and I are now in love, and he's officially my boyfriend in every sense of the word.

Except for the whole telling-people-about-it thing, because it ain't no one's damned business, quite frankly. What we have is so precious and special, I think even Bobby agrees that letting it out into the world is asking for Spruce to come and take it away from us and turn it into something else.

We don't want to be the next Billy and Tanner.

We don't want to be the big, scandalous Cody and Trey.

Bobby and I transcend every box Spruce and all its gossip-hungry hens would try to shove us into. We don't fit into a single one of them, anyway.

Plus, there's something special and powerful about what we have. It's beautiful, even in its secrecy. It's fun. It's exciting.

And it's all ours.

No one else's.

"I'm here to rehearse," Bobby announces, stepping into the garage with cute bravado.

Weeks have passed since that night when Bobby helped me lose my man-on-man virginity.

If that's what it's called.

I extend a hand toward him. "Let's see if you remember all the steps, then. Come here, boy."

"Boy?" Bobby snorts, then struts right up to me and grips my hand with surprising strength. "You better recognize who your *man* is when you see him, Jimmy Strong. I ain't no *boy*."

He snaps into position in front of me, arms locked where they belong, hands clasped to mine.

I smirk knowingly into his eyes. "Alright. Then prove it."

The music kicks on.

Five, six, seven, eight ...

And our dance begins.

Of course, we've been doing more than just rehearsing these past few weeks. Bobby and I have engaged in several productive and important tasks.

Such as secret rendezvous in my bedroom for "studying".

And in the barn for "discussing foot technique".

And out in the woods for ... well, I forgot our excuse for then.

Whatever the reason is, I'm shameless enough to admit that they're all flat-out lies. The simple truth is: Bobby and I can't keep our fucking hands off each other.

The last stroke of music plays, and Bobby and I stop in place, posed, our fierce gazes locked on one another's.

Bobby cracks a smile.

I do, too.

Ten minutes later, we're in my bedroom with the door shut and locked.

Another ten minutes later, we're naked.

Give another ten, the dirty pair of us have made another mess on the bed and our bodies are drenched in sweat.

This is our lives now.

"Are you sure I'm enough for you?" he asks me.

It's around eleven at night, several nights later, and we have climbed out of my window to sit on the small awning of roof that stretches out from beneath it. My mama *despises* when I climb out onto the roof, but she isn't home now, and I'm feeling especially high on cloud nine tonight with Bobby at my side to care.

I turn my face to his. My arm is around his back, holding him against my side in a lazy cuddle. "Enough?"

"I mean, like ..." He lets out half a laugh before he finishes: "Well, you still have feelings for girls, right? Like, you find them attractive, right?"

"Well, yeah. I mean, when I think about them, sure."

"So I was just wondering if ... well ..." He blushes. "I feel dumb. To ask it. I just ..."

I rub his shoulder with the hand I've got around him. "Bobby, let me say a few things. First off, I haven't identified as bisexual for very long, and I'm still not sure if that's the right word or not. Also, I just really don't care."

"Yes, we established that," he agrees with another chuckle.

"Second, yes, I still think girls are hot. I wasn't lyin' to myself about that. Only about what my feelings for guys really were."

"Right, 'cause you thought 'all guys feel this way'."

I give him a look. "You make me sound so dumb when you put it that way."

Bobby lets out a booming laugh that touches the stars and makes the moon itself tremble. "I'm really just turnin' your words right around and saying them back to you."

I shrug. "Anyway, guys or girls, it doesn't matter. I think what you're really askin' is, if I like both, can I possibly be satisfied with just you. Right?"

"Right."

I put a peck on his cheek and his forehead before getting a good, firm look into his eyes. "Does it look like I'm satisfied?"

He's fighting a blush. "Yeah."

"Do I seem like a head-over-heels dude who'd go to any length to keep you happy?"

"Yes. Okay, you've made your point," he decides.

"Not yet I haven't." Then I push him down flat—as flat as one can be on a slanted roof—and tackle his mouth with mine. Bobby's response is a deep-throated groan of approval.

We're so filthy.

Really, our secrecy is about protecting *Spruce* from *us*.

And this obscene, kissy-kissy grossness that the once-pair-of-best-buddies-we-were have since devolved to.

And I couldn't be fucking happier.

The secret is so much fun to keep, too. Especially every time we meet for breakfast in the kitchen with my mama and Jacky-Ann, and we share private, knowing looks across the table.

Especially when my mama asks something like, "Did you catch a lizard in your room last night or somethin'? I heard some loud, strange noises through the walls. And a bunch of thumpin'! I was just certain it was a lizard you'd caught that'd gotten into the house. You used to *love* catchin' them lizards. Was it a lizard?"

Bobby and I couldn't look at each other; we couldn't keep a straight face otherwise.

"Yeah, mama," I answer her. "A big ol' lizard."

A big lizard down Bobby's throat.

A big lizard up Bobby's butt.

We're sure huntin' big, scary lizards, alright.

Sometimes Billy and Tanner join us for breakfast or lunch or dinner, and then it's an even bigger game of keep-the-secret when they ask how our dance rehearsing is coming along. Bobby and I will share one of our knowing looks, then I'll coyly say something like, "There is a lot of sweating and sore muscles involved," while Bobby tries not to laugh.

We're impossible.

But as fun as it is to play mind games with my family, the real special moments are between me and Bobby, and they come when we are all by ourselves in the safety of my room or his—whether it's on the Strong ranch, or cozy in the bedroom of his house out in Spruce's east suburbs. The nights are always peaceful, summer breeze playing against the windows and through the branches of the trees outside. And Bobby's in my arms like always, cuddled against my chest on his bed or mine, two warm bodies, our hearts beating and speaking a language of their own to each other, and the enraptured pair of us whisper sweet things into the darkness of whoever's bedroom.

Things like: *"Jimmy, I love you."*

And I'll say: *"Bobby, you're so dang good to me."*

And he'll go: "*Jimmy, I'm so glad you took a shower, 'cause after all our dance rehearsing, you stank so bad.*"

Then I'll kick him for that.

He'll shove me back.

Then our squirming bodies become aroused from the simple movement, his butt against my crotch, or my butt against his, and our tightly spooning quarters becomes a problem.

A problem resolved by removing our shirts.

And our pants.

And underwear.

One thing leads to another—and *dot, dot, dot.*

We're not just lust-filled horny animals all the time, despite how I might be making it seem. He keeps me absolutely calm when I would normally be stressed out over choreographing a dance for this big Spruce Ball thing. In fact, he makes it so fucking fun that I'm looking forward to showing off our skills to the whole town.

And whenever he finishes a long shift at that movie theater— *where he seems to be dealing with more stress than he tells me about, from the look of it, but I don't press him*—I get him back into a relaxed state by taking him out for dinner at some local place, blowing off steam at the arcade with a few games, or just whisking him off somewhere to gaze at the sunset and chat about nothing.

In no time, I'll have Bobby smiling again.

No matter the shitty customers he likely dealt with.

Or the stress of Mr. Lemon and his mounting list of demands and expectations out of his new totally-underpaid Bobby.

Or that asshole Anthony Myers, who I don't trust for shit.

And sometimes, even despite being advised against this, I go up to the theater whenever he works a late night shift and watch the last showing of whatever movie, not caring what it is, even if I've already seen it six and a half times. I sweet-talked the box office girl, so I don't even get a ticket most of the time. I'll sit in that theater, chow down on some popcorn, and then stick around afterwards to hang with Bobby up in the projector hall where I totally don't belong. And since we've figured out which days Mr. Lemon leaves early, the misbehaving pair of us will kick back, or mess around, or just be a pair of idiots until two in the morning.

"Y'know," I tell him one night as we're sitting in the bed of my truck outside the theater after one of his closing shifts, "I *did* say I was swearin' off girls this summer."

Bobby already finds the humor in that, chuckling. "You did."

"I'm a man of my word, aren't I?"

He looks at me, tired eyes and all. "I can always count on you to make me feel better no matter what, Jimmy."

I lift an eyebrow. "Feel better?"

He shakes his head. It appears he let that particular wording slip out unintentionally. "After a hard day at work, I mean."

I nod slowly, but study him skeptically. "Is there something goin' on at work that you ain't tellin' me, Bobby? Is Mr. Lemon treatin' you right? You looked stressed when I first showed up."

Bobby plays it off with a flick of his hand. "I'm always stressed at my job. It's ... well, my job, after all."

"You sure?"

He makes a movement, as if he's about to kiss me right here on the bed of my truck, on the curb in front of the theater, in front of whoever's possibly out here on the Spruce streets at two in the morning. Then he thinks better of it and settles with a pat on my thigh and a hearty, "Yeah, Jimmy, I'm sure. Just job stress."

"Just job stress." I nod. "Alright."

I privately decide I'll come back to that subject later.

Later that same night, I'm holding Bobby in my arms, it's well past three, we're in his bedroom, and neither of us can sleep.

"Jimmy? You still awake?"

I'm playing big spoon, and he's the little spoon, so I speak to the back of his head. "Yeah, Bobs, I am."

He squirms a bit under the covers to get more comfy, which presses his cute gym-short-wearing butt into my crotch. *If he does that a few more times, we'll be up all night fucking, I just know it.*

"I just wanted to say that you make me happy."

"I know. You make me happy, too."

"You think things will change when we go back to campus?"

"Nah. In fact, they'll be better," I insist to him. "We'll be back in our own dorm. Just us. Hey, we can push our beds together."

"Really?"

"Yeah, make ourselves a big ol' bed. Might have to move one of the desks down a bit to fit them, but ... we'll make it work."

"What'll your friends say when they hang out in our room and find the beds pushed together? Are we ..." Bobby frets. "Are we ... gonna have to come out to everyone? Are you ready for that?"

"I'm ready for anything." I kiss the back of his head, then give his chest a rub with my hand. "Anything for you."

"Mmm." Just that moan indicates Bobby's smile. "You sure?"

He squirms again, grinding his ass deeper into my crotch.

I growl. "I'm *sure* your ass is askin' for some action tonight."

"Is it?" he asks tauntingly, then squirms again.

I flip him over at once. My lips are on his, and the night is lost to our fevered kisses, sweaty bed sheets, and greedy hands.

21

BOBBY

It's the middle of another hot summer night when I open my eyes. We must have separated at some point, like we usually do on account of his overly-sweaty body and the summer heat. Jimmy's busy on the other side of his bed snoring lightly, wearing nothing but a pair of tighty whities—and looking downright adorable with his mouth hanging half open in his slumber. I'm on the other end with an arm dangling limply over the edge, just one innocent roll away from falling clean off the bed.

I'm super thirsty from sweating so much, so I sleepily climb to my feet, pull on my pair of loose gym shorts that rest on the floor in a balled-up clump next to Jimmy's, then slip out of his bedroom.

I don't make it to the kitchen.

Voices from downstairs stop me. I hear Billy asking Tanner where his ma keeps the brown sugar, then the noise of drawers and cupboards opening and shutting. I didn't check the time, but surely it has to be after midnight. Despite being sleepy, I figure it couldn't hurt to be a little social and see if I can help.

Until I hear the words: "But I don't think it should be Bobby."

I stop halfway down the stairs, my hand on the railing, a foot reaching for the next step, now frozen in place.

The words came from Billy.

"Why not?" asks Tanner. "He's been rehearsin' every damned day with my brother."

"Yeah, but ..." Billy lets out a sigh. Some container is set down I can't see, the kitchen (and both its occupants) not fully in view. "You've gotta think about presentation here. The McPhersons—"

"Billy, do you even hear yourself?"

"I do! But think about how it'll look when your brother—who is a *real* dancer—does a little 'for fun' jig with his best friend. Now imagine that you're an investor, or one of the McPhersons' rich friends, or a couple of snobs from Fairview or Brookfield who are coming. Are you going to donate a bunch of money on account of two dudes—one a dancer, one not—doing some awkward show?"

"Well ..."

"I just think Jimmy should be doing his big number with an actual dancer. An actual *trained* dancer. Camille Randall should be his partner. She still dances, Tanner, and she's still in town."

Tanner lets out a sigh. "Maybe that is the whole point. We're raising money to keep the arts in the schools, right? What better way to showcase the effect of studying the arts than to have a choreographed number by a dancer and a non-dancer? It gives it style! Flair! Character!"

"I don't agree. I know these snobs, even more so than your ma knows them," Billy argues, "and they will want top-notch. If they don't get it, they're gonna think, 'Why do I want to support some medium-caliber school?' They're *snobs*, Tanner. They don't think like you and I do."

After a cold silence passes, I hear Tanner take two slow steps toward him. "Billy, I love you. But the only person who sounds like a snob right now is you."

A scoff hisses its way out of the kitchen. "Tanner ..."

I listen to the side door open, then close. Billy's feet shuffle on the kitchen tiles as he paces. A cupboard is shut, then I hear Billy mumble, "This should be enough brown sugar for a proper apple crumble," before the side doors open and shut once more.

Silence finds my ears, thick and empty. I slowly lower my ass on that step halfway down the staircase and stare at my feet.

Is Billy right?

Am I just kidding myself with this whole Jimmy dance number ...?

What if I'm not all that great? What if Jimmy is just indulging me? What if I'm hurting the cause by keeping this up with Jimmy, and he's just too nice (or excited to be dancing with me) that he doesn't want to hurt my feelings?

I return to Jimmy's room without a drink, then lie back down on the bed, feeling defeated and unsure. Jimmy continues to softly snore at my side, blissfully unaware of my emotional state. I stare up at the ceiling, my eyes unfocused, lost.

It's a bad night to get no sleep.

Especially considering that I work an early shift at the theater tomorrow.

Before I know it, I open my eyes to sunlight. I slowly blink the sleep out of my eyes, then notice Jimmy's arm over my chest. He's turned over in his sleep and now half-cuddles me in a lazy sort of sprawled-out-across-the-bed way. After a deep yawn, I take a look at my phone on the nightstand.

My shift starts in eleven minutes.

"Fuck!" I shout out, thrown into a sudden panic as I toss Jimmy's arm off my body and hop out of bed to get dressed. "Wake up, Jimmy! I need to get to work in ten minutes! Fuck, where did I put my suspenders??"

I'm searching under different piles of crap in his big room as he slowly starts to stir from his sleep, groaning and grunting and sniffing loudly. "The fuck ...?" he moans. "What time ...? Mmph ..."

"Jimmy, I'm gonna be late!"

This performance of panic and freaking-out continues for well over ten minutes. Twenty, in fact. It isn't until nearly a half hour after my shift has started that Jimmy finally pulls up to the theater in his truck with a sweaty, frantic-faced me in the passenger seat.

"I'll be back to pick you up at—" Jimmy starts.

I slam the door halfway through his sentence, rushing into the theater to clock in as quickly as I can.

Of course, Anthony Myers is working today, and he is all too eager to taunt me from behind his wide concession stand fortress. "Ooh, boy. You're late. Mr. Lemon is *not* happy. Not one bit."

My heartbeat plays angry music on my eardrums as I burst into the employee break room, punch in for work, then hurry to grab a broom and dustpan from the usher's closet and join Vince or G-man or whoever's working this morning with me.

The day does not improve.

"Dude, did you not take out the front trashcan from the first auditorium we cleaned?" asks Vince just minutes before my lunch break. "It was completely full and Mr. Lemon just bitched me out."

I slap my forehead, confused. "I swear I did, but—"

Vince sighs. "Where is your head at, Bobby?"

"I'll go take out the trash," I tell him. "I just forgot, that's all."

"I already emptied it. Seriously, Bobby, you are in a totally ..." Vince shakes his head. "... *totally weird* place these past few weeks."

We're standing in front of the door to the break room, our brooms and dustpans in hand. I stare at him with a lost expression on my face, exhausted to my core, and utterly sleep-deprived. It's difficult to even form my own sentences, let alone decode Vince's.

"I've not been *weird*," I argue back, annoyed.

And then comes another opinion this already uncomfortable confrontation totally doesn't need: "Yeah, you have been."

My ears practically flatten like a cat's when I turn to face the smarmy face of Anthony Myers. "No one asked you," I retort to him, my tone as civil as I can possibly manage.

Anthony puts himself right between me and Vince, leaning against the break room door. "Mr. Lemon knows all about Jimmy's late-night hanging out with you in the projectionist booth during your closing shifts."

I sigh, then glance back and forth between them. "Really, do you guys have somethin' you need to say to me? Just say it."

Vince, despite having literally nothing nice to say about Mr. Asshole Myers here ever, nods at him. "Well, Anthony said it. You aren't supposed to bring friends up into the booth. I think Jimmy is makin' you lose focus on your job. He's distracting you. You're forgetting some of your basic duties, and—"

"Vince, I already said sorry about forgetting the trash."

"It isn't just the trash," he goes on. "You keep compacting the trash wrong on your closing shifts—always when Jimmy's here distracting you—and then I gotta—"

I gape incredulously. "There's only one dang way to do it! You shove the trash in and press a button!"

"You gotta hold the button down for at least fifteen seconds," he corrects me tiredly, visibly exercising an amount of patience, "otherwise it can stop in the middle of its compacting cycle, which makes *my* job in the morning that much harder when I show up for work and find the compactor stuck halfway through its cycle."

"Hell, even *I* know that," Anthony throws in.

I shoot Anthony a withering glare. It isn't lost on me what's really going on here. I take a step toward him. "Y'know what? I think the issue here isn't my work ethic, or whether I'm holding a damned button for fifteen seconds."

"Oh, here we go," mutters Vince, slapping a big hand to his forehead with a sigh, all too used to the bickering and pissing matches between me and Anthony.

"The issue," I finish, "is that you have some personal problem with me, Anthony Myers."

Vince eyes me. "C'mon, Bobby. Let's not do this right now."

I take another step toward Anthony, ignoring Vince. "You've been on me since day one, and I don't know why, other than Jimmy got over it pretty fast when his prom date ditched him for you, and stole your thunder by asking me to prom instead."

"I don't ... W-What?" Anthony laughs off my words. "What in the hell you talkin' about, Parker? Prom was forever ago."

"Exactly, yet you can't seem to let it go," I retort. "You have been antagonizing me since I was hired here, and for no reason other than you're just a dick." I spread my hands challengingly, putting myself in Anthony's face now. "So what's your problem with me? Just say it and let's get this feud over with."

Vince puts a hand on my shoulder. "Hey, man, it isn't that big a deal about the trash, I'm sorry, I should've just—"

I swat his hand right off my shoulder. "Yeah, obviously it is."

Vince sighs. "Look, can we just finish our duties for the day after you take your break? I didn't mean to make a big deal out of it, I was just letting you know about the trash you forgot in—"

"Obviously you *do* want to make a big deal out of it," I argue back, my temper lost, "because you're siding with Anthony Myers here, who—"

"Wait, wait, no, no," Vince starts, lifting his hands in defense.

Anthony's in my face again. "Hey, don't start goin' off on him just because *you're* the one who can't do your job properly."

"I do my job just *fine*," I spit back.

"Yeah, whenever you bother to show up here on-time," says Anthony. "Or maybe because you're Mr. Lemon's little pet, you think you've got some kinda right to show up to work whenever you want? Do whatever you want? Your fancy ass is so west-coast now, living away from Spruce for so long—you *and* your boyfriend Jimmy—I don't think you even belong here anymore."

For a second, I have to catch myself.

Boyfriend, he said.

But he doesn't know, I remind myself. *He's just being an asshole. He doesn't know. The secret isn't out. Calm down.*

I'm a single breath away from losing my shit and putting my fast-tightening fist right into Anthony Myer's round, flushed, self-important face. I really could do it. I could do it and just be over with all of this for good. I'm quite sure I wouldn't feel an ounce of remorse, either, even if I broke the fucker's jaw. Hell, I might even feel complete and total satisfaction.

Instead, I take one deep, steeling breath and channel some kind of magical fucking nirvana inside me to calm down.

Ignoring Anthony completely, I face Vince. "I'm really sorry for missin' the trash. And I'll keep an eye on the compactor from now on. Fifteen seconds. Heck, I'll even hold the thing for twenty."

Vince gives me a tightened but appreciative smile. "Fifteen will do," he mutters back.

I nod, feeling like the situation is handled and, frankly, being damned impressed with my own patience and maturity. I don't need to mend any fences or right things with Anthony. That boy is a lost cause anyway and isn't worth the trouble. Just another month or so and I'll be back at South Wood anyway. Even sooner if Jimmy wants to make an early departure like we did last summer. *But only after the Spruce Ball, of course,* I tell myself privately, feeling a renewed sense of peace return to me after my chaotic morning.

I gesture at the break room door. "Mind if I clock out for a quick break, buddy?"

Vince steps out of the way with a smile. "Of course, man."

I ignore the noise of Anthony scoffing as I pass by them, enter the break room (which is more of a closet, really), then clock out and proceed to kick back in a creaky plastic chair by a bucket of soapy mop water, all by myself.

After taking another deep breath, I whip out my phone and start to text Jimmy a quick greeting to see what he's up to.

Then I stop.

Suddenly it's the middle of the night and I'm hearing Billy and Tanner talking not-so-privately in the kitchen of the main house.

All over again, worry and doubt and unrest swirl around in my chest.

I've been going nonstop since I woke up, raced to work late, and dove straight into my duties. I forgot about what I overheard

Billy telling his husband Tanner at nothing-o'clock in the middle of the night from the kitchen.

That it shouldn't be me partnering with Jimmy for the dance.

That it should be someone more qualified.

Someone like Camille Randall.

"Don't listen to him," I tell myself. "He doesn't realize what's goin' on between you. You can't blame him. He doesn't know. If he knew, then all of this would be different."

Would it, though?

Maybe it makes better sense that two professional dancers with years of training ought to lead the Spruce Ball with a number that's both polished and impressive. That's more likely to open up wallets than a couple of buddies having fun on a stage.

My face flushes with a whole new wave of insecurity.

I was never a dancer. I'm clumsy when I'm not kicking around a soccer ball. I don't understand grace; I understand scoring goals.

I sigh, then stare at my half-written text to Jimmy.

Gnashing my thumb, I slowly delete the letters one at a time, then replace them with something else:

ME

Maybe you should do the dance with Camille.

Within seconds, I get the notification that he's already seen the text. Then I watch him type, stop typing, type, stop typing, and finally there's nothing.

I frown, curious what the struggle is about.

Then my phone starts to ring.

I answer it. "Jimmy?"

"What the actual fuckin' fuck is that question about??" Jimmy blurts out at once.

"I didn't ask a question. I made a statement."

"Fuck that. I'm doin' the dance with you. No one else."

"Yeah, but—"

"What's got you sayin' this? Something is makin' you say this bullshit to me. This isn't you."

"I mean ..." Billy's words start coming right out of my mouth. "Wouldn't it be better to have two *actual* dancers doing the dance? We're tryin' to raise money here for the schools, and—"

"Did you have a cruddy day at work or somethin'? Is Anthony treatin' you right?"

Strange, how his mind goes straight to Anthony. "Well, after arriving late, it's been a bit of a stressful day, but—"

"He's being an asshole to you? Really? How long has this been going on?"

I wouldn't say Jimmy has a telepathic way to kind of fish these things right out of my head, but that's exactly what the boy does. "Anthony ... is a difficult person to work with, yes. But that isn't the reason I feel this way."

"What is Anthony saying or doing? I'll kick his ass."

"No, you won't. I actually want to keep my job, thank you."

"So tell me what's going on."

"Nothing is, Jimmy! I just—"

"Bobby, something is wrong with you."

I glare at the floor, losing my patience. "I'm perfectly fine."

"You're perfectly not. I can tell when you're hiding somethin' from me, Bobby. I've known you forever. Is it me?"

That throws me off. "You? What?"

"Yes, me. Did I do somethin' wrong, man? Are you mad 'cause I forgot to set an alarm last night? You're doin' the dance with me, Bobby, and that's fuckin' final. It's just two weeks away. We don't have time to deal with a little stage fright or whatever this is."

I sigh and lean forward, propping my elbows on my knees and dropping my head between my knees, tired. "See, Jimmy? It's always gotta be your way or no way. I have a valid point here."

"No, you don't. You're just being weird, or chickening out, or someone said somethin' to you."

"No one said anything to me."

"It was Anthony, wasn't it. It was that fucker."

"Jimmy ..."

He's already made up his mind suddenly. "I'm gonna go inside and deal with that fucker once and for all. He's been a thorn in my ass since senior year. He and Jazzy fuckin' deserve each other."

"Jimmy ... Wait, a sec. Go inside? You're here?"

"Right out front. Was gonna see a movie. Bored as fuck at my house. Now I got somethin' more important to do."

"Jimmy, don't, wait, stop. What are you gonna—?"

He's already hung up.

I stare at my phone, wide-eyed. I glance up at the back of the closed break room door.

Then I hear Jimmy shout in the lobby.

My stomach drops through the floor.

I'm out of my chair and pushing the door open to find Jimmy standing in front of the concession counter—having pushed his way in front of a line of customers—putting his face in front of Anthony Myers.

"What'd you say to him??" Jimmy demands.

Anthony, decked out in his concession apron, hat, and bowtie, lifts his hands innocently. "Didn't say nothin' to your *boyfriend*."

That word sets Jimmy off. "What did you just call him?" A lady at the front of the line says, "*Excuse me*," but Jimmy ignores her, keeping himself right there in Anthony's face. "I asked, what the fuck did you just call him?"

"I'm trying to help some hungry and thirsty customers here, if you don't mind. Step aside, dancer boy." Anthony lifts his blunt eyebrows at the lady next in line. "Hello, ma'am. Welcome to the Spruce Cinema 5. Can I get you a large popcorn and a—?"

"We're not done!" shouts Jimmy, beating a fist on the counter.

I push myself out of the break room, despite the spinning of horror in my stomach at this scene, and put myself between the two of them. "Guys, c'mon."

"What did you just call him?" Jimmy won't give in. "Don't for a second think this concession counter is enough to keep me from beatin' that smart-ass look off your face, Myers!"

Anthony turns to me. "Bobby, would you mind escorting your lost puppy-dog here out of the building? I'm pretty sure Spruce Cinema 5 enforces a strict *no-pets-allowed* policy."

And then a series of nightmares happen very fast.

The second Jimmy lunges across the counter, I'm blocking him with half my body. A large cup of soda gets knocked by my elbow, flinging its contents across the front of Anthony's apron. The woman in front shrieks and backs away, trips over her son's foot, and falls flat on her back. Jimmy, oblivious, keeps trying to throw himself over the counter, hands outreached to grab Anthony by the *anything*. Anthony, in his reflex of backing away, bumps against the loose popcorn machine tray, dislodging it and sending an avalanche of perfectly-made popcorn cascading down to the grimy floor, emptying the whole damned machine.

Pandemonium in a matter of two and a half seconds.

And I'm still trying to hold Jimmy back from adding an assault charge to his nonexistent record.

"The fuck you call him??" Jimmy's still screaming, demanding an answer, scrambling to climb over the counter, completely set off. "The fuck you just call him??"

It's the Jimmy Strong show. In this episode, he seeks a totally unasked-for vengeance for his best friend being called exactly what I thought he was supposed to be:

His boyfriend.

"The fuck you just—??" Jimmy screams, reaching out.

And elbows me square in the nose.

I fling backwards, abandoning my hold on Jimmy to bring both hands to my nose, which stings something awful. I'm struck instantly by a simultaneous and urgent need to sneeze and cry and scream at the same time, and none of those three things happen—except maybe an inevitable bit of reflexive just-got-hit-in-the-nose tears escaping my eyes.

Behind my scrunched-shut eyelids, I hear the commotion stop right away. "Bobby?" comes Jimmy's voice, soft and worried.

"I'm fine," I say, not even sure if it's true. "I'm fine."

"Bobby, fuck, you're bleeding."

"I'm fine." I'm not even sure if I'm facing him anymore, totally blind, my vision blurred by tears every time I try to open my eyes.

"Mr. Parker," comes the drawling voice of my manager Mr. Lemon, appearing at my ear so suddenly, I jump. "Please go to my office. Mr. Strong, if you would kindly leave the theater, I—"

"It wasn't his fault," Jimmy blurts at once. "I was ... Anthony and I were ... I was just—"

"Mr. Strong, please leave. Mr. Myers, a fresh batch of popcorn please. I'm sorry, ladies and gentlemen, for the disturbance." His voice is right in my ear again. "Mr. Parker, please go upstairs and wait for me in my office. I have a fallen customer to assist."

Still cradling my nose, I back away from the scene and make way for the stairwell leading up to the projectionist booth and the office, amidst the tune of Jimmy still protesting: "None of this was Bobby's fault. This wasn't his fault. I'm leaving, alright? I'm going. But Anthony started this, and—Are you listening to me? It wasn't Bobby's fault! It was that fucker, him, that arrogant-faced fucker behind the concession stand. I'm going, I'm going, I said I was going, and I'm going!"

And so am I.

The noise of the lobby shuts when the door at my back does.

Up the stairs, I go.

By the time I'm seated in the one chair in front of Mr. Lemon's desk, my nose is weirdly numb and cold, and it feels like I have a big shard of stone caught in it somehow, like a dumb toddler at the beach who keeps pushing sand granules up his nose for no good reason. Everything's still blurry. The office is eerily silent. All I hear is my own pulse beating in my ears—*thump, thump, thump.* Unable to breathe properly through my nose, I just sit there dumbly, mouth open as I drag in one slow breath at a time. I stare at the back of Mr. Lemon's last-generation Mac, a wormy brain of cables and fat wires and Ethernet cords coming out its back.

I'm totally numb, even in my mind.

I taste blood on my upper lip.

Jimmy didn't mean to hurt me, I remind myself, even though it's a strangely difficult concept to swallow at this point in time. *He was blind with rage and was trying to hurt Anthony.*

I sniffle once.

It sounds gross and clogged and clumpy.

He didn't mean to hurt me.

There's a buzz in my pocket. I pull out my phone and give the screen a glance.

JIMMY
Dude I'm sorry. I'm in my truck. Don't let them blame U. It was that A-HOLE'S fault.

I stare down at the text awhile.

Suddenly a spot of red appears right in the middle of his text.

Oh, it's blood that dripped from my nose.

I grab a tissue from a box on Mr. Lemon's desk, wipe the drop off my phone, then gently apply the tissue to my sore, sensitive nose with an open-mouthed grimace.

The office door opens behind me.

I twist around in my chair to face Mr. Lemon as he comes in. "I'm sorry," I say at once. "Jimmy and Anthony have had this very aggressive rivalry thing ever since—"

"I know. Everyone does. How is your nose?"

"It's ..." I dab a bit more with the tissue and inspect it. "Almost stopped bleeding."

"Here." Mr. Lemon reaches on a high shelf and pulls down a small first aid kit, pops it open, and sets it down. While he leans on the front of his desk, he starts to treat my nose as best as he can.

After a few cotton swabs and a small one-hit-wonder of me hissing and wincing, Mr. Lemon sighs and says, "You'll probably want to make a quick trip to the clinic, just to make sure it isn't broken. I don't think it is, but that's just my opinion. I would still—"

"Am I fired, Mr. Lemon?"

He sighs, then folds his hands in his lap. He doesn't say a word for a while, studying the floor, gathering his words.

I say some first. "I swear, I'm doing my best. I'll tell him not to come here anymore. He and Anthony, they got into a fight about me, and it was stupid and petty, and—"

"I'm sorry, Mr. Parker, but ..." He shrugs, then finally decides to face me. "Some jobs, they just aren't for everyone. Some people don't fit every role. Some of us are better built for one thing or the other. I just don't think this work environment suits you anymore. Maybe next summer, you should consider looking for—"

"W-Wait. I *am* being fired?"

"—a job as a coach of one of the soccer teams at Spruce Park," he finishes anyway. "They're always looking for coaches."

"But that's volunteer," I protest. Tears are coming back to my eyes, but I'm not sure it has anything to do with my nose. "Those coaching positions don't pay. I need money, Mr. Lemon. My ma, my pa, they're depending on me. I need—"

"I'm sorry, Mr. Parker. There's ..." He sighs. This is all taking a lot of effort for him to say. "There's a strict no-violence-in-the-workplace policy I must abide by, and—"

"Then Anthony ought to be fired, too!"

"I'm afraid he wasn't the aggressor here."

I'm out of my seat at once. "This isn't fair! Mr. Lemon, he—"

"Mr. Strong almost threw himself over the counter first."

"Mr. Lemon ..."

"I saw it all on the security camera. I'm sorry, Mr. Parker. I've tolerated the Strong boy's frequent presence here for quite some time—all summer, really—but we've reached a point now where his presence is affecting my business."

"But it wasn't *me* who started the fight. I was just—"

"I'm sorry, Mr. Parker. I have to let you go."

I break eye contact with him, staring down at the box of tissues and the opened first aid kit on the desk, mouth agape, at a total loss of what to say or do.

Maybe there is nothing to say.

Maybe there is nothing to do.

"I'm sorry, Bobby," he murmurs softly.

Somehow, his use of my first name for once elicits a stronger emotional reaction than any other thing right now. As my eyes try to fill up with more tears, a deep and heavy breath draws into my lungs, then escapes right out in a jagged and disheartened exhale.

I lick my lips.

I can still taste blood.

Despite the ball of unsettled emotion in me, I make myself be cordial. "Thanks, Mr. Lemon," I tell him, then proceed to remove my suspenders, bowtie, and name badge. I place all three items on the desk. "I'll drop off the rest of my uniform in the morning."

"No rush. I'll give you a good reference, Mr. Parker."

He reaches to shake my hand.

I take it, then smile past my veil of tears and the pain still ringing in my numb, cold nose full of blood.

When I pass through the lobby on my way out, I don't give the concession stand even as much as a glance. I don't know whether

Anthony is still there, or if Vince took over for him, or if there's a fucking pink English-speaking pterodactyl serving popcorn now.

It's none of my business anymore.

Jimmy's truck sits down the street some ways, almost pulled up onto the curb. I give it a pained look from a distance.

Nothing feels good right now. Nothing at all.

One small turn of events has sent my whole day into a dark, downward spiral. I'm too emotionally exhausted to walk all the way home, and my face is hurting worse by the second.

I pull out my phone and make a call.

My ma answers in her lofty, gentle voice. "Sweetheart?"

"Are you busy? Can you give me a ride home, Ma?"

"Ooh, your shift ended early? Too hot outside today to walk?"

I don't have the heart to give her the story right now. "Yeah."

"And Jimmy's not comin' to get you?"

I glance down the road at the back of his truck. "Not today."

"Mmm, okay, sweetheart. I'll be there in a few."

From the hesitant sound of her voice, I can tell my ma knows something's wrong, but she isn't prying just yet. She'll wait until we're home before she starts fishing.

After we hang up, I plop down right there on the curb, then hug my knees to my chest. The shade from the building at this hour covers me from the harsh sunlight. I stare ahead at the road, catching a gust of wind from the vehicles that whiz right on by.

"Why aren't you answerin' my texts?"

I glance up to find Jimmy standing there.

I shake my head and return my gaze to the pavement. "You can go home," I tell him without looking his way. "I'm gettin' a ride from my ma. She's on the way."

"What?"

His voice has softened, like suddenly he's the one who's been wounded. I continue to hug my knees to my chest while staring off blankly at the road.

He sits down on the curb next to me, his shoulder touching mine. "Bobs, please don't tell me they fired you."

"Alright, I won't. Mr. Lemon simply sent me home for the day, and also maybe I won't come back to work again for the rest of the summer, whatever's left of it."

Jimmy drops his head between his knees and grips the back of his neck. "Aw, no, man, no, no, no. This is my fault. No. Fuck."

"Well, no one's arguin' that." I look away.

I feel his attention on me suddenly. "Bobby, I didn't mean for this to happen. Anthony was being an asshole."

"I know. This may be a shocker, but he's been a douche to me all summer long."

"Why didn't you tell me??"

"Because I can keep my cool. And you clearly can't."

"But he called you my—" Jimmy takes a frustrated breath, and his voice goes soft again. "I mean, you *are* my boyfriend, but he said it in a way that, like ... meant somethin' else."

"I know. I was there." I'm still not looking at him. "You could have kept your cool anyway."

"Look, I'm sorry. I'm really, really sorry. I feel awful. This is all my fault. Me and my ego, right?" Jimmy scoffs at himself. "Me and my stupid, big, fat ego ruining everything."

"And I was serious earlier."

"What?"

I finally turn my eyes onto him. "You should do your dance at the Ball with Camille as your partner. Not me."

His whole face collapses. "Bobs, no."

"It just makes better sense."

"And I told you I'm not gonna do that. We've been rehearsin' so hard, and for weeks! You deserve to be up there with me!"

"Jimmy, you *left* a sport to pursue dance. I was a soccer player since the start. Hell, small town obsessions with sports is half the reason we *need* fundraising for the arts. I belong on a soccer field, not a dance floor. It makes total sense that you do the dance with Camille, *not* with me."

"This isn't about the dance anymore, is it?" The wounded look in Jimmy's eyes is almost too much to bear. "You're just afraid to be thrown into the spotlight again with me. Just like Prom, back in the day. You remember your very first reaction, right after I asked you in front of the soccer team? You were *angry* at me. You *hated* the attention. I had to talk you into actually goin' with me at all!"

"Jimmy, that isn't the same."

"It is! It's exactly the same! You're just afraid, Bobby Parker."

"I just lost my job, Jimmy. I lost my fucking job. I was countin' on this money to help my parents out and pay for my tuition. Now what do I got?" I spread my hands, empty. "Nothin' but a bloody fuckin' nose, that's what."

"Bobs ..."

My ma's car pulls up in front of us.

I rise up off the curb. With Jimmy shouting, "Bobby, c'mon," at my back, I slip right into the passenger seat of my ma's car and pull shut the door, cutting off Jimmy's protests.

My ma's eyes go wide. "Sweetheart, your nose!"

"Just drive," I beg her.

22

JIMMY

He isn't answering my calls.

Or my texts.

What the fuck have I done?

"Seriously, Bobby. I'm so sorry. I was a fuckin' idiot, I made a huge mistake, I lost my temper," I bleat into the phone, leaving him my tenth or twentieth or thirtieth voicemail of the week.

It's been a week since that horrible day at the movie theater.

Worst day of my life, which started the worst week of my life.

My voicemails start to feel like I'm shouting fruitlessly down a well hoping for someone to shout back. But the only thing that comes back are my desperate echoes.

"Please, Bobby. Call me back. I'm dyin' here, man."

My mama keeps checking up on me. I keep ignoring all her questions, even when she corners me at every meal. After a few days, she finally realizes I'm in no mood for her meddling, and has since mercifully backed off. Now the two of us eat in an awkward silence, punctuated now and then by a totally superfluous story my mama tells about her day, which I barely listen to.

I spend shit loads of time in chairs just staring at shit. The walls of my room. The ripples of water in the swimming pool. The distant trees on the edge of our property, swaying in the summer breeze. Clouds in the sky. Wind chimes on the back patio.

My own stupid face in the mirror, staring back at me stupidly.

"You're such a fuckin' idiot, Jimmy Strong," I tell that stupid reflection in the stupid mirror.

Why can't he just respond to a simple text, even if he's totally pissed with me?

He's never done this before. Even that time when I might've been the reason an ex of his dumped him freshman year. (He was no good for him anyway.) Or another time when I made him late to one of his midterms. Actually, that happened twice.

Still, Bobby always comes around, or forgives me, or at the very least answers a goddamned text.

I must've really fucked up this time.

Obviously my mama has made a few presumptions about my friendship with Bobby (or has been talking to Mrs. Parker) and then went and told Tanner and Billy, because one morning I find the pair of them joining us for breakfast, and Billy goes, "I don't mean to be insensitive, but if you and Bobby aren't talkin', then does that mean you're doin' a *solo* now for the Spruce Ball, or—?"

I don't have a proper answer for him.

Even days later, when I peer at the calendar and realize it's just one fucking week until the Spruce Ball.

In my last-minute desperation, I finally suck it up and drive out to his house. I come right around the house to the back door—not the front, since no one who means anything or isn't a solicitor or Girl Scout Cookie Pusher comes to the front door—and I knock until Mrs. Parker's sweet face is hovering in front of mine. She has this pained grimace on her face that breaks my heart when she says, "I'm sorry, Jimmy, sweetheart, but Bobby just isn't feeling well and isn't up for visitors."

"Please," I beg her. "I'm his best friend. I'm not just a visitor. Bobby!" I call, peeking around her and into the house, for a second foregoing my manners in an act of desperation. "C'mon, man! I said I'm sorry! Bobby, just come talk to me!"

She comes out of the house and closes the door behind her. "I know you care about him, Jimmy. You love him more than anyone else in all of Spruce. I know you do. But—"

"You're darned right I do!" Then I remember my manners. "I mean, y-yes, I do, Mrs. Parker, ma'am," I add more meekly.

"He's hurt about losing his job, but he's also ... confused about his ... you know ..." She leans in and, in a scandalous whisper, adds: "*about his feelings for you.*"

"Confused?" I stare at her, worried. "How is he confused?"

"You've got to give him some time, sweetie."

"This isn't fair. This is all that f—" I swallow a curse word. My mama raised me right. "This is all *Anthony Myers'* fault. Did you know he's been mean to Bobby all summer at that movie theater? And then he goes and starts a fight with me in the lobby, and I'm *up to here* with that moron, and then—"

"Jimmy." She puts her hands on my shoulders. "I don't blame you one bit for standin' up for my boy. I don't. You're so brave and ... *valorous*. I just think ..." Then comes the pained grimace again. "Perhaps this time it just went a step too far."

"A step too far?"

"Just give him time, Jimmy. He needs time."

For a second, I'm fighting tears. Then another bolt of rage runs up to my head, causing me to consider literally racing around to his window and banging on it. Then I feel defeated and sad and wanting to drop on the dusty ground.

I close my eyes, take a breath, then slowly nod.

Mrs. Parker's arms envelop me. "You're a good boy, Jimmy Strong," she says as she hugs me. "You're a good, good boy."

And that's how I leave Bobby Parker's house, being sweetly consoled by his mama to the sound of their cat Delilah meowing from between her legs, watching me with giant, curious eyes.

I spend the afternoon in the arcade playing *Mortal Kombat II* for hours trying to reclaim my high score, once again, from some "T-BOY" kid who keeps proving himself better than me.

Another hour later, I'm back home, sulking on my living room couch with the TV playing who-the-fuck-knows while I just stare ahead at the fireplace we use one month out of the year.

I don't know what to do with myself.

Maybe I should just take his mama's advice and give him time.

"You alright, bro?"

The question comes from my brother, who's come into the main house for some reason or another. I don't even answer him, my arms folded, my body sunk halfway into the couch, my ratty red-and-white hat sitting so low on my forehead, the thing covers half of my face.

He sits on the couch next to me. I feel his arm come around my back, where he starts to pat and rub my shoulder.

"Heard what happened at the theater a few days ago."

I sigh. "It was over a week ago."

"Everyone's talkin' about it."

"Let them talk. I don't care."

"Did you really punch Anthony Myers in the face so hard, he lost three teeth?"

I roll my eyes. "Sounds like the Spruce Game Of Telephone is already expert-level this summer. You just believe what you want to about what I did or didn't do to Anthony fuckin' Myers."

"I heard it was over a fight about Jazzy. You still into her?"

My face wrinkles right up. I stare at my brother hard. "What the fuck kind of rumors you listenin' to lately?"

"The kind I get from my colleagues at the school. And Coach Larry, who's worse about gossip than our own mama."

"He won't talk to me."

Tanner lifts an eyebrow my way. It takes him a second or two to realize who I'm talking about. "Bobby?"

"I got him fired. All because of my stupid temper, and the way Anthony was lookin' at me, and all the shit Bobby's probably had to put up with ... all on account of a stupid grudge Anthony's got with me, apparently." I huff and cross my arms even tighter across my chest. "I just feel so ..."

The words escape me. Then all the fight in me escapes, too. My arms slacken over my chest, drooping with defeat.

I close my eyes, exhausted.

I'm running out of anger.

It's so much effort to stay mad.

And when I can't be angry anymore, only one other emotion rushes in, and it's the last one I want to feel right now.

"You feel so ... what?" prods my brother.

I slowly shake my head, overwhelmed. Then a strange sort of gasping starts to happen in the back of my throat.

My eyes begin to sting.

Fuck, don't tell me I'm crying.

"Jimmy ..." comes my brother's voice softly, confirming it.

"I d-d-don't know what the fuck to do." *Why am I letting myself cry in front of him?* This is so embarrassing. "I f-fucked up. And I've told him sorry a thousand times, but he won't listen, and he won't t-t-talk to me, and now what in the *FUCK* am I s-s-supposed to do about the Spruce Ball?? We're the entertainment!"

Tanner's hand presses to my back and starts rubbing. "Don't worry, bro. There's a bunch of other things that can occupy the guests' attention. The Spruce drama department is doing a thing. They're auctioning off a bunch of nature paintings done by the afterschool art program. Even the elementary school is involved. The dance is the least of your concerns, bro."

"B-B-But it was gonna be *our* thing!" I sound like a blubbering toddler whose toy just got taken away. "Bobby and me! And I just fuckin' ..." I bury my face in my hands, losing all composure and sobbing into my palms. "*I ruined it.*"

His arm slides all the way around me, then holds me close to him in a side-hug. Soon, my own sobs drown out anything my big brother might be saying. Every one of my limbs are limp. My lungs are crushed inward. My stomach aches with emotion. My head is a mess of despair.

Then, through all of that noise, my brother's words touch me: "You gotta tell me what's *really* goin' on here."

I swallow my sobs. I blink until my eyes are clear, and then all I see is the floor of the living room.

"There *is* somethin' else goin' on, right?" my brother asks.

Suddenly, I'm not making any sounds. I'm holding my breath.

"Between you and Bobby, right?" He nudges me. "He and you have been sneakin' around all summer, holed up in your room, off doin' this and that all the time. You're not into drugs, are ya?"

I frown. "You know me better."

"Yeah, I usually do, but not lately. You can tell me whatever it is," he assures me. "And whatever the heck you tell me, you know I won't go tellin' mama or papa. I didn't tell her when you were flunkin' calculus, trustin' you'd pick your grade right up. Or when you and what's-his-name broke the barn door your junior year. Or all those nights you'd sneak out to hang with your friends at the arcade. We got a bro code, remember? It's sacred."

Bro code.

Sacred.

"I ..." My voice comes out in a nasally croak. I clear my throat. "I don't even know if ... if I know what it is, yet. Or if I can even put it into words."

"You sure?"

My whole body's tightened up.

Why am I so petrified to say it? Where did all my confidence from this past month go?

I feel so fucking broken.

He hugs me from the side again, rubs my back, then gives it a firm, meat-slapping smack. "I won't push you. You can come to me when you're ready. But don't try to do all of this alone, Jimmy. You have so many people who care about you." He gives me a light and playful smack over the back of my head. "So don't live in that head of yours and sulk for the rest of the summer, alright? It doesn't have to be me, but talk to someone, alright?"

I give him a feeble, wordless nod.

After another moment of empty hugging, my brother lets me be on the couch. I listen to the clattery noise of him fussing with something in the kitchen, probably fetching something for Billy in the main house like they always do, before finally he departs with a, "I'm just a call or a short walk away, bro."

My phone's in my hand suddenly. I stare down at its blank screen, and the countless unanswered texts, and the countless unanswered voicemails I've left Bobby.

I shut my eyes, lean back on the couch, and fall the fuck to sleep right there.

When I open my eyes, I don't know what hour it is, but the whole house is dark, even the kitchen, and there's a blanket over me. I guess my mama must've found me snoring here and laid the soft, fuzzy red thing over me. There isn't a sound in the house, not even a murmur or a whisper or a creak of a floorboard.

My mind is so numb and I'm so exhausted from my emotions, I don't even feel anything anymore. I'm one of those shells lying on the beach that just whistles hollowly when the wind blows, all sandblasted and shiny from the lazy ocean lapping at it.

I push the blanket off of me, rise from the couch, and march across the room.

And straight to the hardwood flooring area of the garage.

In front of the mirror, a ghost of whatever I was a week ago stands there in clothes he's worn for two days straight. The poor guy probably smells bad. Actually, I'm sure of it. He looks tired and dejected and sad.

I face the mirror boldly, despite all of that.

Then I toss my phone onto a nearby workout bench, tap its face to make my music play, and I start to work.

If it won't be a smashing partner piece with Bobby, then it'll be the best knockout solo Spruce has ever seen.

Five, six, seven, eight ...

I pop an elbow in the air, kick a foot, twist my body, and move with the jagged rhythm. Whenever I expect to clasp my partner's hand, I just turn it into a stylish maneuver with my fists.

But in seconds, the music has me picturing his face.

All the times he'd laugh when I grabbed him by the hips and yanked him against me at one point in the song.

Every stank-face he would give the mirror at another part of the music when the beat kicks in.

Then I stop dancing and am just staring blankly at myself, the music still playing.

I need a new song, I realize. *This whole thing is Bobby. It's all just Bobby, Bobby, Bobby.*

The door from the garage to the house opens suddenly.

I look up at it, startled.

Camille's face emerges. Her pretty eyes meet mine, glowing from the subtle purple eye shadow she's wearing. She's in a pair of super-short denim cut-offs and a loose, purple Nirvana tank. A sideways black cap squishes down her short dark hair.

She quirks an eyebrow at me. "Seriously, do you guys *ever* lock your doors here? Literally anyone could just walk right in."

I stare at her. "Camille ...?"

She saunters over to the mirror, gives her hat an adjustment, then peers down at my phone, which still blasts the music. Then she looks up at me. "Is this your song for your dance thing?"

"Was." I cast my eyes down to it as well.

"It's a good song." She starts bobbing her head to it.

I look at her. "What're you doin' here, Camille?"

"Your brother's hubby Billy called me an hour or two ago. He said you might need my help. Something about you losing your partner without any notice right before the big dance." She eyes me. "Sounds familiar, doesn't it?"

I drop my gaze to the floor.

"It's prom all over again," murmurs Camille, sauntering closer to the mirror to inspect something on her shirt—a bit of fuzz or a loose thread.

Even her walking is graceful, like she's crossing some grand stage, toes pointed, legs moving like she's made of air, even if it's just the hardwood dancing area of my garage she's walking on.

Camille peers back at me over her shoulder. "Of course, you can continue doing what I suspect you're busy doing—turning your big piece into a solo act—or ... if you're willing ... I can be your partner instead."

I consider her offer with heavy, dry eyes, even if every inch of my brain aches and doesn't feel capable of such consideration.

My chest is still as crushed in as it was before.

My spirit is broken.

"Alright," I decide flatly, soullessly, uncaring. "I'll go through the piece with you."

Camille crosses her arms, then nods at me and offers a soft, understanding smile. "I'm a quick learner."

Then begins a two-hour session of rehearsing at whatever-o'clock on a don't-even-know-what-day-of-the-week-it-is night.

I don't know what Billy told her. Does she know Bobby and I had a falling out? Does she know how shitty I've felt the past few weeks? Does she know anything at all, or everything?

It doesn't matter. Camille Randall is mercifully asking me zero questions about it.

She doesn't even shoot me any skeptical looks, like my mama does every morning at breakfast.

She doesn't ask me if I'm okay.

Hell, she doesn't even try to hug me, or squeeze my shoulder reassuringly, or give me a wink of encouragement.

In just a matter of hours rehearsing with Camille, I feel more comfortable and at home than I've felt in weeks. I won't say I'm laughing and cracking jokes and feeling confident, but at least I don't feel scrutinized and interrogated and prodded at. In fact, I feel downright *secondary* to the piece Camille and I are working on.

Even after we've had enough, Camille simply helps herself to some water from a pitcher in the kitchen, then tells me she'll be back tomorrow, and with a casual wave, she's off.

Afternoon the next day, Camille's back, just as promised, and we dive right back into work.

For days, we rehearse. We break for a meal here and there. It's especially entertaining on Wednesday when my mama has Jacky-Ann make us some lunch after a particularly exhausting morning of hard-hitting, leg-punishing rehearsal. The entire time that Camille and I eat, my mama is staring at us from across the table, her eyes jumping back and forth, like she's trying to work out some kind of story between us without asking a single question.

Afterwards, when we're back to dancing in the garage, right after completing a series of pirouettes that end in arabesque (which Camille added for flair), she holds the pose and peers at me over her shoulder to say, "I think your mom thinks we're fucking."

And then I let out the first laugh I've had in weeks.

That's followed soon by Camille laughing herself, collapsing from her arabesque to join me in my laughter. We shed tears from laughing so hard.

Rehearsal continues well into the afternoon. We only take one more break to discuss a potential idea near the end which involves me dancing out into the thick of the audience, then letting her charge toward me and lifting her up *Dirty Dancing* style, which we quickly nix with a laugh.

We stop dancing when the music ends for the sixty-third time today. Then, we're both left staring at each other, standing at opposite ends of the mirrors, ten feet of bare hardwood flooring stretching between us.

Both of us are out of breath.

The air in the garage is warm and humid from our efforts.

And then, amidst the gentle noise of either of us drawing slow breaths into our lungs, Camille lifts her chin my way and quietly asks, "Still haven't heard from him, huh?"

My face slowly collapses.

"I can see it so clearly in your eyes. I think I could always see it, even before I moved to Europe, before graduation, before prom, before everything happened." She tilts her head. "You and I both know the truth."

Camille slowly begins to close the distance between us with one of her graceful, toe-pointed, ballerina saunters. She stops in front of me, her bright and beautiful eyes sparkling as she peers into mine. Then she cradles my face gently with her hands, and brings her lips right up to my ear.

And she whispers: *"You know in your heart I'm not the partner you're supposed to be dancing with, Jimmy Strong."*

23

BOBBY

"I don't want to go."

My ma, all dressed up in her pretty blue gown that matches my pa's fancy blue suit, sighs outside of my closed bedroom door. "Bobby, sweetie ..."

"My stomach's still aching. I'm not up for seein' everybody in all of Spruce." I roll over on my bed, hugging my pillow. "C'mon, Ma, you're literally inviting *torture* onto me by making me go."

"Nonsense." I hear her fussing with her dress. "If you don't go, then I'll end up not going, and then this pretty dress I got will go to waste, and—"

"You should go." I bury my face. "*Just go*," I moan, my words muffled underneath my pillow.

I hear my door open.

My bed shudders and squeaks when she sits on its edge.

"*Ma* ..." I groan.

"Sweetheart."

"I thought I locked the door."

"Is this about you seein' Jimmy?" she asks softly and sweetly.

I throw my pillow off my face. It lands halfway across the room on my beanbag chair. "This has *nothin'* to do with Jimmy."

"What else could it be? That silly Anthony boy? Mr. Lemon? He doesn't hold anything against you, sweetheart. He just had to follow company protocol. He could lose his job otherwise."

"Yet *Anthony* is still happily scooping popcorn there. Yeah, sure, policy this and policy that, but we both know certain people are immune to all that." I fold my arms over my chest with a huff.

My ma leans over me, putting her face above mine. "I might be softhearted sometimes, but I'm not dense. I know what's going on has *everything* to do with Jimmy Strong."

"Ma, don't."

"You love him. And he loves you."

"Ma ..."

"Didn't I teach you forgiveness? He's sorry. He's said so about a zillion times." She starts gently running her hand through my hair. "I hate to see you so unhappy, sweetheart. Why can't you just forgive the poor boy and let it all just be in the past?"

"Because he isn't any good for me, Ma!"

She sputters in disbelief. "Jimmy's all kinds of good for you! You're so happy when you're around him! What in the heck are you talkin' about, sweetheart??"

"Me and Jimmy are a fantasy." I sit up and turn my harsh eyes onto my ma's aching, slowly-crumbling face. "He wants to keep the two of us a secret, and I have a good idea it's exactly what I've feared all along: He isn't really gay. He isn't really bi. He's simply ... entertaining some kind of bro-obsession with me. A straight-boy, buddy-buddy infatuation with his best friend. It turned into kisses and ..." My face flushes. "... more. But it isn't love. Not real love."

My ma shakes her head slowly, her eyes detached and looking for the truth between all of my words. "I ... I just don't understand. Bobby, I ... I ..."

"You know what happened at the movie theater, Ma, but you don't know why." I lean toward her, bringing her eyes to mine. "Jimmy tried to attack Anthony because Anthony called me his *boyfriend*. Right there in front of everyone. And Jimmy couldn't handle it. He took offense. He just ... lost his cool, just from that one little word."

She sighs. "Oh, poor Jimmy."

I stare at her. "Poor *Jimmy* ...??"

"It can't be easy for him, having to figure out his feelings for you in a place like Spruce where secrets don't live long lives." She takes my hand, startling me. "It might've hurt you, how he acted, but I say forgive him still. It doesn't mean he doesn't love you."

"He hasn't done anything to prove it," I say, "except freak out when some dumbass at the theater called me his boyfriend, then give me a bloody nose."

"What a romantic story to tell the kids someday," sings my ma in her wispy voice.

I frown at her. "This isn't a time for *jokes*, Ma."

"You know darn well I am *not* going to leave this room until I know you're going to get ready in your cute outfit that matches my dress perfectly. I am *not* going to this gosh-darned fancy-pancy *Ball* without my son at my side."

I eye her severely.

Then she smacks me on the arm. "Get up and shake off this moody mood you've had on you these past seventeen-somethin' days! Yes, I've been countin', but I might be off by one or two."

I rub my arm where she smacked me, surprised. I rarely see this side of my sweet, feathery-voiced ma. "What has gotten into you?? What happened to what you said to me last night, that I can take all the time I need to feel better?"

She shrugs. "Maybe the *Spruce sass* is rubbin' off on me." Then she gives my foot a squeeze and a shaking. "Or maybe I just can't stand to see my son unhappy for another day. You look so cute in blue, Bobby, my boy. Let's be pretty together, and show all of Spruce how the *Parkers* get up after being knocked down." She smiles warmly, then rises from my bed and sees herself out.

I sigh and stare ahead at my outfit hanging on the back of my closet door.

I'm wearing the same pair of soccer shorts and an oversized gray t-shirt I've been in for the past three days. I was completely committed to staying home tonight and watching reruns of whatever's playing on Adult Swim.

Then that reminds me of Jimmy at once.

And all the dumb shows he finds so funny.

His laughter is caught in my ears now.

I shut my eyes. *Forgive him.* My ma's sweet voice keeps circling around in my brain like a buzzard. *Forgive him.* But does forgiving him also mean continuing to suffer as his secret boyfriend? And for how long? *Forgive him,* I keep hearing, but what happens if Jimmy and I don't work out as boyfriends?

What's left? Can we go back to being just friends? Is that even possible after the things we've said and done?

I don't know.

But suddenly, I realize I need to be at the dumb Spruce Ball no matter how I feel.

I need to see Jimmy Strong.

First things first, however: I'm gonna need a shower.

A really, really long one.

An hour and a half later, the sun has fallen, the stars fill the sky, and the moonlight spills over our heads as my ma, my pa, and I make the long drive out to the McPherson's mansion. We park on a long curved driveway lit by paper lanterns. The wind is eerily still tonight, so all the trees look like creepy silhouettes pasted against the sky, not a single one of them swaying or moving. We walk a curved path leading up to the house, which is a glowing three-story beacon in the middle of the impenetrable darkness that is the woods surrounding it.

We're greeted at the door by TJ McPherson, the sixteen-year-old baby of the family who works at Billy's T&S Shoppe. It is clear that the boy is well-off from his stylish shoes to his crisp, tailored pants and smart, formfitting suit. His face, however, is cheery and welcoming as he invites us inside, happy to receive us.

The front doors open to a jaw-dropping spread of twin spiral staircases and a grand room that can only be described as a *lobby*, which leads further into the house. One branch takes you through a gallery of local artwork being (silently) auctioned off. Another leads you through a dining area with a gasp-worthy spread of food catered locally by various sponsors and restaurants.

We make our way for the annex, which opens to a very large outdoor spread of tables set in front of a great stage that's been erected in the yard.

It's a stage that Jimmy and I were supposed to perform on.

Right now, it appears members of the Spruce High orchestra are performing on it instead. A Mozart piece, I think. I'm not sure.

My heart grows twice as heavy as it was before, just looking at that stage.

"You okay, sweetheart?" asks my ma.

I'm not looking at her, my eyes glued to the stage and the scattered guests sitting and walking among the tables, mingling while the orchestra pours over their ears. "Yeah, I'm fine," I say emptily, my eyes as blank as pools.

I follow my parents to a table of catered T&S sweets where, at one end of it, we run into Nadine Strong herself. The tall woman wears the biggest, tightest, most-rehearsed smile in the world as she talks to Mrs. Cissy McPherson, both of them decked out in elegant gowns that look worth a whole semester of tuition for me.

The two women are having a light conversation with glasses of white wine dangling from their long, heavily-bejeweled fingers when we approach.

It is clear that Nadine has done a lot of speaking into mirrors preparing mentally and emotionally for the event tonight, since it was originally supposed to be at the Strong ranch, after all.

"Oh, some friendly faces!" Nadine lets out with delight, giving my ma a big hug. She then presents me and my parents to Cissy McPherson, who greets us and thanks us for coming. Some more pleasantries are made before Mrs. McPherson is pulled suddenly to attend to some other guests, then heads off to the party with an apology and a sweet-voiced goodbye to us.

When the woman is gone, a mask seems to drop right off of Nadine's face, and she looks relieved at once. "Oh, am I *so glad* to see you all here," she says, facing us. "Some *real* friends." She lets out a giggly, nervous, uncharacteristic laugh. "Oh, have y'all seen the art yet? The *paintings*, they're just *beautiful!*"

My ma's voice is just as buttery and soft as it always is. "Are you doing alright, Nadine? We haven't spoken since ... oh, was it church last week?"

"I think it was! And I'm just peachy, thanks for askin', doll."

My parents are approached by some friends from church, and their attention is stolen away with another conversation, leaving me and Nadine standing awkwardly at the dessert table together.

She gives me a reluctant glance, at last turning her eyes onto me—as if she was afraid of addressing me at all until now.

She offers a tiny, shriveled little smile. "Hello there, Bobby."

I'm certain she knows about the fight at the theater involving her son and Anthony, and how it resulted in my losing my job as well as giving me a black eye.

She has nothing at all to do with it, so I put her at ease at once with a warm, "Good evening, Nadine," and a welcoming smile.

It does the trick. The relief is instant. She leans in toward me and, under her breath, says, "If you ask me, I think Anthony Myers is a little shit, and it's *he* who should a' lost his dang job, not *you.*"

She reaches her bony hand out and gives my shoulder a rub. She's got twenty rings on those fingers of hers, and my shoulder feels every one of them.

I smile, despite my stomach spinning. "Thank you, Nadine."

"Don't thank me. It's just the plain truth. You know, so much has happened to me this summer, what with the Cold Spoon goin' under, and all the drama down at the restaurant ... it really makes one reevaluate what's important in life." She bites her lip, then peers off. "Billy has been a ... a *really* great man for Tanner. There was a time when I thought that football-kickin' son of mine would never be happy, y'know that? And now look at him."

I follow her line of sight and spot both of them, Billy and his husband Tanner, dressed up in fancy tuxes standing by the long table full of an assortment of decadent desserts. Billy is feeding Tanner something sweet and chocolaty, and the pair of them look lost in a dream, smiling into one another's eyes.

It pains me, to look at them.

I want to be happy for them. I want to see what Nadine sees. But all I see is what I've lost.

And it hurts.

"Maybe it's about time I let go of the past," Nadine decides. "I've wasted so much time competing with the McPhersons, or the Whitmans, or the ..." She sighs, unable to utter any more names of her alleged rivals. "Really, I ought to just set my eyes on important things. My sons. My husband. My friends. And ..." She nods with resolve. "And the future of *Nadine's*. The Cold Spoon has had its run, and it was a good, long run."

Billy across the room seems distracted by something, then peers our way suddenly, his eyes searching. He finds Nadine, then gives a meek little wave at her.

Nadine returns the wave, though her face looks a bit pained. "Mmm. Life is so funny sometimes, the way things work out." She crosses her arms, then turns her eyes onto me with importance. "You and Jimmy need to fix this thing between you. Him without you? You without him? It just ain't right, boy."

I'm stunned a bit by her sudden shift in topic. "Ma'am?"

"You heard the words I just said." She nods at me assertively. "Jimmy can do only so much with an apology. You also need to do your own part in fixin' things with him."

I clear my throat, then avert my eyes. "Mrs. Strong, I—"

"I won't hear it." She arches her eyebrows. "I *adore* havin' you in my son's life, Bobby. You give him so much happiness. Don't go takin' it all away, now."

I close my eyes. "Mrs. Strong, there's a lot more goin' on that you don't—"

"It's *Nadine*." She gives my cheek a pinch, startling me, then smiles. "Friends and family call me *Nadine*, sweetheart. You know that. Now eat a cherry tart and put a smile on that cute face a' yours, hon." Then, with a wink and a smack of something into my palm, the woman saunters her way around me and mingles among some other Spruce locals, like this is her own party.

I peer down at my hands.

One of Billy's famous cherry tarts from his T&S Shoppe sits on my palm, decorative, flaky, and sweet.

I take a bite from it.

Heaven.

Nadine made a few good points, but she's missing some key information. I can tell just from the way she spoke to me now. If she knew all that transpired between me and Jimmy, I think she would've picked a few other words to say.

I finish the tart by the time I make it back to the house, alone. The tart doesn't sit well in my stomach. I proceed to wander through its halls and exhibits, as my eyes scan the crowds of people around me. Several I recognize, but I don't bring any attention to myself, preferring to keep in my own head.

I don't see Jimmy anywhere.

Not that I'm looking for him. Or worried about him.

Or that the boy is actually the only thing I've been thinking about since we left the house.

Ugh, of course he's all I'm thinking about.

That is, until I turn a corner in the art gallery hall and, after spending a second to admire an awe-striking painting of a lake by a damned third grader (seriously, the talent among our youth here in Spruce is staggering), I find myself face-to-face with Anthony Myers himself, who stands before me awkwardly with a glass of champagne in his hand.

It's the first time I've seen him since the day I was fired.

My eyes flash, startled and scared and angry the second I see his round, stupid face.

Anthony makes a thousand and one thoughts in the space of a second before blurting out, "B-Bobby. Hi there. I ... I didn't expect to see you here. I thought—I, um—well, anyway, I wanted to say to you that—"

"I don't care what you've got to say to me," I cut him off coldly, "or to anyone for that matter."

"Bobby. W-Wait. Really, I was just gonna say I—"

"Save it." I make my way right around him, heading off to view the rest of the exhibit, despite the scramble of emotions that are now all stirred up in my chest just by seeing him.

The last thing I care about is what Anthony wants to say.

He's already said and done enough for a lifetime.

I find a bathroom, shove my way through the door, then shut it behind me with a sigh. My feet shuffle across the tile as I put myself in front of the mirror, then commence in a staring contest.

Solitude and peace envelop me.

The world is far away for now, where it belongs.

Is it really so awful an idea, to just forgive Jimmy, move on, and be his boyfriend again? Even if he hurts me again?

Would it be so bad to let him back in, so I can feel his arms around me again every night when I put myself to sleep?

I lift an arm tentatively to the mirror, then pop it in place, imitating that thing Jimmy always does. It's followed by another little maneuver he taught me, then by a few of the dance steps of our two-man routine we've been working on.

The moves make me smile.

Then I stop.

My arms drop to my sides.

My smile falters.

It's over, I remind myself.

In another twenty minutes, I'm sitting at a table off to the side with my parents. A few friends of my ma's from church are with us, too, but they mostly keep conversation with her, leaving me to stew by myself with my thoughts. I'm in the chair right against the edge of the covered pavilion area by an ornate thatch wall with wallflowers intertwined through it, so I feel pretty much invisible to everyone, which is exactly how I want to be right now.

As the orchestra finishes playing, the majority of the guests have made their way out to the atrium to take their seats. Soon, the crowd quiets, and Cissy and Tim McPherson come to the stage together to greet and thank everyone for coming to the Annual Spruce Ball Fundraiser for the Arts—which is a far longer official name than I remember it being before—then announce proudly how much money has been raised already. A round of applause crashes over the room.

"And now, a word from the director of the Arts program at Spruce High," announces Mr. Tim McPherson, and his name is lost to the applause that fills the room.

As the speeches and numbers and detailed figures continue to be announced, my gaze strays off to the rest of the sea of chairs. I feel strangely out-of-body as I watch everyone with their full and undivided attention glued to the stage.

This would be a lot more exciting with Jimmy at my side.

I mean, raising money for the arts is an amazing thing. But so is the idea of two best friends who, after strings of unsuccessful relationships and fruitless searching, find the greatest of loves in each other.

Isn't that something of a miracle in itself?

"And now for a special performance from an alumni from the Spruce High Dance Department," announces Cissy McPherson. She gestures toward the wings of the stage. "Jimmy Strong."

Applause ripples over the room.

I stay perfectly still as the applause is swallowed in the depths of my ears, which seem to have closed off the world as my eyes zero in on the young man who steps onto the stage. He's a vision in red. He wears a red and black button-up shirt undone a few buttons at the neck, showing off the top of his toned chest, and hugging his slender, V-shaped torso. He's got on a pair of tight dancer jeans, made from a fabric that's as flexible as a second skin, and shiny shoes on his feet. His hair is uncharacteristically swept up in a perfectly-styled light brown wave with spikes here and there for accent—or it's just one of those super cute Jimmy-Strong accidents that simply *happens*.

My heart breaks, melts, and is mended the instant I see him.

I miss him so fucking much.

The same music we had been rehearsing to for the past month plays over the loud speakers, but Jimmy doesn't take his position.

He marches across the stage and comes rights up to the center stage microphone, which a stagehand was about to take away.

Jimmy takes hold of it. "Good evenin', ladies and gentlemen. Please cut the music."

The music stops.

The audience look among themselves, confused, excited, and curious.

Jimmy takes a breath. His breath is broadcast to the whole room, his slow inhale, then his short and determined exhale. "One of Spruce's many charms is somethin' I think we take for granted too often. It's a charm you don't often find in a small town, I think some of you from Fairview or Brookfield or some other Texan towns might agree. It's what makes Spruce such a great place to live. It's the fact that we accept our friends and family for who they are, no matter the color of your skin, or your gender identity, or 'who you like to kiss', as my lovin' mama once put it."

The crowd titters with warm appreciation.

"But beyond that," Jimmy goes on, "this amazing town we live in also made an environment in which some small town boy who is the younger brother of a major football star can take dance class with a bunch of girls and not be judged for it."

Applause of approval mixed with a cheer here and there from some familiar voices—mostly Tanner and his friends Joel, Kirk, Harrison, Robby, and whoever else is out there in the crowd that I can't see—erupt across the pavilion.

Despite my mixture of emotions, I feel a pinch of pride for my Jimmy Strong.

"Now I know you're all expecting a dance from me, and you're gonna get one, I promise. But ..." He takes a deep breath, then flits his eyes over the room. "But I can't perform it without my proper dance partner."

With that, Jimmy hops right off the stage, ignoring the steps off to the side. And amidst the murmurs and whispers and stares of confusion from the crowd, Jimmy cuts straight through them, making a beeline through the tables and aisles.

I hold my breath.

Oh my God, he's coming right for my table.

Jimmy emerges from the neighboring aisle, now on the far edge of the pavilion, where he comes right on down toward me, a smart twinkle of confidence in his eye, and a knowing smirk on his lips. Every eye in the room follows him.

Including my own.

Jimmy stops in front of my table. His eyes fall on me, beautiful and brave and full of his boundless strength and confidence.

Then he says: "No one puts Bobby in the corner."

I stare at him. "You didn't just."

"I did." With a humored smirk, he extends a hand toward me. "You belong on the stage with me. You're the only partner I want. The only true one I have. Do this dang dance with me, will ya?"

I'm not ready.

I'm not confident.

I'm terrified out of my bones.

And I take Jimmy's hand anyway, putting all of my trust into him as I rise from my chair.

Jimmy keeps holding my hand as he takes me down the aisle. So many faces and eyes and stares and dropped jaws follow us the whole way there. So do the murmurs. And the whispers. And the gasps and glances and noises.

And then we're ascending the steps to the stage. Lights spill over me as I follow Jimmy right to the middle of the stage. The microphone has already been taken away. The crowd is starting to quiet down. Silence falls over the entire world.

All focus is on us.

Every bit of it. All of Spruce is watching.

Jimmy holds me in place, then takes my hand, and just like that, we're in position, ready for the music.

Jimmy looks into my eyes. "*Just like we rehearsed,*" he whispers to me. "*It's just you and me.*"

"*Jimmy ...*"

"*Yeah?*"

Something about his strength makes me find my own.

At once, I'm at ease.

Jimmy Strong. This is where I belong. This is who I belong with. This is where I begin and where I end.

The beat kicks in. Those first eight counts play where the pair of us stand perfectly still in our pose, hands in hands. We stare intensely into each other's eyes.

A smirk finds my lips. "*I'm not scared.*"

Jimmy's smirk mirrors my own. "*Let's dance.*"

Five, six, seven, eight ...

And then we dance.

He takes a step, leading the way, and I take my step.

Our bodies twist, I slide under his arm, then we're in position again, hips slammed together, our eyes fierce and focused.

Another beat hits.

Another foot slaps the stage with resolve.

Jimmy makes a move that's as light as air.

His elbow pops in place, opposite mine that mimics his own movement.

Every time we spin away from each other, our eyes lock right back on the other's, and we find home again in each other's arms, or hands, or another beat of the music.

There is no audience.

No parents.

No idiots at a movie theater.

No past. No mistakes. No worries. No sulking. No tears.

There's just Jimmy Strong. And there's just me.

And the music that carries the love-drunk pair of us away.

Four and a half minutes goes by a lot faster than I expected. And when Jimmy and I hit that final winning pose, I doubt either of us hear one bit of the whole audience exploding into riotous, screaming applause.

We don't even see them, either.

All we see is each other.

And through all that noise, Jimmy softly murmurs to me: "I love you, Bobby. I can't live without you in my life."

"Life isn't life without you in it, Jimmy," I say right back to his strong and striking face.

Then to everyone's surprise—including my own—Jimmy goes and swings my body right around, dips me with charismatic gusto, and presses his soft lips to mine, kissing me right in front of the whole goddamned world.

24

JIMMY

I doubt the town of Spruce was ready for that final unplanned move.

When we separate, new music is playing, and just as planned, the rest of the dance department floods the stage to take over the spotlight with a group number of their own. Even as they start dancing around us, Bobby and I stay right where we are, staring into each other's eyes.

Through the music, I ask him, "Are we alright?"

Bobby stares back into my eyes. Slowly, a smile spreads his face apart. "Yes," he answers. "Though, I gotta admit—"

"The kiss freaked you out."

"It was surprising," he admits, "but I think we might've just freaked out your ma more than anyone else."

"I got no idea how I'm gonna explain this to anyone." I tug on his hands. "Maybe we should step off the stage and let the girls have some of the spotlight, yeah?"

"Yes, please."

And hand-in-hand, I lead Bobby off the side of the stage.

But we don't go back into the crowd under the pavilion.

I take him off the stage the back way, and slip back into the house, which is mostly empty except for some caterers and hired servers who are cleaning up after guests who have left glasses and small plates of unfinished food here and there, as well as a few stray guests loitering around the food tables. Still gripping his hand, I take Bobby to the least populated room: the art exhibit, where just about all the paintings except one or two have little "SOLD" signs hung near them.

We stop under an unsold painting of a ranch with a sunrise breaking out behind a long line of distant trees. It has an uncanny resemblance to my house. *Maybe that's what it is.*

"What did we just do?" asks Bobby finally, wide-eyed.

I shrug. "I think I might've just come out to the whole fuckin' town, that's what I did."

"Yeah, I think you did!" agrees Bobby laughingly.

I break a smile, then kiss him again, silencing his laughs. His hands slip around my back, and I do the same, pulling his hips against mine and holding him close.

When we separate our faces, I give him a warm rub up and down his arms. "You look really, really good tonight."

Bobby smiles, then nods at me. "You're lookin' fairly dapper yourself, Mr. Strong."

"So what do you say? Are we ready to face the music?"

"I've been ready all night."

With that, we hold hands and head right on back to the noise of the pavilion, where everyone is mingling and chatting amongst themselves. I reckon a common question most—if not all—of the tables are asking is what the heck that kiss was "between the Parker and the Strong boy". Bobby and I pay no attention to it, caring instead to hang with our parents, who have gathered at a big table right by the wall where I found Bobby in the first place.

That's where we belong: among friends and family who don't buy into all the scandal and craziness of Spruce's gossipers.

Okay, maybe that's a bit naïve of me to say.

Did I forget whose son I am?

"What in the goose-lovin' hell??!" exclaims my mama when we first approach the table. She's trying to keep her voice down. It isn't working even a tiny little bit. "I've got two gay sons now? When were you gonna tell me?? Why am I bein' denied over and over again the opportunity for a fabulous comin' out party?? *Why do my sons hate me so friggin' much??*"

I have to hug and console my mama for several minutes and give her a hundred soothing, apologetic sentences before we're back to rights. Also, I set her straight about the fact that I'm not sure what exactly I am, but know I'm attracted to women *and* men.

Or maybe more accurately: women and *Bobby*.

Of course, Patricia has to brag (in her soft-voiced, sweet kind of way) that she knew way ahead of time about the pair of us, and is now so excited for the world to know, too. That seems to change my mama's tune, turning her from a caught-off-guard mess to a, "Well, I mean, of *course* I saw the signs, yes, I was quite sure, I just, I just didn't know *for sure*, yes," as she anxiously sips her wine.

Soon, people start to get braver and make their way over to our table to offer their congratulations on our performance. One woman in a purple dress says our dance inspired her to attend more dance recitals and shows at the school, even though her daughter graduated years ago. Another woman proudly tells us that she just donated an extra hundred dollars to a silent raffle after seeing our "impassioned dancing". There's a young man who approaches us and is especially impressed that Bobby isn't even a trained dancer, but "just a soccer player jock", in the young man's words. Bobby smiles especially brightly at that and thanks him, his face burning its usual shade of red when he's complimented.

At first, months ago, I had thought maybe Bobby and I were just doing a fun dance to help support the movement of working to keep the arts alive in the schools.

I had no idea how much our little performance would mean to so many people in Spruce. Husbands. Wives. Their inspired kids. Relatives. Teachers and administrators, and about everybody else.

And more importantly: to so many people *with full and heavy wallets—as well as full and heavy hearts.*

It's overwhelming.

Billy looks like he's hyperventilating when we encounter him by a tall vase of multicolored tulips. "We've raised over three times as much as we did last year, and the night's not even over." He wipes sweat off his forehead that's not even there, knocking a hand into the bowtie of his smart-looking tux on accident. "I have no idea how we managed this. We sold all the art. We got over two hundred more donations after y'all's dance alone. And now there's talk about rebuilding the decrepit Spruce High auditorium that's probably at least a century old. I ... I ..." He looks at us suddenly. "I haven't even had time to process what you guys did. Are you two an item now? Did I miss something? When did this happen?"

Bobby smiles, then gives him a shrug. "Under everybody's nose is probably the most accurate answer."

Billy lets out a nervous laugh. Then he studies Bobby as a deep thought circles in his brain. "I owe you an apology, Bobby ... but I don't even think you realize I owe it to you. I ..." He sighs. "I may have had some doubts about whether you could hold your own, especially with Jimmy as a partner. Boy was I wrong. Dead wrong." Suddenly Billy wraps up Bobby in a hug, then slaps his shoulders. "And I would say somethin' like, 'Hey, welcome to the family!' with regard to you and Jimmy, but you've basically already been a part of it for quite some time. I'm so proud of you. Both of you." Then he gives me a wink. "When Spruce High has its brand new auditorium, I wouldn't be surprised if they slap your name on it. *Strong*, that is," he adds quickly. "Not Jimmy. That'd be strange."

Billy isn't the only person to find us. While chatting with some girls from the dance department who find us and offer their congrats on our performance, one particularly special girl breaks through the crowd to offer her own words.

Camille.

Despite her grunge/punk look she's usually rocking, tonight she is absolutely radiant in a low-cut black satin gown that hugs her every curve. She wears some long black gloves that reach her elbows with jewels adorning them on the tops of the hands. It's a mixture of artwork and fashion, what she's wearing tonight.

She moves with grace when she approaches us, and all her focus is on Bobby. "I swear, Bobby, if I didn't already know better, I'd say you were a dance student already, training for months on that spectacularly moving piece you just performed."

Her words make Bobby smile. "Thanks, Camille. I appreciate that. It ... really means a lot, especially coming from someone as talented as you."

"Talented? Or do you mean clumsy and uncomfortable in this gown?" She rolls her eyes and picks at her gloves. "These things might look pretty, but they sure as pig shit aren't practical to wear while eating."

Some girls titter behind her, and Bobby lets out a full-on belly of laughter.

I shake my head, smiling appreciatively. "You can take the girl outta Spruce, but you'll never take the Spruce outta the girl."

Camille gives me a wink. Then, after a second's hesitation, she leans toward Bobby, bringing her lips right up to his ear. Words are whispered, and I watch Bobby smile.

She gives him a squeeze on his arm, shoots me one more sly and knowing look, then says, "Enjoy your success, boys. The whole town's got their eyes on you now." Then with a kind smile, she is off with the other dancers, who were apparently in the middle of speaking excitedly with her about what schools in Europe are like.

Like some kind of fairy of inspiration, Camille waltzed back into my life this summer, and much in the same way she came in, she saunters right out with that graceful stride of hers.

I turn to Bobby, curious. "What'd she whisper in your ear?"

Before he can answer, we're approached by someone else.

Someone who makes all of the muscles in my face and body stiffen with tension and anger.

Anthony Myers, in a white dress shirt with a loose vest over it, approaches the pair of us cautiously with his hands stuffed in the pockets of his slightly ill-fitting, tight gray slacks.

His head is bowed slightly when he addresses us. "Hey, Bobby. Hey, Jimmy."

Bobby doesn't say a word. He only stares the boy down like he could cut him into twenty-two pieces with his laser eyes.

I lift my chin. "Myers."

"I ..." Anthony clears his throat, shuffles his feet, then finally manages to say, "You both performed pretty amazingly. You guys, uh ..." He clears his throat again, sounds almost like he's gagging on nothing but air for a second, then resumes. "You guys should be really proud of your efforts."

Bobby rolls his eyes.

I take a protective step in front of Bobby. "If that's all you got to say to us," I start, "then I'll say thanks for your compliments, and you can head right on off now."

"That isn't all I got to say." Anthony straightens his back. "I'm also here to say I ... I-I'm sorry." His eyes shift nervously back and forth between me and Bobby. "About what happened."

"Sure ya are," grunts Bobby, not having a word of it.

"I am. I really am. In fact, I ..." Anthony swallows hard. "What I was tryin' to tell you earlier, Bobby, is that ... I had some words with Mr. Lemon. Some important words. I really, uh ... gave it a lot of thought. After that day. And I realized—"

"He means he went to *church*," Bobby sasses privately to me, which makes me smirk, amused.

"It *was* church that I went to," Anthony asserts, having heard Bobby's aside. "And Trey Arnold gave a sermon-thing on assumin' responsibility for the things we've done, even unconsciously, and that we should know that a secret is somethin' that eats you from the inside-out. And I realized I had a big ol' secret ..."

"*Aw shoot, Myers is about to come out to us,*" mumbles Bobby.

"My secret was that I *was* jealous of you two, all the attention you got, and how it made me and Jazzy look like these villainous creeps our senior year. I never got over it. And I used it against ya, Bobby, ever since you were hired. And I instigated the fightin' at the theater. And ain't none of it was right, and—" Anthony's eyes tear up suddenly, which sobers both Bobby *and* myself, our humor and jokes swallowed up. "And so I spoke to Mr. Lemon, and I told him the truth, and ... a-and I got let go instead."

Bobby's face wrinkles up. "Say what?"

"You got your job back if you want it," Anthony explains. "I'm outta there. And Jimmy, you aren't banned from the theater any longer. I took the blame, which I *shoulda* done in the first place." He bows his head even more, nearly showing us just the top of his messy head of hair. "And I'm sorry."

Bobby and I share a confused look. We don't say anything, our eyes doing all the talking.

Anthony glances up at us, as if to check if we're still there. Then a look of confusion clouds his face, too. "Wait. D-Didn't Mr. Lemon call you? He said he'd call you and offer you your job back."

Bobby bites his lip, then shoots a glance at me. "Actually, uh ... I kinda have been ignoring all my calls."

My eyes narrow.

Okay, that's fair, I reason with a shrug.

"Anyway," Anthony goes on, "I kinda realized, like, maybe the movie theater isn't for me, anyway. It was kinda holdin' me back from lookin' for a serious job I can advance in, you know?"

Bobby shrugs. "Well, you could have kept it up and run your own theater someday."

"Actually, I kinda always wanted to be a veterinarian. I saved up some money from the theater. So maybe I'll, like, go to school in the fall. I've been lookin' up programs." Anthony smiles with a faint glimmer of hope. "So, uh ... I guess also I, uh ... kinda want to thank you two as well. I'm sorry, and also thank you."

Bobby, to my surprise, is the first to extend a hand to Anthony Myers. His face is flat and emotionless, showing strength. "I accept your apology, Anthony, and I wish you well."

Anthony looks as stunned as I am right now when he accepts Bobby's hand, shaking it cautiously. "Thanks, man."

Then he faces me, a nervous glint in his eyes.

I smirk smartly, then extend my hand toward him. "You treat my man right, then you're alright with me."

Relief washes over Anthony's face so fast, I might've thought he just let loose a gallon of pee down his leg that he's been holding this whole time. "Thank you, Jimmy," he exclaims, taking my hand and shaking it.

"Actually, I ought to thank *you*, really," I throw back.

Anthony's face freezes. "Why?"

"Because if it wasn't for you stealin' my prom date, I'd never have found the real one I should've taken all along." I give Bobby a smart look, which warms his face at once.

Anthony tries to find that funny. The laugh he makes falters quickly, and then he hastily adds, "Your dancing was incredible. And I'm not just sayin' that. You. Bobby. Really, an inspiration."

"He's the inspiration," I say, turning my face to Bobby and giving my man a wink.

Bobby's face brightens with accomplishment.

And just like that, everything in my world is right again.

We spend the better part of another hour greeting people, thanking people, listening to congratulations and compliments, and holding each other's hands proudly. I've never in my life been more happy to have someone at my side than I am right now with Bobby Parker in front of the world of Spruce.

"And right there in the most silent part of the movie, the guy farted so dang loud," my brother's in the middle of saying when we approach, "it sounded like applause! Like ... quick, staccato applause. I literally stopped what I was doin' and looked around to see if someone had performed a dance or made a toast."

I don't know what that's in reference to, but after a burst of laughter from his crowd of former football buddies and new ones, my brother Tanner faces me for the first time since the dance, and his eyes are alight with pride. The pride turns into emotion. And then he's nearly in tears when the big brute hugs me tight.

"Bro, if I'd known ..."

"Known what?" I blurt, muffled against his shoulder. "That I was in love with my best friend? Hell, I didn't even know until my heart near burst to flame when I kissed him this summer."

Tanner pulls away and gives me a teary-eyed look that could be him crying or laughing hysterically, I can't tell. "Nah, bro. I meant I would have given you the name of a better gay bar instead of the crappy one I sent you both to." Then he guffaws heartily and slams me back into him for a hug. "G'damn, and to think of all the boobs Mama found on your phone over the years ..."

"*Tanner, you're suffocatin' me,*" I groan against him, red-faced.

He lets go of me, fusses with my hair, then goes in for a much gentler hug with Bobby. "Take care of him, will ya?" he tells him loud enough for me to hear. "My little brother Jimmy here's the most high-maintenance guy I know—" "*Am not!*" I interject feebly. "—and I happen to know a *lot* of high-maintenance guys, so you've got your work cut out for ya."

Bobby laughs, then gives my brother an assured nod. "I'll take great care of him, don't you worry."

Tanner throws an arm over Bobby's back, taking him off to talk to him about who-knows. I cross my arms and watch them, feeling completely out of my own body right now.

How quickly everything changes, just from letting out a little secret from my heart.

I realize now after having come out that I care a whole lot less about what people think of me than I thought I would. Maybe it's part of my privilege of living in a place like Spruce that gives me such confidence. In other places in the world, it isn't as safe to come out. In some places, it isn't safe at all.

I wish the whole world could embrace people for just being themselves like this special place does, and the only thing you get judged for is wearing last season's shoes to a party.

I peek down at my own.

Nah, mine are in the clear.

"J-Jimmy, sir?"

I glance behind me, startled. The person who stands there is a young fellow, a teenager, maybe sixteen or so—TJ McPherson's age. He's got a baby face, a cute upturned nose, and big eyes. He's pretty slender, too—a total swimmer's build—and cheeks that look permanently flushed. He's in a fitted dress shirt and slacks, and his light brown hair is flipped up in the front.

"You look familiar," I tell him, thinking on it suddenly. "Have I seen you at Biggie's before?"

"I work there. I-I'm new there. My name's Toby. I just wanted to say that I really liked yours and Bobby Parker's dance. It was ..." His eyes flash with a thousand dreams and hopes and wishes. "It was really ... uh, *sharp*."

"Sharp?" I smirk. "You hopin' to be a dancer someday, Toby?"

"Not really. I mean, it's cool and all, but ... I think my thing is painting. I really like to paint." He smiles nervously. "You and ... and Bobby did a great thing today. It gives me hope."

At once, it clicks in place.

My mama mentioned a kid at school who's getting bullied, a kid who just came out as gay and was just hired at Biggie's Bites. *Didn't she mention his name was Toby, too?*

I give Toby a reassuring pat on his shoulder. "Thanks, Toby. I appreciate that. Y'know, the secret to findin' yourself is to just be strong, trust your own mind and heart, and ..."

I peer off at wherever Tanner has taken my Bobby off to. My heart feels tickled suddenly, like I worry I'll never feel happier than I do this day.

Then I finish: "... and when you make a friend, you *stick* with that friend 'til the end."

Toby's eyes light up. "A friend ..."

I give his head much the same kind of fussing that my big bro gives me, feeling suddenly like an older brother to this budding, goodhearted teenager. "Stay strong, Toby. Your friends are your home away from home, no matter where you are."

That's exactly what Bobby is to me.

And it's what he'll be forever, no matter where our future takes us.

It isn't much longer before Bobby and I are together again and peering out over the pavilion full of happy and inspired faces.

"Ready to sneak outta here?" I ask Bobby, squeezing his hand.

He turns to me. "I thought you'd never ask."

Hand-in-hand, we scurry out the back of the pavilion and make our way up the long curved driveway to my truck for one last adventure to end our night.

25

BOBBY

The stars pour over our bodies.

We lie side-by-side on a pile of soft blankets in the bed of Jimmy's truck, right on the outskirts of the Spruce woods.

"You ever wonder why this town's called Spruce?"

I chuckle lightly at his question, my eyes lost among scattered constellations. "Not once, ever."

"I mean, spruce trees are more common in the north."

"I can't even tell ya what a spruce tree looks like," I admit.

He relaxes against me, his head resting on my chest, and my own resting atop his head. His hair smells so clean and inviting.

Then he goes and asks, "What did Camille whisper to you?"

I don't recall what he's asking at first. "Huh?"

"Camille. She leaned into you and whispered something just before she left. What'd she whisper?"

A smirk finds my lips as I hear her whispering in my ear all over again. I kiss the top of Jimmy's head, then reply, "Ah, nothin' much. Just that I need to take care of you." I bite my lip. "And that I was the perfect guy ... up for the job."

"Job? What job?"

"Of taming *the* Jimmy Strong."

"Taming? I don't need no tamin'. I ain't a wild animal." Jimmy chuckles lightly to himself, amused. Then, after a spell of thought, he whispers, "*So ... do you forgive me finally, then?*"

The tight squeeze of my arms around his body is my answer.

He smiles against my chest, relieved at once, and for the first time in weeks, I think the both of us feel whole again.

Then he adds, "*You danced like a fuckin' star out there, Bobs.*"

"Only 'cause I had you as a partner."

He lifts his head off my chest and gives me a kiss, then he leans back and peers into my eyes in wonder.

I tilt my head. "Can you do me a favor?"

"Anything."

"Promise me that you'll work on this *it's-the-Jimmy-Strong-Show* spotlight complex of yours?"

He bites his lip, considering it. "Well ..."

"Haven't I proven I can stand up for myself?" I give Jimmy a tough, challenging look. "You might be a Strong by name, but I'm strong in my own way, too. And if we're gonna do this ..."

"Do this?"

"Us. You and I. If we're going to make this work, I need to know that I can trust you'll let me handle my own situations, and that you'll control your temper. Y'know, as my ..." I catch myself smirking. "*Protector.*"

Cuddled up on the bed of this truck with Jimmy in my arms, my world's perfect again. I know Jimmy will do whatever it takes to make me happy.

And I'll do the same for him, so help me.

"I'll try to be the best version of myself for ya," he tells me, then tilts his head cutely into mine, "but my rambunctious ass can't promise I won't mess up now and then. I've got a tendency to get hotheaded. Or run my mouth. Or say the wrong thing."

"More than a tendency," I sass at him.

He chuckles, gives it a second's thought, then sits up to get a good, strong look at my face. His pretty brown eyes turn sincere. "But if there's one thing I *can* promise, it's this."

He runs a hand down the side of my face, then lets it settle at my chin where he gives it a soft, loving pinch.

I smile into his eyes, adoring him utterly, and listening to his words with all my heart.

"You'll always have someone to run to when shit get tough," he says. "You will always have a good, reliable fella to hold in the night when you're feelin' lonely and just plain need a warm body to snuggle right up against. Bobby Parker, you will always— *always*—have a special guy in your life who adores you for every fuckin' part of you—good, bad, and everythin' in-between."

Warmth rushes through my body by his words alone.

I've never felt more fucking complete than I do right now in this little moment under the stars, with nothing but the whispers of distant trees touching our ears.

And Jimmy's sweet, loving words.

I take his hand into mine, pulling it from my chin, then gaze into his eyes. "Jimmy," I say, then cock my head. "What '*bad*' parts of me are you talkin' about exactly ...?"

The hint of a grin plays on his crooked lips. "What we're 'bout to do on the bed of this here truck out in the middle a' nowhere."

I bring a hand to his chest, feeling his heartbeat.

It's fast.

My lips are caught by Jimmy's so quickly, I hardly see the kiss coming. Then my eyes close, and I'm drifting among the stars as he takes me away with the strength of his kiss.

His hands find the buttons of my shirt, opening it up.

My fingers find his belt, and off that comes, along with his pants, and just about everything else.

Out here in the middle of nowhere, under the night sky, with nothing for company but the trees and the playful breeze and the wild animals.

A pair of wild, untamable animals, indeed.

And when Jimmy and I make love tonight, it's clear to me that there is something absolutely eternal about the special thing we have between us, something everlasting, something undeniably fateful. It's as if every star in the night sky above us has been waiting patiently for these two silly small-town boys to finally end up together in this vast, unknowable universe.

Well, them stars up there sure don't have to wait any longer.

EPILOGUE

JIMMY

The ceremony is long and unseasonably blazing hot.

Especially in these dumb gowns we gotta wear.

Bobby Parker sure looks cute as hell in his, though. Long blue cloak like a wizard. Square cap, all scholarly and accomplished. His extra Honors College tassel. The crisp and shiny look of his shoes, which I lent him from my own supply since his had scuff marks on them and just wouldn't do.

Two years fly by really fast.

And now Bobby Parker and I are graduating from South Wood University at long last, our eyes set on the future.

But whatever's in store for our future, neither of us can know yet.

Out here in the windy pre-summer heat, over a thousand miles away from Spruce, I turn to my man, my two-years-going-on-forever boyfriend, my lover, and I mumble, "Dude, did I forget to put on deodorant?"

Bobby quirks an eyebrow at me. "Seriously?" Then he leans in and shamelessly gives my pit a sniff. He smiles up at me. "Smells like all man to me."

I frown. "That could mean I didn't put any on."

He slaps a hand to my shoulder. "You're just nervous 'cause we're about to leave our safe haven of South Wood University for the past four years and start our lives. All our friends and family are out there, waitin' for us to walk across that stage."

"Yeah, yeah, that's it." I shake off the nerves. Then I look at him. "Also, I don't think none of 'em know yet."

Bobby looks at me. "Know what?"

I take his hand, interlock our fingers, then bring them up to our eyes. On my ring finger, I wear the bright, silver, polished band Bobby gave me.

"That I'm yours forever," I answer, "and you're mine."

Bobby smirks. "Well, after our big-ass *weddin'*—whenever that is—I sure will be." Then he puts a kiss on my lips, both firm and soft at the same time with that special Bobby Parker flair only he is ever capable of.

The big question was popped earlier in the semester, right in the heart of springtime. We had both finished strenuous weeks full of exams, and I was rehearsing like crazy for a performance I was starring in at a big local theater. Bobby was acting funny, but in a way that didn't worry me; I simply felt clued in to the fact that he was up to something.

I just didn't know how *big* that something was.

He drove me to my opening night in his new car: a white sedan he bought with all his saved-up money that had a long black racing stripe over its top. (I jokingly refer to it as his Soccer-Ball-On-Wheels.) I *should've* been suspicious of my cast members acting strangely attentive to me, but I was too focused on the big show. It was my first time to perform on a stage that big, and with a whole company of professional dancers, some of whom have made a serious living out of it (and from whom I was eager to learn).

The show was amazing. Every step and hit felt perfect. The audience even gave us a standing-O at the end. I was on top of the world as I hopped into Bobby's car afterwards to head to the after party. I wouldn't shut up about the performance, and Bobby had a grin ear to ear as he listened to my play-by-play.

It was at the party that my life changed forever.

Right in the middle of all the dancing, chatting, and drinking, suddenly the music cut off, and the lighting in the room changed. I seemed to be the only person startled by it. As I clutched my glass of wine and glanced around the room, all the other dancers parted and stepped aside, creating a giant circle with me at its center. Confused, I asked someone what was going on, but that someone took my glass right out of my hand and joined the circle just as fast, not giving me an answer. Bobby was nowhere in sight.

Until he was.

From the end of the aisle of dancers, Bobby emerged. He was nervous, I remember. But as he came down the aisle of dancers, confidence began to swell with his every step, and each dancer to his left and right bowed, as if this whole thing was intricately choreographed ahead of time.

Of course it was.

And when Bobby finally reached the end—right in front of me—he had his hands behind his back, and his adorable brown eyes met mine, excited and full of anticipation.

"What ... What's goin' on?" I asked, completely beside myself.

I knew damned well what was going on.

And I knew what was about to happen.

My heart was beating so hard in my chest as Bobby then revealed his hands, and I saw the bright, bold silver ring pinched between his fingers.

My lips were parted.

I couldn't move.

And there in front of all of my fellow dancers, Bobby dropped to a knee, and smiled up at me.

Then began the speech I'll never forget: "You are and have always been the love of my life, Jimmy. It never mattered to me if our love never became romantic or physical. Not truly. I've always only ever wanted whatever would make you happy, regardless if it was with me or someone else. What exists between us is more intimate than friendship. It's the forever thing."

His hand, confident and self-assured, extended toward me with the ring pinched between his skillful fingers.

Oh my God, this is really happening, I thought to myself, stunned.

"You knelt before me in a locker room one day, in front of all of my soccer teammates, and you stole my heart by giving me a prom-posal I would never forget." A heart-crushingly beautiful smile had spread across Bobby's face, his cheeks turning rosy. "I felt it only fair to do the same to you, and ask you to be mine in front of a roomful of *your* 'teammates'."

The room warmed with the sound of all my dancer friends chuckling, clutching their mouths, hiding their smiles and tears of joy for the two of us.

"Jimmy Strong, I want you to be my forever thing officially," said Bobby. "Even if you already are, in so many ways. Will you do me the honor of being my husband?"

I don't cry.

Ever.

But on that day, staring into the bottomless pools of Bobby's warm brown eyes, I felt tears resting at the tops of my Strong-boy cheeks. Even all of my friends seemed to hold their breath, waiting for my answer, waiting for this perfect moment to pass that would promise us to each other in mind, body, and soul.

I took his whole hand into mine—ring and all—and pulled him right off his knee and up toward me for a kiss.

That was my answer.

The room exploded into applause I didn't hear, because I was consumed with my beautiful man who knew just how to sweep a country boy like me right off his dancing feet.

And I can't wait for the day to come that I can finally call the boy Bobby Strong, my man, from here until the end of my days.

"Are you ready?"

Bobby's gentle word in my ear snaps me back to the present. I give my fingers a wiggle in between his. "For this? Or just to get a rolled-up piece of paper and throw my cap up in the air?"

He just chuckles and kisses me, taking my lightly-spoken words for an answer.

I fucking love this guy.

Soon, Bobby and I are sitting in a sea of chairs full of caps and gowns and a whole lot of blue. After a long procession of names and speeches and obligatory congratulations passes, each of us have our turn to walk the stage.

I feel the eyes of my family and Bobby's on me as I proudly strut across that stage like my walk is just another choreographed dance of mine. My chest bursts with pride when I accept my diploma, shake the dean's hand, and join the rest of my graduating class back in our seats. It's a lot of hard work that pays off in a culmination of cheers, proud smiles from the audience, and a fancy bit of paper.

In time, the magic words are spoken over the speaker, then the sky becomes painted in swirling graduation caps, dancing blue tassels, and screams that shake the heavens.

When Bobby and I reunite with our friends and family, we do so with our hands held and beaming smiles on our faces. Even from a distance, I can already see my mama and papa with my brother and Billy, and even Grandma who flew in with my family to see my graduation. Bobby's mama and papa are among them, too, both of our families having united over the years into one big mishmash of happiness, zaniness, and all kinds of craziness.

"Joel and Mindy would've come," my brother assures me after his due congratulations and a too-tight, bone-crunching hug, "but they've got their hands full with *twins*, Lord help them both. Oh, and your little pen-pal buddy Toby says hi, by the way. He starts his senior year at Spruce High in the fall. That boy is Mr. Tucker's right-hand man, I swear. He's damn near runnin' the place, same as Billy was years ago."

"He's a good kid," I say with a smile. "Too bad Spruce is still full a' little shitheads who won't leave him alone."

Tanner shakes his head. "Don't get me started on how full of misbehavin' little shitheads *our* high school careers were. Shit, I'm still recoverin' over here from Billy's and my ten-year high school reunion last summer. Lance even flew in for it—he cut his hair all short, lookin' like some kind of Hollywood movie star—and *that* was an explosion in and of itself. Phew! Oh, and speaking of Lance, did you know that he—?"

"Tanner, dang it!" comes Billy after finishing up a quick little convo with Bobby, interrupting whatever it was my brother was going to say about Lance. "Don't hog your brother! Jimmy, Jimmy, Jimmy," he then greets me cheerily, a warm smile on his face. "There was a time I had thought I'd never see this day, that Jimmy Strong graduates from college. I'm so damned proud of you."

"Is that a tear in your eye?" taunts my brother.

Billy shoots him a look, then pulls me in for a hug. "Congrats, Jimmy. We're all so proud of you."

I hug him back, then slap a hand on my man Bobby and pull him over to us. "It's all thanks to this man for gettin' me through the hard times over the years. Lord knows we've both had them."

Bobby looks me in the eyes, bursting with pride and joy. Then, with due attitude, he goes, "Better *bet* it was all because of me."

Billy and Tanner laugh at my expense while I give Bobby a playful swat on his blue-gowned ass, then yank him up against me for a hug and a peck on his cute lips, clasping my hands tightly around his back.

That's when my mama notices it.

"What is that?" Her voice slices straight through the noise of everyone making a fuss. She completely just cut off something Grandma was saying and makes a beeline straight for us. She grabs hold of my wrist and lifts it up in the air. My ring glimmers in the sunlight. "What is this shimmery thing??"

My brother and Billy drop their jaws.

Our papas, who were chatting together, are both staring at our hands now, unsure what they're looking at.

Patricia, however, gives my mama a coy little shrug and a knowing smirk.

Of course, she already knew.

And my mama is quick to notice that very thing. "You knew about this??" She turns on Patricia at once. "You already—?" She lets out a huff of exasperation. "*WHY* does everyone always know everythin' before I do?? Goodness gracious, I'm so happy and mad at the same time! Augh, my mascara's runnin', ain't it? I'm cryin'. My mascara's cryin'. Oh, heavens, have y'all set a date? We need to set a date! Oh, gosh darn it, now I'm full-on cryin'! *There's so many plans to be made!*"

My mama's gonna need a few moments to recover.

Or a few hours.

Or a few days.

But regardless, Bobby and I find ourselves caught in a whole new wave of excited, wordy congratulations by my brother and his husband, as well as our papas. Laughter is shared, smiles are made bigger and brighter by the second, and even my completely blindsided mama is uncharacteristically quick to recover, hugging us both repeatedly as her eyes spill with boundless tears of joy.

Bobby and I are whisked away with the family to enjoy a nice post-graduation dinner at a big restaurant, which is kind of like the Biggie's Bites of Arizona, a favorite spot that Bobby and I always frequent. With our parents and my brother and his man and my feisty grandma, we all share a spread of the greasiest, sloppiest, best damned food we've ever had.

And with every burst of laughter at the table ...

And every knowing look from one of my parents down the table at me ...

And every nudge of my brother's big, obnoxious arm into my unsuspecting side ...

I'm certain my future will be full of more surprises, love, and happiness than I could have ever dreamed, because I have Bobby Parker at my side.

Now, and forever.

Then an all-too familiar song comes on the restaurant radio, a song I've heard many times over the past two years ever since we first danced to it at the Second Annual Spruce Ball—as well as our reprise for the Third Annual Spruce Ball, and probably this coming summer for the Fourth.

Bobby eyes me importantly, then extends a hand my way. "Will you have this dance with me, Mr. Strong?"

I take his hand with pride. "You bet your *Lightnin' Leg tushie* I will."

Then, with a sweep of feet and a graceful maneuver of Bobby into my arms, we do our dance right there in the middle of the whole restaurant to the tune of happy strangers clapping, fellow graduates cheering, and our families beaming proudly at us.

It's a dance I will be doing the rest of my life—a dance with Bobby Parker, the best gosh-dang partner a lovesick, puppy-eyed dancer-boy like me can possibly wish for.

The End.